DEARES

SAW T... STO

& TH...

& YOUR CRAZY DREAMS.

Border 7

LOVE YOU,

BUMBLE.

x

Pauline Kirk

Stairwell Books

Published by Stairwell Books
70 Barbara Drive
Norwalk
CT 06851 USA

ISBN: 978-1-939269-25-6

Printed and bound in the UK by UK Russell Press
Layout design: Alan Gillott

www.stairwellbooks.co.uk
www.paulinemkirk.co.uk

Also by Pauline Kirk

Waters of Time
The Keepers

Written with Jo Summers as PJ Quinn

The DI Ambrose Mysteries
Foul Play
Poison Pen
Close Disharmony

For Pete

With thanks to Jo, to my publishers and editors, Rose and Alan; and to Kate Marshall who proof read the final drafts.

Chapter One

The alarm was too painful to bear. Throbbing inside Jude's ear, it set her pulse racing.

"Emergency on level 252," the electronic voice barked, over and over again.

"Emergency Support!" Jude shouted. "Let me through!"

Dwelling 252:99b was at the end of a spur from the main corridor. A group of whispering neighbours stood outside the door.

"It's OK. Security's here," a man said.

Jude tapped her code into the corridor control and the alarm in her ear stopped. It was like having a hammer taken from her head.

"Problems?" she asked.

"Locked herself in. Got her child with her."

"Height sick if you ask me."

"Says she wants moving back down to level 23 -"

The explanations were garbled and noisy. Inserting her pass, Jude switched on the surveillance.

At first the visi-screen showed only an empty bedroom. A quick scan of the lounge revealed nothing there either. Finally the camera swept across a pair of shoes, and then some leggings. Sabbattica Collins was sitting on the floor, almost hidden behind the workstation. Her eyes were wide open, fixed on the front door. Wrapped in body foil, her baby slept in her arms.

A whisper of surprise passed among the onlookers. "She's got some scissors," one of the neighbours whispered. "Look!"

"All right," Jude said, coolly. "Tell me what's been happening."

The neighbours began to talk at once, interrupting each other. They were typical Class Seven Operatives, apart from the man who had spoken first. Jude turned to him. "Let's have your version," she asked. "How long has Sab Collins been inside?"

"We're not sure, Officer." The networker was uncomfortable, aware that he should have taken control. "A couple of us called to see why she missed Contact Session. She wouldn't let us in - kept shouting she wanted to go back where she was."

"She hates it here," the woman near him volunteered.

Her lapel badge marked her as a probationer. So junior a member should have waited to be asked to speak.

Sabbattica Collins remained completely still. On the table beside her was a beaker and some crumpled wrapping. Jude enlarged the image. The foil could belong to either a mood enhancer or a sedative. Since it was yellow, it was not the usual purple-wrapped Tranquil.

There were several medications in yellow foil. An overdose of Quorzac would do little harm - make the woman happy for a while, then send her to sleep. Lubitzin would destroy her liver. Survival depended on treatment being given within the first hour.

Urgently, Jude focused on the woman's face. Enhancing the image still further, she looked at the lips. There were faint signs of discoloration around them. Tucked inside his body foil, the baby was asleep. The whole line of his body suggested peace, though he looked very hot. Little beads of sweat covered his forehead. Jude's alarm increased.

For a few seconds the neighbours were silent, awed by the image above the door. "She's suffocated the poor thing!" one whispered.

"No. She's stabbed him. Look at the scissors!"

"Don't talk stupid!" the probationer retorted. "Sab Collins wouldn't harm her baby. There's no blood anyway."

There was indeed no blood, just a silent mother and child.

Softly Jude reported back to Control. The surveillance images would have been relayed already, but local details helped. Then she turned to the neighbours. "Go back to your dwellings please," she asked. "As you can see, Sab Collins is quite well and the baby is asleep."

Reluctantly the crowd began to move away. Only the young probationer lingered. "Is there any way I can help?" she asked.

Jude considered the offer. Probationers were becoming uncommon. Despite the failure of the cloning programme, most Refuges could meet their human resource requirements from within. Under the Family Eugenic programme, a whole generation was being produced. Sabbattica Collins' friend must have unusual skills to be admitted from outside.

"Stay if you like," Jude agreed. "What's your name?"

"Probationer Linda Vass, Ma'am. Programmer, Class Two."

It was difficult to overcome the young probationer's fear. She was convinced Family Support was a branch of surveillance, whatever the official line might be.

Surprisingly, the communicator was still switched on. Stopping incoming calls was usually the first sign of trouble. Opening the channel, Jude spoke Sab Collins' name very softly. If she had taken mood enhancer, startling her could be dangerous. Jude knew a little about such bad awakenings herself. After one, she had broken every fingernail trying to climb a cliff that proved to be her own front door.

"Sab Collins -" she repeated.

Suddenly the communicator responded.

"Go away!"

"This is Support Officer Shah here," Jude persisted. "I've come to visit you."

"I don't need you."

"I have Linda with me. She's worried about you. All your friends are."

"My friends are on level 23. Get me moved back there, then I'll talk."

"There aren't any dwellings free at present. Besides, your partner is needed here. That's why they promoted him."

"Then why keep sending him off somewhere else?"

Jude sighed. She should have been warned that Team Leader Collins was working away again. "He's a clever man," she replied. "When people have problems on other levels he sorts them out. He'll be back soon. Let me come in. I haven't seen your baby."

"Keep out of here! If you so much as unlock that door, I'll kill us both!"

Jude was too surprised to answer. Snatching up the scissors, Sabbattica Collins lunged towards her baby's head. Her friend cried out, then put her hands over her face.

Catching her breath, Jude held firm. Sab Collins was not the sort to kill her baby, even if she threatened it.

Disturbed by his mother's sudden movement the baby began to cry. Torn between concern for him and her own misery, Sab Collins hesitated, the scissors now angled towards her child's eyes.

Slowly her grip on the scissors weakened. Then, as if only just realising what she was doing, she threw them to the floor.

Jude let out her breath in relief. "I won't come in if you don't want me," she promised. "Let Linda in though. She's longing to see you."

"Tell her to bring my moving orders. No one comes in until they do." An expression of understanding, even cunning, came to the woman's face. "I really will kill Jamie, you know," she said. "You wouldn't want to lose one of your precious babies, would you?" Snatching the communicator control, she ended the conversation.

The silence afterwards was appalling. "What do we do?" Probationer Vass whispered. "I've never seen Sab Collins like this. Is she height sick?"

"Perhaps. Has she shown any signs of paranoia?"

The probationer was near to tears. "She was a bit low last week. Her partner's away a lot and she'd applied to go back to level 23. Not that moving would solve much..."

There was a wistfulness in Linda Vass' voice that told Jude a great deal. The probationer could remember ordinary human companionship, the chatter and jokes, the friendship. She might not have been a good influence. It was easy to glamorise life beyond the Refuge.

On the screen above them, Sab Collins had closed her eyes. Her mouth was definitely going blue. Jude should either leave the woman to whatever fate she had chosen, or get inside.

"Go back to your dwelling," she instructed. "Sab Collins will get bored and she can't have much food. It's purchasing day. She'll come out when she's hungry."

"But what about the tablets? There's a packet on the table. Can't you see?"

"Quorzac," Jude assured her. "Nothing to worry about. Off you go. I'll call back every half hour to check your friend's all right. She'll come out when she's ready."

Reluctantly Probationer Vass returned to her dwelling. Along the corridor a couple of doors opened slightly. Too well-disciplined to disobey orders, the neighbours stayed inside, but they were watching all the same. Jude walked back to the main corridor, and out of sight.

She flicked her communicator. "Any hope of that transfer?" she asked.

Overseer Pera's image appeared on the lenses above Jude's eyes. "None at all," she replied. "We can't have people threatening to kill their children whenever they want a move. Team Leader Collins is needed on level 252."

"I gather he's working away at present," Jude replied carefully. "Could I have him here for an hour - to talk some sense into his partner?"

"Request denied. Collins' services are required until this evening."

"This evening may be too late," Jude pointed out.

"The Adjustment figures are not ready. We have a glitch on 168. Payroll figures must be complete by fourteen hours."

Jude did not attempt to argue. Sabbattica Collins could not have chosen a more inconvenient time. Payroll Day was always a panic. Every account must be balanced by midnight, or council salaries would not be paid, and families would go hungry. Then politicians - and the press - would demand that the contracts be taken from SecureCity Incorporated, and given back to the regions.

Overseer Pera was waiting. “I may be able to gain entry to the Collins’ dwelling,” Jude suggested. “From the fire ladders at the rear. Is it your wish that I proceed?”

There was a pause as the risk factor was assessed.

“The situation is costed at a ratio of 187 to 71,” Pera replied. “In your favour. You are ordered to take only medium risk, but if you can save the child it will be appreciated.”

“Could you arrange medical assistance? The mother may need it.”

“Sabbattica Collins is of little value. We will have an incident team ready, however, in case you or the child need it.”

Jude nodded. “As you wish,” she agreed. “Patch me into Directory please.”

Jude stood memorising the plan for that sector of the Refuge. Since none of the neighbours could see what she was seeing, her stillness must have looked odd. Dwelling 252:99b faced towards the inner pleasure area and was near a fire assembly point. To reach that point, she would have to drop down from level 254. At a costing of 187 to 71, the risk was worth taking - but only just.

*****

The family at 254:84b were startled by a visit from Security, especially during the morning rest period. Judging by the number of empty beakers, Networker Dallow had been struggling with a pay roll that would not balance. His voice was tired as he acknowledged Jude’s greeting.

“Dunno what the fuss is about,” he whispered to his partner. “They’re always causing trouble on 252.”

He had underestimated Jude’s hearing, but she let the complaint go unchallenged. “It’s only a routine check,” she assured him, smiling sweetly. “The fire officers are short staffed at present and they’ve asked us to lend a hand. Your access points should have been tested two weeks ago.”

The windows around the Dallows’ balcony were covered by screens portraying a pleasant little harbour. The couple evidently preferred not to be reminded of the sheer drop to the pleasure area a hundred and fifty levels below.

“Rather you than me,” Sab Dallow said, laughing nervously. “It’s a long way down.”

“Thanks for the encouragement,” Jude said wryly.

Used as she was to the heights of her daily work, she had to steady herself before opening the fire door. Then she stepped out onto the platform beyond. For a second her breath swelled in her chest and her head swam. Holding onto the rail she closed her eyes. "Lord, be with me," she said softly. She was never quite sure who she was praying to, but it helped.

Still holding onto the bar, she looked downwards.

The drop was sickening, the swimming pools and play area below almost invisible. Above, another hundred levels circled upwards, on and on, to the struts of the stayglaze roof and an illusion of sky. From all around her, above and below, came voices, echoing and re-echoing until she felt her ears must explode. Breathing deeply, she waited until the view around her steadied into circular sweeps of doors and balconies. To her left, a man was standing on one of the terraces, fifty metres away on the curve of the circle. He was wearing something bright red, a shirt or an overall. For a second Jude was mesmerised by that splash of colour. Then the man noticed her. He came to the edge of his balcony and pointed.

Uncoiling her harness from the equipment capsule, Jude anchored herself to the rail. Then she leant forward and examined the route below. Now that the dizziness had passed she felt wonderfully, eagerly alive. However dangerous her position, she would not swap places with any one of the thousands of operatives bent over their workstations below her. Free to come and go around the whole Refuge, she felt as if she could reach up and touch real sky.

The route was not going to be easy. A creeper had almost overgrown the top of the ladder. After that, an air vent on level 253 jutted out, too close for comfort. Even more worrying, the safety rail near Jude felt damp and sticky.

East Five was one of the most modern Refuges in England, but its engineers had still not solved the problem of condensation. With so much water in the pleasure area, when the sun shone onto the skyscreen, the central void was like a greenhouse. Plants loved such days. Maintenance crews dreaded them. Moisture settled on everything. In such conditions, even catsoles would not hold firm.

Given a ratio of 187 to 71, the risk was probably too high. Yet no assessment was ever simple, Jude reflected. A lot of eugenic skill had gone into the creation of Sabbattica Collins' child: genetic screening and matching, preconception counselling, pregnancy support... all to produce an ideal Refuge member, more individual and intelligent than any clone. However many surrogate mothers might be available, wouldn't he as an adult wonder about his own flesh and blood, and wish that he had known her?

As for the mother herself... Jude could never value any human being solely in terms of current benefit to the Refuge. The woman had agreed to give the Corporation a son. Before that, she had been a good worker. She deserved some thanks, or at least the chance to prove herself once her mind was clearer. Living at the end of a spur often made members miserable.

Stepping back within contact range, Jude called central control. "I'm about to descend," she reported.

Overseer Pera's expression remained impassive. "We have a condensation figure of four, and rising," she warned.

"I shall go slowly," Jude promised.

"Very well. We accept your judgment. When do you want the medical team to go in?"

"Five minutes from now."

"That doesn't sound long enough. We'll make it ten."

The overseer's image faded.

Unclipping her safety harness from the rail, Jude stepped backwards, onto the ladder. Then she attached the harness again, around the top rungs. Very carefully, refixing the clips every few steps, she lowered herself down.

The creeper was a nuisance. Within minutes Jude's hair and sleeves were soaked. Just above the recycling point, she paused to check where the ladder finished. The levels circled round the lobe below her, as if she were a fly hanging on a bottomless shaft.

The Collins had not closed in the whole of their balcony. A small sun area was filled with potted plants and lounger seats. It should be possible for Jude to jump across from her ladder and land between the seats. To do so, she would have to completely unhook the safety harness. The least slip and she would not stand a chance. The plant pots could be a nuisance too. If she knocked into them they would clatter and alert the woman inside.

By now, a small crowd was gathering on the balconies opposite, watching. Firmly Jude put them out of her mind. As soon as she was level with the Collins dwelling, she unhooked the harness for the last time and turned herself round.

"One - two -" she said to herself. Then she jumped.

*****

There was a gasp from the onlookers opposite. The balcony rushed towards her.

Catlike, she landed between the chairs.

For several seconds, Jude crouched, listening. Her knee hurt but otherwise she was intact. It was doubtful that Sabbattica Collins would have heard anything. Two sets of doors separated her from the balcony. The greatest danger was from the neighbours. They were probably already calling on the friendship net to warn that prowlers were about. Hopefully, central control had cut off the terminal.

Bent as low as possible, Jude crossed softly to the door. She set her pacifier on full stun. Very carefully, she slid her pass into the lock.

Within seconds, Jude had run across the inner balcony and opened the door into the dwelling. The scissors were still lying on the carpet. With a scream the woman tried to reach them, just as Jude kicked them to one side.

After that, everything seemed to freeze. The Sabbattica remained in the doorway, clutching her child. Her eyes were still fixed on the pacifier in Jude's hand. The child began to howl. Suddenly the scene came alive again

"Give me your child," Jude ordered. Her voice sounded strange in her ears.

Mutely, the woman did as she was told, too shocked to resist. The emergency was over.

Beginning to cry, Sabbattica Collins sat on the floor with her head in her hands. Taking no chances, Jude kept the pacifier pointed towards her. It was not easy trying to soothe a grizzling baby held in one arm, and she began to feel foolish. Finally she lowered the weapon, though keeping it ready.

Still the woman could not speak. Pushing the body foil back with one hand Jude examined the child. His face was flushed. "The poor thing's too hot," she said.

At last Sab Collins found words. "How did you get in?" she whispered.

"I came down the fire ladder."

There was a long pause. Jude began to wonder what had happened to the medical officers. When she glanced at her timepiece she was amazed to see only six minutes had passed.

"What will you do with me?" the woman asked.

"That's up to my superiors."

Sabbattica Collins' fear turned to misery, and she rocked herself back and forth on the floor. "Happiness ever after!" she jeered. "That's what they promised me. Then they said I was one of the chosen... Chosen to be stuck here with a man I hate!"

Startled by his mother's raised voice, the baby began to howl again. At once Sab Collins was on her feet, wanting to comfort him. "Why did you put him in foil?" Jude asked.

"He was so cold last night," the woman answered. "I couldn't warm him."

"You should have called a medical officer."

"I did, but he said I should wait until morning - that I was always worrying. They're all against me. Even the children whisper about me. Listen! You can hear them now!"

Jude listened. There was no sound but the whine of the air control.

"They say I don't look after my baby. That's why he's sick."

Jude sighed. Sabbattica Collins was showing classic symptoms of height sickness, though an overdose of Melodine or Tranquil could lead to the same behaviour. Whatever the cause of her paranoia, she was not imagining the baby's illness. The pulse in his throat fluttered like a butterfly.

"Did you give him anything?" Jude asked. Meaningfully, she glanced towards the empty packet on the table.

"No! That's what I've had - to keep me going."

Edging over to the table, Jude looked at the packet. It was Melodine, not Lubitzin. An overdose would certainly not improve Sab Collins' state of mind, but it would do no permanent damage. Jude put the packet down. She had overreacted as far as the mother was concerned, but not, she feared, for the child. It looked as if they had another case of fever on their hands, though how the infection could have reached level 252 Jude could not imagine. Since the last outbreak, the quarantine locks had been checked daily.

"I think your little boy has a fever," Jude warned. "Do you care?"

"Of course I do!"

"Then why did you threaten to kill him?"

"I never did such a thing! I wouldn't hurt him!" The woman clearly believed what she was saying. Jude found herself wondering how she herself would cope with being stuck on an upper spur with a man she detested. Already she dreaded the idea of being cooped up next year, with nothing to think about except her partner and her child.

In annoyance, Jude pushed such thoughts away. "They won't move you back to level 23," she warned, "No matter how much fuss you make. It'll only get you conveyed for treatment."

"I don't need treatment!"

"The doctors will send you for therapy now," Jude warned.

"Will they punish me?" The woman's voice had dropped to a whisper.

"No." Relaxing a little, Jude smiled. "They'll try to help you - talk you through your fears. Get you mixing with people again. You may only need a few sessions."

"Do you think I'm ill?"

"It's not for me to say."

Taking a deliberate risk, Jude handed back the baby. At once his mother was cuddling and comforting him. Watching them together Jude smiled. Her trust had been justified.

"I think you're recovering," she said gently. "Once you come down off the Melodine, I'm sure you'll be a normal but very lonely woman. If there are signs of height sickness, I shall argue that you deserve a second chance. You were right to attract attention. Your baby is sick. The medical officer should have come when you called. I shall say that in my report."

In amazement Sab Collins stared at Jude. "Why should you help me?" she asked.

"That's what family support officers are for. Besides, I understand a little how you feel."

"How can you?"

"I too have been chosen."

"Oh yes, they'd want your gorgeous red hair," Sab Collins said, "but you're not -" She was about to say 'perfect', but stopped herself.

Jude could not help bridling a little. "My hair isn't red," she insisted. "It's officially copper." In embarrassment she laughed. "And I know I'm not perfect. My eyes are too large. Apparently I've been chosen for other attributes."

"When does your sabbatical begin?"

"I'm to be bonded in two months' time - the sixth of September."

For a second both women were silent. "If they offer you Tranquil the night before, don't take it," Sab Collins said suddenly.

There was something in her voice that made Jude look up sharply. "Why?" she asked.

Sab Collins shrugged. "I was so frightened and tense," she said. "They said it would make me feel more relaxed, but I shouldn't have agreed. It made me all confused. Afterwards I kept getting horrible ideas..."

In concern, Jude looked at the woman's face. It was hard to say what her expression was - fear... self-disgust... "What sort of ideas?" Jude asked.

By now Sabbattica Collins was shivering. "People nudge and smile when I go by," she replied. "Especially the men. It's as if they've seen me in a reality game... the horrid sort you get on the black market. It makes me so ashamed." Turning away so Jude could not see her face, the woman dropped her voice until it was little more than a whisper. "When I told them at the clinic, they said I was imagining it. If I told anyone, I'd be sent for treatment. Jeff wouldn't even let me talk about it. He got so angry. Not even my mother believes me." Turning back suddenly, Sab Collins looked directly at Jude's face. "Do you?" she asked.

Jude did not know how to reply. The implications of what the Sabbattica had said were too frightening to take seriously. "I believe something has made you very upset," she said carefully. "Tranquil can do some funny things, just like Melodine, and you've had too much of that now."

"You don't believe me either." Her expression hardening, Sab Collins walked away, into the bedroom. Fearing some sort of outburst, Jude followed her, but the woman merely gathered up her baby's things, ready to leave.

"You see yourself in me, don't you?" Sab Collins asked unexpectedly.

"I see what I dread becoming," Jude admitted.

The medical officers were definitely late. Flicking open the communicator, she re-established contact. "Where's that help?" she demanded. "I have a sick baby here."

Chapter Two

There was always a sense of anticlimax after such incidents, and this one left Jude feeling troubled for some time. She waited to see Sabbattica Collins and her baby taken away, reassured the neighbours, and then went into central control to make out her report.

To her surprise, Overseer Pera was almost complementary. "Good job you got that baby out so quickly," she remarked. "We don't want fever round again. He must have picked it up at the clinic. They'll have to tighten their procedures."

"And the mother?" Jude asked.

"Silly woman! Still, there are extenuating circumstances. They'll have her back in her dwelling in a week or so."

Marsha Pera's world had no room for height sickness or loneliness. For her, everything was as brisk and simple as her own life. Doing one's duty and maintaining the ideal of the Refuge... Those two principles were all that any member needed. The troubles of the last year were due solely to a failure to observe them strictly enough. People had begun to put the wishes of the individual before the good of the many.

It was a theme Jude had heard expounded many times, and she continued typing in her report while agreeing in the right places. Her mind was still on Sabbattica Collins and her baby. It would be good to know what happened to them, but Jude rarely heard the end of the stories in which she became involved.

Transmitting her report, she prepared to return to her normal morning duties patrolling the levels. Only then did she discover she was soaked from her climb down the ladder.

"Take an extra break," her overseer instructed. "You can return at fifteen hours."

For once Jude was grateful to be ordered to rest. Going back to her dwelling, she took off her wet clothes and put on a wrap.

There was a message on the visi-recorder waiting for her.

Kurt's image was as handsome and charming as ever. "How's my future partner getting on?" he asked. "There's a rumour about an incident on '252. That's your patch isn't it? No trouble I hope. Let me know you're OK. Message timed at fourteen hours exactly."

Kurt would be back on duty by now. She could reply later. Running the image again, Jude froze it on a particularly good view of his profile. Yes, Kurt Hammel was good-looking. He was also kind and attentive.

The family development officers had chosen well for her. So why could she feel so little for him? She had only ever cared about the well being of two men, and one of those was her father and the other was barely more than a boy. All the talk in the world about perfectly-matched genes and shared interests did not make Jude's stomach lift or her cheeks go hot. That was what love did to you - at least according to her mother.

Though her mother had had some peculiar ideas, Jude admitted. "Tends to romanticise," the character profile had said. When Jude first read those words she had not known what they meant. "My Mum doesn't romanticise!" she had shouted at the personnel officer. "She was brave - braver than you'll ever be!" Poor man, he had not known how to reply. Furious, filthy little thirteen-year olds were not normally part of his job.

Smiling at the memory, Jude went into the kitchen to prepare a meal. Then she started the in-dwelling entertainment system. As usual, there was nothing much that interested her, but she settled for a tourist programme. If she was going to be bored, she might as well sit on a balcony overlooking the Mediterranean. Her reconstituted food was out of keeping, but apart from that, for a few moments it was possible to believe she was warm and relaxed and enjoying a good holiday.

The bleeper on her workstation interrupted her. Reluctantly, Jude returned from the Mediterranean and put on a dry uniform. There was just time to acknowledge Kurt's message. "I'm OK, thanks," she replied. "Yes, it was my patch. I'll tell you what I can tonight. How did your assessment go, or has it been postponed again?"

Pausing, Jude put the transmitter on hold. She never knew how to end her messages to her future partner. It was noticeable that Kurt also avoided signing off with any term of endearment, merely giving a time or a request for further contact. Whatever he might say, he did not feel love for her. Sitting in front of a visi-screen seemed to make people more careful, as if they feared a machine could tell they were lying - which it often could.

"I'll call at about twenty hours," Jude added. "I'm off duty at sixteen but I have a session in the gymnasium booked after that."

Setting the system again on 'record', Jude prepared to leave. Then she hesitated. She had a peculiar feeling that there was something more she ought to do. Glancing round her apartment, she checked that things were properly put away, and that all private cupboards were secure. Still she felt as if she had forgotten something.

"Oh, give over!" she said to herself. Closing the door firmly, she went out.

*****

A children's party had been arranged for that afternoon, and Jude had agreed to help. The mental health Assessor was concerned that some of the younger ones on level 251 were spending too long in their dwellings, and failing to develop social skills.

After half an hour trying to get a couple of games going, Jude saw what the Assessor meant. The children had no idea how to relate to each other. They would sit happily on the floor and play with their toys, but in isolation. Getting them to share a game was difficult. The ring dances that were the staple of children's parties elsewhere fizzled out, almost as soon as they started. Clearly, the social contact organiser had not been doing his job. Teatime was brought forward. There was no point in forcing things, and some of the children were beginning to squabble.

Sighing, Jude went back to her normal duties. She had an hour before the social contact session on level 249. It would be wise to spend it talking to Sabbattica Collins' friend.

Jude paused at one of the public viewing points, jutting out over the central void. Though she had seen such a view most of her life, it never failed to impress her, and East Five was the tallest Refuge. With firm chalk for a foundation and the latest building techniques, its architects had been able to reach higher than earlier builders had dared imagine. The central tower was a vast circle, the topmost levels often enveloped in cloud. Since most members rarely left their Refuge, few ever saw that cloud, but Jude had seen it, and felt privileged. Many of her colleagues lived and worked - and died - never looking outwards, not even seeing the city they serviced. Their view was of the inner void within the central lobe, where the weather was perpetually kind, and the horizon was an unending cliff of window and balcony.

Now, the vast sweep of that inner lobe encircled Jude, two kilometres high. Enclosed within that circle, the public pleasure area covered the roof of the hundredth level, half a kilometre across. Faint echoing squeals rose from children in the play area, while all round the circle, conversations floated from balconies and open windows, so crisp they could have come from the other side of a mountain valley. Joel had described the Refuges as "Human ant nests", but he was wrong - at least about East Five. That was home, Jude reflected, to those who had chosen to live there. Already, the families in the domestic sectors were turning their levels into vertical suburbs. With the usual English desire to be an individual, they had painted their outer doors, added ornaments and tables and chairs, or filled their sun decks with so many potted plants they looked like hanging gardens. Everywhere, creepers flowed downwards like green waterfalls.

Marked by the red balcony and white lounger seats, Sabbattica Collins' dwelling was just distinguishable. The fire access point above was visible too. Seen without the urgency of crisis, the route downwards looked terrifying. Jude should not have taken such a risk. Even with her safety harness attached, if she had fallen, she could have hurt herself badly, swinging around as she tried to get back onto the ladder. Control had given her a higher value than she had expected. Until the Collins child showed what potential skills he might have, he would only be costed at basic rate, as a future male member of the Refuge. Whereas she had cost a lot of money to train...

Calling herself a couple of shades of fool for taking an unjustifiable risk, Jude turned away. She had never been able to judge life according to numbers.

*****

Doors opened surreptitiously along the corridor as Jude waited for the probationer to answer. "It's the support officer," someone whispered. "What do you think she wants?"

"Perhaps they're going to send Linda for treatment too? She always was a bit peculiar."

The probationer's door slid back.

"I thought you'd like to know how your friend is," Jude said loudly. "May I come in?"

Probationer Vass' dwelling was above a delivery point, and overlooked a lounge. People were constantly coming and going outside, yet once the outer door slid shut, it was like a sealed box. Not one of the windows looked out. Each gave a view of another part of the dwelling, or of the gardens above the concourse lounge. Light reflected around the rooms without any definable source. The effect was unnerving, which was no doubt why so large a suite had been allocated to a newcomer. In surprise, Jude glanced round.

"Excuse the mess," Probationer Vass apologized. "I'm battling with a new programme."

Empty beakers lay on the floor near the workstation, and run-offs were strewn around the chairs. In embarrassment, the probationer picked up a pair of shoes. "Thank you for helping Sab Collins," she said. "Most security officers would have said she wasn't worth the risk."

Realising the remark might be viewed as criticism, Linda Vass looked uncomfortable. “She probably wasn’t,” she added hurriedly, “But you’ve given her a chance to sort herself out. They say the baby has a stomach upset.”

“So I’ve heard,” Jude replied vaguely. “He’s a nice little thing, isn’t he?”

“Yes. Ever so intelligent, you can tell.”

There was a pause. Clearly the woman was wondering why Jude had come.

“How long have you been in the Refuge?” Jude asked.

“Three years.”

“You must find things very strange still.”

The probationer shrugged her shoulders. “Sometimes,” she agreed.

Jude tried again. “How do like being on this level?” she persisted. “It’s mostly families.”

“I don’t mind children. In any case, I don’t see much of my neighbours. I’m usually here slogging away.” Probationer Vass glanced towards the workstation. “Are you sure you only want a coffee?” she asked. “You must be exhausted. They say you came down the fire ladders.”

“A coffee will be fine,” Jude assured her. She noticed how few ornaments stood in the display cases. Linda Vass had lived there for six months, yet she clearly still did not regard it as home.

Finding some comfits and sticking them unceremoniously on a tray, the woman brought their drinks through to the rest area. She was not used to entertaining visitors. “Will I be able to visit Sab Collins?” she asked.

“As soon as the baby’s better. They’ll both be kept in quarantine a few days, in case it’s catching. It might be an idea for you to have a check-up yourself.” Jude took her beaker from the tray and smiled. “Nothing to worry about - just a precaution.” It was difficult to know how to continue. On her next few sentences a fellow member’s future could depend. “Tell me about Sab Collins,” she added. “You two were friendly, weren’t you?”

The woman flushed. “Bek was very kind to me after I was posted here,” she replied.

“But she wasn’t happy herself?”

“No. She’d applied for a transfer. They were near the social area in their last place, with people coming and going. On a spur like hers, no one passes your door. She had little Jamie of course, but you need adult company sometimes.”

In understanding, Jude nodded. "She could have used the family net," she suggested.

"All they talk about is medications and toilet training. Before she was chosen, Bek was a class one operative - earned bonuses and awards. She had nothing to work towards anymore. You can't keep going to the pleasure area, and she'd played all the reality games."

"I doubt it," Jude replied dryly. "Not all ten thousand."

"But the dreams are all the same, aren't they? Winning in love or work. None of it is real. Not like the world outside." Aware that she had said too much, Probationer Vass stopped. "Not like Bek could remember," she added lamely. A deep flush spread across her face.

"The world outside is not a pleasant place," Jude reminded her. "Did you enjoy being followed every time you left your boundary wall?"

Mutely the woman shook her head.

"You have a nice view of the hanging garden," Jude remarked. "It's good not to be reminded of the height all the time."

"I don't mind the height."

"Then what do you mind?"

The question surprised Probationer Vass, as Jude had intended. "Miss Vass, you are clearly not happy here," she continued. "Why?"

Nervously Linda Vass put down her beaker. "I'm very happy," she said. "It's what I've worked for all my life."

"Yes, you did very well in the entrance exams," Jude agreed. "And you've been promoted twice since you were admitted. You're fulfilling your ambitions, and the Corporation has kept its side of the bargain, yet still you miss your home. Why?"

"I can't answer you. You know I can't," the woman's expression replied. She was becoming increasingly frightened. "I'm very, very happy," she repeated aloud.

"It's all right. I haven't switched on the surveillance," Jude said softly. "You can talk." Taking out her communicator, she laid it on the table between them. The switch was set at 'off'. "Check if you want," she instructed. "Go outside and look at the screen above the door. You can pretend to be expecting a visitor."

Afterwards Jude sat alone in the dwelling. If her superiors knew what she was doing, she could be in trouble. Family support officers had the right not to relay conversations if they were private, between friends or family. This hardly fell into either category. If Probationer Vass was not in sympathy with the ideals of the Refuge, then Jude should be reporting the matter.

When the woman re-entered the room she was calmer, but puzzled. "Why do you want to talk to me?" she asked.

"Because you seem discontented, and it worries me."
"Why?"
"You're trying to look two ways - back to the world outside, and inwards to your success here. You can't do both. Ultimately the strain will break you. You've seen what happened to your friend. She wants the benefits of a Refuge, but she also wants her freedom. It's impossible to have both."
"I don't agree." The probationer's tone grew sharper. "When I joined the Corporation I agreed to serve its ideals, not to become a slave."
"You knew what you were signing up for," Jude persisted, "guaranteed safety, work, medical benefits - in return for your skills and total commitment. You enjoy a much higher standard of living here than you did outside. Everyone misses their freedom, but with so many people in so confined a space, we have to abide by the company's rules or there would be continual conflict."
"How dare you lecture me?" Linda Vass flared out. "How do you know what it's like outside? You've spent your life in a box!"
"Actually, that's not true," Jude replied quietly. "I was born in a Refuge, but I spent a lot of my childhood outside. My parents were engineers. We went from place to place, camping rough while they investigated sites for future complexes. They were killed on one such expedition."
"I'm sorry," Probationer Vass said uncertainly. "I didn't know. What happened?"
"Our base was attacked by local tribes. They didn't want us in their territory."
"I think I've heard about that. It was up north wasn't it?" Sitting down again, the probationer looked at Jude curiously. "There were no survivors, except a few children," she recalled. "The eldest was only thirteen, but she led them back to their Refuge. We were told the story when I was training - to illustrate how anyone can survive in the open, if they have to."
Jude nodded. "We wouldn't have made it without help," she admitted. "A squatter family nearby took us in - fed us, and looked after one of the little ones who had been hurt. They were very kind."
"Squatters? How could they afford to be kind?"
"They couldn't. But that didn't stop Mr. and Mrs. Denovitch. They even sent their eldest son with us as guide." Pausing, Jude considered the past. It was a long time since she had allowed herself to talk about it. "Joel was barely fifteen himself," she added. "Yet he got us to

safety, right across the Border Country. Don't ever let anyone tell you squatters are scum."

There was an awkward pause. "I don't know how you can talk about it so calmly," Linda remarked at length. "To watch your parents being killed... You must hate the people who did it."

"Not now. I can understand their anger. Would you want a complex as big as this gobbling up your land?" Trying to be honest, Jude paused. "I still have nightmares, but I've come to terms with what happened."

"I still don't know how you can be happy cooped up here," the probationer insisted. "Not after you've lived outside. I long to walk with the sun and the wind on my face - instead of round and round an endless corridor."

"I share your discontent at times," Jude admitted. "But my parents believed in the ideal, and they brought me up to do so as well. My grandparents were founder members. The Refuges kept civilized life going when the country was falling apart..."

"I know, like the abbeys did long ago," Linda Vass interrupted. "I've heard it all before. But we have democracy now, and the government should be allowed to run things again."

"But it's still too weak -" Jude began.

"While the Corporation controls nearly everything it's bound to be! How can you have a state within a state and share things round properly? The English Refuges aren't even efficient - not compared to the European ones. I've been to one of them."

"I am not going to argue with you," Jude replied firmly. "The Corporation has been mother and father to me since my own died. When the Reivers are brought under control, there won't be the need for such places as this. Until then, ordinary people need protection, and the daily business of running the cities has to go on." She tried to soften her reply with a smile. "Make up your mind what you value most," she advised. "Your walks in the open, or your career and comforts. Then abide by your choice. Otherwise, you are going to be very unhappy." She got up to leave.

"I suppose you'll have to report this visit," Linda Vass said, rising too. "What will you say?"

"That I called to advise you to go for a check-up. That's all."

At the door Jude paused, wondering if she could have worded things better. She had meant to give friendly advice and had preached a sermon instead.

"Were you the girl?" Linda Vass asked. "The one who led the children to safety?"

Nodding slightly, Jude opened the door. The subject embarrassed her. She could not think why they had come to be discussing it.

"I always wondered how someone so young could have reached your rank," Linda admitted. "It's because of what you did."

"I hope not," Jude replied. "It probably got me on to the high-flyer course, but I'd like to think my progress after that was up to me."

*****

For the rest of the afternoon, a vague sense of dissatisfaction remained with Jude. She performed well in the gymnasium and was praised by her trainer, but still the unease remained. By the time she returned home, she was glad to lose herself in an utterly trivial comedy show.

Halfway through, the programme was interrupted by a series of public announcements. The first warned everyone to observe anti-viral procedures when passing between levels. An extension of the curfew on city visits followed, virtually confirming that the fever was around again. It was a mistake putting the two announcements together. People were bound to fear another epidemic.

Then followed a series of personal messages, reminders to individuals to attend social contact sessions or get their work up to date. Everyone dreaded being disciplined so publicly. It was like having to stand in a foyer with a placard round your neck.

Suddenly Jude sat bolt upright. She was sure she had heard her own name mentioned.

A man's voice came over clearly, though for some reason the accompanying image had been lost. Urgently Jude pressed the visual control. A faint outline of a figure appeared, but no more. The voice repeated the message.

"Call for Officer Judith Shah, serving number 11690, member of the Family Support Corps. You are asked to meet your father urgently at Border Seven. Repeat. Family Support Officer 11690, please meet your father at once, at Border Seven."

In bewilderment, Jude stared at the screen. The comedy series had returned. It must be some unpleasant joke, she decided, beginning to feel angry. Her father was dead. She had seen him die with her own eyes. "What a horrible, hateful trick!" she said aloud.

Pulling herself together, she flicked on her communicator. "This is Officer Shah," she said. "I've just received a peculiar message on the in-dwelling display. I'd like an explanation."

“No announcements have been put out for you tonight, Officer - or any other member of the corps. You must have been dreaming.”

“But I know what I heard!” Pausing, Jude considered her reply more carefully. “You’re sure?” she asked.

“Positive,” she leaned forward, “we keep careful records of all public service announcements directed at our staff. Have you been using too much Tranquil?”

“No. I must have fallen asleep. Sorry to have troubled you.”

For a long time afterwards Jude stared at the screen. She had not been dreaming.

Chapter Three

Jude slept badly that night. The events of the day seemed to have conspired to bring her childhood back to her. Between fitful dozing and wakefulness, she recalled the expeditions with her parents - the fun they used to have, cooking meals under a makeshift shelter, with a real sky above them and a real wind on their faces. On winter days their voices used to echo from the hills. The beauty of snow-covered fields had stayed in her memory ever since.

There were less pleasant memories too. Crowds passed backwards and forwards across her mind: people on their own, people gathered in raggle taggle armies they called tribes, all coming to plead with the survey party to go away. "This is our land!" The cry echoed in Jude's head.

"But SecureCity has bought it," Jude's father would say, trying to soothe them. "Your leaders sold it to us. If you don't like what's been done, talk to them. We're just surveyors. All we want is to do our job..."

Finally Jude fell into a deep sleep.

At once she was back in her childhood, playing in the woods. One of the older boys had hung a swing from a branch, and she was pushing Carrie backwards and forwards on it. "More!" Carrie shouted. "More!" Jude's arms were beginning to ache and she stopped for a moment, letting the child swing under her own momentum.

Then they heard the shooting. "What's that?" Gary asked.

They ran to the edge of the woods to see.

Riders were charging down the valley, from both sides. Some had old-fashioned guns in their hands, other waved scythes and spades. They were shooting towards the camp. The horses were mangy and dirty, but they galloped so quickly they were already among the first tents. People were running everywhere, trying to get away. They had nowhere to run.

Sonja screamed. "Down!" Jude shouted. Carrie was about to run towards her mother but Jude pushed her flat into the wet leaves. Gary and Sonja threw themselves beside them.

"Who are they?" Gary whispered. "What do they want?"

"It's those tribespeople," Jude whispered back. "The ones your Daddy was talking about."

"Don't worry," Joel replied. "Everything will be all right. Trust me..."

With a jolt, Jude woke up.

Rubbing her hand across her eyes, she sat on the edge of her bed. It was some time since she had had one of her nightmares, and she felt sick.

Her dreams usually followed the same pattern. All that varied was the point at which she managed to struggle awake. This time however, something had changed. For a moment Jude could not think what. Then she recalled Joel's words.

Joel did not belong there. He came on the scene much later, after she had found Iphegenia and Koko. Nor would he have spoken aloud like that. He was far too careful. Trying to rationalise her dream, Jude controlled her emotion. She had mentioned Joel to the probationer earlier. That was why she had mixed him up with Gary. It was odd all the same. For all she knew, Joel could be dead. In so troubled an area, with his parents driven from place to place, he would be lucky to survive. Even if they did meet again, she would probably not recognize him. After fourteen years struggling to make a living on a stony hillside he would have coarsened and aged. Those squatter families bred young and produced many children, whether they could feed them or not.

Sighing, Jude took her drink and returned to her rest area. Joel deserved better than the typical squatter's fate. She had never known a boy with so much native intelligence. Though he had fled from the city with his parents, he had learnt how to survive in the Waste better than most country children. He knew how to trap a rabbit, or bind a wound to stop it bleeding. Even when there were no stars or sun to guide him, he could tell the way he was heading just by examining the moss on a tree trunk. Without his help, they would never have got back to Refuge Six. Only one thing had frightened him, and that was the Refuge itself. He had taken one look at the vast tower looming on the horizon, and disappeared.

The message transfer clattered into life, startling Jude. Obediently she transferred the image onto her entertainment screen.

"Central Control to Officer Shah, 11690," the message read. "Please report to main office at nine hours precisely."

"I wonder what that's about?" Jude wondered as she flicked the screen clear again. Since sleep was impossible, she settled back to watch the insomniacs show.

*****

No one seemed to know who had given the order summoning her. Feeling foolish, Jude waited in the briefing room.

Finally a courier appeared at the door. "Officer Shah?" he asked. "The Chief Secretary wishes to speak to you. Would you accompany me please?"

In amazement, Jude got up. No one ever met the chief. He - or she - was a faceless, godlike figure located somewhere in the depths of Admin. Communications from so senior a member usually took the form of a general homily circulated throughout the Refuge on Budget day. The likelihood of Jude being called for a personal audience was about as high as getting the final adjustment figures right first time. It had been known to happen, but only to other people.

From Central Control the quickest route to Administration was through the main atrium. The courier led the way. Since Jude rarely had occasion to go through the reception area, she looked around her curiously. A sense of unreality began to afflict her. Jude Shah could not be on her way to visit the Chief Secretary. She must be dreaming again.

The main atrium of East Five was famed throughout the sector. Built to impress visiting politicians and financiers, it created a vast sweep of luxury, a hundred metres wide and three levels high. Its bright and airy foyer echoed with the splash of fountains and the murmur of soft music. Beyond the foyer, marble stairways led upwards, tier upon tier until they were almost out of sight. From each tier, ornate marble arches led to marble lounges, beyond which carpeted corridors waited, each covered with a different coloured design to mark the route that was beginning. If you wished to head towards Finance, you took the blue route. The corridors of Purchasing Department had yellow carpets, Distribution a tasteful green. Administration, being the central department, merited deep, royal purple. Where routes crossed, the colours ran side by side until they ultimately diverged along their separate moving pathways. There was no excuse for any menial getting lost - which was fortunate Jude reflected, as it must take an army of maintenance men and women to keep all those carpets clean.

"This way," the courier said, indicating one of the smaller elevators. In surprise, Jude followed him. It was not at all how she had imagined the entrance to the Chief Secretary's suite. The elevator displayed no numbers. Judging by the time they stood there, it took them well above level 200.

Finally, they arrived at a small waiting room with a hatch and a bell. The courier spoke into an intercom. "Wait here," he said to Jude, and disappeared through a door.

For half an hour Jude waited, becoming increasingly nervous. Had she done something wrong? Until then, she had assumed it was a privilege to be called to the chief's office. Supposing it was nothing of the sort? She tried to recall the courier's expression. Was it friendly or pitying? The waiting area was suffocatingly hot. Jude's lips dried out with nervousness. No one asked to speak to her. There were no magazine discs to amuse her, or refreshments. Beyond the hatch she could hear people talking easily to each other, but indistinctly. Every so often a buzzer sounded, and twice a trolley rattled down the corridor outside, startling Jude so much she nearly yelped. She found herself longing to bang on the reception window and demand to be allowed to leave.

An hour slid slowly by. Urgently Jude tried to think what fault she might have committed. She could have been summoned because she was in a great deal of trouble. Perhaps they had found out about her talking to Probationer Vass.

"Don't be daft," Jude told herself firmly. The Highest of the High would not waste time on so trivial an offence.

There was her annual personality probe, though... Sometimes lately, she had found herself feeling on the edge of things, as if she did not quite belong. Such feelings were always strongest after she had been outside the complex. Perhaps her sense of being slightly different had been picked up in her probe? Or her occasional irrationalisms registered? She could have been called because she had symptoms of aberration...

The idea appalled Jude. She came very near to leaping up and running away. The Refuge was her life. If she were expelled from it, she would have nowhere to go...

Controlling her fear, Jude sat upright, staring ahead of her. Whatever the reason she had been summoned, running was not going to improve matters. The long wait could be some sort of test. No matter how long she had to sit there, she decided, she would not run.

At eleven hours exactly an intercom crackled into life. By then Jude's mouth was so dry she could hardly reply. The door near the hatch swung open.

"Come in please," a disembodied voice invited. Steadying her breath, Jude walked through.

She found herself in a vast office. Operatives sat at terminals or stood beside store shelves. One woman was cleaning her shoes, rubbing the toes with a cleanser. Another was talking to her neighbour about her holiday in the hologram suite. The very ordinariness of their actions bewildered Jude. How did they all enter the room? Not through the waiting area, that was certain. There must be more corridors reached from the other side of the lobe. Uncertainly, she paused.

"Straight on," the woman with the cleanser said. "Through the far door." She looked at Jude curiously. "Only Family Support," Jude heard her whisper afterwards. "Wonder what the chief wants with her."

The courier was waiting. Where he had been for the last hour and a half he did not say. Nor did he apologise for the long delay. "Come along," he said briskly. A panel in front of them opened. "Step forward."

He gave Jude a little push, and the panel closed, behind her.

*****

Jude could hardly see. Sunlight blinded her. The outer wall of the Chief Secretary's room was almost completely glass. Even part of the floor was made of stayglaze, so that the desk and chair seemed to float. After the darkness of the waiting area her eyes hurt. Then, as she grew used to the light, she let out her breath in pleasure. Ordinary dwellings looked inwards, towards the central pleasure area. The Chief Secretary's view was wide open, far over the city, to the hills on the horizon a hundred kilometres away.

The room was empty. Cautiously Jude moved to the window.

From so high a level, the menials' lodgings and the service buildings were hidden, too close against the foot of the tower to be seen. It was as if the room hung on invisible threads. Despite the soundproofing, the force of the wind against the lobe made the glass moan. The struts between the panels shuddered. If one of them snapped, the whole outward wall would burst inwards.

Below Jude, the city sprawled like a brightly coloured fungus. The line of the security fencing around it was clear, lapping around the outer edge. As if spores of the fungus had blown over the fence, smears of shantytown spread around, densest wherever there was a patch of flat land. Even from such a height, she could see that one of the transportation routes had collapsed, the coil of a pass-over leaning at an odd angle. "Cheap materials," Jude thought angrily. A factory was burning in the old industrial area, smoke blotting out the streets downwind and then rising in an angry black plume. As it blew towards the east, it thinned into a dull haze, almost hiding the valley below. Beyond the haze she could just make out the fortified homes of the wealthy, each nestling in its ring of carefully planted trees.

"You like my view, I gather."

Turning in alarm, Jude found she was not alone. Near the desk was a woman of such ugliness, she was almost as striking as the view outside.

"Yes, Ma'am," Jude replied. She could not imagine how anyone could have entered so silently.

"I could spend hours at that window. I have to be firm with myself or I'd never do any work."

Ugly people were allowed to stay in the Refuge only if they had quite exceptional abilities. Ugliness could give offence, and in so confined a space, all sources of potential friction must be avoided. This woman was barely five foot six. She had heavy, deep-set eyes, a large jaw and a forehead that rose in an unattractive sweep towards a sharply defined hairline. Yet intelligence filled every feature. After the first shock, Jude saw character, not defect.

"I'm sorry to have kept you waiting so long," the chief continued. To Jude's amazement, she offered her hand in greeting. "To be frank, I wanted to see how long it would take you to run, but after an hour and a half I got bored. You were obviously going to stay put."

The remark seemed to be meant as a compliment and Jude smiled nervously. "I assumed you would send for me when you were ready," she replied.

"Come and sit down," the woman invited. "I prefer people to sit. You're not too bad, but most people here tower above me."

In surprise, Jude went to the chair indicated to her. It was next to the window, giving her an uncomfortable sense of swinging above empty space. "What is your wish, Ma'am?" she asked.

"First of all, to congratulate you. You handled yesterday's incident well - with compassion as well as firmness."

"Thank you." Glancing round her, Jude wondered how a senior officer could know a minor event so quickly. There were no surveillance screens on the walls, or on the desk.

"Holo-reality, my dear," the Chief Secretary said, anticipating Jude's question. She touched a pad beside her. At once, a man and woman appeared in the middle of the room, arguing fiercely.

"Don't you dare say that!" the woman shouted. "I know my job as well as anyone!"

"I'll teach you to make a fool of me!" Raising his hand to strike, the other operative lunged forward. In alarm Jude leapt up to stop him. At once the couple vanished.

Jude stared at the space where they had stood. It was an ordinary stretch of carpet. Foolishly, she sat down.

Before she could gather her thoughts, the space filled again. This time, three women appeared. Two were as real as if they had just walked into the room, but the one on the outer edge blurred eerily into the plant pots. They too were arguing. "Come on! Where's the rest?" the nearer figure demanded. "Those antibiotics sold well. Don't kid me that's all you got!"

The image snapped off again. Jude looked round the office, wondering what other facilities it might conceal.

"Interesting," the Chief Secretary remarked. "Level 159 could do with a visit. There's not much I can't see from my eyrie up here," she added, "Including you, my dear. I've watched you in action several times. You have qualities that could be useful to me. Your background is unusual too. You're one of the few officers we have who can cope outside." Thoughtfully she consulted a prompter on her desk. "Let's see, you've been out of the Refuge three times this year: once guiding maintenance crews and the second time as bodyguard for one of our representatives. The other occasion is merely noted as 'translation duties'. What did that involve?"

"Escorting a delegate to the Scots Federation. He was travelling incognito."

"He required a translator?"

"Yes, Ma'am. The Reivers are developing their own language. I spent my childhood in the Border sector," she added, by way of explanation.

"Of course. It's recorded on your file." The Chief Secretary paused, as if considering her next words. "Tell me - what impression do you form of Border Seven nowadays?"

In surprise Jude looked away. Hearing the place mentioned again was unnerving. "That's -" she began, and stopped. Describing a public announcement no one else had heard, and that had supposedly come from her dead father, would make her sound ridiculous. "It's some time since I've been there," she said instead.

"But you've retained a - special interest I imagine. What rumours do you hear? Good or bad?"

Jude began to wonder where all this was leading. "That it's very beautiful," she replied. "And people like to take their R and R periods there - some of them very senior I gather. Some say it's risky, though - with the Reivers getting active again..."

"Ah -" the woman replied, though whether in agreement or not, Jude could not tell. "What other things do you hear? That there's a lot of corruption for instance?"

"I've heard suggestions," Jude replied guardedly. "It wouldn't surprise me if they were true. When you're on the edge of the civilised world, you come to understand what's beyond. That can tempt you to slide into it yourself - if you see what I mean."

"I do indeed. But it's not only at the outer edges. Medications find their way into the cities from most Refuges. You saw the clip from '159 a few moments again. Food, antibiotics, contra-virals, equipment, games... you name it, if it's worth having, it's turning up in the hands of the local warlords. People in high places are making a lot of money, while ordinary Refuge members die of fever."

"That's awful!" Jude protested. "The Refuges were supposed to help people - bring peace, and a higher standard of living..." She tailed off, feeling foolish.

The wind rattled the window beyond them. "You still believe in the ideal," the Chief Secretary commented. "Good. As I said, you could be very useful to me."

"In what way, Ma'am?"

"Do you really want to know? Once I've told you the details you'll have no choice but to accept. I couldn't let you go away, knowing - certain things."

"I'm willing to do my duty in any way you require," Jude replied, as she had been trained. She was not sure she meant it.

"Are you, my dear? To take any risk?"

Jude paused. She would be wise to find out more before committing herself. "May I ask how long you need me?" she replied.

"Is time important?"

"I'm due to be pair bonded on the sixteenth of September."

The Chief Secretary looked up in annoyance. "I was not aware that the date had been fixed," she said. Then her manner softened. "Well - that's one prior obligation I can't ignore. I could, however, ask for a postponement. How do you feel about it, my dear? Are you looking forward to your sabbatical, or would you like to continue working a few months longer?"

Staring out of the window over the city, Jude tried to think how to answer. She dreaded not working, but she had been brought up to believe duty was important, however uncongenial. She had given her word to the Futures department, and to Kurt himself. Though she had no family to disappoint, he had a dozen relatives, all busy buying bonding gifts. Besides, bearing a child would be an experience, an aspect of womanhood she had not yet tried. What alternative was on offer? Something so vague, only a fool would accept it.

And yet... Jude could not overcome that 'and yet...' She would love to be able to put off her bonding for a while. There had been no suggestion that she would have to break her promise to Kurt, only that a postponement could be arranged.

The more Jude thought about the choice, the easier it became. Kurt would be disappointed, but it would do him no harm to wait a month or two. "I'm satisfied with the choice made for me," she replied carefully, "And I'm grateful for the privilege of bringing a new member into the world. If you have something else that needs doing first, however, I think my partner would accept a short delay."

Leaning back in her chair, the Chief Secretary smiled. "I hoped you'd say that," she said.

"May I have the details now?"

"Go and stand by the window. We'll look at the view together."

Puzzled, Jude did as she was asked. Silently the Chief Secretary disconnected the holo-pad on her desk, and then getting up, pulled out the leads of the main terminal. "This place has been checked a dozen times," she whispered, "But I'm never at ease while these things are on. An expert could feed off their power." Joining Jude, she stood beside the window. "Move a bit further out," she instructed. "Right against the glass."

They stood side by side, nothing but toughened stayglaze between them and oblivion. All around them the wind moaned and howled, shaking the glass. The situation was so strange, Jude did not know where to begin. "What do you want me to do?" she repeated.

"Go to Border Seven."

Startled, Jude looked across the city.

"I know it will mean returning to where your parents died, but there's no one else I can trust. You know the area already. You speak the language, can blend in. I need someone like you."

Anxiously the woman looked back into the room. Taking a scanner from her pocket she passed it over the blinds and carpet near her. Either she had good cause to suspect eavesdroppers, or she was suffering from height sickness. Satisfied at last, she continued. "Border Seven is particularly important at present. Central Administration has been temporarily transferred there, following an attack on Refuge Two." Jude had to strain to hear her voice above the wind. "Admin. decided Border Seven was the safest place to move to. No Reiver would dream we'd move anything vital so near their territory."

Smiling slightly at Jude's surprise, the woman paused. "No, it hasn't been publicly admitted," she agreed. "But in principle it was a good idea. The trouble is, moving has solved nothing. The same stupid policies are being followed, the same isolationism, the same callousness to outsiders - all the things that led to the Troubles when you were a child, and are leading to almost monthly attacks on our Refuges now. Of course, the local managing board prefers not to inform those at the top, and they're too busy trotting round Europe to know what's going on. We have to alert them somehow... and failure is the one thing people at the top do notice. If we could show how much corruption there is - and at the very Refuge chosen as a secure place... Well, we might unseat the present management. Then more - able - officers will have the chance to turn things around."

The word "we" worried Jude. It suggested some nameless, faceless group that was somehow including her. A phrase from an old hologram story returned to her: 'Palace Coup'. Though that story belonged to two centuries ago, it seemed to fit the moment. "I wouldn't be any good at - political things," she said carefully. "My experience outside is as a translator, or bodyguard."

"But that's just what I want you for - to accompany my best Assessor. Let me explain. Six months ago an accountant made a routine visit to Border Seven. He found discrepancies in the returns. Unfortunately, he didn't find out why. A gantry fell on him. It may have been an accident - cleaners can be so careless - but it was a little too convenient. So we sent a second inspector. This time we gave no warning of her visit. The only people who knew were here."

Looking out of the window, the Chief Secretary watched the plume of smoke. It was beginning to die down, turning from black to grey. "Inspector Henderson failed too," she continued. "Just as she was beginning to send some interesting reports, she was taken ill, and had to return. Two days ago she died. Once again, it may have been coincidence. On the other hand, it may not."

Jude's whole body was going cold. She wanted to say she had been foolish, should have asked for details before making a commitment, but there would be no point. She would not be allowed to refuse now she had been told so much. "And you want me to protect the next one?" she asked.

"Yes - but discretely. If you assume the role of a menial, no one will notice you, and you'll have free access to the outer buildings. I'll arrange for you to have security clearance to move into the central lobe if necessary. Don't instigate contact, but keep an eye on her as much as you can. If she passes any messages to you, you'll have codes to enable you to relay them straight to me. You end up doing nothing but cleaning sanitary units, but you could be my only eyes up there."

"It shall be as you wish," Jude acknowledged. Her voice sounded odd in her ears.

"Excellent. I'll arrange for you to be sent officially to Mid Two, so no one here knows your true destination. You'll get sent on a roundabout trip after that, covering your tracks, until finally you get to Border Seven. Any questions?"

"What shall I say to my partner?"

"You'll need to explain to a lot more people than him. Even the operatives outside will be wondering who you are, and why you've been with me so long. Tell people you've been disciplined, and had your privileges withdrawn. As part of your retraining, you're being posted to Mid Two. If you acquit yourself well there for three or four months, you'll be allowed to return for your bonding."

Something seemed to have stuck in Jude's throat. "I would rather have another cover," she admitted, "if that's possible."

"I'm sure you would, but I'm afraid you're going to have to stick to this one."

Already Jude could hear the comments of her colleagues, the sneering consolations. "But what should I say I've done?" she pleaded. "Until now I've had a good reputation."

"Tell them you're becoming too friendly with your clients."

The lump in Jude's throat was swelling. "But I've always tried to keep a balance," she insisted, "to be firm as well as fair."

"You haven't always told us what they've told you, though, have you? Probationer Vass now - I can understand you feeling sorry for her, but she's a bad influence. You really should have switched the surveillance on when you went to see her. You seem to have trouble deciding where your loyalties lie; to the families you support, or to the Corporation."

There was no reply Jude could make. She was being trapped, as effectively as any rabbit out in the fields. But she had walked into the trap - run into it even. Any assignment had seemed better than her coming bonding. She should have accepted Kurt and stayed safely home.

The Chief Secretary touched her arm. Her hand was colder than the window beside them. "Go back to your duties, my dear," she said. "I suggest you cry a little as you leave. It will convince the operatives. Cry a bit more when you're with your colleagues. They'll be most sympathetic. Then at eighteen hours precisely, take yourself off to your local games room to forget your sorrows. Booth number eight will have been out of order for the previous hour, but it will come back on line just in time for you to go in. You'll receive your travel directions there."

Releasing Jude's arm, the woman smiled. Jude found herself recalling the ice they used to break at the camp each morning.

"Take Officer Shah back to her duties," she heard intoned into the intercom.

The door to the main room swung open. Immediately the courier appeared again. "This way please," he said.

As they walked past the rows of tables, faces turned in Jude's direction. "Been disciplined," one of the operatives near the door whispered. "You can tell from the chief's expression."

"Wonder what for?" her companion whispered back

Putting her handkerchief to her face, Jude pretended to cry.

Chapter Four

It would have been easier if Kurt had not been so angry. As they sat together beside one of the fountains, Jude had to warn him to lower his voice.

"You're one of the best support officers we've got," he insisted. "Fair, but never soft. As soon as I saw you at work, I knew I'd struck lucky."

His praise surprised Jude. "Thank you," she replied simply. "I'm sorry I've let you down."

"Of course you haven't. It's not your fault."

Cautiously Jude watched his expression. "You were disappointed at first," she remarked.

To her surprise, a slight flush spread across Kurt's face. "Maybe," he admitted. "I hoped you hadn't noticed. I tried not to let you see."

"Why? I know my features aren't perfect."

"Not by Refuge standards, no." Tentatively Kurt took her hand. "But every woman's the same here," he continued. "Altogether too perfect, if you know what I mean. They're like the women in reality games, not real people. You're flesh and blood, someone I want to touch."

In embarrassment Jude withdrew her hand. "Shush -" she warned, glancing towards a group of operatives nearby. She wished Kurt could have met her in a less crowded place. Private meetings between intended pair bonds were discouraged, however. They could lead to passion, and anticipate the Futures Department's careful timing.

"But I do want to touch you," Kurt whispered back. "I never asked for a partner. I was complimented of course. Any man'd be - well, proud to be chosen - but I didn't want to settle with any particular woman. Now - I dunno. I enjoy your occasional calls. I almost like the idea of being with you for a few years. I don't mean to question our superiors, but from my point of view it's cruel - making me care and then saying I can't have you."

"They'll let me come back," Jude assured him. "They have to honour our bond. It has precedence over other orders. All they're doing is sending me away, to teach me a lesson."

"But what have you done? Got a bit too friendly? With whom? You're up and down the levels all day. How can you get close to anyone? You're not even close to me."

Jude searched for an answer. The meeting was proving more difficult than she had expected. "I should have switched on the surveillance," she replied. "Not let the Vass woman talk in private."

Kurt shook his head. "If they're going to discipline anyone who gives members a bit of privacy, we'll all be in trouble," he replied. "I've left the surveillance off many times. How else can you get people to talk freely? Besides, I've no wish to invade people's lives. This place is changing Jude, and I don't like the way it's going. We're being watched; all of us, not just when there's a staff appraisal - all the time."

Out there, in the middle of the pleasure area, it would be difficult for anyone to be monitoring their conversation, but even so, Jude felt nervous. "Don't you start getting paranoid," she whispered.

"I don't think I'm imagining it, Jude, but how can you tell? Sit on your bed, touch a little pad and you're on a desert island. Everything's right. You can see it, hear it, even smell it, but it isn't real. Go down to the games room and you can turn yourself into a world war three ace, in a second. But when the game's switched off, where are you? Sitting in a booth no bigger than a cupboard. Nothing we do is natural. We're so used to looking down corridors, wide open views make us sick. When you think about it, that's no more normal than trying to kiss Queen Cleopatra in a holoroom. None of us here know what's real and what isn't."

"I've never heard you talk like this before," Jude whispered.

"We've hardly ever met like this before - just the two of us." Glancing towards the operatives, Kurt smiled. "And a dozen or so neighbours," he added wryly. Taking Jude's hand again, he put it to his mouth.

"Perhaps it's a good thing we don't meet too often," Jude suggested gently. "You mustn't say such things, even to me, unless you're absolutely sure no one can hear."

"You sound like you're frightened."

"I am. I'm sure it's not just height sickness. There's no reason for me to develop it. I go out of the Refuge too often, and I'm not shut in a little box when I'm here. I shouldn't have thought you'd sicken either. Resource officers are always coming and going and meeting people."

The operatives were beginning to return to their duties after their lunch break. It would soon be time for Kurt to return also. Picking up his jacket, he prepared to leave. With the light from the sunscreen catching his hair, he looked like one of the figures in the holograms, tall and dark and very handsome. Jude smiled at the image created in her mind.

"Oh, to Hell with it," he said, sitting down again. "I can stay another minute." Putting his arm round her shoulders, he drew her close to him. "I don't think you are being disciplined," he whispered. "They're sending you away - to stop you seeing things."

"What sort of things?" Jude asked in bewilderment.

"Things they don't want ordinary members to know." Still holding her so that others would not hear, Kurt touched her face. "You're too sharp," he whispered. "You look at people and work them out. Then you don't let them out of your sight. It's one of the reasons your levels have so few problems. You spot the troublemakers straight away." He laughed slightly, as if nervous in her presence. "You've even done it to me."

"When was that?" Jude could not look at his face.

"The day we were introduced. I didn't think much of the choice they'd made for me. I was wondering if there was some way I could get out of it... You knew. I'm sure you did."

In silence they sat beside the fountain, still close to each other. "I don't want you sent away," Kurt said finally. "I've grown to like you."

Awkwardly he kissed her mouth. One of the operatives near them giggled. Feeling a fool, Jude pulled away, just as the bleeper on her uniform signalled the end of her break. "I have to go now," she said. "I'll try and see you again before I leave, but if I don't manage it, take care."

Getting up again, Kurt nodded. "Will you keep your bond to me?" he asked.

"Of course. I swore I would, and I don't break my word."

Without replying, he turned and walked away.

For several moments Jude sat beside the fountain, watching Kurt cross the pleasure area. She was surprised how little she had felt when he kissed her. No thrill, but no aversion either. If he had been introduced to her as her future senior officer she would probably have liked him - respected him at least. He was a decent man, a bit brash in public, but with a gentler side she had not until then seen. He was also intelligent. No one rose to the rank of senior resource officer otherwise. That in itself was worrying. If Kurt believed they were being watched more closely, then he was probably right.

*****

The receptionist at the rehabilitation suite smiled. "Room 9, Ma'am," she said. "It's your last session isn't it?"

Jude nodded. "I leave in two days," she replied.

"Are you allowed to tell me where you're heading? It'll help me choose your programme."

"I've been posted to Mid Two," Jude lied.

"You'll have to cross the Capital Zone. I suggest you take one of our city link stories. They say the mass transit system gets worse, and it'll help to be well prepared." The receptionist called up a menu and invited Jude to make a choice. "Done much travelling outside before, Ma'am?" she asked while she waited.

"A bit," Jude replied vaguely. "It's always a shock at first though."

"Isn't it? I couldn't get over how wide everything was - I mean, all that space, and all of it full of people." Taking a key-pass from one of the slots, the receptionist passed it through the hatch. "You can go straight in if you like. The last occupant couldn't manage the full hour."

Jude tried to smile. No matter how often she came to the rehabilitation suite, she was always nervous. What was about to follow was totally unpredictable, one day pleasant, and another terrifying - exactly like being outside the Refuge.

The first test took Jude by surprise. As soon as she entered room 9, the door shut mechanically behind her, leaving her in darkness. There was a faint scuttling sound, like insects running for cover. Jude held her breath to steady it. She had come across that illusion before, and knew it in reality also, from a hotel up north. Every time she entered the shower cubicle in her room, she used to hear the cockroaches scuttling away. Recognising the sound did not make it anymore pleasant however.

To her relief, the darkness did not last long. With a faint hum, the image-maker came on, to reveal four blank walls and a blank, white floor. After the luxuriance of the pleasure area, it was as if Jude had stepped into a void. Patients had been known to start banging on the door for release simply at the sight of those featureless walls. For them rehabilitation began at the most basic level.

Jude waited a little longer until she was mentally prepared, then inserted the lenses. She took more trouble than usual over the left one, having scratched her eye during the previous day's session. It was still sore and watered under the disc. In concern, Jude tried again. Any discomfort could be magnified by the rehabilitation programme, and make the illusion more disturbing.

As soon as she was satisfied the lenses were safely inserted, Jude attached the pulse pads and gloves, checking the sound and sensory levels several times. An electronic voice spoke somewhere in her head. "Welcome to the rehabilitation suite," it intoned. "The programme about to follow will introduce you to some of the situations you may encounter on leaving the Refuge. The story line is interactive. Players are thus enabled to learn which responses are the most likely to ensure their safety. Should you make a seriously wrong choice, death is possible, but only within the reality of your programme. Please press the square pad on the left to indicate this has been understood."

"Oh get on with it!" Jude thought impatiently. She pressed the left hand pad.

The voice continued. "Thank you. The scenario you have chosen is City Two. During this illusion, you will travel by public transport to visit friends in a large northern city. If at any time you wish to discontinue your journey, press the 'abort' triangle firmly. May we respectfully remind you that all damage to the illusion room must be paid for.

"Now, if you are ready to catch your transit capsule, press the circular pad on the right."

Jude pressed the pad. A burst of music followed, like the lead-in to a family amusement strip. "Welcome to the outer world," the voice continued. "Have an interesting illusion."

The music began to fade. As it did so, the blank walls filled with colour and movement. Sound throbbed in Jude's ears. Voices, voices... Everywhere people were shouting and laughing. Something hard shunted against metal. An engine roared. After the quiet of the Refuge the noise was almost unbearable. She was waiting at a departure terminal, crushed against a hundred or more passengers on a boarding deck. It was suffocatingly hot. Already sweat dampened her face.

With a squeal that made Jude's ears hurt, a transit capsule approached. At once everyone surged forward. Jostling and pushing, they forced their way past passengers trying to leave. Jude had to fight to find even a place to stand.

At once the capsule set off. Though Jude told herself that it was all only an illusion, the sense of speed was nauseating.

The scenario continued, focusing on a filthy window beside her. She could see nothing but open space through it, a black formless plain where a few lights glittered. The scratch under the lens on her left eye was beginning to hurt, and the real discomfort it caused began to blur into the illusion. Her mind wrote it into the scenario, creating an imaginary explanation for the pain: that she had been attacked by Hawkboys on her way to the transit station, and her money taken...

As suddenly as the illusory capsule had started, it stopped. "All change!" a voice announced. "All change!"

The scenario became increasingly unpleasant. No one knew why they had to get off, and there was a great deal of grumbling and confusion. The passengers poured onto an already crowded deck. Hundreds more workers were streaming towards it along the walkways, many of them wearing the grey uniform and blank expression of the clone. A muffled announcement came over the loudspeaker. A replacement capsule had been arranged, but it was leaving from another deck. All passengers for the north must cross to deck six at once.

By now Jude was becoming totally absorbed in the imaginary world being portrayed. She began to push through the crowd. Her father was ill and she must return home immediately. The walkway was packed solid with people. She struggled through them. Her head throbbed. Her left eye kept going misty and she rubbed at it, only to wince with pain. One of the Hawkboys had hit her with his flail. It must have hit her eye...

Each time a capsule came in, the crowds pushed forwards, carrying Jude with them. The walkway was slippery and her soft Refuge shoes would not hold. She had to struggle to keep upright. Suddenly a fight broke out ahead. People surged sideways to avoid it. Near Jude, a huge, thickset woman was elbowing her way through. She was wearing the protective clothes of a rodent controller and smelt of sweat. "That's my Geordie!" she shouted. "Let me through to him!"

Grabbing people by the shoulder or arm, the woman hauled them out of the way. Jude tried to avoid her, but there was a safety rail on the right blocking her path, and no space for her to move to in front. Remorselessly the rodent controller pushed against Jude, crushing her against the metal bar.

It was no use part of Jude's brain telling her she was standing in a room no bigger than three metres by six, or that she was attached to various wires and pads. The transit deck and the rail were as real as herself. Real crowds pressed down on her. Her arms were too weak to hold her away from the bar much longer. Slowly, painfully, her elbows began to bend. Her chest was being pressed against the metal, tighter and tighter. Soon her ribs must crack under the pressure. Breath swelled in her lungs. The sense of suffocation was overpowering, however unreal.

"Go under the rail," a voice called beside her. "It's your only way."

As soon as she slid downwards, hands were pulling her from the other side, dragging her under. A man was kneeling beside her, lifting her head so that she could breathe more easily. "You're safe now," he said.

Painfully Jude turned her head so that she could look round. "My poor Jude," the man said. "You've been hurt. Don't you know me? I'm your father. You were coming to visit me."

"But you're dying," Jude replied in bewilderment.

"No! You must have got the message wrong. You were going to meet me at Border Seven. Now we'll have to arrange another day, when you're stronger."

"I've seen you before!" a voice shouted. It was the rodent woman. Leaning over the barrier, she pointed at Jude's father. "You're Tuecer! You killed my Geordie!" Turning back to the crowd, she shouted, "It's that unifier man!" Furiously she waved them towards the rail.

Some of the passengers near her began to take up the cry. "Tuecer! Tuecer!" they shouted. The cry became a chant.

"He'll give us water!" a voice shouted above the babble. "Let him be!"

But the crowd was not listening. "Reiver!" someone shouted, and voices all around began to take up that word too. "Reiver! Reiver!" they called.

The shouts filled Jude's head. "Tuecer... Reiver! Tuecer...!" Urgently she tried to struggle to her knees but she was too dizzy. With a howl, the crowd rushed forward, knocking the barrier forwards.

Screaming, Jude was trampled under their feet...

*****

"Poor woman. She must have had a bad illusion," a voice said, but from far away. "Lucky she knocked the 'abort' button."

Vaguely Jude heard the receptionist reply. "I heard her screaming on the intercom, but there was nothing I could do. I mean, if they won't press 'abort', how can you help?"

A technician was undoing the sensor pads and leads, while a medical orderly was injecting stimulant into Jude's hand. Jude could not work out whether they were part of the illusion, or real. Frowning with the effort of concentration, she watched them. Then the stimulant hit her brain. With a start, she tried to get up, only to be held back.

"Oh no, you don't," the medical orderly said firmly. "Not until you've had a thorough check-up and a rest."

Feeling a fool, Jude sat against the wall. "Did I faint?" she asked.

"Yes, officer," the receptionist said. "You gave us all a fright."

"I'm sorry. It was hot in there," Jude said lamely. "And my eye hurt."

"Why?" the orderly asked. "Do you have an injury?"

"Just a scratch. I caught it when I was inserting the lens yesterday."

"You should have reported it. You know the rules."

"It didn't seem important enough. It wasn't hurting then."

The orderly examined her eye. "Just a minor scratch," he agreed. "That shouldn't have caused you much pain." He passed the diagnostic reader over her throat. "Do you have low blood pressure?" he asked.

"In the bottom band I believe, but not exceptional. It's quite useful for sporting activities. Why? Is that why I blacked out?"

"I don't know." Once again, the orderly examined the reader. "Do you meditate a lot?" he asked.

"Most days. It helps me to relax."

"You don't have fits do you?" the receptionist asked.

"No - I don't." Jude was beginning to feel annoyed. Since she outranked everyone in the room, she decided to wait no longer. "I'm perfectly well thank you," she said coolly. "I passed out, because I was hot and having an unpleasant illusion. That's all. Thank you for your concern, but it's time I returned to my duties."

The orderly shook his head. "I can't stop you doing so, Ma'am," he replied. "But you'd be wiser going home to rest."

As soon as she stood up, Jude saw the wisdom of his advice "All right," she agreed. "Perhaps an hour or so in bed would be sensible."

Though it was still only mid afternoon when Jude returned to her dwelling, her bedroom felt unusually cold. Shivering, she changed out of her uniform and put on a warm lounger suit, before lying down on the couch.

Half an hour later, she was still cold and lying wide awake. Sighing, she got up and rummaged in her closet for a wrap to put round her. Then she made a hot drink.

Afterwards, as she sat at the table, Jude tried to recall the illusion which had proved so unnerving. Border Seven. The name kept turning up, though this time there was an obvious logical explanation. She was worrying about her forthcoming journey and what she might find at the end. But why did her father appear again? And who on earth was Tuecer?

As far as Jude could recollect, she had never heard the name before. And what was a unifier - apart from the obvious implication? Was it some sort of rank? She had not the faintest idea, yet the word niggled at her memory as if she ought to recall something. Why should it be associated with water? Anyone who could bring water would be a hero indeed, but if such a man existed the government did not know about him, or he would have been forced to help at once. The drought in the south grew worse with every month. London had not seen rain for five years; the Eastern Sector for more than fifteen. A whole generation was growing up who thought water came only in pipes.

Yet in her illusion the crowd had wanted to destroy the man... Because he was a Reiver.

Ah - there was a link of course. Silly worries and concerns often got caught up into the interactive stuff, and turned into drama. Getting up, Jude went to her workstation, and called up the cylopaedia.

The word game referencer did not include 'Tuecer' or 'unifier', jumping from 'unification' to 'unified'. Jude tried the historical and mythological listing.

To her surprise a whole paragraph appeared, headed 'Greek myths':

'Tuecer: Legendary brother of Ajax, hero of the Trojan Wars, and himself a courageous archer. Banished by father for returning home without body of dead brother, though had struggled valiantly to give him honourable burial. Heartbroken, sailed east to found city of Salamis, on island of Troodos (former Cyprus). Probable site now under sea.'

Bewildered, Jude stared at the entry. To her knowledge, she had never heard of Ajax or Tuecer before, or any other Greek myth come to that.

She returned to the word game referencer. Perhaps she had not made a specific enough request. This time she typed 'Tuecer, the unifier'.

The referencer took longer than usual to activate. In the corner of the screen a code appeared - 'R100'. In surprise, Jude stared at the numbers. R100 indicated restricted access. She was about to press 'clear' and try again, assuming there to be some error. Then she stopped. If the entry genuinely was restricted, keying it in again could activate some sort of alarm. It would be unwise to persist.

By now Jude was thoroughly intrigued. Why should an illusion lead her to a restricted entry? If the authorities did not wish people to know something, why put it in a rehabilitation programme? There was of course, another possibility. Her own mind could have added the reference. Interactive experiences were the sum of the prearranged programme and of one's own memories, fantasies, fears...

One last route might be worth trying. If a term was historical in origin, a patient researcher could scan the main events of the last few centuries to see if it turned up along the way. That could take hours however, which Jude did not have.

She had long enough to call up her own records however. Her parentage, qualifications, and admission to SecureCity Incorporated as a full member, were all recorded, as were the various promotions that had followed. A note had been made of her slow heartbeat and low blood pressure, but not as cause for concern. An early entry did suggest witnessing the death of her parents might make her unstable, but as she had been admitted to officer training corps at the age of fourteen, and then to the 'high flyer' course the year afterwards, that worry had clearly been discounted. Jude had read it all before. There was nothing to explain her panic in the rehabilitation suite.

Suddenly Jude saw the obvious point she had missed. The man in her illusion had called himself her father, but she had not recognized him.

Quickly she clicked back to her birth details:

'Father: Joachim Shah (2084-2126), engineer grade five; killed by tribes people while on survey expedition. Awarded posthumous declaration of honour. Mother: pair-bond Claudia Shah, formerly Artuso, (2086-2126), survey officer grade three; killed ditto. 'Dignity of motherhood' award (posthumous).'

Though taken nearly fifteen years ago, the photo line images were still crisp and clear. Fixing her parents just under a year before their deaths, their portraits still made Jude's throat go tight. They looked so happy, both of them bronzed and healthy after one of their trips outside the Refuge - just as she recalled them in her dreams. There was no question about it. The man in the illusion had had auburn hair, like hers. Her father was dark.

Jude prepared to shut down the file. Then she paused. It might be a good idea to play with the cyclopaedia a while longer, as if she were completing a word game. Reference requests were presumably logged somewhere, if only to prove that the service was well used. Leaving her entry as a single inquiry could arouse interest.

For another half hour Jude keyed in entries, finding as many words as she could beginning with 'T' and then 'U'. At least the monotony was relaxing. Closing down the cyclopaedia, she lay down again on her couch and slept.

Chapter Five

By the time Jude woke it was sixteen thirty. Someone was at the door. Grabbing a hairbrush, she smartened herself up a bit, and then went to see who was calling. She was not altogether surprised to find Probationer Vass. In such a close environment, news travelled quickly.

"I wondered if I might talk to you for a bit," the woman asked. "I know you'll need to switch on the surveillance. I'm quite prepared for others to hear."

Puzzled, Jude invited her in. "Can I get you anything?" she asked. "I wouldn't mind a drink myself. I was asleep when you called."

"I'm sorry - I disturbed you."

"It was time I got up." Pointedly, Jude flicked open her communicator and laid it on the table between them. "What can I do for you?" she asked.

Linda Vass hesitated. She was evidently nervous and judging by the redness of her eyes, had been crying. "I came to apologise," she began. "I'm sorry I've caused you so much trouble. They say you're being disciplined."

It was as hard to lie to a probationer as it had been to deceive Kurt. Jude paused at the kitchen door. "You mustn't blame yourself," she replied. "It was my error of judgment, not yours. Besides, I doubt if it's only one mistake that's being punished. My behaviour in other matters must have already given cause for concern."

"How can you accept it - so - passively? Aren't you angry? I know I would be."

"I have had to learn to accept discipline." Jude spoke truthfully, but the words sounded pious in her ears. "When I became a full member of the Refuge, I promised to accept the wishes of my superiors," she added. "Besides, as a security officer, I know the importance of obeying orders. In so confined a space, there would be violence if everyone insisted on having their own way."

"But it's so unfair! Making an example of you -"

Glancing towards the communicator on the table, Jude gave an unspoken reminder. Linda Vass was not in the mood to be careful. "It's me who should be being disciplined!" she insisted. "Not you. You've always done your duty - and more. No one else would have got Bek out of her dwelling like you did. Everyone I know speaks well of you. What does Admin. want? They tried clones and went back to human beings - said clones didn't know who they were... But human beings will always make the odd mistake, however good they are at their job, and there should be room for them to do so. Otherwise, we're no more than insects slogging away in our nest." She laughed. "Yes, that's just what this place reminds me of - an ants' nest in the sky."

"You mustn't talk like this," Jude warned. "It'll do you no good."

"I can talk how I please. I'm leaving tomorrow."

In alarm, Jude came back into the main room. "You're giving up your apprenticeship?"

Linda nodded. "Yes," she replied firmly. "But I don't see it as giving up - more as starting afresh. My whole-life contract comes up for signing next week. I've thought and thought about it, and I know that it would be wrong for me to sign. I don't belong here."

"Have you told your line manager?"

"Of course, or I wouldn't be talking to you now."

"Where will you go?" Jude asked more gently.

"Back outside."

"How will you cope?"

"I shall have to learn. The longer I stay here, the harder it'll be. That's why I'm going tomorrow, while I can still remember how to feed and clothe myself, and have a chance of earning my living alongside everyone else."

Jude could not help admiring the young woman's courage. "Your resistance will be low," she warned. "You could go down with fever or tuberculosis. Without our medications, your chances of survival won't be good."

"Which is all the more reason I have to go now, before my body gets too soft." Getting up, Linda offered her hand in farewell. "I've made up my mind," she insisted. "Please don't try to dissuade me. Once I sign that contract, I shall have promised to serve the Corporation, right or wrong. I can't make that promise. Listening in on private conversations doesn't seem - decent to me. Nor should people be cooped up in tiny rooms with no human company, day after day, just so targets can be met. I used to believe being admitted to a Refuge was the best thing possible, the one thing you could work for at school. Even having to promise total commitment sounded a good bargain. The trouble is, the practice doesn't live up to the theory. When they discipline someone like you for an act of kindness, the ideal looks a bit thin."

Not knowing how to answer, Jude stood in silence. "I'm sorry if my situation has coloured your judgment," she said finally. "You don't know all the circumstances, and I'm not able to tell you. Your going will be a loss to us all, as well as ruining your own career."

"Don't worry, I made up my own mind - out of a need to be honest I suppose. Haven't you ever thought of leaving?"

"No," Jude replied honestly. "I signed the contract, and my parents did so before me. I'm not happy with how isolated the Refuges are becoming - we should be sharing our knowledge - but if the ideal isn't being kept to, then it's up to members like me to make sure it is - from the inside." Again Jude wished she did not sound so trite. "Now let's have that drink," she suggested. "To wish you luck."

They sat together in the lounge, drinking and talking. Jude found herself enjoying the younger woman's company. Now that she had made the decision to leave, Probationer Vass was full of hope and enthusiasm. "Mum and Dad'll be dreadfully disappointed," she conceded. "They were so pleased when I passed the entrance exams, but they wouldn't want me to stay with something I couldn't believe in. Dad's a biologist you see. He teaches at the university - when there are any lectures that is. Half the time, the building's closed for repairs. He works in a plant factory a lot of the time, cloning new vegetables. Dead boring, just cutting up bits of tissue, but it's money. He might be able to get me some work there - if he can find something the human resource manager wants badly enough." Linda laughed. "We've still got a nice little table left."

"Have you told your parents?" Jude asked.

"Not yet. I wanted to tell them in person and I haven't been able to get them a pass to visit me. I shall just have to land on their doorstep."

Looking at the woman's eager expression, Jude did not have the heart to ask anymore. "With your skills, you ought to be able to get a job with Manu-web," she suggested. "Their grid's not much different from our Groundnet, and you'd have the advantage of knowing how our purchasing system works. I'd give them a try."

Linda looked into her drink. "My uncle may know someone there," she said thoughtfully. Unexpectedly she laughed. "Yes. I think he does! I'll talk to him. Thanks for the idea."

Jude smiled. There was a chance the woman might survive. Despite her talk of honesty, Linda Vass realized she would need influence to stand any chance of finding work.

"You go out of the Refuge quite a bit don't you?" Linda asked. "If you're ever in Sector Three and need help, don't hesitate to call on us. Here's our address." Taking out a crumpled hard-copy, she wrote along the side of it, and then handed it to Jude. "Now I'd better get back," she added. "I've got a lot of packing to do."

Jude got up with her. "May your God be with you," she said and offered her hand.

*****

Kurt came to the departure room to wish her good-bye. Awkwardly they stood together while Jude's travel permits were checked and stamped.

"You're a few moments early," the transport officer said. "Wait over there please."

Two other Refuge officials were leaving that day, sales representatives, judging by their casual dress and smart cases. Jude and Kurt stood a little to one side, so that they could say their farewells privately.

"Call me as often as you can," Kurt asked.

Smiling, Jude nodded. "I don't know how much access I'll have to the inter-Refuge server," she replied. "But I'll call at least once a week. I promise." That much she could guarantee, having already recorded the messages that would be sent. The Chief Secretary had spotted the need to keep Kurt happy, even before Jude raised the issue. Come to think of it, there wasn't much the Chief Secretary had missed. There were arrangements for almost every contingency.

"What will you do with yourself while I'm away?" Jude asked.

"Work. Swim a good deal. Play badminton. Much the same as I did before I met you."

"No you won't," she teased. "You'll lounge around in the officers' games room. Keep me up to date with the gossip. I shall get out of touch otherwise."

"Oh, yes. There's one juicy bit you can take with you now."

For the second time that hour, Jude unclasped her travel sac and felt for her medical cards and food vouchers. They were exactly where she had put them. "What's that?" she asked.

"The Chief Secretary's been dismissed."

In amazement Jude stared at him. "What do you mean, 'dismissed'?" she demanded. "You can't dismiss a Chief Secretary!"

"Apparently you can. Or rather, the Intergovernmental Employment Agency can."

"But they don't usually interfere in Refuge affairs. I mean, we operate under licence. How can they fire our staff? And senior ones at that? "

"They must have had good reason." Glancing towards the other travellers, Kurt lowered his voice. "The rumour is, she's been charged with corruption. That's one crime the Agency does have the right to act on."

Appalled, Jude stood with her wallet still in her hand. "I don't believe it," she insisted. "I met the woman. Not under pleasant circumstances, I'll admit, but I ended up respecting her. I would have said she was totally honest."

"I can't say," Kurt admitted. "She never came near any of us. Whatever the reason, she's gone."

Jude began to feel alarmed. "Where to?" she asked.

"Another Refuge perhaps. Maybe outside. Nobody seems to know. They were all talking about it in the officer's rest room this lunchtime. With you packing and everything, I didn't think you'd have heard. The official line is that there's been a reorganisation, and the post is being amalgamated with comptroller. Our line management reckon the deputy will act up for a while. Well - it saves money. If you ask me, it'll be months before they make an appointment."

"At least," Jude agreed vaguely. She was not concentrating on what Kurt was saying. Apart from the Assessor she was to meet at Border Seven, no one knew her role, or could offer any support. Her sole channel of contact was the Chief Secretary, direct. Now even that link had gone. A transport was about to arrive, to take her to a place where no one knew her, to do a job no one wanted, and which could cost her her life. Jude had never felt so alone.

"You look a bit pale," Kurt remarked. "Are you all right?"

"I hate waiting," Jude replied.

Kurt looked up at the indicator above them. "Your transport's due any minute," he said. "You will take care, won't you?"

Urgently Jude tried to think what to do. Her passage out of the Refuge was arranged. If she announced now that she was not leaving, there would be questions asked. The whole fabrication about her being disciplined and sent to Mid Two would emerge, and that would inevitably link her to the former chief. Jude had no doubts about the reason for the Chief Secretary's sudden dismissal. Someone - with a lot of power - had realized the woman was trying to discredit them, and had arranged her removal. If they knew Jude was involved, they could well arrange for her to disappear also, from her own Refuge.

A disembodied voice filled the room, making Jude jump. "Members, your transport is ready," it announced. "Please take your seats as allocated, and have your travel passes ready for inspection. We hope you have a safe journey."

For a second longer Jude hesitated, then she put her arm round Kurt's shoulders. "Good-bye," she whispered. "I'll keep my bond to you - if I survive - but none of us knows our future."

Trying to smile, she turned towards the waiting transporter.

*****

"Identify yourself please," the automatic voice intoned.

Jude swiped her cards through the reader beside her seat. "You are clear to continue," the voice responded. Her mind had begun to work again, with the rush of ideas that follows panic. Before the hood had closed over her head, she had decided on her most sensible course of action.

The Chief Secretary had ordered her to travel to Mid Two, and then from Refuge to Refuge until she was lost in the system. After so many transfers no one would notice her disappearance for at least a month - long enough for her to travel to Border Seven by ordinary public transport, assume the role of a menial, and provide support for the Assessor there.

Providing those travel orders were still in place, Jude decided she would follow the plan as far as Mid Two. Otherwise she might be regarded with suspicion. Once at Mid Two she would abandon an assignment that was now too dangerous to complete. The human resources officers there would have no idea what to do with her. It should be relatively easy for her to persuade them to make out the necessary orders for her to be sent back home.

Feeling a little easier, Jude began to notice the world around her. The transporter was slowing down, the walls of the tunnel taking form after being no more than a blurred streak of lights. They were approaching the transit station. Rapidly the Refuge terminus came into view. The capsule shuddered slightly, then screeched to a halt. Even inside the protection of the passenger pod, the effect was like being thrown at a brick wall. Silently the hood slid back. "All change," the automatic voice intoned. "All change. Refuge jurisdiction ends here."

A little shakily, the three passengers stepped out onto the platform. Beyond the private gates, Jude could see crowds of workers waiting for the city line. From now onwards, she would have to remember how to push and shove, how to hold her own. Not even her uniform and first class travel warrants would protect her from the heaving, sweating mobs of ordinary citizens. If the link to the transit station were above ground she reflected, the shock to the system would not be quite so bad. Being able to look back at the complex and watch its lobe gradually diminish, would at least give some warning of the change from cocooned protection, to chaotic reality.

*****

All three Refuge travellers paused a minute on the safe side of the gates, gathering strength. "It doesn't look any better," the older of the sales reps remarked.

"No," his companion agreed. "Apparently there were riots on a couple of lines yesterday."

"Not again!" Jude commented. It would be wise to join the conversation and ensure herself some company. "What were they rioting about this time?"

"The new order isn't going down well."

"Oh?" Jude asked. "I thought it went through parliament without opposition. We have to save power somehow."

They began to walk through the gates, sticking close for mutual protection. "So I heard," the younger man agreed. "Still, what this parliament agrees and what the people will support are two different things. No one's going to welcome giving up the right to travel where they want, when they want. It's one of the basic human freedoms. Don't get me wrong," he added hastily. "The Exclusion Order was much needed. I mean, just look at this lot, and everyone with a permit, even under the new legislation. There are just too many people trying to move about, and too little transport - or power - to take them."

"A year or two and they'll get used to it," the older man agreed. "When the Personal Transportation Bill was passed, there was no end of trouble. I was serving in North One then, and there were riots every day. It's amazing how reluctant people are to stay in one place. It was just the same when they banned the automobile."

By now they had reached the city-link deck. Though their travel passes gave them access to the reserved area, away from the main crush, the five minutes' wait for the next capsule was uncomfortable enough. The seats had been vandalised and in the stifling heat, standing was tiring. Jude began to find the ever-present odour of bodies and transporter fumes unpleasant. She had a strong sense of smell - more a liability than an advantage in such crowded conditions. Pretending to push the hair away from her face, she held her cuff near her nostrils. Just before leaving her dwelling she had soaked a handkerchief in freshener and hidden it up her sleeve. It was a luxury she would have to forgo later, or it would destroy any attempt she might make at disguise.

The capsule came in at last, and Jude joined the two men at the rear, in the first class accommodation. The ordinary travellers seemed to watch their arrival with more than usual resentment. There were more guards around too, not just on the platform, but riding on the transporter itself. Jude sighed. It was not going to be a pleasant journey. She did not like feeling she was one of a privileged few, but at least she was safe while she was in uniform. SecureCity Incorporated had the power to protect its members effectively. Charges of assault would be brought rapidly against any attacker, and whole councils made to pay for failing to protect Refuge travellers. It would be a different matter if she went up north as a menial - the lowest of the low, and considered by many as fair game for a bit of sport. She would be mad to go.

The two sales representatives parted company with her at the central station. There was an elite express link to London, once a day. Jude decided to take that rather than risk travelling to Mid Two by normal public transport. She spent the two hours' wait playing reality games in the first class lounge, and watching the latest news on the overhead viewer. There was no reference to any riots. Indeed, the Private Transportation Order was claimed to be universally welcomed, a long-overdue measure to save power. Without it, there would be more - and longer - power cuts, and everyone would suffer. A couple of tame citizens were paraded to recommend the government's far-sighted action. "We can all travel if we need to," the woman said, smiling to camera. "Passes will be easy to obtain. All we have to do is provide proof that our journey is necessary, and produce our identity and medical cards. Oh - and you also need a letter from your employer, giving permission."

A woman near Jude snorted loudly. "What if you don't have an employer?" she asked, of no one in particular. "Or your boss doesn't feel like giving you a letter?"

Other travellers murmured agreement. "First it was medical sanctions," one remarked, "'To prevent the transmission of infection' - now it's virtually everything you can think of. If this goes on much longer, we can forget about visiting dear old Ma and Pa."

Their comments surprised Jude. It was not often one heard such outright criticism of the government, and certainly not in a first class lounge. "Do you know how long I had to wait for a pass?" a woman asked. "Four hours! They reckoned it was a 'temporary hiccup' - everyone had panicked and applied, whether they needed one or not."

Another woman laughed scornfully. "I bet our elected members aren't waiting four hours," she retorted. "Or Refuge officials either."

The last comment was obviously intended for Jude's hearing, but she pretended to be too absorbed in her luggage to notice.

Chapter Six

"Didn't they tell you before you left?" the reception officer at Mid Two asked, quite kindly. "The order was changed. You've been sent on to Mid Three."

So the Chief Secretary's plans for her travel were still intact, Jude thought in surprise. She hadn't bargained on that. "But I was told I'd been posted here," she said aloud, pretending annoyance.

"No. Your posting was transferred. I've checked twice."

"How infuriating!" Jude said, still holding out her ID wallet.

"I can't understand how East Five came to make such a mix-up," the young woman continued. "Making you travel so far out of your way! The last time I went out I was appalled. The civil police have warned us there are rape gangs hanging round the stations. Any woman leaving here is advised to be in a group."

"That doesn't sound good," Jude replied, becoming genuinely alarmed. If the rape gangs were back, no woman with any sense would travel alone if she could help it.

"I'll have to get new travel passes issued for you. You'll have to wait until they're ready, so I'd leave in the morning," the reception officer suggested. "I can arrange accommodation under our emergency budget. The hospitality suite's fully booked, but '240a is free. Why don't you have a meal while I sort things out? My name's Holly Newton by the way. Pleased to meet a fellow northerner."

Smiling, Officer Newton extended her hand.

Two officials were already standing at the food panel as Jude entered the refectory. They looked like representatives on the way to an important meeting. Their minds were clearly on more urgent matters than food, for they were talking instead of concentrating on the menu. Patiently Jude waited for them to decide what to order. "I tell you it isn't safe," the first man was saying. "I intend to contact Head Office, and tell them I'm stopping here."

"With respect, Commissioner, you'll just be told the situation is 'under control'," the other replied. "The best thing we can do is prestex our papers ahead of us, leave everything distinctive here, and then go on as ordinary citizens. That's the safest way."

In alarm, Jude turned towards them. "I'm sorry," she said. "But I couldn't help overhearing. I'd heard there were riots, but I thought they were only in the northwest sector."

"It depends who you talk to," the first representative answered. Older and more polished than his companion, he shook his head in concern. "The guard at the transit gate reckons it's right across the north. Are you planning to go up there? I wouldn't if I were you. Personally, I intend to hang on until things have settled down."

"We could be stuck here weeks," his companion reminded him. "There are a lot of people out there with grievances. If we go now, we'll be all right. Tomorrow, who knows?"

Another traveller came in, a childcare officer, escorting a girl of about ten.

"I'm fed up with hanging around," the girl complained. "Why do we have to stop here?"

"We can't go on just yet, dear," the officer replied, "It's not safe."

"There! What did I say?" the older representative demanded. "Our colleague doesn't think it's safe either."

"Not with a child," the woman agreed. "I thought it wiser to stop off here." Leaving her charge sitting alone at a table, she joined the queue at the servery.

Looking at the child's face, Jude forgot her own anxieties. She could vividly recall similar journeys she had made as a teenager. They had not been fun either. Deciding to let the others order their meals first, she went across to the girl. "May I join you?" she asked. "I'm on my own too."

"If you want. I don't see why Dragon's Breath should mind. Who are you anyway?"

Glancing at the escort, Jude smiled to herself. 'Dragon's Breath' looked appropriate.

"My name's Jude," she replied. "What's yours?"

"Loreen. Loreen Carpenter."

"Hello, Loreen," Jude said and offered her hand. The childcare officer looked across. Obviously she did not like her charge talking to strangers, but in view of Jude's seniority, she said nothing.

"I'm just passing through too," Jude explained. "It's scary outside, isn't it? Did you have any adventures getting here?"

"A great pile of men came onto our transporter, and shouted things at us. I stared out of the window and pretended not to hear."

"Very sensible. What did they do then?"

"One of them waved a bottle at me. I couldn't make out whether he wanted me to have a drink, or give him one. It was empty anyway. In the end, he got bored and went to bother someone else."

Jude smiled. The girl had spirit. "I'm not surprised your escort's worried," she commented. "She only wants you to stay here until things are safer."

"I'm sick of staying with people I don't know. Besides, I don't like this place. It stinks of disinfectant."

"Doesn't it?" Jude agreed. "They keep cleaning it, in case people like you and me bring nasty germs. Did they spray you when you arrived?"

Loreen giggled. "Like I was covered in creepy crawlies. They even sprayed her." Glancing towards her escort, she grimaced. "I don't know what for. Bugs wouldn't dare grow on her."

"Where have you come from?" Jude asked.

"Leodis One. My Gran lives there, only she can't have me anymore. She's poorly." Loreen's eyes had gone very bright. "I'm going to stay with my auntie instead."

Jude's heart went out to her. "You'll be fine once you get there," she promised. "At least you have an aunt. I didn't, and I've survived OK."

"Didn't you have any parents either?"

Smiling, Jude shook her head. "It's not quite the end of the world," she advised. "Though it seems like it at the time."

The girl's companion was coming towards them, carrying two meals on a tray. "I wish you were going with me - not her," Loreen said suddenly.

"It doesn't matter who you travel with," Jude replied gently. "You can shut them out and think your own thoughts. Once you make up your mind you're alone, it doesn't hurt half so much."

"Afternoon, officer," the girl's escort said, and set the tray on the table. "Do join us."

"It's very kind of you to invite me," Jude replied, "But I need to think. I don't know whether to continue my journey or not."

"It's not my place to say so," the woman replied, her expression suggesting exactly the opposite. "But I wouldn't if I were you."

Sitting on her own, Jude tried to decide what to do. Her travel pass would only be valid for a journey to Mid Three - presumably she would find another there, arranged by the Chief Secretary, or her allies. But the situation outside was getting worse all the time. She must find a way of getting back home. Then she thought of the woman she was supposed to be protecting, stuck at Border Seven. She could imagine the Assessor's growing alarm, looking every day for her assistant to arrive. Jude began to feel very guilty at the idea of abandoning her assignment.

Sweat began to prickle on Jude's upper lip. Feeling increasingly worried, she pushed the remainder of her food away from her. To her annoyance, the older of the representatives was crossing towards her table. Introducing himself as Commissioner Markham, he sat beside Jude and began to talk about himself.

As Jude had thought, he had been on his way to an important conference. "HQ will have to cancel of course," he predicted. "They've got representatives coming from all over Europe. God! What they must think of this place! All the way from Barcelona in a couple of hours, to get stuck at an interchange here!"

Politely Jude smiled, and tried to listen to him. "What have you decided to do?" she asked.

"Stay the night. I've finally got my hotheaded friend to see sense. What are you doing?"

"I don't know, Sir."

Commissioner Markham smiled. "There's no need to call me, Sir," he assured her. "We're both off duty. After all, I'm your representative, appointed to serve you and your colleagues. I'd much rather people called me John."

Warily Jude nodded. She did not like the man. Despite his charm and distinguished bearing, there was something about him that repelled her.

"You look tired, my dear," he continued. "Why don't you take a bit of advice from your representative and stay the night too? We could keep each other company. Let me arrange a room for you. I have a good deal of influence here."

With a start, Jude realized Commissioner Markham was leaning across the table rather too closely. Apparently he fancied her. The idea amused her, but also filled her with distaste. Something about him was not right. She had a distinct impression that if she could part the skin across his chest, she would find rotten flesh inside.

Drawing back, she kept a polite distance between them. "That's very kind of you," she replied. "But my partner will be worrying about me. Maybe I'll go straight home."

Disappointed, the man left her.

Wearily, Jude got up and fetched herself a cup of coffee.

Afterwards, she went back to reception, and asked for the key to dwelling 240a.

*****

As soon as the domestics had prepared her bed, Jude settled in front of the in-house entertainment. At twenty hours exactly, she called the communication centre and asked to put through a message to her intended partner. Rather to her surprise, she was allowed to speak to Kurt in person, and they talked for ten minutes about the mistake in her posting. Then the 'please terminate' sign came on screen, and they wished each other a good night, and a safe day to follow.

Flicking through the channels, Jude looked for something to watch until she was ready to sleep. Nothing appealed to her, so she went to the workstation and decided to play a few in-house games. "Choose your century," the first invited. "With our unique enhanced imagery, you can be anything you wish, in any time you please."

"Of course!" Jude said to herself. Closing down the games programme, she opened the learning package. 'History: twenty first century; religious and social' she typed.

"Please give your reason for requesting this category," the synthesised voice responded.

Jude chose 'c': private research. Irritatingly, the programme required further details before it would proceed. "To assist in developing a new reality game," she answered. Since Jude had written three games already, two of which had been accepted by the Entertainments department, her reply ought to satisfy.

A menu appeared. Jude stared at the screen. The phrase, 'that unifier man' suggested a wish for compromise. Pro-democracy groups had been common at the turn of the century, and a major force in the fight to re-establish parliament. 'Tuecer' could have been the leader of one, and his name might have surfaced from memories of her history classes. Hoping she was on the right track, Jude chose 'political parties', and then gave the names of five pro-democracy groups. So that it did not appear to have any special significance, she left 'unifiers' almost to the end.

Patiently Jude plodded through the first three sets of references, at the pace of a researcher making notes as they read. At last, the fourth search began. Holding her breath, she watched the screen. A single extract appeared:

"In the mid twenty first century, cult leaders like Guru Naagarssa had strong support among the masses. The Jupitarians turned to the past, particularly ancient religions and so-called earth magic. The unifiers, a pro-democratic group which emerged during the early years of the Junta, were reputed to have established a special relationship with the Reivers. In 2089, General Rowles introduced the Cult Control Bill, which made membership of any unapproved group an imprisonable offence, and specifically named the unifiers. The new government has not yet repealed this legislation."

Failure to repeal the Junta's legislation was not remarkable, Jude reflected. Legalising banned groups would not be high on the agenda even now, ten years after the Junta was overthrown. There were far higher priorities for a novice government - like learning to run a country and re-establishing basic services. Still, it did mean that the unifiers remained on the banned list, and membership would be an imprisonable offence.

Typing in the cross reference, Jude waited for a link to the Reivers to appear. Again, there was only one brief entry:

Reivers: 1) Families who robbed and plundered along the Border, following the Battle of Flodden in 1513 and the defeat of the Scots. 2) Present day lawless groups of Borderers who follow warlord leaders, and are popularly named after the above.

For several moments, Jude waited for more to appear. Nothing else came on screen. She began to feel uneasy and closed down the programme.

She might as well go to bed and get a good night's sleep.

When Jude woke, it took her several moments to recall where she was. She had been dreaming again, not her usual recurring nightmare, but about Joel.

"Oh, for heaven's sake!" she said aloud. If being unable to stop thinking of someone was love, she was in love with a boy she had not seen for years. She was as bad as her mother.

Staring back into the past, Jude sighed. She was being unfair. Her mother had not been a foolish romantic, but a sensible, practical woman, who had fought bravely until the end. Her marriage to Jude's father had been an arranged pair-bonding like Jude's own, and she had no chance to watch too many reality games. When she had spoken to Jude of love, it was at Jude's insistence, after some silly chatter amongst the menials they had overheard. There had been a wistfulness in her voice too, as if she knew from experience what she was describing.

And Jude herself - if she could not get a fifteen year old boy out of her mind, it was not necessarily foolish. She and Joel had endured a great deal together, led a group of fractious children day after day, and made them keep silent when the merest sneeze would have helped murderers find them. By the time Joel had guided her back to her Refuge, she had known and respected him like a brother. There had never been chance for her to form so close a relationship with anyone - other than her parents - before or since.

That of course was part of the problem, Jude admitted. Both Joel and Probationer Vass had called the Refuge an ants' nest in the sky, but ants communicated with each other. Members of a Refuge were more like solitary bees. Each of them had their own comfortable little nest and did their work in it, solitarily. Even their amusements were solitary, shut inside a cubicle or plugged into an illusion their neighbours could not share. Pair-bonding had its uses, however callous the business of screening and matching might seem. How else would couples meet and mate?

Impatiently Jude got up from the bed. She was getting morbid. Too much time for thought never did her any good.

As she ate her breakfast, however, her mood would not lift. Her decision not to go on with her assignment began to look cowardly. Reason said her assignment had become too risky to continue. But where did that leave the Assessor stuck at Border Seven? If Jude felt alone without the Chief Secretary's support, how did that woman feel?

Letting out her breath slowly, Jude came to a decision. Her new travel pass would get her to Mid Three, and then she would see what happened. If she could get to Border Seven, she would. She had known danger many times, and though she had never taken needless risks, she had never run away from it. She would not do so now. What was she planning to do after she ran back home? Sit in her room and play reality games? Reality was out there, however dirty and dangerous.

*****

If the Public Transportation Act had been intended to make people stay at home, it had failed, abysmally. The interchanges were seething, every transporter packed to suffocation. Workers who could not obtain travel permits walked, carrying their tools. While Refuge members complained they could never leave their dwellings, outside it seemed half the population lived in one city and worked in another. Even whole families seemed to be on the move, their household goods stuffed in bags or piled on trolleys.

As Jude waited for the Midlander Express, she looked around her warily. In such crowds anything could happen. A discarded drink canister could contain gas, the travel sac near her feet could explode in her face. Such terrors had happened to others. There were half a dozen sects who might decide the Government should fall today, and that they had a divine right to bring it about.

To her surprise, Jude noticed Commissioner Markham on the opposite platform, waiting for the Southern Express. At breakfast, he had announced that he was going to stay at the Refuge for a few days, until conditions improved. His colleague had certainly cancelled his journey. Jude wondered what had made the man change his mind, and why she had disliked him so much. Her aversion to him was so strong that when he sat down at her table that morning, she could scarcely look at him.

The Southern Express was due, but the Commissioner was not facing in that direction, but across to Jude's platform. Intrigued, she turned to see what had caught his attention. He seemed to be looking towards the back of her platform, watching three men and a woman clustered around a single, very fat man. Jude smiled. She could tell fellow Security officers when she saw them. "I wonder who they're minding?" she thought.

There was nothing about the fat man to indicate rank or position, but his bearing suggested he was accustomed to be being obeyed. Though he was dressed quietly, the cut of his clothes looked too good for England. His mannerisms were not English either. Whoever he was, he was travelling incognito, and judging by the anxious way he kept looking about him, he was not happy travelling across England at such a difficult time. Jude remembered the Commissioner's reference to an important conference, and wondered if the foreigner was heading there too. Such high ranking officials were rarely seen in England, and if the Commissioner knew who the man was, his interest would be understandable.

A tall, dark-haired man in military uniform was standing on the same platform as Jude, almost next to her. He too seemed interested in the fat man, but Jude formed the impression that he was anxious about something, and uncertain what to do. She glanced at his face. There was a faint scar above his left eyebrow. But for that scar, he would have been handsome, though in a thoughtful, quiet way, rather than by Refuge standards. She could not work out why he seemed familiar to her.

Coming to a decision, the soldier tried to move towards the group at the far end of the platform, but he was given a hard nudge by a woman beside him. "Wait your turn!" she snarled. The crowd closed tighter.

Anxiously, the young man looked across to the Southern deck, towards Commissioner Markham. For a second he hesitated. Then he turned away from Jude, and began pushing his way towards the footbridge over the gyrocaust. "Let me through please!" he shouted.

Jude glanced across to the other deck. Commissioner Markham was standing in exactly the same position as when she last looked. There was something odd about his silent, fixed gaze towards the fat man - something that made her feel uncomfortable.

By now, the soldier had managed to reach the footbridge. Virtually lifting a woman out of his way, he ran up the steps two at a time, onto the bridge. He was very fit, an athlete or a runner, spare but strong.

The four minders were watching the crowds around them, and looking everywhere except at the platform opposite. Clearly they considered anyone on it too far away to pose a threat, but a very skilled assassin, with a long-range weapon... He - or she - might aim between the minders just as the transporter was arriving, and then vanish as it came alongside, blocking their view.

Jude's curiosity became alarm. Like the dark-haired soldier before her, she tried to push down the platform to warn the man's guards. The Midlander was being signalled and people near her were surging forwards. When she shouted, her voice was drowned in the babble. Increasingly concerned, she looked back towards Commissioner Markham. If she could make him understand the danger, he might be able to call a warning across the gyrocaust. The crowds were thinner on his deck.

Then, in bewilderment Jude paused. The Commissioner was still standing watching the fat man, smiling to himself. The thin, hard line of his mouth sent a chill through Jude's mind. There seemed to be a direct relationship between his amusement and the minders' ignorance.

The soldier had managed to reach the southern platform now, and was approaching the Commissioner from behind. Trapped in the crowd opposite them, Jude could do nothing but watch. She felt as if she was involved in a reality game, compelled to wait for its ending.

In seconds, the soldier reached Commissioner Markham. Putting his hand on the man's neck he whispered something in his ear.

An expression of absolute terror came to Markham's face. He tried to turn round, but the grip on his neck was too strong. Then the other man gave him a little push.

There was no way the Southern Express could brake in time. In the instant before Jude's view was blocked, she saw the Commissioner falling forwards, still struggling to regain his balance. With a great roar, the transporter threw itself into reverse, just as the Midlander drew in alongside it, two minutes late.

Absolute chaos followed. On both platforms people started to scream. Jude caught a glimpse of two of the minders dragging the foreigner to safety, then they too vanished in the confusion.

"Security!" she shouted. "Let me through!" Scrambling up onto the bridge, she tried to see where the soldier had gone. He was already running past the main transit lounge.

Dropping down behind the Express, Jude ran along the gyrocaust, to cut him off. As she did so, she suddenly knew why the soldier had seemed familiar to her. He looked like an older Joel. The memory of a similar chase flashed through her mind. Then they had been running together, with transport police pursuing them across a platform. The blood had pounded in her ears just the same.

"Joel!" she called frantically.

Even as she shouted, Jude prayed the runner would not give any sign of recognition. To her horror, he looked back. She had guessed correctly.

It was impossible to catch Joel up. What would she do if she did? She was unarmed, and a man who could coolly push someone in front of a transporter must surely be carrying a weapon. Stopping at the end of the platform, Jude watched Joel leap down from the edge of the deck. Darting to the side as if expecting to be fired upon, he ran across the wasteland bordering the interchange, and out of sight.

For several moments Jude could not steady her breath. Shock, rather than effort, exhausted her. "Did you see what happened?" a voice called.

Turning back to face the officials approaching her, Jude nodded. "Refuge Security," she said, and took out her pass.

Chapter Seven

"Carrie!" she almost said aloud, and stopped herself. Fourteen years ago Carrie Lawson had been a four year old with pretty blond hair and a sweet manner. Today she was a woman, and not necessarily to be trusted. Meeting her was an unexpected complication, and after seeing Joel earlier too, a very odd coincidence.

Sadly Jude turned back to the window. They had endured a great deal together. It would have been nice to catch up on each other's lives since they parted. The local government officials were still talking. "You're absolutely right, George," the woman was saying. "Something will have to be done." Since neither knew what that something was, their conversation faltered.

"Scotland and Wales don't have gangs terrorising their cities," George insisted. They won't even let English tourists in anymore, not without a visa. Last time I went up to Scotland I felt like a poor relation."

"I've never been," Carrie said wistfully. "They say it's lovely. I don't like mountains though. They're cold."

The treasury official smiled indulgently. "Have you ever actually seen a mountain, my dear?" he asked. "A real one I mean."

Flushing slightly, Carrie shook her head. She had retained the naive sweetness of her childhood, and Jude found herself drawn to her again. Of all the children in her charge, little Carrie had quickly become her favourite.

"No, I don't suppose you have," the official continued, answering her own question. "Only an image of one. That's where we do have an advantage over you. Even when I'm at work, I can look out of my window and see the real world, and that's more than you can do."

"But our gardens are real," Jude protested. "Only the wealthy can afford those outside -."

"Jude!" Without warning, Carrie threw her arms round Jude and hugged her.

In surprise and pleasure Jude held the girl to her, while the other passengers watched in amazement. "Hey-" she said at last, freeing herself gently. "Don't cry. You'll have me crying too."

Laughing now in confusion, Carrie sniffed and looked for her handkerchief. "It is Jude, isn't it?" she asked. "I'm going to feel an awful fool if it isn't."

Taking Carrie's hands in hers, Jude nodded, looking at Carrie. The blond hair was still fine, though controlled under a Refuge band. The mouth was full and the eyes a perfect oval, but the effect now was of beauty rather than mere prettiness. "My, how you've grown!" she teased.

"So have you." Drawing back a little, Carrie considered Jude's uniform and insignia. "Internal Security," she remarked with approval. "That takes some getting into. Mind you, I'm not surprised. They picked you out as a leader immediately we got back."

"I'm not really in Security," Jude insisted. "Family Support's quite separate."

Carrie smiled. "So you lot always say. You'd be good at it. You'd care for people, not just enforce the rules."

It was Jude's turn to flush with embarrassment. Recalling the two other passengers, she began to feel some explanation was needed. "I'm sorry," she apologised. "Carrie and I haven't seen each other for years. I'm afraid we got carried away."

"You must have been very close," the man replied. Public expressions of emotion were clearly not to his taste.

"Jude saved my life," Carrie replied. "And my friends."

"Really?" the man asked. His tone annoyed Carrie.

"Yes, Sir" she insisted. "There were five of us, none of us over ten years old and Jude led us to safety, right across Border territory. I was only four then, but like you said, memories stick."

With a faint 'humph' the man turned away, towards the window. His companion was intrigued, however. "Do tell me about it," she prompted.

For the second time in a few days, Jude listened in embarrassment while an old story was told.

"We were staying with our parents, Ma'am," Carrie said, "Near the border with Scotland. They were engineers, you see, investigating a site for a new Refuge. The local people hated us." With an attempt at a smile, Carrie steadied her voice. "The authorities hadn't consulted anyone who lived on the land, and the compensation was hardly worth having. There were several local gangs - tribes - whatever you like to call them, and they attacked our camp. Jude and I were playing in the woods at the time. We survived, with a few other children. I can't remember a lot - I was too young, but I can still see my mother being hit about the head with a stick."

"How dreadful!" The woman was beginning to feel uncomfortable. "Didn't anyone help?"

"The police never did a thing. When Jude went to see them afterwards, they weren't interested. They just told her to go back where she'd come from. So that's what we did - walked the whole way. It was Jude who looked after us and kept us going."

"I was the eldest. That was all," Jude insisted.

Pausing, Carrie glanced at the woman's companion, who had been listening, though pretending not to do so. "So you see, Sir," she concluded, "Even if Jude and I are safe inside our glass towers most of the time, we know more about trouble than you think."

"She has you there, George," the woman admitted, and tapped her companion's arm. Then she turned to Jude. "My dear, I am pleased to meet you!" she enthused. "You must be a very resourceful young woman."

It was all Jude could do to keep her temper. She loathed being patronised. "No," she replied. "No more than any other thirteen year old girl trying to save her skin. I didn't do it all on my own either. We had help from a family of squatters nearby."

"Squatters?"

"Yes. Riffraff like the ones your colleague dislikes so much." As she spoke, Jude thought of what she had just seen Joel do, and her eyes stung. To her infinite relief, the transporter was approaching Birmingham Central. Getting up, she reached for her luggage.

"Are you getting off here too?" Carrie asked in delight.

"I've been temporarily posted to Mid Three." Turning to the two officials, Jude nodded in farewell. She had been rude to them both, but there was nothing she could say in apology. "Good morning," she said stiffly. "May you have a safe journey."

With an effort at dignity, she left the compartment.

Carrie had to run to keep up along the deck. "Are you angry with me?" she asked.

"Yes, I am," Jude retorted. "You embarrassed me intensely."

The girl was becoming breathless. "I'm sorry," she panted. "I wouldn't have said anything, only I was so surprised to see you, and that stupid Councillor got up my nose."

Jude relented a little. "They were both thoroughly annoying me," she admitted. "But it's safer to smile sweetly and say nothing."

"Why? What right have they to be rude to us? They want what we can provide. Not one of them have the first idea how to keep the Groundnet going, or even how to keep their water and power going. They don't even want to learn. They're like parasites feeding off our knowledge, but we've got to be reminded every minute of the day how lucky we are!"

"Hold on," Jude warned. "You're talking to the converted." Instinctively she had lowered her voice. "Don't talk so loudly," she warned. "There's a funny atmosphere today."

At the Refuge transit station, Jude felt more at ease. The refreshment machine was actually working, and the next capsule was due to arrive within thirty minutes. Settling down to wait, she sighed in relief.

"I'm sorry I snapped at you earlier," she apologised. "I know what you mean about feeling unwanted. Refuge members are a useful target. The public can vent their anger against us, rather than the authorities."

"The Public Transport Act's made things worse," Carrie agreed. "Last time I travelled, people didn't seem half so angry."

They sat in silence for a few moments. "I'm awfully glad we met like this," Carrie said at last. "I intended to travel on Thursday, but my pass was changed. I don't know why - a mix-up in the Travel Department."

In surprise, Jude considered Carrie's remark. "It is quite a coincidence," she agreed.

They were joined by another Refuge official. A senior programmer, he was accompanied by his personal assistant and a stack of luggage. "Glad I'm on my way back," he remarked. With a gesture of the head, he indicated the crowd beyond the gates. "Have you heard?"

"I'm not sure, Sir," Jude replied carefully.

"It's on all the news flashes, girl. The plebs are burning things down. If the authorities had any sense, they'd do a bit of fire raising themselves, and teach the rabble a lesson."

Carrie was about to say something impulsive, but she managed to stay silent. The new arrival was five grades senior to her.

Mercifully, the capsule arrived, preventing further conversation. "How long are you here for?" Carrie asked, as she and Jude took their places.

"Only a few weeks."

"You'll spend this evening with me, won't you? We have so much to talk about."

Smiling, Jude nodded. Carrie was definitely going to be a problem.

*****

Reception at Mid Three were apologetic. There was no position for Jude there either, but North One could use her. Would she mind awfully going up there that afternoon? She could stay for a meal and a rest first.

Jude's heart sank. She seemed to be trapped in an everlasting journey around the country. Whatever had happened to the Chief Secretary, all her plans for Jude were still in place.

Making a pretence at exasperation, Jude agreed. Then she went to find Carrie.

The girl was still unpacking. "But they can't do that to you!" she protested.

"I'm afraid they can. I'm a supernumerary. If I'm not needed, they don't have to take me. Budgets are tight this year."

"But why were you sent in the first place?"

"I've been suspended."

At once Carrie put down the clothes she had been unfolding. "No!" she protested. "I'm so sorry. What on earth happened? I can't believe you could do wrong."

"In their view I have."

"What was the charge?"

"That I was too lenient."

Uncertainly Carrie watched Jude's expression. "I don't know you now of course," she admitted. "I only remember you from when I was a child. But I wouldn't have thought you'd do anything other than your duty."

Together they went back to the living area. "It's very disappointing," Carrie admitted. "I should have loved you to stay. It's been so long since we last saw each other."

"Do you know where any of the others are?" Jude asked.

"Sonja and I see each other on the friendship net occasionally. She's at Mid One. Gary died. Did you know?"

"No! What happened?"

"He never really recovered from his wounds. When he was at junior academy with me, he was always ailing. About a year ago he died of some sort of fever."

"What about the others? Do you ever see them?"

Carrie nodded. "Mark's doing managerial training like me," she explained. "We communicate sometimes. Koko's working in Entertainments. Spends most of her time posing for reality games. Have you ever played 'Find the Maiden'? That's her."

"Really?" Jude laughed. "You've all done well, except poor Gary of course. I feel like a mother - proud of her children's achievements."

"Why didn't you keep in touch? We often used to talk about a reunion."

"I wanted to put what happened behind me. It dogs me a bit."

Carrie looked up quizzically. "Why?"

"It's a mixed blessing having done something terribly worthy. You end up being remembered for that one action, and nothing in the present can live up to it. I feel a bit of a failure - that I haven't achieved much as an adult, only as a child."

Carrie was surprisingly easy to talk to, her eyes full of understanding. "That's why you were cross," she suggested. "I never thought. People were just sorry for me, and that soon wore off. Besides, I had uncles and aunts. You only had the Refuge. That must have singled you out. Still, I don't think you should feel you've failed, whatever's happened now."

There was a reflective pause. "Do you know what happened to Joel?" Carrie asked.

For a second or two, Jude could not think what to say. There was no point in upsetting Carrie, however. "No," she replied. "I've often wondered."

As soon as Jude went down to the visitors' refectory, the communicator crackled. It was the transport manager. "I'm afraid we can't get you out of here until seventeen thirty, Ma'am," the woman apologised. "All the earlier departures are full. We can offer you a night's accommodation if you prefer."

"I think I'll press on," Jude replied. "It may be even more difficult tomorrow."

"As you wish Ma'am."

Afterwards, Jude tried to think why she had refused to stay. Not even the Chief Secretary - wherever she was - would be likely to grudge her a good night's sleep before continuing her journey. Yet the more Jude thought about it, the more convinced she was that she had given the right answer. In a few days the situation could be very much worse. At the height of the troubles twelve years ago, no one had been allowed to move anywhere. She ought to go straight to Border Seven, and miss out the third leg of her journey altogether.

There was one major problem with doing that however. The accommodation officer at North One would be expecting her. If she did not arrive, Admin. would become concerned. She might even be reported absent without leave. Urgently Jude tried to think how to get round the difficulty. The only way she could avoid travelling around the country for the rest of the week, was for someone to send an order cancelling the Chief Secretary's plans.

"Who?" Jude asked herself. "Who could send such an order?"

The only person she knew at Mid Three was Carrie Lawson, and Carrie owed her a great deal. Perhaps it was time to call the debt in, and risk taking Carrie into her confidence?

*****

Fortunately Carrie was still in her dwelling.

"I can't get a capsule out until seventeen thirty," Jude explained. "We can spend a couple more hours together if you like."

"That's wonderful! What would you like to do?"

"I'll pop up to your place," Jude offered. "Then you can take me for a walk in the gardens."

By the time she reached level 82, Carrie already had a coffee waiting for her.

"I had one in the refectory," Jude began.

"You don't call that coffee!"

"Could you do me something to eat?" Jude asked. "I couldn't face the meal they gave me."

"Of course. I haven't eaten myself yet."

"I'll give you a hand."

Casually Jude followed Carrie into the kitchen area, and stood against the work surface. Like a lot of the equipment in Mid Three, the food preparator was old-fashioned and made a noise. It would mask their conversation for a few vital minutes.

"Listen to me," Jude said urgently. "Don't reply, unless the preparator's on to cover your voice. When we were children, I saved your life. Now you may have to save mine."

In surprise, Carrie looked up, and for a second Jude's heart raced. If they were being watched, the girl's reaction could give them away. To her relief, Carrie lowered her eyes almost at once. "How?" she asked softly.

"I'm supposed to be moving on to North One, but I need to go somewhere else instead. Could you find a way of getting a transfer order through, so that my absence isn't noticed? There would have to be another to my home base as well. Give me your answer when we're in the centre of the gardens, not before."

"There's no surveillance here," Carrie whispered. "They only use it when there's trouble."

"How do you know? I work for Security. I've seen what can be done. Carrie, I've a feeling I'm being watched. I certainly have enemies, though I don't know who they are." Jude saw the girl's disbelieving look. "I'm not height sick," she insisted. "I've been given an assignment. It's safer for you not to know what it is. Just think if you can help me."

"To send a couple of orders? That should be easy enough."

With a ping, the preparator came to the end of its cycle. Taking out the meals, Carrie laid them on the table. She said nothing more about Jude's request.

They ate their meal in the lounge, while watching the afternoon lottery. "I've got an invitation for you," Jude said brightly. "To my bonding party. I don't have the exact date - it's been put off a bit - but I hope you'll come. In person if possible."

"I'll be delighted," Carrie said. She glanced at Jude uncertainly. "I can't imagine you settling down," she admitted. "What's your partner like?"

"I could have done worse."

"Is he very good looking?"

"Very," Jude admitted. "He's called Kurt. We ought to be able to get on for a few years."

Carrie nodded. There was a wistfulness in her expression that intrigued Jude. "You're lucky," she replied. "It must be wonderful to know you're going to have a child."

Flushing slightly, Jude looked away. "I imagine you'll be chosen," she remarked. "When you reach the age of maturity."

"Yes," Carrie agreed softly. "I imagine I will. That's not meant to sound conceited. I've only got to look in the mirror to know they'll want to perpetuate my features. I wish it didn't have to be with a stranger though. That seems so - callous. Still, it's not my place to question our superiors. The Futures Department is one of our big successes. Much more humane than all that cloning stuff must have been."

Though she spoke lightly, a flash of anger brightened her eyes. Jude was intrigued. "I'll write my address down for you," she replied casually. "Messages so often go astray. If you haven't received a formal invitation within a few weeks, contact me direct."

Taking a message pad and stylus from her pocket, Jude bent over it so that a viewer would not be able to see the words. As if setting out an address, she wrote:

'International conference cancelled because of unrest.
Officer Shah needed to guide delegates.
Intercepted en route to North One.
Cancel all other commitments.'

Above them, Jude had already printed her rank, number, transfer codes and personal identifier, as well as her address at East Five.

"I'll put this in my file as soon as you've gone," Carrie promised. Her voice shook very slightly. Getting up, she slipped the sheet in a drawer of her workstation. If they were being watched, it was a terrible risk for them both, but Jude could think of no other way of giving Carrie the codes she would need.

"Let's go for that walk," Carrie suggested afterwards.

All the way down to the pleasure gardens, they talked only of old friends. Neither felt it was it was safe to speak otherwise, until they were in the centre, beside the fountains.

"Any ideas?" Jude asked. "How can I get that message through, without being detected?"

"Easy enough." Carrie laughed softly. "Mark can send it. He'll bounce it off a couple of times, and no one will have the faintest idea where it originated."

"Mark?" Jude asked in surprise.

Carrie nodded. "We keep in touch," she said evasively.

"But how can you send him the message in the first place? It'd be intercepted."

"We share a private room on the Main Web."

"Isn't that against the rules?"

"Of course it is, but how else can we talk to each other privately? Mark and I have been friends as long as I can remember - since we played in the camp, and when we were walking all that way back to safety. He was the one who looked after me when you couldn't. I can't remember when I first started loving him, but I know it was a long time ago."

In pleasure, Jude smiled. "I'm glad," she said. Then she paused. "But Mark's deaf -"

"Exactly," Carrie retorted. "He has an implant of course, but the problem's genetic. Whereas I'm perfect, in every way - apart from being a bit thick. As you say, I shall be chosen. He won't. Even if we put in for a special dispensation, it wouldn't be approved. Mark will never be allowed to breed." Carrie's voice had begun to take on the strangled note of emotion tightly controlled. "And we would never be allowed to become lovers. Not in a Refuge."

"You're not thick," Jude replied gently. "To have found a way of tapping into the Main Web, you've got to be good. I'm not even going to ask how. Are you sure I'm not putting you at risk?"

"If we can't take a risk in return for what you did for us, we're not worth much. Mark will pad your message - make it sound official - and send it on tonight. He'll only dare do it once."

"Once should be sufficient."

They took another loop around the flowerbeds. High above them, small clouds passed over the sunscreen, dappling the lawns. The day could not have been more pleasant, the controlled temperature neither too hot nor too cold. Voices echoed around the levels, while children laughed in the play area just beyond the lawns. A sense of unreality began to trouble Jude.

"Have you and Mark ever thought of leaving?" she asked. "You could be together outside."

"And what would we live on?"

"You're very sensible," Jude replied sadly.

"It was you who taught us to be. If we'd all stayed together in a group, like we were the first few years, I doubt if Mark and I would ever have considered breaking the rules. After we got back from the camp, we were like a happy family together. Remember? But you were sent away on your high flyers' course, and one after the other, we were posted around the country. Management knew how close we were to each other, and why, but they still split us up. I don't think any of us has forgiven them. We don't have the courage to give up our comforts, but we go our own way, as far as we can."

Beginning to feel bored with walking round and round the same flowers, they sat near the children's play area. "Perhaps you can answer a question for me," Jude remarked casually. "Have you heard of a man called Tuecer?"

"You're the second person to ask me that." Carrie's expression suggested nervousness as well as surprise. "Mark got me to run a search last Tuesday. He was afraid of putting in too many requests himself."

"Did you find anything?"

"That's what's so odd. First I found something. Then I didn't."

Looking away to hide her anticipation, Jude waited.

"What was the reference about?"

"Soil erosion." Carrie smiled. "Honestly. The whole file was about ways of conserving soil. I can only remember one sentence." Closing her eyes, Carrie paused to get the quotation right. "'Several successful schemes in the border area appear to have been instigated by the warlord known as Tuecer.' There was something more about him teaching people to terrace the hill slopes, but when I came to look a second time, the whole paragraph had gone."

"I got a security warning when I tried the referencer," Jude admitted. "Whoever Tuecer is, someone is trying to stop us knowing about him."

"Why?"

"I haven't the faintest idea. I don't even know who we're talking about, except that he's connected with a group called the unifiers, and probably the Reivers too."

"That's what Mark said. It was the unifiers that interested him initially. Someone on one of the chat lines accused them of causing trouble up north. There was only one reply, but it was so strange he followed it up. The unifiers don't cause trouble, it said. They're much too clever. They only predict it, and then use it for their own ends."

Children's voices filled the air, echoing off the levels above the play area.

"What ends?" Jude asked at length.

"Money and power," Carrie retorted. "That's what most people want, isn't it?"

She reconsidered her reply. "Maybe that wasn't always true," she conceded. "Mark found a fact-finder file - that's gone too now. Several banned groups were described. Apparently, the unifiers was banned for trying to re-establish democracy, and for 'repeated crimes against the state.' One of them was helping non-persons to get ID - rejected clones and people like that. Another was 'providing shelter for undesirables.' They don't sound like crimes to me. I mean - it depends on your definition of 'undesirable' doesn't it? And who's doing the defining."

Uneasily Carrie sighed. "I wish Mark wouldn't meddle in such things," she admitted. "But he's always been interested in peculiar groups, and he's bored out of his skull. He's running a risk though. The government's clearly afraid, or they wouldn't be censoring whole files." She paused. "Do you recall learning anything about any unifiers? I don't. Mind you, I slept through most of my classes."

"No. Not even the name."

There was another reflective pause. "How did you get interested?" Carrie asked.

"I had an unpleasant illusion in the rehab suite. Tuecer featured in it."

"How odd!"

It was time Jude prepared for her journey. "By the way," she began casually, "Could you lend me some grey trousers? And a grey tunic if you've got one?"

"Whatever for?"

"To make myself look like an andryne. I reckon that'll be the safest way for me to travel."

Carrie laughed. "You'll never look like an andryne," she commented. "For a start, you have too much - well, shape."

"I've done it before, I have a knife-proof vest under this lot. It's standard issue. If I do the laces up tight, it hides a great deal."

Shaking her head, Carrie stood up. "Come back to my dwelling and I'll find you something," she promised. "You've come a long way in the last decade. When I knew you, you were a paragon of virtue."

"I doubt it," Jude replied, laughing. "Only on the outside."

Chapter Eight

As soon as she arrived at the interchange, Jude changed into the clothes Carrie had lent her, and bought a standard class ticket. The man in the office gave her a funny look, but that was all. On the transporter itself she was left severely alone. Catching a reflection of herself in the window, Jude was not surprised. With her hair greased back, and the andryne's two bars of black paint across her cheeks, she was unrecognisable.

Near Leodis the problems began. Ten minutes before they were due to arrive, the transporter threw itself to an abrupt halt. Baggage flew everywhere. Passengers facing forward were thrown against the seats in front of them. One screamed. A baby began to howl.

Afterwards everyone sat still, afraid to move in case they destabilized the cabin, but ready to run as soon as the fire indicator flashed an alarm. Nothing happened. Carefully they picked up their things. "Oh my god!" the woman opposite Jude exclaimed. "What happened?"

Dressed in the red of a respectable citizen, she had done her best to avoid Jude when she boarded. Though it was her civic duty to tolerate all religions and categories, clearly she did not speak to deviants if she could help it. They were the only passengers left in the end section however, and fear overcame prejudice.

"We hit something." Looking out of the window, Jude tried to see where they were, but the transporter had come to a halt on a raised stretch of link-way. Fog was settling. She could just make out the Leodis conurbation in the distance, but how far they were from safety it was hard to tell. Shapes blurred into an orange haze.

The transporter was unusually empty for a Friday evening. With such wild reports circulating, most people had either decided to stay at home or travelled earlier, fearing darkness. Apart from the mother and baby, and the woman opposite Jude, there were only two other passengers in the compartment, possibly father and son. Everyone looked from one to the other, waiting for an official announcement.

There was no apology for the delay. Suddenly the transporter set off again. A peculiar smell filled the air. "The reverse thrust," Jude decided. She sincerely hoped it was nothing else.

Nervously everyone settled back. "We definitely hit something," the woman opposite Jude repeated. "A suicide perhaps. They often lie down here. It's accessible from the road."

"I'm afraid that was too hard for a body," Jude replied. An uncomfortable lean was developing to the port side.

Once again the transporter stopped, but with more warning. There was a long pause, as if damage was being checked. Then they began to inch forward again. The standard class accommodation was in the middle, sandwiched between Elite and Tourist. It was difficult to know what was going on at the front, but a frightened buzz of voices came from the rear compartments. In their own the toddler's howling was becoming unbearable. Bouncing the child up and down on her knee, the mother tried to quieten him.

They were approaching an outlying subchange. Normally mainliners pounded through so fast it was impossible to see the decks, but now Jude could make out the advance sign. 'Leodis Three' it announced. Slowly they limped towards it.

At first everyone thought the transporter was going to make an unscheduled stop, and in relief prepared to leave. It kept going however, jerking through the subchange. Amazed, Jude looked out. The decks either side were crowded to the point of overflowing. Even the steps were packed with waiting travellers, though the rush should have been over long ago.

"What's going on?" Jude's neighbour demanded. "There can't have been a suburban through for hours."

"Must be industrial action," the older of the men shouted.

"Industrial inaction!" his son replied. He was the sort who would find a witty remark in a holocaust.

They all stared at the crowds with alarm. Watched by at least a thousand resentful faces, the transporter struggled through, towards Leodis centre.

Four kilometres outside the security fence, it came to a halt again.

This time the electronic monitor did intervene. "We regret to inform passengers there will be a short delay," it announced cheerfully. "Please accept our apologies."

Everyone relaxed, relieved to know something, however vague. Within minutes a kind of camaraderie was developing.

"My partner works for Transportation," the young mother admitted. "I'll give him what for when I get back."

"I don't think it's altogether his fault," Jude replied, smiling.

The woman in the corner coughed politely. "Would you answer a personal question?" she asked Jude. "Being as we're stuck here together. Are you a man or woman?"

"I was born neither," Jude lied. "Now I'm mostly woman."

There was an awkward pause.

"Why don't you change properly?" the young mother asked.

"Sex wastes such a lot of time. You can achieve more if you concentrate on other things."

"Don't I know it!" The baby began to howl again. Judging by his mother's expression, she would not have minded becoming an andryne herself.

They waited half an hour. Nothing whatsoever happened. Without the central power system, the compartment began to go cold. Despite the fog, there seemed to be a wind getting up outside, for the cabin swayed several times. It was an uncomfortable sensation.

Jude began to worry. If the whole system had been shut down they were safe enough, though likely to become increasingly uncomfortable. If it had not, there was a real danger of another transporter hitting them from behind. Sector control was becoming more and more unreliable. Rather than sitting there obediently, they would be safer getting out and walking. "I reckon we've been deserted," she whispered to the woman opposite her. "I'll go up front and see who's around."

As soon as she stood up, the other passengers called out in alarm. "You're supposed to stay put," the older man snapped.

"One of us has to find out what's happening," Jude insisted. "Give me a hand with the emergency door."

The two men pushed the emergency exit. It was stiff, but they managed to open it.

In the next compartment, others were disobeying the rule too, scrambling out onto the walkway beside the gyrocaust. "No sign of any staff - not even security," a student whispered furiously. "I've been right up to the control room."

Quietly, Jude returned to her compartment. Five pairs of eyes turned towards her in anticipation. "What's the news?" the young man called out.

"There isn't any. There are no security staff left on board and the control room is empty. I'm going to walk into Leodis. Anyone coming with me?"

The young man moved forward so that he could talk to Jude. "Dad and I will," he said. "There's some steps down to the road. We can make our way along to them."

"What about me?" the woman with the baby demanded. "How can I carry Laban?"

"We'll help you," Jude offered.

Hesitantly the other passengers considered Jude's suggestion. Taking the lead from a deviant was as difficult as what she was asking them to do.

"Others have done it," the young man said brightly. "There was an accident near us only the other week, and at least a dozen people walked to safety."

"We're not too high up," the woman opposite Jude said encouragingly.

Finally it was agreed. They would try to walk to Leodis.

The younger man slid down and then helped his father. Though a north-easterly wind blew across the moor, orange tinted fog streamed over the stricken transporter. Darkness would come early that night. The sooner they set off the better. Already Jude could barely make out the ground level below her.

Voices echoed from further along the transporter. People were looking out of the emergency exits, watching their progress.

"Pass Laban to me," Jude called to the child's mother.

The woman lowered the child down to Jude, and then jumped down herself. She was very frightened, but willing to try anything to get to safety. Jude had brought a small personal illuminator with her, and picked out the gyrocaust track ahead.

One by one the others followed, forgetting every difference in the need to help each other. Grasping the child firmly so that he could not unbalance her, Jude began making her way forwards. Voices blew on the wind behind them. Several other passengers were following.

Ahead of them, the men had spotted the steps downwards and were flashing a light to indicate their position. Passing the child back to his mother, Jude began to descend to ground level.

At the bottom of the steps there was a poorly maintained service route, following the line of an old road. On either side of it was a vast tip, covered in the remains of ancient petrol-driven vehicles. Bits of spring and crankshaft lay in the mud, their edges ready to trip an unwary walker. Over the whole area hung a smell of decay. Half a dozen brigands could be lurking behind the heaps of rubbish. Jude was glad she was not alone.

A few meagre dwellings appeared in the mist, squatters' shacks built out of panels from the tip. Children rushed to the doors, excited by the sound of so many voices, and several adults stared suspiciously.

"How much further is it to the security gates?" Jude called to one of them.

"Two kiloms. Maybe ten." The old man seemed to have no idea of distance.

By the time the line of passengers reached the boundary fence, it had begun to straggle out into twos and threes, the men from Jude's compartment still leading. As they approached the city gate, two guards came out to see what was going on, but did not seem particularly surprised. It had been a day of surprises apparently, and yet another was greeted with weary resignation. There was not a lot they could do.

"Everyone's getting stuck," one said, shrugging his shoulders. "Mass walkout. Good job you had the sense to walk."

"What do you mean?" Jude demanded. "Strikes are against the law."

"So everyone says, but Transport's orf tonight, all th' same. Staff reckon it's too dangerous to work. Too many attacks."

"What if another transporter comes up behind?" Jude warned. "There'll be an accident."

"Aye," the guard replied phlegmatically. "We'll warn the authorities, but I dunno as they'll pay much attention. They probably know already. What with riots and strikes, this whole sector's a mess today. If someone don't come to relieve me soon, I'm off meself. Why should I be the only one left on duty?"

By now, another twenty or so passengers were clamouring for attention, demanding to know what had happened, and how they could contact relatives or superiors.

"Patch me through to your head office at once," a large man in a heavy overcoat ordered. "I have to attend an important meeting."

"Sorry Sir," the second guard replied. "Not a hope. The air's jammed. You can give us your details if you like, and we'll do what we can later."

An angry discussion began to develop, with several people insisting that something be done about the stricken transporter, and others trying to give their details before they were asked. Jude edged towards the door.

"Aren't you staying to give your name?" the young mother asked her.

"I'd rather not," Jude admitted. "Good luck with the rest of your journey."

"And you. You're a good sort, whatever you look like."

Softly Jude slipped away into the darkness.

*****

Just inside the security gate, a featureless housing estate sprawled, dominated by three vast blocks of dwellings. A peculiar stillness filled the area. Groups of workers were still making their way through the streets, like Jude caught by the sudden strike. Most walked in silence, their faces ashen with tiredness. No one spoke to her. If any did glance in her direction, they looked curiously for a second, and then lowered their eyes. The Leodis conurbation had grown rapidly since Jude's childhood. Rather than risk turning in the wrong direction, she crossed to a small shop opposite, and asked the way to the central interchange.

As she was offering to buy bread, the owner was reasonably helpful. "Turn left," he said, indicating with the loaf. "If I were you though, I'd get indoors as soon as I could. There was a lot of bother last night. The tribes are moving into town again."

Jude began to feel alarmed. "I'm not from round here," she admitted. "Is it bad?"

"Getting that way. If you see any gangs hanging around, don't try to pass. Some of them wouldn't even leave your sort alone, not if they fancied a bit of fun."

Thanking the shopkeeper, Jude walked on, pulling chunks off the loaf as she did so. Following the man's directions, she turned left and walked towards the centre of the city. She would be wise to find accommodation for the night, and continue in the morning.

The houses were becoming older around her, the streets emptier. Apart from the occasional police patrol hovering above, there was almost no traffic. Jude did not pass a single hotel - not even a cheap lodging house. Fog thickened around her. Behind locked palisades and shutters, lights glowed, but it seemed every decent inhabitant was hiding. Finally, just ahead of her, she saw a small square opening off her route. Like animals hunched in the cold, a couple of seats crouched in the fog. It would be good to rest for a few moments.

A police searchlight suddenly scanned the square, the craft coming in so low as to be in danger of hitting surrounding buildings. Almost too late, Jude saw the two men lounging on a bench. Nonchalantly they got up, just as Jude flattened herself into a doorway.

Outlined in the searchlight, their appearance was grotesque. Each was wearing the coloured shirt of the tribesman, his head shaven into bands of scalp and hair, his right cheek marked with a fine pattern of scars. Jude held her breath as they came towards her. Hidden on her person she had a small fortune in Refuge tokens.

The men were standing right under one of the lamps now, scarcely more than a metre from her. One of them raised his right hand to wave derisively at the departing police. Blue marks decorated his fingers. Without seeing, Jude knew what those tattoos meant. Each was a letter, spelling "Hawk" on one hand and "Boy" on the other. At once, a wave of revulsion and panic passed over her. She had to force herself not to run away. Her only safety lay in remaining completely motionless.

For an eternity the two men stood under the lamp, joking and spitting. Another joined them. It seemed they were meeting by arrangement. He too was dressed in the same blue shirt, with the same bands of scalp showing through his hair. Like Jude, the square held its breath, windows and doorways shuttered against those who had invaded it. Then kicking over one of the benches, the tribesmen set off, on whatever amusement they could find.

Sitting down on the doorstep Jude breathed properly again. Her whole body was shaking. She felt physically sick.

The extremity of her reaction bewildered her. It was out of proportion to the event. Her fear was not only to do with the present, but came from the past too. Somewhere, deep down in her memory, there were two more men with that distinctive pattern of scars and shaven hair. One was a huge mountain of flesh, the other stank of alcohol.

No matter how hard Jude tried, she could not recall anything more. Her mind seemed to have closed around the event, sealing it from her, but she was sure the memory was real. It had turned up in the rehabilitation scenario before she set off on her journey, as if the programme had accessed her innermost thoughts, when her conscious mind could not.

For a little longer Jude crouched on the step, trying to think what to do. A river ran through the centre of Leodis town. Somewhere to the east it joined the main shipping canal leading out to the sea. Border Refuge Seven was near a river too, Renewal Lake opening off its estuary. If Jude could find a waterman willing to take her to the coast, she might be able to reach her destination by boat. By cutting across the suburbs, she should find one of the western wharves, without going into the city centre. It was worth a try.

Travelling as an andryne had not proved as useful as Jude had hoped, and she disliked feeling she was an outcast. Taking the first-aid kit out of her pack, she soaked a pad of lint in cleanser, and removed the black bars from her cheeks. Then she loosened the laces of her tunic and set off.

*****

It took her over two hours to reach the river. By the time she saw water glinting in the sickly glare of a row of lamps, her head was pounding. Through the fog, she could just make out the shape of several craft moored beside a jetty.

An elderly pleasure cruiser was just casting off, a shadowy figure loosening the mooring. Jude took out her Refuge security pass and held it flat in her hand, so that she could show it without having to reach into her pocket. "Going down river?" she called.

Startled, the man stood upright. Light from the cabin fell on his hair and beard. Both were braided with hundreds of small beads. He looked nervously towards the cabin. His craft was carrying something he did not want Jude to see.

"What's it to you?" he demanded.

"Could you give me a lift down to the coast? Further if possible."

Suspiciously the man considered her. She must have looked very odd Jude realized; a woman on her own, dirty and poorly dressed. The man on the boat probably thought her as strange as she thought him. "I can pay," she added, "But not a lot."

"How do I know you won't steal my boat?" the man shouted back.

"You don't. Get yourself a weapon if you want. Then I can come on board to discuss terms."

"Are you the police?"

"Sort of, but I have no jurisdiction here. You're safe."

Intrigued, the man watched her face. Finally he bent down and took something from beneath a tarpaulin. Metal flashed in the light. Then he kicked the gangway back into place with his foot.

Stepping forward, Jude held out her pass. "Refuge Security," she said.

The man looked at the disc closely. "What are you doing outside?" he asked.

"I'm on the way to a job. I need to get to the border sector urgently. Could you take me down to the shipping canal? There may be a bulk carrier going up north."

The waterman considered her dubiously. "What can you pay?" he asked.

"A hundred tokens to the canal. Five hundred if you can take me anywhere near Oldcastle Town."

"Refuge money's no use to me."

"It's worth a fortune on the black market. Don't pretend you haven't heard."

"Why should I help you? What's SecureCity done for the likes of me?"

"Not a lot," Jude admitted. "Without our skills, there'd be even less employment, and fewer people with money to buy what you sell. For you directly though, I don't imagine it has done much."

"How do you know I sell something?"

"You have a cabin full of stuff, packed in boxes. Medicines I imagine."

It was a lucky guess, based on the small size of the cruiser and the man's guilty manner, but it unnerved him. "You psychic or something?" he growled.

"I'm not bothered what you're carrying," Jude replied. "Even if it came from our Refuges, it's the people inside who sold it to you I want, not you."

There was an uneasy silence. "Can you take me down to the canal?" Jude repeated.

The waterman came to a decision. "For five hundred tokens I'll take you right to Oldcastle," he replied. "You'll have to stay below though, out of sight."

"That's fine with me," Jude agreed.

Grunting in acknowledgment, the waterman pushed open the hatch. "Turn to port at the bottom," he ordered. A small galley opened out beneath the steps. It smelt of chips. As soon as Jude entered, the hatch shut behind her.

"Help yourself to biscuits," the man called. "You can cook us both a meal later."

On the table was an open box of biscuits. Hungrily Jude ate, and then found the water carrier. She would be all right for a few hours.

The cruiser stopped twice as it travelled down river, but Jude stayed in the galley. Voices came and went in muffled echoes, and there was the sound of boxes being off-loaded onto a jetty. Suddenly the boat began to pitch and roll. They were out to sea. For so elderly a craft, the cruiser could get up a fine turn of speed.

"I could do with that grub," a voice called from above. "Bring it up when it's ready."

Jude explored the larder. Quite what she was meant to cook she was not sure. All she could find was a bag of potatoes and some elderly oil. Chips it would have to be. With a fine sense of absurdity, she started cooking dinner for a smuggler.

Scrambling up a fight of steps with a plate was not easy. Carefully Jude stepped out on deck. At once she caught her breath in surprise. The fog had gone, leaving the night so clear she felt she could reach out and touch it. Ahead of her, lights climbed upwards, high into the air, in a dazzling pyramid of buildings. At its heart, a circular tower of silver seemed to touch the sky. They had almost reached Oldcastle. The pyramid of light was Border Refuge Seven.

Chapter Nine

The pleasure cruiser glided on, up river. Jude passed the waterman his food in silence. It would be wise not to indicate her exact destination.

Reflecting the lights of the Refuge in a shimmering mirror, the inlet to Renewal Lake emerged from the darkness. Either side, in the shelter of the mud flats, a motley assortment of small craft was moored. Further along the channel Jude could see other, indistinct shapes.

"You didn't say how close to Oldcastle you wanted," the waterman remarked.

"Take me a few more kiloms," Jude replied. "I'll find my own way after that."

"That'll suit me. The more checkpoints I avoid the better. You make good chips, by the way."

Jude smiled. She rather liked the man. "Why do you wear so many beads?" she asked.

"These are my fortune, lady. You'd be surprised what they're made of."

"Ah - I see." Smiling, Jude returned to the galley, to eat her own food.

Twelve kilometres beyond Oldcastle, the cruiser slowed right down. Very carefully the waterman steered into a muddy inlet. A landing stage was tucked behind a bank, almost invisible from the river. Jude settled her bill. She had a shrewd suspicion the man had been coming north already, and had been well paid for a short diversion. Still, he had brought her there safely, and that was all that mattered.

The rest of her journey was simple enough. There was a suburban line only three kilometres away. By seven hours, Jude was standing on a jetty beside Renewal Lake, looking across to the Refuge her parents had died to build. The view was so beautiful it made her heart lift with pride.

Water was the reason for Border Seven's existence and its chief delight. Even at such an early hour, boats crossed and re-crossed the lake, weaving their way between islands lush with trees and flowers. Less official looking craft were busy with people too: cleaning decks, scrubbing clothes, emptying slops. Some boats appeared to be inhabited all year round, for vegetables and flowers grew happily in barrels on their decks. Judging by the number of small jetties, the whole area was becoming a pleasure zone for the neighbouring city. It was difficult to believe that twenty years ago there had been nothing but spoil heaps, and a grey, poisoned desert. SecureCity Incorporated was justly proud of this, its greatest reclamation project.

A group of canoeists were passing between two of the islands, their brightly coloured helmets and life jackets standing out against the blue of the water. Delighted by the splash of colour they made, Jude watched their progress. In close formation, they moved quickly, cutting through the water with swift, rhythmic strokes, and reminding Jude of swans she had seen as a child.

Joining a crowd of other women on the jetty, Jude sat on one of the benches. A Refuge official appeared and checked their identity cards. "You're here early," she remarked. Pursing her lips, she studied Jude's contract closely.

Jude managed to stay calm. "My previous employment came to an end, Ma'am," she explained. "And my starting date here was flexible. With so much trouble down south, I decided to come straight away."

"I imagine we can find you something," the official agreed. "Domestic services are short staffed at present. Report to Reception."

With a sigh of relief Jude sat down again. After such a journey, she was not sure she could have coped with being told to wait another week.

At seven thirty exactly, the first ferry to Border Seven left the city. Within minutes, it had reached the Refuge jetty and was unloading another consignment of contract workers to service the needs of the privileged. As she looked up at the tower of windows filling the sky, Jude felt her stomach tighten. A new life was about to begin, such as a few weeks ago she would never have dreamt of having to lead.

*****

If she had thought at all about where Refuge menials stayed, Jude had assumed it was in a cheaper version of a member's dwelling. The prospect of having to share a dormitory with fifty other women had never occurred to her. The rules on the wall stated that a minimum space of one and a half metres must be allowed between each bed. In practice that also meant a maximum. In such a crowded room it was virtually impossible to keep a secret from those nearby. An old-fashioned manual screen could be drawn around each woman's area while she undressed, and if desired, during the night. The only storage facility was a wardrobe at the foot of the bed, and a small cupboard beside it.

Which left Jude with a problem. In her travel sac she had direction finder, magnifiers and memo stylus, besides several smaller items of specialized equipment. She was also wearing a knife proof vest. One of the other women would be sure to see her undress sometime, and the vest would give her away immediately.

Pulling the screen around her bed, Jude hurriedly changed into domestic uniform. She disliked being unprotected, but she dared not keep the vest on. Wrapping it around her equipment, she stuffed the lot into her travel sac, afterwards pushing the bag to the very back of her cupboard. If anyone picked the lock, they would find some very odd cleaning materials.

"You'll have to finish unpacking later," her supervisor called. "We need you on level 92."

"Already?" Jude called back.

"We're short staffed. Hurry along."

Catching her breath to steady it, Jude rubbed her eyes. She was tired, and would have liked to explore the Refuge to see if the layout was different to her own. Evidently that was going to have to wait, and so was planning her assignment. From now onwards, she was a menial, and must always remember to behave as such. Opening the curtain again, she smiled at the supervisor, and then followed her down the room, remembering to keep the regulation two paces behind.

On level 92, a charge hand gave a rudimentary introduction to the automatic cleansers, then Jude was on her own. She had never been so conscious of her ignorance of worldly matters. At every dwelling, she was ignored. She could have had three heads and six feet and still would not have been noticed. If they did deign to look up from their work, members made it clear that they preferred not to think about such trivial matters as floor cleansing. Only the knowledge that her new life was temporary got her through the day. It was useful to see things from the other side Jude told herself - a lesson she must never forget.

By the end of her shift, Jude was exhausted, too tired to sleep. The last time she had shared a bedroom was at Officer Training School, and then there had only been five women to a unit. In the menials' quarters, she could hear fifty women breathing. Drawing the screen around her bed was no help. Within minutes the air was stifling and she had to push the screen back.

As she lay listening to the snores and snuffles around her, Jude was overcome by an appalling loneliness. What was she doing there? For the past few days she had pushed herself on, when any sensible woman would have given up. A menial, three beds away, began to cough, waking several people around her. Mutters of annoyance mingled with the snores. Sighing, Jude pulled the pillow over her head.

"Did the wretched woman wake you too?" a voice asked softly.

With a rush of gratitude Jude turned towards her neighbour. It was good to know someone was concerned about her welfare. "I wasn't sleeping much before," she admitted.

"It's always the same on your first night. Haven't you worked in a Refuge before?"

Unwilling to lie outright, Jude replied vaguely. "I've had other contracts," she said, "But never with Refuge Domestic."

"It's not too bad. At least they feed you well. Try to sleep. You'll feel rotten tomorrow otherwise, and you've got to keep up with your team. They'll have you out if you don't. Olive'll be gone soon."

"She's got a nasty cough," Jude agreed.

"Hope it's not TB. We'll all be screened if it is. Where are you from?"

"Down south."

"What 'you doing up here?"

"I wanted a fresh start." Jude had her story worked out. "I was in a relationship that broke up, and needed to earn money quickly."

"Got any kids?"

"No. My parents managed to buy me a contraplant."

"Lucky devil! I had my first kiddie when I was sixteen. I vowed I was never going to get caught, but you know how it is. Don't get me wrong. I love all three of mine dearly, but once you've got children, you can never get your head above water."

"It must be very hard," Jude agreed.

"You sound a bit posh for this place. Couldn't you get anything better?"

"I've got no experience. My parents belonged to the Religious. They didn't permit me to work, except in the commune." It occurred to Jude that her answer was in a way truthful. Her parents had served SecureCity Incorporated as well as any god.

"You're going to find it a bit rough here," the other woman predicted. "My name's Feda, by the way. What's yours?"

"Sara."

"Nice to meet you, Sara. Hope you don't snore." Yawning, Feda settled to sleep again. Stuffing some tissue in her ears, Jude tried to do the same.

*****

By the end of the first week, when there had still been no contact from the Assessor, nor any sign that such a person was present at the Refuge, Jude began to worry. What if that woman too had been dismissed, or worse still, simply disappeared? What would happen to Jude herself, left alone with an assignment no one else knew about? Already she was permanently exhausted. It was galling to realize that despite her training and physical fitness, she did not have the strength of an ordinary menial. She would have to develop it soon, or her contract would be terminated. Her days were becoming merely a question of survival.

Then, to her relief, a name on the bulletin board caught her attention. As casually as she could, she read the message.

"Pied Piper of Hamlyn" it was headed. "Will all children interested in this production please attend an audition at nineteen hours - children's theatre three, level 54. Parents are assured younger members will not be kept up late."

The Chief Secretary had warned her to expect the code 'Pied Piper of Hamlyn' but the means of contact seemed odd - too public, and yet also likely to be missed by Jude herself. It was worrying, suggesting the Assessor was in difficulty. Apprehensively, Jude returned to the dormitory, and behind the shelter of her screen took her supervisors' ID from the travel sac hidden in her cupboard. At eighteen hours she slid into in an empty storeroom and smartened herself up. Then, since questions might be asked if she crossed the main atrium, she went to the side entrance, near the menials' quarters. Walking purposefully, she re-entered the lobe and took the first corridor to the right.

Several times people passed her. Jude nodded to them politely and walked on. Only once was she actually spoken to - in the rapido lift to level 50.

"Excuse me," a young girl asked timidly. "Are you from Domestic Supervision?"

For an instant Jude's heart pounded. "I am indeed," she acknowledged cheerfully.

"My sanitary unit's on the blink. I've put in several requests, but no one's been."

"I'm afraid that's not my department," Jude apologised. "Tell me your dwelling number though, and I'll see if I can hurry things along."

She was still smiling to herself as she took the escalator to level 54.

Half a dozen children were hanging around near the theatre, attracted by the idea of a new activity. One of their parents asked Jude if she knew anything about it. "I'm always watching for something my Robin can join," she confided. "He gets so bored with reality games."

"I'm afraid I don't know anything about it, Ma'am," Jude replied. "I'm only checking the cleansing. You know what children are - always dropping their sweet wrappings."

Pretending to check the floor and stage, Jude walked around the theatre. Every minute she expected one of the women to approach her with a whispered message, but they all stayed beside the stage. No one else came. Disappointed, the children began to drift away.

"You'd think they'd let people know it's cancelled!" one of the mothers complained. "Come along, Minta. If this is how reliable they are, I don't think you want to be in their production."

It was nearly twenty hours. The Assessor was not coming. Jude dared not stay longer or Security would wonder why she was hanging around. Urgently she looked to see if something had been left for her. What would she choose if trying to pass on a message or gift unobtrusively? Apart from a few sweet papers, there was nothing on the floor or the seats - except a Tranquil pack lying near the waste basket.

A Tranquil packet... Everyone had them - and left them lying about amongst their things or tossed into waste baskets. What could be more - and therefore less - obvious? Casually she swept up the sweet papers and the packet, and tapped them down into her litter collector. Then she left the room.

In the safety of a store room Jude opened the packet. Several folded memos had been wrapped around a key and stuffed inside. Carefully she smoothed each of the sheets and then examined the key. Since it bore the number M122 it would probably open one of the lockers in the menials' rest area. The first two memos meant nothing to her, just drafts of various batch returns. The third nearly stopped her breathing. It was a list of city officials and grants made to civic societies. Entry number seven read, "The Oldcastle canoe club: training officer Joel Denovitch, treasurer J. Simeon."

It could not be a coincidence. A message had indeed been left for her, but what it meant she had no idea, except that for the second time in under a month, Joel had entered her life. Was she being warned against him, or directed to make contact? Were all the other groups connected with him, or just randomly listed to divert attention? Nothing on the memos offered an explanation.

Jude's hands were shaking so much she dared not leave the store room yet. During the past few days, all she had cared about was survival, and somehow completing her assignment without attracting suspicion. Now, with Joel turning up again, she seemed to gain a new burst of energy. Before she left, she had to know what he was doing, whether it was good or ill.

She must return to her quarters or she would be missed. So long as she could find her way, there was just time to call at the Menials' lockers. Pushing the Tranquil pack deep into her pocket, Jude slipped back into the corridor.

The key fitted locker M122. Inside were some training shoes wrapped in a towel. In the shelter of the ladies' toilet Jude examined them. Tucked in one shoe was a pair of miniaturised enhancers, so small they would fit into an overall pocket, but more powerful than any binocular. The other shoe held what appeared to be a make-up compact but opened up to something far more sinister - the smallest and most lethal of pacifiers.

Urgently Jude stuffed both items back into the shoes.

*****

Crossing to the city was not allowed, even for menials. Though they had been inoculated on appointment - it was one of the most coveted perks of the job - Refuge authorities were not going to risk them carrying infection when they returned. There were several man-made islands however, linked by walkways to the floating platform that supported the complex. Domestic staff and visitors were permitted to walk round them, and in a large area of gardens in front of the reception area. The second week Jude was at Border Seven proved unusually still and pleasant, and most of her colleagues took the opportunity of an evening break in the fresh air.

Though she would have preferred to rest, Jude joined them. If her assignment was to be successful, she had to find evidence of corruption at Border Seven. Even a menial might see goods being smuggled out, or a group of canoeists passing the complex. Discreetly, she watched the lake. Occasionally she was able to slip away from her companions, and risk using her magnifiers.

There were two regular arrivals at the Refuge jetty. The first was the waste collector. For an hour it moved steadily from one waste shoot to another, docking with a great deal of clatter and shouting. While it was being loaded it was impossible to see what was going on behind it. The process took about ten minutes at each outlet - ample time for someone to slip onto a boat with half a dozen boxes of Refuge goods. A supply boat arrived soon afterwards. Though its berth was clearly visible, a corrupt official could easily arrange for goods to be labelled as innocent exports to local firms, or food parcels for relatives...

Then there were the boats belonging to the water folk. Evidently the land to the north was still subsiding, settling into the ancient mine shafts that pitted the area. When Jude was a child, the flooded hollows used to be known as 'ings' and provided sanctuary for all sorts of wild birds. Now they were home to a thriving community of traders and fisher people. No doubt some of those water folk might be willing to provide a service to Refuge members, for a fee of course. It would be hard for the authorities to keep an eye on every small boat at night.

Finally there was the Oldcastle Canoe Club. Every evening, as dusk began to settle across the water, a group of kayaks appeared, the same ones she had noticed when she was on the mainland. Each wearing a brightly coloured life jacket and helmet, the canoeists paddled briskly across the lake in an arrow shaped formation. Passing behind two of the islands, they went up into one of the ings, and then vanished. Ten minutes later, they reappeared from behind another island, cut straight across the lake, and back to the city. Any goods they might be smuggling must be very small and loaded within minutes.

Working out who was part of each night's group was difficult. Though Jude made a mental note of the colours of their jackets and helmets, she had no way of knowing whether they swapped them around. One figure seemed to be constant however, and as he usually led the formation, she dubbed him the Training Officer. Try as she would through the enhancers, she could see no similarity between him and Joel. The shoulders were too broad, the waist too thick.

On the fourth night, though, she felt her whole skin shiver. On the way out the leader was no different to the previous evening's. On the return he was less strongly built, but more skilful, his paddle cutting through the water so cleanly that there was hardly a sparkle of water. One of the novices was beginning to fall behind. Immediately he dropped back to provide support, turning his canoe so tightly a waterman could not have done better.

Urgently Jude watched through the magnifiers. As the leader neared the Refuge, she focused on his face. Only his mouth was visible. The rest of his features were obscured by the webbing of his helmet. Even after so long a crossing, he had the energy to laugh.

Once again, the group passed behind the islands, and then disappeared.

Of course! It was people they were smuggling, not goods. So long as each member of the team was replaced by someone wearing the same lifejacket and helmet, no one would notice that a switch had been made. But it had to be done quickly, during the missing ten minutes.

Was it Joel who was leading, Jude asked herself - Joel who had been picked up behind the shelter of the islands? The canoes had passed quickly, and the face was obscured. Besides, she had only seen him once as an adult, and then briefly under stress. Even so, that sudden laugh, and the concern for a weaker companion reminded her of him.

But whoever the man was, what could he have been doing up there, behind the islands, so near to the Refuge complex? Whatever it was, it involved being brought back into Oldcastle afterwards. The most likely answer was theft, something of high value that would fit into his kayak with him. That suggested money or more likely still, medicines.

Jude tried to put herself in the position of a thief seeking access to the Pharmacy. The laxity of the guards, and the predictable sweep of the lights would help her, but she would not be able to hide her kayak too close to the Refuge. She would have to leave it on one of the artificial islands, and then swim the rest of the way.

But a dripping wet figure would be noticed immediately. She would need a towel and a Refuge uniform, with a waterproof pack around them. And of course, she would need Refuge ID. That would be difficult but not impossible. No matter how many times the authorities altered their codes, or swapped cards for buttons or buttons for skin implants, there were always experts outside who could catch up.

Something still did not fit, however. Where could an intruder pause long enough to get properly dressed? She would need to look smart, or suspicions would be aroused. The whole idea was getting too complicated. In Jude's experience complicated plans never worked. There must be a simpler solution - particularly if Joel was involved. He was too intelligent for scenarios such as she was imagining.

Hoping to get a better view, Jude crossed back onto the Refuge platform and walked round it.

She only managed a few hundred metres. The bridge to one of the artificial islands had been blocked off. Beyond it, the path round the platform had collapsed. An attempt had been made to give the impression water erosion was to blame, but to Jude the break looked deliberate. It was possible however to slide down the bank near one of the grey-water outlet pipes. From there, she found she could walk along the mud flats. Keeping close to avoid being seen from above, she began making her way towards the northern side of the lobe.

Suddenly her path was barred by a tightly meshed fence, running straight into the water. Judging by the sullen ripple, it continued into the lake for some distance. Jude had no choice but to turn back. Whether there was a similar fence on the eastern side of the platform she did not dare investigate. She strongly suspected there was. Something management did not wish visitors to see, was being kept at the northern end of the platform, out of sight.

Chapter Ten

The following morning, Jude was called to Domestic Control. She was to be taken off Emergency Supply, and assigned to level 163, a sheltered area for seniors.

"You'll like it much better," the allocations officer predicted. "It's nice having your own round, and getting to know the people you serve. One of the older menials has been sent for medical examination, and the team's one short."

Recalling the coughing that had disturbed her at night, Jude nodded. Her neighbour's illness was unfortunate, but Jude could not help but welcome the change of duties.

Working on level 163 was indeed much easier. All the residents had been unable to keep up with the Refuge's frenetic pace of work, and had been transferred from their normal levels. Many were missing colleagues and friends, and glad to talk even to a menial. One elderly woman was particularly welcoming. For her part, Jude liked her at once.

Adviser Nyall was the epitome of the absent-minded lecturer. When Jude first entered the dwelling, she found it in chaos, the Adviser moving her things frantically from one pile to another.

"Now what on earth did I do with it?" the old woman demanded, before Jude had time to announce herself.

"What, Ma'am?" Jude asked.

"My identity button. Such a nuisance! Why do I need ID after all these years? Don't people know me well enough by now?"

"I suppose it's to stop outsiders coming in," Jude suggested gently.

"Nonsense! How can anyone get in? It's bad enough being transferred up here, without being confined to my room because I can't find my ID."

"May I help you look?"

"If you would - you'll have sharper eyes than mine." Laughing ruefully, the Adviser sat down to rest. "It comes to something when your body disobeys orders," she grumbled. "What's the use of education, if you can't find things when you look for them?"

Adviser Nyall was clearly twice as intelligent as her new neighbours, and judging by her rank had held an important position in the education service. It was hardly surprising she was impatient with the frailty that had brought her there. "You've probably put the button in a safe place," Jude suggested.

"Of course I did. The question is, where? Don't let people tell you the human brain is better than a computer. Mine's a dead loss nowadays. At least when your workstation goes wrong, you can call a man in. I've been calling men in ever since I was fifteen, and not one of them's improved my circuits."

Jude smiled. With her restored hair and new teeth, Adviser Nyall's appearance contrasted endearingly with the chaos of her room. She reminded Jude of her own director of studies at Junior Academy. "I'm sure your memory's still very good, Ma'am," she replied politely.

"No it isn't. Not anymore. I forget things, and then people stare at me. They stare at you a lot here you know. Some of them whisper behind your back. I know I should be grateful for the move. I wasn't keeping up on 251, and people were getting impatient. All the same, I don't trust this lot."

Though Jude tried to introduce safer topics, the Adviser returned to the same theme. "They watch me all the time," she insisted. "I've seen the real world outside, and they hate me for it."

"I'm sure they don't," Jude replied brightly. It was not her place to ask whether the woman was imagining things, but she could not help feeling concern for her. Though it was only halfway up the lobe, according to the other menials, level 163 was well known for height sickness. Perhaps it was something to do with spending a lifetime inside a Refuge.

They began to search the dwelling together. Within minutes Jude found the identity button in a wardrobe drawer, still attached to the Adviser's leisure suit.

"You're a friend for life!" the old woman exclaimed. "Now I can go and have my afternoon swim. You're to call in here whenever you want a coffee, understand? I know how tiring your job must be. You're a different class from the others. You'll feel the work more."

Concerned at the turn the conversation was taking, Jude excused herself and continued on her round. It would be good to have somewhere to rest occasionally however. Adviser Nyall probably needed a visitor too, though as Jude reminded herself, it was none of her business. She must stop thinking like Family Support.

The Adviser was right about the odd atmosphere. At first glance a visitor would have thought level 163 the semi-retirement paradise it was considered by younger, more hard-pressed workers. Yet many of those Jude served had a worried, insecure manner. When she came to their dwellings they looked up in alarm, as if fearing a sudden inspection. Others seemed suspicious of each other, keeping to their rooms as much as possible, though careful to attend social contact sessions. As she went from dwelling to dwelling, a sense of unease began to trouble Jude.

*****

On the fourth day after she was transferred there, a medical examination was called. Jude was cleaning the corridor near the clinic, and saw the queue forming outside the door. Outwardly everyone was cheerful enough. Their cheerfulness reminded Jude of the mood after the transporter accident: a kind of wartime bonhomie. The people in the queue were afraid.

Following the examination, three of her clients did not return to their dwellings. Doors were sealed and external surveillance activated, pending their return. When Jude asked how long the dwellings would remain empty, she met bland reassurance. It could be some time. Their occupants had been sent to Rest and Recuperation. They might not ever come back. Some did. Some didn't. Who could say? Level 163 was not the sanctuary the authorities promised. It was a place of unspoken fears and unexplained events.

Such an atmosphere bred superstition. On other levels, Refuge members spoke with the fervour of dedication. On 163, a frightened trust in routine replaced belief. As Jude was pushing a mechanical polisher across a lounge, she overheard some very peculiar remarks. A group of operatives were talking about what happened if you broke Refuge rules.

"They're watching you, even when the ordinary surveillance's off," one of the women warned. "If you do anything wrong, our Managers always know."

"Don't they just?" her companion agreed. "They don't punish you outright though. They're much too clever. They use your own guilt. You see things you're afraid of."

"My neighbour saw a figure from the reality games," one of the men replied. "The Warlock. Standing right in the middle of the corridor. He didn't half give her a fright."

"Sidespillage. Sometimes the games leak and images are transferred to vacant spaces nearby. That's why it's usually a corridor. There's nothing in the way, you see."

The explanation was mumbo-jumbo but sounded convincing. "Really?" a woman remarked. "I've never known what caused it." There was a faint irony in her voice which Jude recognized. Discretely, she looked up. Adviser Nyall was sitting in the middle of the group, trying to look interested.

Jude sighed in sympathy. She knew only too well from her evenings in the dormitory, how necessary it was to appear to belong.

"My partner swore blind she'd met a real warrior," another man remarked, "Near the bottom spur. Wouldn't go down there for ages. Management says it's imagination, but you ask around. Dozens of figures have been seen this last year. There's a woman in black who crosses the hanging garden. Our neighbours reckon it's a ghost - some woman who threw herself off the balcony years ago."

That night, Jude dreamt about strange figures. A woman in black was walking towards her along the corridor. "I have a message from Joel," she said. Reaching out, she took Jude's hand. Her fingers were ice-cold.

*****

At breakfast that morning, Jude tried a few careful questions. Several of her companions had noticed the security fence towards the north of the platform. They offered suggestions as to what lay beyond it, ranging from a private club to a pleasure beach.

"Nah!" one of the younger women retorted. "It's where they dump the people they don't want. Haven't you noticed how your clients vanish? I've had two of mine disappear this month. One minute I was doing for them regular, the next, someone else was in their rooms."

"But none of this Refuge lot could survive outside!" another woman protested.

"So? No employer can keep useless staff, and this place is a business like any other..."

"What an awful idea!" Jude interrupted. Her horror was genuine.

"Don't get so upset," Miriam advised. "It's only a few old folk. They've had their time - more than we'll get, too. I reckon Dana's right, though. Some sort of eviction order's been given. I doubt if the really sick even make it outside. Have you seen the north facing windows? They've all been blocked off."

"I've only been on the inner levels," Jude admitted. "The windows there seem normal enough."

"When you do get on the north side, check it out. It's weird. Every window's coated in some sort of fabric. It looks like there's a view, only there isn't."

"'For the good of the members'," Maeve repeated, mockingly. "They mustn't be distressed by the contrast between what they've got and the world outside. I mean - what's distressing here? The lake's gorgeous."

"But you can't ever see the north bit under the lobe," Dana persisted, "Like Sara says -"

Feda pursed her lips warningly. "Don't talk so loud," she warned.

"Especially when Maggie Roland's around," Maeve added.

In alarm Feda looked up. "What do you mean?"

"Molly's been sent on a course for a few days. Maggie's replacing her."

"Oh Lord!" Feda said. "I'm in for it now."

"Why?"

"I used to be in Maggie's team. There was one little clone who was a bit slow. Maggie kept on and on at her, making the poor girl's life a misery. In the end I made a complaint and she was reprimanded. I could do without her following me here, even if it is only for a few days." Turning to Jude, Feda shook her head warningly. "You want to watch Maggie too," she advised. "You're the sort she goes for - a bit different, and not keeping up too well."

Feda was right. All the following day the temporary supervisor was checking on Jude, finding fault. Jude had learnt to accept discipline, but this was victimization. By the time she finished her afternoon shift, she was exhausted by the effort of trying to meet the woman's demands, and so angry she could not trust herself to speak. Furiously, she drew the screen around her bed and threw herself down to rest.

After a few moments, she became aware of someone moving in the cubicle next to her. Assuming Feda had returned, Jude turned over.

Something about the movements did not sound right. Becoming curious, Jude looked through the gap where the screen met the wall. The new supervisor was standing near Feda's wardrobe. Softly Jude lay back and waited until Maggie left.

As soon as Feda returned, Jude pushed the screen back slightly. "Check your things," she warned.

"Why?"

"Maggie's been round your wardrobe."

"If she's taken anything, I'll have her!"

"More likely she's added something."

In horror, Feda rummaged through her clothes. "Try your pockets," Jude suggested.

"Oh Hell!" Bending forward so that no one could see, Feda took something from her leisure suit. "Where's this come from?" she whispered. Opening her hand slightly, she showed a glint of gold. "I didn't take it. Honest I didn't. I just cleaned, and put it back."

"Your DNA will be all over it."

"What do I do?"

A message was coming through on the screen near the far door. Maggie was talking to someone in Security.

"Pass it to me," Jude whispered urgently.

Quickly she took the timepiece. It was obviously valuable. Either Feda's client was exceptionally careless, or he trusted her a good deal. Thinking quickly, Jude dropped it into her bodice, next to her skin. If she was strip-searched it would be found, but there was no time to find anywhere safer. Beyond the screen, Maggie's voice was already approaching.

"Feda Minowsky?" she called. "Where's that timepiece?"

Another voice joined hers - one of the deputies. As if just waking up, Jude pulled the screen back. A crowd was beginning to gather round the cubicle beside her.

Maggie made no attempt to presume innocence. "You thieving bitch!" she snarled.

"I don't know what you're talking about," Feda replied.

"Officer Gray has reported his timepiece missing."

"The last time I saw it, it was on his table. The man's always leaving his things around."

Maggie began searching the wardrobe. She was no good at hiding her surprise. Twice she checked the same pocket. "You've passed it on to someone," she snapped.

First she tried the woman on the other side of Feda, who did not appreciate being accused. A furious row developed. Then she turned to Jude. Angrily she rummaged through the wardrobe, and flung the nightfoil off the bed. Finally she looked at the cupboard. "Open it up," she ordered.

For an instant Jude could not move. In her concern for another, she had not considered the danger to herself. Sitting in her cupboard was a bag of equipment and a knife-proof vest. There was nothing she could do but obey. Any other response would arouse suspicion.

"Look through if you want," she invited, opening the cupboard door. "You won't find anything that's not mine."

The travel sac lay squashed at the back, just showing behind a pile of folded clothes.

"Oh give over, Maggie," the deputy advised. "The man's probably mislaid it. You know what these Refuge people are like - their heads in some electronic cloud. I've worked with Feda for months. She's too sensible to steal."

Furiously, Maggie kicked the door of Jude's cupboard shut. Grumbling about members who made complaints without checking first, she went back down the room. The crowd of women dispersed, but not before there had been a lot of angry talk. "She's after you, Feda" one of them said. "It's a good job you didn't take it."

"What do you think I am?" Feda shouted. "I don't steal. Nothing's worth the risk. Who'd feed my kids?" She avoided looking at Jude.

With the timepiece pressing against her skin, Jude could hardly eat her evening meal. The incident had badly frightened her. She must find a better hiding place. The lock on her cupboard might not be left unpicked much longer.

As soon as she could, Jude returned to her cubicle and pulled the screen round her. Quickly she took the bundle of equipment out of her cupboard, and stuffed it into a real-time postbag, as if she was mailing something home. Just before dark, she buried the mailbag in a patch of sand on one of the artificial islands. It took her half an hour to feel satisfied no one was near, and even then someone might be watching through magnifiers. By the time she had finished, Jude was shaking with relief.

When she returned, Feda was waiting for her in the rose gardens. "Why did you help me?" she asked.

Sitting down with her, Jude tried to find a reason. "You were kind to me," she said.

"Anyone with any sense would have kept quiet." To Jude's amazement, the woman began to cry. "What would have happened to my kids?" she repeated.

Tentatively Jude comforted her. The grief she heard was not just for one shabby incident, but a lifetime of humiliation.

Sniffing, Feda looked for her handkerchief. "If you ever want anything," she said, "Just ask."

"I don't expect any return," Jude replied. "I acted on impulse. It's one of my failings."

"It's that religious upbringing of yours." Feda tried to smile. "I meant what I said. I don't have much, but whatever I have, is yours."

"I need your friendship most," Jude admitted. "I hate it here." She pushed the timepiece into Feda's pocket.

*****

That night, Jude slept the sleep of the exhausted. When she woke, she was convinced it was morning, and was surprised to find darkness instead. The cupboard to the left opened quietly. Feda was getting ready for bed.

"Where have you been?" Jude whispered.

"For a walk."

"You've been with a feller," Jude guessed, "Haven't you? Is he nice?"

Carefully Feda pulled the screen round them and sat on Jude's bed. "It's not what you think," she insisted. "I love him."

"Honest?"

"Cross my heart. Yakim's the kindest, gentlest bloke I've known."

Sitting up against the pillow, Jude found Feda's hand in the darkness. "It sounds like you've done all right," she whispered.

"I have. We met when I was working up river. He's stuck with me ever since."

"How have you managed to keep seeing him?" Jude asked in bewilderment.

"He calls for me - like a gentleman should."

At once, Jude's interest in a friend's good fortune sharpened. If there was a way off the complex, she might be able to use it herself, to cross to the city and find Joel. "Do you see your friend often?" she asked.

"Every few days." Feda laughed softly with happiness. "He's asked me to live with him."

"Will you?"

"As soon as my contract finished, I'm out of this wretched place, up the ings."

Jude smiled into the darkness. "What about your kids?" she asked.

"Yakim says they can help him, while I see to things below. He's been struggling to cope on his own for a year. His partner died having their first child."

Jude tried not to question too obviously. "Aren't you afraid of being caught?" she whispered. "I thought there were security lights."

"They only sweep across every few minutes, and if you know the pattern, you're safe. As for the guards, they're too busy trying not to see their own partygoers."

"Partygoers?" In one conversation Jude was learning more than weeks of investigations might have told her.

Feda laughed quietly. "You don't think our bosses sit around playing reality games, do you? Not when there's half a dozen pleasure domes across the water. You almost feel sorry for them. They're so excited they're like children on an outing."

"You've actually seen them?"

"You can't hardly miss them. There's some steps down to the mud flats, just beyond the rose gardens. You see little groups running across to them, trying not to make a sound. Half of them end up bumping into the benches. Then there's the women from town squelching around under the platform. They're a scream."

"Women?" Jude repeated in amazement.

"Even Refuge officers need a change of face." Feda's tone was scathing.

"I wouldn't have thought a boat could come so close," Jude admitted.

"A skimmer can. I'll tell you what, he's on to a nice little number. Yakim reckons it's like taking comfits from babies."

"Does Yakim take them across too?"

As soon as she spoke, Jude sensed she had probed too hard.

"No. He doesn't trade in people."

"I'm glad," Jude said, recovering the situation. "I wouldn't have liked him if he did."

She framed her next question more carefully. "Do you know if Yakim has a friend?" she asked. "Someone nice? I'm sick of being stuck here."

"He might. He'd only be another waterman though. Isn't that a cut below you?"

"I'm hardly in a position to choose nowadays. If he's nice I don't care what he is."

"I'll see what I can arrange." Getting up, Feda ruffled Jude's hair against the pillow. "Don't say anything to anyone," she warned. "Or we'll both be dismissed."

Chapter Eleven

The public announcement flashed at thirty-second intervals on the bulletin board. "All service personnel to the main atrium," it ordered. "Attendance is mandatory. Teams will proceed to their afternoon duties directly."

"Bloody nuisance," Kylie grumbled. "They're always cutting into our break."

Maeve could be relied on to know what was happening. "It'll be about the epidemic," she said.

"Epidemic?" half a dozen voices repeated. A buzz of alarm spread round the refectory.

"That's right, ladies." Molly's voice cut through the babble. "Plague! But not here - not if I can help it."

In a chattering, anxious stream, the service workers poured into the main reception area. Mechanics, domestics, laundry personnel, even sewage operatives crowded under the trailing plants and marble landings. There was no other space big enough to hold so many people. Carried along in the flow from dormitory five, Jude joined one of the rows. Supervisors walked up and down purposefully, keeping order.

It took fifteen minutes for everyone to file in and be accommodated. Since it would be impossible for those at the back to see a speaker on the podium, a huge screen was lowered, ready for the Service Manager's arrival. Few of those waiting had ever seen so important a person, and there was whispered speculation as to whether a man or woman would arrive.

Finally the screen lit up. A thin figure appeared. "Must be an assistant," Therese whispered.

Passed in a corridor, the newcomer would not have attracted a second glance. Yet when he spoke, a hush settled on the whole atrium.

"Fellow workers," he said. Though amplified around the room his voice was soft and polite, the voice of a man who had never needed to shout and did not intend to do so now. "As some of you may have heard, there is an outbreak of Binasha Fever in the city nearby. I am asked to assure you the infection has not reached here.

"We intend to ensure it never does. Anti-viral procedures are being strengthened, and infection locks strictly monitored. Each of you will be given a Provene injection. Recent trials have shown this to be more effective than inoculation. Unfortunately, we do not yet have supplies for everyone, and Refuge members will, of course, have priority, but their laboratories are working full strength to engineer further supplies.

"Until the emergency is over, the following measures are to be observed, without question: No one who leaves this complex for any reason is to be allowed to re-enter it. Those of you who are nearing the end of your contracts will be required to stay until the epidemic is over. We cannot admit new staff to replace you -"

A growl of dissension passed along the rows. Supervisors stepped forward in warning.

"I appreciate these restrictions will be inconvenient," the soft voice continued. "But you will be paid for any extra time you serve.

"The Directorate have asked me to make one further point. It has been brought to their attention that service personnel are making unauthorised trips to the city. This is strictly forbidden. Under article seven of the Resident Workers' contract, members of staff leaving without authorisation may be summarily dismissed. Any person found to have visited the infected areas and returned to the complex, will be regarded as wilfully putting the lives of their colleagues at risk. Offenders will be handed over to the civilian authorities, with a recommendation that a term of imprisonment of not less than two years is served."

There was a whisper of disbelief.

"You have not yet been allowed to talk," the little man reminded. The whisper died back to sullen silence. "It's unfortunate that such measures have to be taken, but they are needed against the irresponsible few, to protect the many. Don't underestimate the Corporation's willingness to defend itself."

The rows of workers waited, heads down. Jude could feel the anger around her, a furious, bottled-up resentment. Every worker standing there was united in hatred of the man on the podium. He was one of them, a contract employee, who had risen up the ranks. They could not hate a whole organization, but this man was visible before them.

"Thank you for listening so patiently," the soft voice concluded. "Now you may return to your duties. There will not be time for you to resume your break."

"I know what I'd like to do to him," Therese whispered.

"I can't think what you mean," Kylie mocked. "Would it involve an automatic cleanser?"

There were many similar comments. Jude shared the fury around her but felt worn out by it. There was nothing any of them could do, complain as they might. In such battles, SecureCity Incorporated always won. She was glad to leave the main group and head up to level 163, and a cup of coffee with Adviser Nyall.

To her surprise, however, when she arrived at the Adviser's dwelling, she found two members of the mental health support team waiting.

"Ah! The menial!" one of them said curtly. "We've been expecting you. Our patient seems to think you can help her."

In alarm Jude put down her cleansers. The second orderly was trying to persuade Adviser Nyall to drink a glass of sedative.

"How do I know what's in it?" the old woman snapped. Seeing Jude, she sighed in relief. "Tell them there's nothing wrong with me," she demanded.

"What's the matter, Ma'am?" Jude asked.

"They say I have to go to the assessment centre."

"It's only for a check-up," the auxiliary said reassuringly. "You could do with a little rest."

Adviser Nyall almost shouted. "Rest?" she demanded. "Until two months ago, I was running a whole schools' Inspectorate. Having too little to do's my problem."

"You can tell your counsellor all about it," the staff nurse suggested. Like her colleague, she was discretely dressed, a model of quiet efficiency. Only the restrainer in her breast pocket marked her as any different to other workers.

Jude's own heart missed a beat. Restraining officers were feared by everyone. They were supposed to be just another branch of the medical service, but they had powers others did not, and the means to ensure that their requests were obeyed.

"How can I help?" Jude asked, very politely.

"Tell them I'm perfectly well," Adviser Nyall pleaded. "I have no need of counselling."

Even if she had been standing there as a member of Family Support, Jude could have done little. Once the restraining officers had been sent in, treatment was usually inevitable. Even so, she tried to win the old woman a reprieve. "Adviser Nyall has always been pleasant with me," she said, keeping her own eyes respectfully lowered. "I've found her very kind, and to the best of my knowledge, totally normal."

"I'm afraid we have reports to the contrary." The staff nurse's smile was cold around the edges. "We're obliged to check. Don't look so worried, my dear. Whatever we decide will be in Senior Nyall's best interests, as it is of all our patients. In the meantime, we'll arrange for the dwelling to be secured. You'll be notified when your services are needed again."

The Adviser's eyes showed her despair, as clearly as if she had opened her mouth and howled. The old woman's reply was restrained however, a valiant effort at dignity. She even tried to smile. "I'm absolutely fine," she repeated. "There's been some malicious gossip, that's all. Nothing that can't be sorted out."

"I'm sure it will be," Jude replied. Her throat was going tight. "Thank you for the cups of coffee. I look forward to serving you again soon." Gathering her dusters, she turned to leave.

The restraining officers moved either side of the old woman. "Come along now," one said brightly. "Let's go and have a nice chat with your counsellor."

In a sudden, terrified gesture the Adviser snatched at Jude's hand. "Don't leave me," she pleaded. Her eyes were wide with fear.

"Really!" the staff nurse reprimanded. "The woman's only a menial."

"She cares more about my interests than you!"

Warningly Jude looked towards the Adviser. Such outbursts would only make her position worse. Pulling Jude closer the woman whispered, "Look outside... For God's sake, look outside..."

"It's time you left, my dear. Your presence seems to be upsetting our patient."

The staff nurse's tone was pleasant enough, but the threat behind her words was obvious. Jude had no choice but to pull her hand free and leave.

Afterwards, in the corridor, Jude found she was nearly crying. Trying to overcome her emotion, she glanced out of the window. There was nothing to see except the balconies opposite, and the central pleasure area beneath. She had not really expected anything different. If the old woman's reason had been affected by something she saw, it was likely to be on the outer corridors of the lobe, to the north.

*****

That night, the dormitory was buzzing. "I'm not staying shut up here," Feda insisted.

"Nor will their own people," Kylie warned. "You watch, the skimmer will be full tonight, just as usual. If anyone brings the infection back, it'll be one of their own."

Though such talk was probably true, it was foolish. Jude decided to leave them to it. "I'm going for a walk," she said. "All this is getting me down."

She found the steps Feda had described. A path from the bottom of them led across the mud flats, towards the lakeside. Since illicit partygoers would be unlikely to wait in the open, Jude chose instead a fainter route alongside the hydraulic platform. In wet seasons it would be swirling with water, but winter had been dry that year, and the few sunny days had already cracked the mud's surface.

After twenty metres or so, the path turned directly under the platform. Checking no one was watching, Jude followed. At first she could see nothing but blackness ahead. Then her eyes adjusted to the darkness. Row upon row of pillars stretched ahead of her, each set firmly into the mud and vanishing into shadow above. Every one was strengthened by an outer mesh of steeltite rods, so that it could take the huge weight that rested upon it. At the top, gears of reinforced steeltite were just visible. When the cavity beneath the platform filled with water, they would enable the Refuge to move upwards with the rising level.

Shuddering slightly, Jude paused. The place had a dank, unpleasant smell. Mounds of rotting vegetation had been swept against many of the pillars. They probably harboured half a dozen species of rat.

Other watchers had waited where she stood, for the mud had been trodden hard. There was even a nub end of Tranquil phial. "This way to funtime," Jude thought cynically. "Get your skimmer here..." The evening was going cold. Even if the smell left much to be desired, under the platform's edge it was sheltered from the wind. She decided to stay a while and watch the lake.

The canoeists had already crossed and were approaching the city. Training her magnifiers on them, Jude checked who was with the group that night. The skilful one was once again bringing up the rear. Not matter how hard she looked, she could not see his face, or tell whether he was indeed Joel. Then they were gone, into a harbour beyond the beacon.

*****

Adviser Nyall did not return that day, or the next. She would be home soon the neighbours said, but Jude could hear fear in their voices.

On the Tuesday morning, removal men came and unlocked the Adviser's door. They began to pack up the property inside.

"Is Senior Nyall moving out?" Jude asked, trying to sound unconcerned.

"Going to level 40," one of the men replied.

"How long for?"

"Dunno Love. We just move people's stuff. Nobody tells us anything."

Jude began to feel relieved. At least she now knew where the Adviser was being sent. If she could discover the dwelling number, she would pay the old woman a visit.

Yet when she called up the grid at the end of the corridor, Jude's anxiety returned. There was no level 40. It existed theoretically, but was taken up by activity rooms and other facilities. The removal man must have got it wrong.

Jude decided to ask her supervisor at lunchtime. Molly was not a bad sort, and knew what was going on. "If someone's sent for treatment and doesn't return," she began. "Where are they transferred? I want to visit one of my old ladies."

Molly rubbed some rough skin on her fingers. "There's a lot of questions we don't ask," she warned. "And that's one of them."

"The removal men said she was going to '40, but that's just service facilities."

Once again Molly pulled at the piece of skin. "They always tell you '40," she agreed. "I tried to visit several of my old dears a few months ago. I wandered round and round, and never found them. Take my advice, love. If you're going to get fond of your clients, this place isn't for you. Serve your contract out, and then find another job."

All afternoon, Jude thought of Molly's advice as she worked. It sent a chill through her soul.

She had never felt so alone in her life. There had been no further contact from the Assessor, and Jude had no way of knowing whether the woman was still at the Refuge, or even alive. Now an old woman she respected had simply vanished. Soon, Jude herself could disappear. No one would care. Even Kurt would merely wonder why she did not return, then assume she had left the Corporation rather than be bonded to him. He might be surprised that she had not kept her promise but he would not grieve. By evening she felt as if the menials' quarters were suffocating her, and had to go outside.

The gardens were empty. Night was closing in, the orange fog from the city floating in banks across the water. It was too cold to stay out long, but the fresher air calmed her. So long as she kept enough people around her, it would be difficult for anyone to pick her off. For the first time since she arrived, Jude was glad of a crowded dormitory. With fifty or so other women around her, she ought at least to sleep safely.

Anger began to replace fear. People were getting away with things in Border Seven - not just theft and corruption, but the inhumane treatment of frail or older members. It was not just a question of cruelty, but of broken contracts. When people signed their lives away to the Corporation, provision in their old age was part of the bargain. Whatever the Chief Secretary's motives, she was right to want to expose such a betrayal. Since Jude seemed to be the only one left to do so, she would find out exactly what was happening to the old people - and what was going on to the north of the complex, then send a report to the very top, to the Triumvirate itself. Having no way of knowing whether even the Triumvirate could be trusted, she would give each member a copy. One of the three might ignore her, but the other two would surely act.

But how could she get the reports to them? If she was being watched, she would be intercepted long before she got to Headquarters.

Lying on her bunk later while the other women slept, Jude tried to think of a way. If she could get to the city, she might find a real-time collection point. Unreliable and old-fashioned, RT delivery would be the last route any observer would expect her to use. Addressing a packet to the Triumvirate direct from the Refuge would surely attract attention, though. Who could she trust to forward her evidence? Carrie would help, but since she was inside the Corporation herself, her mail might be opened. It had to be someone outside.

"Linda Vass!" The name came to Jude just as she was drifting into a troubled sleep.

The young probationer must have left the Refuge by now, but her address was somewhere in Jude's travel sac. Once a packet reached Linda, it would be safe. It took integrity and courage to leave a Refuge of your own free will. Was it fair to involve her, however? The woman had chosen to leave the Corporation. Whatever was going on in it was not her worry.

That, however, was precisely the reason Jude had to call on her, despite her unwillingness to make use of her. What could be more natural than a former probationer receiving a package from a friend, still a member? Even if Jude's report were intercepted, SecureCity Incorporated had no jurisdiction over those who had not signed their lifetime contract. They could do nothing against Linda - nothing legally that is. At the back of her mind Jude had an uneasy feeling she was putting another woman at risk, but she could think of no alternative.

Her head was beginning to pound. If she thought much more, fear would get the upper hand again. For the first time, she swallowed some of her Tranquil allowance.

Immediately after breakfast the following day, teams five, six and seven were summoned for their Provene injections. In a giggly crowd the women waited at the medical centre until an officer came into the room. He was very good looking. A murmur of comment passed amongst the women, making him flush with embarrassment.

"Thank you for coming so promptly, Ladies," he began. "You're about to receive Provene treatment. It will take only a few seconds, and you have nothing to worry about. The medication is perfectly safe, based entirely on flowers. A few of you may experience a mild reaction, but only a very few. After twenty four hours, you'll be protected not only against Binasha, but cholera and Morial Fever too."

The medical officer smiled. "We're very proud of Provene," he confided. "It was developed by one of our own medical researchers. It's been used throughout the Refuges for a year now, and has saved many lives." He smiled again. "We have a very strong research team here."

As soon as he had stepped down, the supervisors marshalled the women into lines. Feda joined Jude. "You still want to meet a bloke?" she whispered. "Yakim's coming for me tomorrow."

"Are you going to risk it? I mean - if we're caught..."

"We won't be. You game to join us?"

For a second, Jude could not think how to answer. She had been praying for a chance to search for Joel. The list of local officials the Assessor had passed to her had included his name, as well as other members of the canoe club. That suggested they might be useful to her. Now that the Assessor herself seemed to have vanished, Jude must contact them - whether they were stealing from the Company or not. But leaving the Refuge now would be an awful risk. Having a friend of Feda's around would be awkward, too... She came to a decision.

"I've realized I already know the bloke I want," Jude lied. "I'd like to cross to the city and look for him."

"You don't waste much time," Feda commented. "Who is this mysterious fellow?"

"Someone I met on my way here."

Feda looked disappointed.

"Can you help me?" Jude persisted.

"If it means that much to you. How far into the city do you want to go?"

"Only to the waterfront. He's got friends there. They'll tell me where he lives." Jude doubted if any canoeists would be at the club after dark. Still, looking round their premises might be useful.

Feda had it all planned. "We'll leave the dormitory an hour after lights out," she explained. "Pretend to be asleep until then, but have your clothes on under your night things. I'll go first. Count to sixty and then follow me out. If you're not at the door to the gardens within two minutes, I'll go without you."

"How do we get outside?"

"No problem," Feda mouthed, and smiled.

Chapter Twelve

Getting off the complex proved remarkably easy. As they had arranged, Jude followed Feda out of the dormitory, and found her waiting at the outer door. "Stick close," Feda instructed. "We'll have to go through like one person."

To Jude's amazement, Feda had her own Exit ID. It let them through without question.

"Where did you get that?" Jude whispered afterwards.

"Yakim got it for me. You can buy anything on the black-market here - so long as you know who to ask."

Instead of turning towards the steps to the mud flats as Jude expected, Feda took a path to the east. It wound around the outside of the service buildings, through thigh-high weeds. With only a pale moon to guide them, the route was difficult, but Feda almost pulled Jude along. Every few minutes she dragged her back against the wall, anticipating the sweep of the security lights.

As they rounded the curve of the complex, a patrol came towards them, skimming across the mud flats. Jude dropped down amongst the reeds.

Just before its lights swept the platform's edge, the vessel veered off to the west. "They don't usually come that close," Feda whispered. "Must be looking for someone."

"Not us I hope."

"Naw - we don't matter." Feda laughed softly. "Saboteurs - that's who they're after."

Abruptly she turned off the path, towards the edge of the platform. "You can get down here," she explained. "It's steep. Don't rush."

Between the platform struts, the spoil mounds on which the complex had been built were still intact. It was far easier to find footholds in ash than on metal. Feeling for roots and rubble to assist her, Jude lowered herself down. Soon her feet touched mud. All around her, water shone in the pale light. It came right up to the platform's edge ahead of her, and then seemed to pass under it in a sullen, silvery river.

"Not bad," Feda commented. "You're pretty fit. Now we go inside."

Taking care not to slip, Feda led the way under the platform. The river flowed beside them, and on, out of sight into the darkness. They were beside the old deep-water channel, but it flowed so sluggishly it made little sound. The running water Jude had heard on the other side of the complex, came from the pipes and gullies that flowed in a hundred small streams and rivulets, draining the platform above. Ahead, light filtered in from the service buildings, around ventilation shafts covered only by perforated grills.

"Who showed you this place?" Jude asked curiously.

"One of the mechanics. His girl used to call for him sometimes. She was a dab hand with a rowing boat. Then the silly man got caught stealing from the kitchens for her. He's doing Remedial. They give him six months - just for taking a joint of meat."

"Do others come here?"

"Not that I've seen. Roddey told me he was the only one who knew about it. He watched the Refuge being built when he was a kid. People assume the old river was culverted, but it wasn't. SecureCity just built over the top. Better than having to wash your cellars out."

Joel Denovitch would know about the river too, Jude thought uneasily. His family was driven off the land when the Refuge was built. If his thoughts ever turned to revenge, he would know exactly the place to come.

A faint throbbing sound began to echo around the pillars. A skimmer on low power was approaching. "Here's our lift," Feda said brightly. "Watch your step as you get on board. If you fall in the water, the current will take you right under the lobe. There's only room for two, so you'll have to lie on the floor. Keep your face and hands out of sight. Flesh shows in the dark."

Jude smiled. Feda would have made a good security officer.

Scarcely under power, the skimmer turned into the channel, using the current to carry it forward. The light at its bow had been covered in cloth, so that it shone only a few metres ahead. Behind it, Jude could just make out the figure of a man. Skilfully he turned the skimmer against the current and up the side of the muddy bank, to a slithering halt. Feda kissed him briefly, but neither of them spoke.

It was a remarkably uncomfortable ride. Pressed flat against the deck, Jude could see nothing but slats and a puddle of stagnant water. Water sluiced around her. She could sense when they hugged the mud flats, and when they struck off across the lake, but little else about their route. Once they turned right about, as if avoiding a patrol. Another time they floated in the darkness, waiting for something to pass.

"We'll drop you off near the waterfront," Feda shouted. She had emerged from under a tarpaulin. Evidently they were beyond Refuge jurisdiction.

"Can I get up?" Jude shouted back. Above the noise of the engine, normal conversation was impossible.

"Don't move too sharply or you'll have us over," Yakim warned.

The skimmer was already losing speed. Feeling as if she had been bounced against a wall and had buckets of water thrown at her simultaneously, Jude struggled to her knees.

"Be at exactly the same place by two thirty," Yakim instructed. "If you're late, you'll have to make your own way back. Look for a skimmer with a blue band along the side. A mate of mine called Jonah will pick you up, then I'll take you and Feda back to the Refuge."

Feda laughed. Her voice carried on the night wind. "Jonah's the one I was going to match you with," she teased. "If you can't find your own boyfriend, you might have a look at him instead. Bit old for you, but doing nicely. You could do worse."

They were already weaving in and out between moored craft, the lights of the waterfront forming a bright band ahead.

*****

The quay was deserted when Jude landed. Taking her direction from the harbour beacon, she set off around the lakeside.

Finally she came to a second, much smaller harbour. Safety lights cast an orange glow, but the only person around seemed to be a security guard dozing outside some gates. Behind a fence, a row of canoes had been stacked for the night. Just beyond them, a cluster of small yachts strained at their moorings, their davits chinking and rattling in the wind. Jude had not really expected to find anyone around. At so late an hour, decent people would be home in bed.

A notice board announced that Oldcastle canoe club was open from six thirty to ten hours in the morning, and seventeen to twenty-one at night. New members were welcome, and could pay for a series of lessons, or take advantage of a one-off free introductory session. For a second Jude stared at the sign in surprise. She had memorized the Assessor's list - learnt it over and over again - and she was certain the names of the training officer and treasurer of the Oldcastle Canoe Club were Joel Denovitch and J. Simeon. Neither name was on the board. She had risked leaving the Refuge for nothing.

The Assessor must have had a reason for adding those names to her list, Jude decided at length. She would try enquiring about the second man, in case asking for Joel put him at risk.

Waking up, the guard watched Jude suspiciously. He reached for his protector.

"I'm looking for a man who comes to this club," Jude called quickly.

"Bit late in't it?"

"I've only just arrived in the city," Jude replied, and smiled, as a worried stranger might. "I have an urgent message for my cousin, Simeon. I thought he might be here. He stays at the club house sometimes."

Out of the corner of her eye, Jude noticed a movement among the yachts. Someone had lifted one of the tarpaulins and was watching her. She could just see a small white face.

"They'll all be asleep by now," the guard replied. "Simeon you say? Never heard of him. You'll have to come back in the morning and speak to the secretary. It'd be more than my job's worth to wake him now."

Thanking him, Jude turned away. There was definitely someone moving among the yachts. Taking care to keep herself in the light, she crossed the yard. Another figure had joined the first, darting between the moorings.

There was no way of staying in the light all the time. The road around the waterfront plunged into a pool of darkness and then re-emerged just beyond some sheds. Jude began to feel angry with herself. She was doing it again - getting herself into danger, because she had not worked out what might be waiting for her.

"Looking for someone?" a voice whispered.

The question had come from among the casks behind Jude. "I might be," she answered, keeping her voice steady.

"Happen I could find him for you."

"Then show yourself."

The voice was that of a boy, but the tone was far older. Jude relaxed a little. "You startled me," she admitted. "How many more of you are there?"

"Dozens and dozens."

Jude smiled. "You and your mate," she said. "I don't have any money on me, but I do have a little food. You can have that, if you come out and talk to me properly."

There was whispering behind the casks, then a boy came out, into the light. He was no more than thirteen, his clothes three sizes too big for him, and his feet bound in cloth strips instead of shoes. In the orange glare his face was white and pinched, with the sharpness of a child who has learnt to survive on cunning. "Who you looking for?" he asked. "Someone from the club? I know them all."

"A man called Simeon."

"Never heard of him," the boy replied. "What's he like?"

"About thirty - strong looking," Jude said vaguely. "Belongs to the club here."

There was a whisper to the side. Jude smiled. "Do let your friend join us," she said. "She's bursting to tell me."

Sheepishly a young girl crawled out. A couple of years younger than her companion, she had the same pinched face and old manner. "How did you know I was there?" she demanded.

"I know lots of things," Jude said, wishing she believed it. "I'm his friend," she added reassuringly. "I have an important message for him."

"How do we know that?"

"I came to warn him something."

Once again the children exchanged glances. They were reluctant to talk. "The doctor en't been around for days," the boy replied. "We could give him a message. But what's in it for us?"

Jude had seen feral children before, but only at a distance. Her heart went out to them.

"Why don't you go to the Children's Office?" she asked. "They would give you food - far more than I can."

"They'd shut us up and make us work. I'd rather go hungry."

Jude sighed. She hated trading on the children's hunger to make them betray a friend, but they were her only link to Simeon. In case she found herself stuck in the city, she had taken two bread rolls from the evening meal and put them in her pocket. Unwrapping one from the napkin, she broke it in half and passed the pieces to the children. They ate ravenously.

"You can have the other later," Jude promised. "What are your names?"

The boy glared back defiantly. "Big and Littl'Un," he said.

"Don't you have any others?"

"Forgot 'em. She's Littl'Un. I'm Big."

"All right, Big. Where do you meet the doctor? I have to see him myself. My message is too important to trust to anyone else."

"You won't lead the police to him?"

"Cross my heart and hope to die."

"And you'll give us summat when we get there?"

"I promise."

Uncertainly the children looked at each other. For a minute they held a whispered argument. Intently Jude listened, catching odd words. "Take her to the hospital," Big suggested. "We can warn the doctor not to go there for a while." It was a solution worthy of an adult.

"OK," Littl'Un agreed, turning back to Jude. "You can come wi' us."

"I have to be back here by two hours."

"No problem. Mind you give us summat though, or the Reivers'll get you. They'll burn you up, until you're nowt but a black puddle!"

After that, Big and Littl'Un led Jude down the waterfront, beyond a jumble of old warehouses and sheds. There was a strong smell of fish. Big spotted some discarded carp heads, and stuffed them into his clothing. Another time he found a drum with a broken bottom and lay on his side trying to feel what was inside. He came up with a handful of grain. The waterfront was evidently a regular route for him. Jude began to feel nervous. As they passed, she noted every landmark. Just before the lake petered out into mud and reeds, they turned up a side street, near a building with a distinctive green tower. Even the children were uneasy now, checking each alleyway. Finally they came to an imposing building, with a vast, ornate portico.

A huge sign had once been illuminated across the front. Now dead filaments marked the letters. In the light from the street, Jude could just make out what they spelt. 'Oldcastle Health Enterprises' she read. 'Serving Your City'. Every window was shuttered; not a light showed. Even the air vents were still. Grabbing Jude's hand, Littl'Un guided her round the side of the building. 'People's Dispensary' a direction board indicated. Someone had scrawled a message along it. Straining her eyes, Jude read, "At least you can eat pigeons."

Bewildered, she looked around her. There seemed to be no guards. Alarms had been fitted all over the building, but when Big pushed firmly on one of the windows, everything remained quiet. "Come on!" he whispered. "Before anyone sees us."

Wondering if she was completely mad, Jude scrambled through the window after the children. She found herself in a long corridor, lit only by transom lights spaced every few metres along the roof. The moon shone through with a cold, blue light. A bitter stench filled her nostrils. Ahead, something burbled and shuffled.

It took a few seconds for Jude's eyes to adjust to the poor light, and she could see nothing. Then one of the transom lights banged in the wind. At once, a dozen shadowy forms shot up from the floor. The surprise made her gasp.

"It's only pigeons," Littl'Un said. "There's thousands of them! Look!"

A public sanitary area opened off the corridor. Its door hung askew, revealing a row of sinks and taps. Every one of the sinks was filled with bits of twig and feather. White splashes covered the bowls and slimed the floor. On the window ledge above, twenty or thirty pigeons were nesting. Judging by the flapping in the darkness, more were flying above, disturbed by the unusual human presence nearby.

"How do they get in?" Jude asked.
"Through the windows, cracks in the roof - any way they can. Filthy things!"
"There's loads more down there," Big added.
Jude looked where the boy had indicated. At the end of the corridor was a large waiting area, with rows of seats arranged neatly. It was as if the hospital had closed one evening and never reopened. On every available ledge, along the door runners, on top of the monitor screens, even on the surveillance cameras themselves, pigeons had taken over. From a distance, the smell was bad enough. Inside, it must be overpowering.
"Do we have to go through there?" she asked uneasily. She hated pigeons. When they flew towards her they made her flinch. They always seemed to go for her face and hair. Besides, they carried disease. It was no use her telling herself they were just birds...
"No. This way."
The children turned through one of the doors off the corridor. It led into another, smaller waiting room. There were a few pigeons in there, but it looked as if their nests were regularly cleared off the ledges. The smell was less overpowering, too. Cubicles were ranged all along one wall, their curtains hanging limply in the pale light. Big led the way past them.
Suddenly one of the curtains twitched, startling all three of them.
For an instant Jude had a glimpse of a small head. Even in such poor light she could see the unmistakable weals of Binasha on the boy's cheeks.
"It's only some kids," Big jeered, as if he had never doubted otherwise. Turning to the boy, he waved him back inside. "The doctor' en't here today," he said. "Go back to sleep."
Jude would not leave it at that. Softly she opened the curtains.
A small boy had made a bed on the floor of the cubicle with an old coat. Crouching there, he glared back at Jude in fright. Another child had been asleep on the bench. Disturbed by the sound of voices, he was waking up, whimpering slightly. In pity and horror Jude looked at them. The weals on their faces were old ones. They would survive. Only the gods knew how many others they had infected. There was nothing she could do for them except offer some water.
"Let me come in," Jude said. "I'm not going to hurt you."
Unclipping the bottle from her belt, she gave it to the first boy, though keeping hold so that he could not snatch it from her and gulp too much. Then she helped the other boy to drink. He was much weaker and leant against her arm.

As he drank, Jude noticed a name in the graffiti on the wall behind him. It surprised her so much that she let the bottle drop a little. The boy pulled it urgently back to his mouth.

Tuecer... There was something about Tuecer on the wall. In the poor light, Jude had to strain to read the words: "Tell Tuecer how we were cheated here!"

Underneath, another hand had written the despairing reply, "What can he do? Or anyone?" And overlapping that, in a different colour was a third comment: "Only the coward gives up!" Whoever Tuecer was, he existed - was real enough to feature in people's graffiti.

In her amazement, Jude had almost forgotten the boy sitting on the floor. "Are you the doctor?" he asked. His accent was unexpectedly good. The jacket he wore was expensive too, though too small, and ragged at the cuffs.

Sadly Jude shook her head. "Just a friend," she replied. "You must go to the Children's Office. They have drugs there."

"Mebbe," the boy agreed. Sighing, he settled back to sleep.

All the while, Little'Un and Big had watched impassively. "Aren't you afraid?" Big asked.

"What of?"

"Catching t' plague."

"No."

"Have you had some of the doctor's magic too?"

Big jabbed his elbow sharply in Littl'Un's ribs. She had said too much. The remark intrigued Jude. The doctor's magic sounded suspiciously like Provene.

Near them was a sliding screen, enabling patients to be called through for examination. Through it Jude could see light reflecting on metal. Getting up, she went to investigate.

She found herself in a treatment room. The table and lamps still stood in the centre of the floor. It amazed Jude that such expensive equipment should have been abandoned. Everything was spotlessly clean, smelling of antiseptic. There were no other signs of occupation, but the room had clearly been used in the past few days.

"How often does the doctor come?" she asked.

"Saturdays mostly, but he en't regular. Since the plague started, he's been coming more. Mike tells us first, and we pass the word round."

"Are there many with the fever?"

"Dunno." The boy's manner became evasive.

"'Course there are!" Littl'Un interrupted. "Loads and loads. Doctor Simeon's real mad about it. He says no one should die from Binasha now -"

"When did he come last?"

"Sunday. I know it were, because he don't normally come two days in a row."

Passing them the remains of the bread, Jude kept her side of the bargain. To her surprise, the children put it in their pockets, saving it for later.

"I have to get back," she said afterwards. Finding some comfits in her pocket, she laid them on the palm of her hand as bait. "You can have these too," she promised, "if you answer one last question. Where can I find a real-time collection point? One that's safe?"

Big shrugged his shoulders. "There in't one," he said.

"Aren't any of them safe?"

"They're all closed up. Nothing's working round here. Everyone's on strike."

Jude's stomach seemed to drop inside her. "Is there no service anywhere?" she asked.

"You could try further south. They reckon the army's moved into Leodis."

"Then I'll have to try there, won't I?" Though she tried to smile, Jude could have wept.

The walk back to the waterfront turned into a nightmare. Littl'Un was getting very tired and began to trail behind. Her brother tried to carry her, but he was not strong enough to do so for more than a few minutes. Jude had to take the girl from him, piggy back, but it slowed her down. By one thirty she had no choice but to go on alone.

Chapter Thirteen

In the darkness, every street looked the same; every alley equally confusing. The children had given Jude directions, but they had continually corrected each other and confused her. All Jude could do was head for the green tower, and then for the harbour beacon. Cutting through alleys and down the back of warehouses, she ran towards the shore. Twice she had to climb over a wall to avoid a furious dog. Alarms sounded behind her.

She only just reached the waterfront in time. The blue skimmer was beginning to turn back towards the lake.

"Wait!" Jude called desperately. Her feet slipping on the mud, she ran towards it. To her infinite relief, it slowed long enough for her to scramble on board.

"You cut it fine!" the driver said.

In amazement Jude stared at the man. His beard and hair were threaded with beads. Even in the dim light of the waterfront, she recognised him. Quickly she grabbed the safety bar.

For the first few minutes Jonah was too busy concentrating on getting the skimmer through the craft at the lake edge, to notice her silence. "Had a good evening?" he asked.

"Not bad." Jude prayed the man would not remember her.

"Find your bloke?"

"I found people who knew him."

Jonah turned to look at her. Though the moon had begun to go behind clouds, it gave enough light to see a face. "Don't I know you?" he asked.

"We may have met some time," Jude admitted.

"Like Hell we did! You paid me five hundred tokens to bring you from Leodis." Jonah laughed, but without humour. "Not bad, considering I was coming here already."

"I paid you for your help," Jude replied.

"So now you spy on me." Cutting the engine back, Jonah let the skimmer float uneasily.

Jude began to feel nervous. "No," she replied. "I have no interest in you whatsoever." She nodded towards the column of light ahead of them. "That's the lot I came to watch."

"What are you doing tripping around, then?"

The skimmer began to roll sickeningly. "I came to ask a friend to help."

"Does Feda know you're a spy?"

"Does she know everything about you?" For an awful few seconds Jude feared she had miscalculated. The man was big and powerful. It would be easy for him to push her overboard, and then drive straight into her. Forcing herself to smile, she added, "We both have our secrets." Her voice sounded odd in her ears. "If you'd like to earn more tokens, I could use your help again."

"Oh aye?"

To Jude's relief, Jonah restarted the skimmer. Quietly it moved into open water. "How much are you offering?" he asked.

"Fifty tokens."

"Not enough."

"It is as a down payment. I need you to take a packet to Leodis - in about a week's time." That would have to be long enough Jude decided. She ought to be able to find out what was happening at Border Seven by then. "I'll give you another fifty when you collect the packet from me."

In the moonlight she saw Jonah glance towards her. He seemed satisfied she was telling the truth. "All right, Lady," he said. "My credit's a bit low at the moment. Fifty tokens in advance would be useful. Do you have 'em on you?"

"And risk someone attacking me? No. I'll give them to Feda." Steadying herself against the safety rail, Jude wondered if she was mad to trust such a man, but he had dealt with her honestly on the way from Leodis.

The skimmer was nearing the ings. Lights still glimmered on some of the houseboats. Watching them, Jude felt an overpowering desire to run, to tell Jonah to turn around and take her back to Oldcastle. She was a fool to risk the same end as Adviser Nyall. She should leave now, while she could, and take her chance in the world outside.

Then she thought of Feda. As her closest friend, Feda would be questioned. Her visits to Yakim would be discovered. Jude could not be responsible for another woman being sent to corrective training. She would have to find a way of leaving that did not implicate her. "I might have another job for you later," she added. "Would you be willing to take me back down south?" She laughed. "I fancy eloping with you."

"When?"

"I don't know. As soon as I've done my job - and can get away without hurting Feda."

"Can you pay?"

"Another hundred tokens?"

Jonah turned the skimmer towards the waiting boat in the centre of the lake. "Feda was trying to match me and you off," he said gruffly. "You're not my sort, but I could have done worse. Keep your money. You'll need it. Just cook me some chips."

*****

After so little sleep, keeping up with her duties the next day was not easy. Jude envied Feda's stamina. Her own head pounded. Over and over again, she tried to make sense of what she had learnt the night before. By the time her shift had finished she was exhausted, and fell asleep leaning on a table in the rest room. When she awoke she was cramped and hungry but her head had cleared.

She could not understand why she had not made the link earlier. According to the children, Doctor Simeon last visited the hospital on Sunday. On Sunday evening Jude had seen another man take the place of one of the canoeists. That man had looked like Joel. The two men were surely one and the same. The Assessor had tried to alert her, writing the two names together on one line.

So what could Joel be doing coming to the Refuge? Stealing Provene? If he had any sort of medical training, he would grow very angry watching children die when just across the lake there were enough medications to share. But how could he get past Security?

When she finally saw the answer, Jude was standing on one of the little bridges in the evening sun. Fortunately she was alone, for she laughed out loud.

At least a year ago, Overseer Pera had pointed out that the grey-water outlets at East Five were vulnerable. Their pipes were so huge, an intruder could virtually walk into one, and by pressing against the sides, push gradually up the incline. Management had told her she was worrying unnecessarily. Such an entry would require considerable strength, and an ability to withstand repeated rushes of water. No thief would consider it worth the effort. After all, what was worth stealing in a service area? They had missed the point entirely. The pipes were easy to reach from the outside. Jude herself had stood under Border Seven's western outlet only a few days ago. Joel could put up with a good deal of discomfort, if the goal were important enough. From the service area he could gain access to the whole lobe.

Looking over the lake, Jude hesitated. It was not her business if someone from the city was stealing medications. All she needed to do was report the fact. The trouble was, infection was not choosy how it entered. A man climbing up a pipe would do as nicely as a partygoer returning home. If she let Joel come and go at will, she could be guilty of a crime against the whole Refuge. She had to stop him. Besides, she desperately needed to talk to him.

Big and Littl'Un had said Doctor Simeon usually went to the hospital on Saturdays. It was Saturday tomorrow. If fresh supplies of Provene were needed, Joel might cross to the Refuge tonight, under the cover of darkness. To intercept him, Jude needed to enter the lobe now, while a domestic supervisor could conceivably still be doing her rounds.

The dormitory was empty. Calling up one of the information displays, she worked out her route. The ID button should operate security doors on the way. Once she reached the recycled water zone however, she would have to pray there was no surveillance. Not even a domestic supervisor would have cause to go there.

For a second time, Jude hid in a storeroom and smartened herself up. Then she went through the side entrance to the lobe, and took the rapido. No one seemed to notice her. At each security point along the vast, curving walkway of level six, the identity button on her coverall let her through. Even as she turned down the corridor towards the recycled water zone, Jude was left unchallenged. With a silent prayer, she tried the service entry. That door, too, opened to her code.

Blinking in the darkness, Jude found herself on a walkway around a vast cavern of a room, stretching six levels below her and at least another five above. It was taller even than the atrium, and lit by a strange blue glow that seemed to have no particular source. The whole place throbbed and gushed with noise. Holding on to the rail, she steadied herself, then looked upwards.

Not even so vast a space was big enough to purify the outlets from so many showers, so many swimming pools. The main processor had been placed on another level above, out of sight. The tank it fed filled half the ceiling. Every minute or so, hundreds of litres of water flowed from it, down unseen coils of pipes, into one of the vats beneath.

Hurrying down several flights of metal steps, Jude reached a control centre, suspended on a gantry. The peculiar blue light came from permastrips around it, and from the dials and panels that monitored the cleansing processes day and night. In other circumstances, she would have found them interesting, but not now. Leaning over the gantry, she looked down.

The floor of the room was still so far below her, it must be level with the mud flats around the lake. A single huge tank stood in the middle, waiting to receive any water that could not be recycled. Suddenly, as Jude watched, a valve opened and a deluge cascaded out, towards three funnel-headed pipes. That was the weak point - the same flaw in the system Officer Pera had noticed. To cope with the volume and the suddenness of the downpours, each pipe had to be several metres in diameter. If the system had been completely sealed, there would have been no security risk, but the funnels had been left uncovered. An intruder could easily scramble out.

Her shoes clattering on the stairs, Jude ran on downwards.

She had only just reached the last gantry when she saw a dark shape emerging from the western funnel. Urgently she stepped back, behind a column.

Another cascade of water tumbled down the funnel, just as the figure dropped down to the floor and disappeared. In horror, Jude tried to see where it had gone. The shadows from the pipes above her confused everything, suggesting forms that did not exist. Her hand shaking slightly, she reached for her pacifier and set it at 'disable'.

At last the man appeared again, near the tank. He was dressed in a wet suit, black from head to foot. Water dripped around him, staining the floor. With obvious relief, he peeled off the hood that had covered his head, and undid the neck of his jacket. Then he stretched out his arms, and eased his back. In the strange blue light, his shoulders and chest looked almost white, and as firm and muscular as one of the statues in the atrium. Jude felt a pang of attraction and called herself a fool.

Turning slightly, Joel checked the stairs behind him. As the light fell on his face Jude stood with the pacifier in her hand, unable to think. He was so like she remembered... but harder around the mouth, as if he had seen a great deal of trouble in the past fourteen years...

Though she hesitated only a few seconds, it was too long. Sensing that he was being watched, Joel almost threw himself into the shadows.

Helplessly, Jude stood with the pacifier pointing at empty space. For the first time in her adult life, she could not see what her duty was. The man was an intruder. She should kill him before he had chance to infect the Refuge. Yet when they were younger, he had saved her life...

Finally, she came to a decision. "It's me! Jude!" she called. "Wait! I'm not going to hurt you. I need your help again."

There was no reply. "I'm leaving my pacifier on the steps," Jude shouted, her voice echoing round the pipes. "Look!" Moving into the light, she held her arms open to show that her hands were empty. Then she began to climb down the steps. If she had been mistaken and the man was not Joel, he would probably kill her as she walked. Even if it *was* Joel, he might. She hardly cared. Everything she valued - all her certainties - had crumbled during the past month. What did it matter what happened to her now?

By the time Jude reached the bottom level Joel was sitting on the floor half concealed by the side of a tank. He had dressed, in a dark tracksuit. "It's a long way down," he said.

"It'll be further back, up," Jude replied.

Awkwardly she stood beside him, not knowing how to behave. "Sit down," Joel invited. He indicated the space beside him. "You'll be out of sight."

With a sense of unreality Jude slid under the shelter of the tank, close to him. "I'm not going to ask you what you're doing," she said, "Otherwise I'd have to arrest you and..."

"And I'd have to - avoid it," Joel replied. "I could ask what you're doing as a menial, but I don't want to know that either." Sighing, he looked away. "Was it you at the station?"

"Yes."

There was a long silence. "I'm sorry you saw what you did," Joel said at last. "I could justify myself, but it would involve others. If I tell you I was protecting someone, can you leave it at that?"

"What I think is irrelevant," Jude replied. "You have to leave here. You could be bringing infection in. And I need to get back before I'm missed. Only... I wish we had time to talk"

"Some time in the future perhaps. I've thought a lot about you - wondered how you're getting on - "Abruptly Joel's tone changed. "You said you needed my help," he reminded her.

"You go up to the islands regularly. What's on the north side of this complex - the bit that's barred off?"

"You can't see. There's a groyne with outbuildings on it. The forbidden area is enclosed by them."

"Have you any idea what's in there?"

"There are lots of rumours- a pleasure beach for top officials, a testing area for weapons, a graveyard..."

"What do you think?"

It was some time before Joel answered. "Some of the water folk say it's a dumping ground," he said quietly, "for things - or people - that are no further use."

"People?" Jude repeated in horror.

"Members who drain the system. Take care, Jude. Perhaps opponents end up there too."

"Opponents of what?"

"Of those who run this place - and make fortunes from the work of others. The idea of the Refuges was a good one. Unfortunately the founders didn't take human nature into account."

They sat in silence together, while water gushed through the pipes beside them. "If you've any sense you won't ask questions," Joel advised at length. "But you wouldn't be the girl I remember if you didn't."

Tentatively he touched her hand, tracing the shape of her fingers. "I've thought a lot about you," Jude admitted. "For years."

"It's time we left," Joel warned. "There's something I ought to do, though, first. Something I should have done when we parted, but never had the courage."

"What?"

"This." Drawing her to him he kissed her.

In surprise Jude would have pulled away. Lovemaking outside bonding was forbidden in the Refuges - though it went on of course. Besides, Joel had been like a brother to her and it was strange thinking of him as more. Then a small voice inside her head asked, "Why not? Why not find out what it's like?" Sliding closer to him she returned his kiss. Even the sounds of the water around them faded from her mind.

Afterwards Jude sat up again and touched her mouth in bewilderment.

"I gather you're not angry with me," Joel said, smiling.

"No - though I wish you could have chosen somewhere more comfortable." Jude also smiled. "This isn't how I imagined meeting you again, but it's certainly interesting."

Smoothing her coverall, she got up to leave. "I won't watch how you get out of here," she promised. "That's something else I don't want to know."

*****

For an hour, Jude hid herself away in one of the game booths, trying not to think about Joel, and failing entirely.

At fifteen, he had been a typical squatter boy - undernourished, determined rather than strong. Now he could haul himself up a pipe and withstand frequent deluges of water while he did it. Fitness required food, money... There was a confidence about him too, the sort that comes from education and responsibility. Nothing short of a miracle could have turned his life around so completely since she knew him.

In Jude's experience miracles were rare. They usually involved an expectation of return. However valuable Provene might be, stealing it from a Refuge was hardly sufficient repayment for a changed future. Why take such a risk anyway? Even viewed in humanitarian terms, protecting a few hundred individuals would not achieve much. Far better to learn how to make the drug yourself. In an epidemic, that would have much greater effect.

With a start, Jude realised that could be what Joel was doing - stealing from the Refuge so that a vital drug could be replicated. Quite why he should give some of his precious resource to children was less clear - except that in them he must see himself, barely twenty years ago.

As for herself - her own conduct had been beyond excuse. Furiously Jude thumped at the reality game, eliminating half a dozen warriors and a support crew. By the time she had finished, her head and eyes were aching, and she had notched up the highest score that week.

"A highly commendable result," the electronic voice intoned. "You have above average hand/eye co-ordination. May we suggest you consider joining the armed services?"

Jude had the grace to laugh.

Even as she did so, she paused. She had been assuming that Joel lived in the city. But what if he had fooled her? What if he were returning home? It would be easy to hide a uniform under all those pipes, and a senior officer's ID would get him back into the lobe.

However apparently absurd, the idea would not go away. Provene was plant based. Joel knew a lot about plants. He had also suffered from plague himself, less than a year before they met. His mother had said he almost died. If there was any cure he would wish to find as an adult, it would be for Binasha.

The details of every member of the Refuge were recorded on the central database. If Joel was at Border Seven, Jude ought to be able to trace him.

As soon as she returned to her quarters, she went to see her supervisor. "I've received a letter from home," she said. "My father thinks we have a relative here. He would like me to pass on family greetings. Is there any way I can speak to one of the members?

"Do you know the dwelling number?" Molly asked.

"Dad wasn't too sure of the patronym," Jude lied. "My aunt took another partner, and we don't know which name my cousin uses. Are there any lists I could check first? I'd hate to make a fool of myself."

"There's the central record. I could arrange for you to scan that if you want."

"I'd be really grateful."

To Jude's surprise, Molly winked. "Is your cousin male by any chance?" she asked.

As Jude waited outside the record terminal an hour or so later, her hands were sweating. Knowing where to start was the problem. Molly would expect her to have just two names to check. Pretending she was unused to info-searches would give a few moments extra, but no more. If she acted too ignorant, Molly would want to come into the booth to help.

'Denovitch' produced nothing. On the top four levels there were thirty men called Joel, and another twenty called Simeon. Urgently Jude typed in the cue, 'Joel Unknown: Medical.'

Only one response appeared: 'Joel Anderson, Medical Research Officer, Grade Six, ESA, Ord. SF. Member Number 095678127'. Quickly Jude obtained a printout.

Molly appeared at the kiosk door. "Any luck?" she asked.

Jude smiled. "My cousin works in the medical laboratories," she replied. "I never realised he was so clever."

"What's his name?"

"Joel Anderson."

"You lucky girl! Researcher Anderson has a lot of influence. You know the stuff they gave you against the fever? He developed it." Molly seemed genuinely pleased. "They say he's a real nice bloke too," she added. "Runs a swimming club and teaches canoeing."

"What does 'Ord SF' mean?" Jude asked. She could not believe she had read the entry correctly.

"Order of SecureCity Fellowship. It's a great honour. Your cousin's one of management's blue-eyed boys. I'd try to get the right side of him."

Jude had to dig her fingernails into her palms to prevent herself laughing. "All I want is to take my father's good wishes," she said demurely.

"Of course," Molly agreed. "But knowing someone like him could get you a few privileges. You're a good worker. I'll see if an appointment can be made for you to meet him. While you're at it, you might put in a word for the rest of us."

Chapter Fourteen

Menials did not often know senior Refuge officials. Such requests had to go through proper channels. Then the member concerned had to give permission for a meeting. Otherwise they could have all sorts of riff raff bothering them. It was evening before a reply to Molly's request appeared on the message screen. MRO Anderson would be pleased to meet with his cousin. He could spare a little time at twenty-one hours the following day.

Jude could think of nothing else. To help pass the time, she spent the hour before lights out in the menials' amusement area. When a woman in black spoke as she left the games room, she started violently. She had been too preoccupied to notice anyone in the corridor.

"Officer Shah?" the woman asked her.

In horror Jude stared at her. "My name is Sara Davison," she insisted. "You must have made a mistake."

"I have a message for you, Officer. From your father."

Anxiously Jude looked around her. There was no one nearby. Every door was shut. "I'm just a menial," she insisted. "Why do you address me as Officer?"

The woman smiled. "Your father would like to meet you. I'll be your guide."

"My father is dead," Jude retorted. "If this is a joke, I don't find it funny."

"I'm not in the habit of making jokes."

Jude looked at the woman. There was nothing about her to suggest she had ever joked in her life. In a black outer wrap and heavy shoes, she looked a model of good sense: a nursing officer perhaps, or a clerk. "Then if you're not joking," Jude asked. "What do you mean?"

"I'm inviting you to meet your father."

"I go nowhere with strangers. Tell him to come to me," Jude replied. She was beginning to feel frightened.

"Very well. I'll see if he's willing." Briskly, the woman walked away.

For five minutes afterwards, Jude could not stop shivering. She had been hallucinating, she told herself. The silly chatter of the old people had affected her imagination. Either that, or there really was such a thing as side-spillage from the reality games.

*****

Molly was permitted to act as escort. They sat together in the visitors' lounge, both of them feeling conspicuous. At exactly twenty-one hours a senior officer entered. It was Joel. Until then, Jude had never quite believed he and Officer Anderson were the same man. Steadying herself, she waited for him to greet her.

Joel's control was immaculate. Everything about him suggested success, the perfect Refuge scientific officer. There was no indication in his manner that he and Jude had ever had more than a passing acquaintance, or that he regarded her branch of the family as anything but unequals. Jude did not have to pretend embarrassment. In the company of so assured a man she felt utterly inferior.

"My father asked me to bring his greetings," she said awkwardly.

"How is he?"

"Well. Thank you. Apparently he saw Aunt Julia recently, who told him you were here."

As Jude fed the lines, Joel responded perfectly. "It's a long time since I saw any of you," he agreed. "Not since I was eleven I think."

Molly was getting bored. "Would you like me to leave, Officer?" she asked. "I feel I'm intruding."

"Of course not." Joel's politeness was all one could ask. "But if you would like to return to your duties, I'm sure my cousin can find her own way back."

Molly almost curtseyed as she left.

Raising his eyes slightly, Joel indicated that the surveillance might be set. "Would you like to walk in the pleasure area?" he asked. "I don't imagine you've been allowed there."

"A menial can't go without a special invitation," Jude agreed.

"Then be my guest."

All the way down in the turbo lift and across the children's zone, Jude could feel the tension within her increasing. Finally they reached the pleasure area. Though it was evening, the artificial sunlight gave the impression of a summer afternoon. People were talking and walking, enjoying themselves.

"Keep up the act," Joel said quietly. "We're probably being watched, but with so much noise around us, they shouldn't be able to pick up what we say."

As soon as they were in the central area, Jude allowed herself a quiet laugh. "You fooled me for a while," she conceded. "But only an hour or so."

"I wondered how long it would be before you worked it out," Joel replied dryly. "I gave you a couple of days. You're better than I thought." Then he turned towards her. "But don't get complacent. A menial has no one to protect them. Don't walk under loose equipment, or lean on balconies."

Jude felt her skin go cold. "Are you warning - or threatening me?" she asked.

"Why should I threaten you? If anyone else had seen me the other night, they would have killed me at once. I'm giving advice. That's all."

The quietness of Joel's voice increased Jude's unease.

"You've grown up well," he remarked afterwards.

"I don't know what to say about you," Jude admitted. Trying to think how to word her question, she bent a flower towards her and savoured its scent. "I don't know you now. How has your life changed so much? Even your accent's gone. Who did you sell your soul to?"

"No one, I hope." Joel's voice was as cold as the fountain beside them. "Jude, you're a security officer," he pointed out. "You must have to do things you hate. If I'd let Commissioner Markham have another few seconds, a member of the Triumvirate would have died, and the country would have been in an even worse mess."

In amazement, Jude stared at him. "The Triumvirate?" she repeated. "No wonder the man had so many guards." Frowning, she let the flower bend back. "What were you doing down south?" she asked.

"Attending the conference - as a medical representative. The riots were useful to Markham, and a nightmare for those of us trying to protect senior officials."

His explanation made sense, yet still did not answer Jude's questions. "But why should you - a medical officer - act as a guard?" she persisted.

They were approaching the seats beside the fountains. "Come and sit down," Joel invited more loudly, for the benefit of anyone who might be listening.

"I feel more like hitting you," Jude admitted softly. "You kissed me to distract me. That was all it was. Wasn't it?"

Joel smiled wryly. "Initially," he admitted. "Then it began to mean more to me. You said you'd thought a lot about me. Were you just distracting me, or did you mean that?"

"I don't say things I don't mean."

"Then you're a very unusual woman." He was only half joking.

"Can you at least tell me how you ended up here?" Jude pleaded. "When I knew you, the idea of being in a Refuge scared you stiff."

"It still does sometimes," Joel replied and smiled. "I was spotted by one of the Refuge scouts and invited to apply for a scholarship. I signed my whole life contract six years ago."

"The Corporation doesn't usually recruit squatters."

"By then I was at medical school. A friend had lent me the money to study." Pausing, Joel looked towards a group of volleyball players returning from a match. "I meant to let you know I'd joined. But somehow I kept putting it off... I was afraid you might tell people my background. There's nothing more prickly than a scholarship boy."

With a faint tightening of the lips, Joel waited as one of the group moved away from the others and crossed the gardens towards them. In other circumstances, Jude would have diagnosed the early stages of height sickness, but the expression in his eyes was far too rational. She, too, allowed the man to pass before she spoke again.

"You seem nervous," she remarked. "Surely you're too important for anyone to harm? Unless, of course, they know what else you're doing?"

"I have a habit of speaking my mind. It doesn't go down well."

Getting up, Joel offered her his hand. "I need to take you back to the lounge," he said. "Distant relatives don't usually find much to talk about."

They went back into the visitors' area together. "It's been very pleasant seeing you again," Joel said politely as he wished her goodbye.

"Thank you for your time," Jude replied. "My father will be delighted we've met."

Drawing her to him, Joel gave her a cousinly kiss. "Go up to level 64c," he whispered. "Look out of the window, and you'll see our future."

*****

Like all the areas used by important members, the corridor on 64c ran around the outer side of the lobe. It was pleasant to have natural light for a change. The atmosphere had a diffused, yellow tinge, however, which puzzled Jude. She associated such light with higher levels, where the sunscreen acted as a filter. Pausing at the window nearest the conference room, she looked out. There was something peculiar about the view. No matter how one angled one's head, there was no change in perspective. The smudge of horizon and scrub remained exactly the same.

Glancing down the corridor to check that she was not observed, Jude picked at the corner of the window with her fingernails, wondering if there was a coating that might lift. There was no movement, but she thought she could feel a raised edge, as if a film had been stuck over the stayglass. The window further along felt the same, and the one next to it. On the fourth window however, she found a slight crease. Someone had peeled up the coating and then pressed it firmly back into place.

Jude had no idea what she expected to find when she lifted the film from the glass - an illicit pleasure area perhaps. What she saw, stunned and appalled her.

Level 64 was high enough for its north facing windows to see over the roofs of the service buildings. It was also low enough for a viewer to distinguish what lay just beyond.

Between the complex and the lake's edge, a hundred or more hovels were just visible in the dusk. Those that could not find space in the shelter of the service wall, had been built with their entrances turned towards the lobe, away from the pitiless northerly winds. A few had even been erected on the mud flats to use the platform itself as shelter, though the first storms would send water swirling through them.

Every hovel had been built from something different to its neighbour - bits of discarded machinery, fragments of cloth, spars from broken boats. Open fires burnt between them, sending up a haze of smoke. Around the fires, figures sat in groups on the ground, or walked aimlessly about. Almost hidden by the lobe, others were scrabbling in the mounds at the foot of the waste shoots, looking for anything that was edible. There must have been a thousand people, too small from such a height to identify as individuals, but all of them apparently without purpose. Their clothes were of one colour, a drab, dirty blue.

For several minutes Jude watched, forgetting everything except the horror of what she was seeing. Taking the magnifiers from her money belt, she focused on the nearest group. All but two were old. Their hair shone white in the firelight. One sat huddled so close to the flames, the heat must have been burning his face. Someone had put a piece of cloth over his shoulders. It was slowly slipping onto the mud.

Bewildered, Jude looked for a boat that might have brought so many people there. She could not even detect a jetty. If they were squatters from the nearby city, why had the Refuge authorities not moved them on?

The answer was so appalling that at first Jude was not willing to consider it. The people beneath her were not city dwellers. They belonged to the Refuge itself. The blue of their clothing was the colour of detention, the blue of the mentally ill. Sick and old, perhaps genuinely mentally unstable, all had been categorised as the same and expelled from the lobe. She was looking down on level 40. The people huddled round the fires or searching for food were the unwanted ones, of no further use because they could not, or would not, play their allotted part in the communal effort.

Footsteps approached along the corridor. With a start, Jude dropped the film back into place.

For the rest of the evening and into the night, the memory of what she had seen lay like a dead weight on Jude's mind. A few corrupt officials - trips to the city, medicines sold at a profit, they were nothing compared to what was being done to those cast out of the lobe.

Management at Border Seven could no longer afford to give space to those who did not meet targets. There were too many skilled applicants waiting for admission, too many eugenically created babies growing up into adults, with all the talents a manager could require. Every dwelling must be allocated to those of value to the Corporation. The economically valueless must be cast out, to die on the mud. That was the fear Jude had sensed along level 163. Each of the old people she served had been warned that if they could not keep up, they would be reassessed. They knew that very few returned from such assessment. Where their neighbours went afterwards they dared not ask, but they had their suspicions. That was why they tried to walk so youthfully, why they observed every rule.

The ideal she had believed in - had risked her safety to protect - turned to dust in Jude's mind. Anything became possible, no matter how hateful. Perhaps a few members of Border Seven were deliberately allowed to see the view outside - to frighten them into co-operation. The shock could easily turn the more sensitive insane. What more effective way was there of removing someone? "Height sick" people would say soothingly, and pat them on the hand.

This was what Adviser Nyall had meant. The old woman was intelligent and observant still, with a tendency to ask awkward questions. She also believed in the Refuge ideal. Instead of going quietly insane after seeing out of the window, she had tried to warn her former colleagues. Her friends had begun to believe her, so she had had to be removed. No wonder the old woman was so frightened when the restrainers arrived. She knew that the very place she had tried to tell people of, was to be her own end.

Urgently Jude considered what she herself could do. She had never felt so helpless in her life. By keeping silent she would save her own skin, and countenance something her whole being abhorred. In speaking out, she would have the satisfaction of expressing her horror, and achieve absolutely nothing. Even as a Refuge officer, she would probably be able to do no more than warn a few members, then she too would find herself on level 40. As a supposed menial she could do even less. Criticism of her employers would be regarded as disruptive activity, and her contract ended at once. With the Corporation exerting so much power over local authorities she was probably not safe outside either.

Her assignment, the Chief Secretary's disappearance, Joel, none of them mattered to Jude anymore. The Refuge her parents had died to build had become hateful to her. However beautiful the lake, however charming the little islands or sweet-scented the roses, all she could see was mud. Even Sabbattica Collins' vague fears began to sound credible. What if her bonding had been recorded, and then used in one of the illicit reality games rumoured to sell for vast sums? Sab Collins might not be imagining that strangers recognised her - might indeed have overheard cruel whispers.

But the worst thought of all was that Joel might have told Jude where to look, hoping that she would give up her mission - or even lose her mind.

*****

For the first time since she set off from East Five, Jude grew careless. As she went about her duties the following day, she hardly glanced around her. If she could have talked about what she had seen it would have eased her pain, but she dared speak to no one, not even Feda.

That evening, Molly gathered her menials together in the refectory. An extra shift was required. The windows around the main atrium were being cleaned. It was a colossal job, only undertaken monthly and at quiet periods, when the atrium could be closed. There was always a good deal of mess. A team was needed to mop up the spillage after the autowashes had passed overhead, then buff the marble tiles back to their customary splendour. She called out the names of those who had been chosen. To Jude's surprise, hers was included.

It was rotten luck Feda whispered - a beast of a job. Still, there was nothing any of the women listed could do, but return to the dormitory and put their coveralls on again. Then Molly led them back into the lobe.

Without the usual bustling crowds crossing back and forth, the atrium seemed even more overpowering, a vast shining cavern, pushing upwards towards unfathomable shadows. It reminded Jude of a holo-reality image she had seen, displaying a medieval cathedral. With a new cynicism, she stared around her. What God did this cathedral serve? She wondered if He was pleased with the daily sacrifice on the mudflats outside.

One automatic cleaner was already working, swinging about from the hawsers that suspended it from the ceiling, far above. As it scraped over the stayglass, it made an awful lot of noise, spraying and washing as it passed. "We'd better get cracking," Molly said cheerfully. It would take more than an empty atrium to overawe her.

Another autowash started up, doubling the noise. By the time all four were working, it was difficult to hear a voice right beside you. The more experienced women had learnt the art of mouthing, and could hold a soundless conversation above the racket, but Jude was too exhausted to do more than plod on behind them, guiding her automatic buffer backwards and forwards. The motion was almost restful, so repetitive it required no thought. Her whole mind was filled by the constant hum, until she was scarcely aware of what was going on around her.

By the end of the first hour, the autowash Jude was following was descending gradually down the stayglass. With a faint surprise Jude noticed that the other women had moved over to the far side of the atrium. There were only herself and Didor left on the eastern side.

For another half hour, Jude and her companion worked together, the one mopping, the other buffing. Finally the autowash came to a halt. It had finished its progress altogether. Molly signalled that Didor should assist the others, leaving Jude to finish polishing the tiles.

Uneasily Jude looked around her. The vastness of the atrium was intimidating, her colleagues too distant to provide any company. Thirty metres up the stayglass, the autowash swung on its hawsers like a pendulum, gradually coming to rest. The other three machines had finished. There was only the one area of tiles left for Jude to finish, right under the nearest autowash. For the first time, she hesitated. The autowash was a huge piece of equipment, too far above her to distinguish as more than a confusion of brushes and hoses. Clearly it was very heavy. As it swung, the hawsers looked slight to carry such a weight.

Unable to explain why, Jude began to feel afraid. She did not want to step right under the autowash. No one would notice if she left one bit of the floor unfinished. Switching off the buffer, she prepared to join the others.

Molly had other ideas. Seeing Jude had stopped, she came over to inspect.

"Call that finished!" she said. "Get that last bit done!"

With a sense of dread, Jude switched on the buffer again, and moved forwards. All the while, she kept glancing towards the autowash swinging above her. Her stomach tightened with fear.

When she heard the shout, she did not even have time to scream. Throwing the buffer to one side, she flung herself forward on the marble. Sliding and rolling, she tried desperately to get out of the way.

Chapter Fifteen

The autowash hit the floor just behind Jude, and disintegrated into a thousand separate parts. Water cascaded over her. She could not breathe. A huge brush crashed down near her arm. Another hit the marble to the left of her.

Desperately she tried to crawl further out of the way. Someone was holding onto her feet. Pain flared through her body. All around her, objects flew off the tiles, or imbedded straight into them.

It seemed to last for hours. Then slowly the world settled back into place, as cold as the floor on which Jude lay. Water still poured onto the marble, but in a steady stream rather than a cascade. As if from far away, she could hear women screaming.

In relief, Jude tried to turn towards them. She could not move her head.

"Oh my God!" a voice was shouting. "What happened?"

Someone had switched off the power. After hours of noise, the silence was almost tangible.

Feet ran across the marble. "Let me through!" someone shouted. That was Molly's voice, taking control as usual.

Jude felt cold fingers on her throat.

"She's alive."

"Of course I am," Jude wanted to say. Her mouth would not open.

"Don't move her!" Molly ordered. "If her neck's broken you'll snap the spinal chord. Help me shift this stuff. Quickly!"

With a sense of bewilderment, Jude listened as half a dozen people scrabbled around her. She had not realized how many pieces of the autowash had hit her.

"Thank God it's only the soft stuff!"

That was Phoebe's voice.

"If one of them bolts had struck her -."

"Look how deep this one's gone."

Painfully, Jude tried to see what Mary had indicated. It was somewhere ahead of her, in the marble itself.

The medical team had arrived. So too had Security. New voices echoed around the cavern.

"Is she alive?" a man shouted. It sounded like Joel.

Sighing, Jude gave up listening. Joel did not belong there. She must be getting her dreams confused again.

A medical orderly was injecting something into her hand. Joel leant over her. "Oh, Lord, it's my cousin!" he said.

"Get her to Emergency," another voice ordered.

"May I go with her?"

"If you wish, Sir."

Jude managed at last to speak. "You nearly killed me," she said to Joel. "Why?"

"The poor woman's delirious," the orderly apologized quickly.

"You must forgive her," Molly pleaded. "She's only half conscious." She sounded frightened.

Joel himself said nothing.

*****

Jude had been very, very lucky. Nurse Millom kept repeating the fact. Such a terrible accident! From that height, even a hairbrush hitting you could kill, never mind one of those huge autowash things.

As it was, Jude had broken her wrist when she threw herself forward, and suffered so many cuts and bruises, she could scarcely bear to move.

The wrist was mended quickly enough, fused in less than ten minutes' surgery, and the cuts were carefully sealed, but the bruises were more difficult to get at. They were deep within her tissue. The only comfortable way Jude could lie was on her front.

"It's wonderful what we can do nowadays," the nurse enthused. "I've tacked people together after half a dozen breaks. Mind you, it's a good job this happened to you here, and not outside. If you'd had to pay for so much treatment, you couldn't have afforded it."

Jude shivered. She had hardly stopped shivering since she came round from the anaesthetic. "No," she acknowledged. The memory of what had happened took her breath from her chest. If she had not heard someone shout, she would have been right under the autowash when it fell.

"There's no need to distress yourself, my dear," Nurse Millom said kindly. "Maintenance won't accept liability of course, but there's no way what happened was your fault. There will have to be an inquiry."

A vase of flowers stood on the side unit - beautiful parrot orchids that could only have come from one of the inner gardens. The nurse saw Jude look towards them. "Your cousin sent them," she said.

"My cousin?"

"Researcher Anderson." Nurse Millom gave a knowing wink.

Though half drugged, Jude had the wit to cover her error. "I didn't think he would bother," she said. "I haven't seen him for years."

"He was very concerned. Came with you when they brought you in, then insisted on staying until you went into surgery."

Jude could remember nothing of that time. "It was very good of him," she said awkwardly. "We hardly know each other."

"Don't sound so surprised, my dear," Nurse Millom advised. "You're not bad looking, and seeing you so hurt must have touched him. I'd play on it if I were you. You might need an influential friend."

For some time after the nurse had gone, Jude lay staring at the wall beside her. Through a haze she could see Joel leaning over her. "You nearly killed me," she had said. "Why?"

When she had spoken, she had been barely conscious. She had not known what she was saying. Yet the conclusion she had come to then made sense. There was no way the autowash had fallen accidentally. Even the nurse had implied as much. Having removed the Chief Secretary and the Assessors before her, someone had tried to get rid of Jude too. Whoever it was, must have been watching, waiting until she stepped under the mechanism. Then they had cut the hawsers.

Joel had to be involved in some way. He had appeared on the scene far too quickly. A research officer had no reason to be near the atrium when it was being cleaned. Her mouth drying with fear, Jude turned towards the orchids. In her imagination she began to see deadly clouds passing across her as she slept.

Carefully she pulled herself up and examined each flower head, as if merely enjoying its beauty. All looked and smelt perfectly normal. A gift card had been placed in a delicately stemmed holder. "To my cousin," it said. "With best wishes for a speedy recovery." No matter how many times Jude turned the words over in her head, she could make nothing significant out of them.

The orchids troubled her even so. When the nurse came in again, Jude asked for them to be taken out of the room while she slept. "My mother used to insist we took flowers out at night," she explained. "Something to do with using up the oxygen."

Nurse Millom smiled indulgently. "You needn't worry about having enough oxygen here," she assured her. "The atmosphere is monitored the whole time. Still, if it'll make you happier..." She carried the orchids outside.

Turning back onto her front, Jude finally managed to rest.

When she awoke, the other patients were still asleep. A jug of fresh orange juice had been put beside her bed. She had not tasted fresh orange juice for weeks - since she set off on her assignment. In delight, she drank slowly, savouring the flavour. She might never have known such sweetness again. Nor would she have seen the light reflecting from a jug, or the beauty of dust motes dancing in a lamp's warmth.

The day before, Jude had not cared whether she lived or died. Now simply to open her eyes and watch people sleeping gave her pleasure. The walls were a pretty pastel blue. A hologram opposite her was the most delightful image she had seen, the waterfall in it shimmering like a thousand perfect diamonds. She would have missed not being able to see a real waterfall again. Even the ache in her back was a reminder that she had another day to experience.

An hour or so later, the doctor called at the beginning of his round. He was very pleased with Jude's progress he said. Her wrist had fused nicely, and the cuts were healing. He would allow her to get up, so long as she took care. In a day or two she should be able to go back to work, though he would ask her supervisor to put her on light duties. After such a spectacular accident, no one could accuse her of shirking. Since the bruises on her back must be sore, he would allow another day's supply of painkillers, but that was all. They were expensive.

"Why don't you spend some time on the sun deck?" he suggested finally. "Let your body absorb the warmth. You can entertain visitors there, and your supervisor has asked to see you."

"Thank you, Officer" Jude replied politely. She would have felt a great deal safer on her own.

*****

Molly was full of concern.

"If I hadn't made you finish those wretched tiles, you'd have been well clear," she said. "I feel awful about it, but we have to meet our targets. You do understand?"

"Of course," Jude replied.

"They're saying it couldn't possibly have been an accident. Have you made any enemies?"

"Not that I know of."

Reluctantly Jude began to consider Molly's part in what had happened. It was she who had called the other women away, leaving Jude alone. Then she had insisted on the job being finished. Until then, Jude would have said she trusted the woman - that as supervisors went, Molly was one of the better ones. Now she would trust no one, not even Feda.

"I've been advised to go onto the sun deck," she said. So far outside the main building, there should be no surveillance. "I'd be grateful if you'd come with me. I feel a bit unsteady."

They went out and sat on a couple of the loungers. With the roof amplifying the heat from the skyscreen a hundred levels above, it was possible to imagine they were sitting on a pleasant beach. "It's nice here, in't it?" Molly remarked. "Shows you how the other tenth live."

"It's almost worth being ill for," Jude agreed. "But not dying for." She shook her head. "If it wasn't an accident, I honestly don't know who could have done it. Unless you have a reason for wanting me dead."

"Why on earth should I?"

"It was you who gave me the job."

Molly flushed. "I was given a list of names," she insisted. "Management always decides that sort of thing."

"Every day?" Jude asked disbelievingly.

"No - just for special jobs."

"Were you told to get me on my own?"

"I wouldn't kill anyone. Don't talk so daft!"

Jude felt sure Molly was telling the truth. When the autowash fell, she had been as horrified as everyone else. Yet the woman had been acting under orders, Jude was equally sure of that.

"No, you wouldn't kill," she wanted to reply, "But if your job depended on it, you wouldn't notice what others did." It was wiser to pretend to be reassured however. "Forgive me," she said and smiled. "I'm being silly. It's just that when something like this happens, you start suspecting everyone. You've always been very fair to me."

Molly's relief was so obvious, Jude almost smiled.

The morning lottery result was showing, and they paused to see who had won. "Only two digits out!" Molly boasted, as if being so near today, improved tomorrow's odds. Then she glanced at Jude. "Do you really think someone tried to kill you?" she asked.

"No," Jude lied. "I'm sure it must have been an accident."

Satisfied, Molly went away.

The more she thought about it, though, the more sure Jude was that Joel had been involved. She remembered the expression of terror on Commissioner Markham's face at the transit station - and Joel's warning about loose equipment. Her father used to repeat a local proverb: "Your best friend may also be your worst enemy." It seemed horribly appropriate now.

Feda came later that afternoon, bringing a box of comfits from the women in the dormitory. "You must have been a cat in your last life," she said.

"Why?" Jude asked. "Oh I see - nine lives. I hope I haven't used up the other eight."

"Phoebe and Mary haven't stopped shaking yet. They reckon that autowash missed you by centimetres. It's made an awful hole in the tiles. You should see it." Sitting down, Feda shook her head. "Maybe you shouldn't," she added. "It'd terrify you."

"They say I can come back to work the day after tomorrow."

"What do you have to do to get three days off? Break both legs?"

Jude laughed. Taking out some mending, Feda busied herself while they talked. For several minutes they chatted about the latest gossip from the menials' rest room, then Jude looked around her. They were sitting on the balcony of the sun terrace, well away from any possible eavesdroppers. "I need to send a message to Jonah," she whispered.

Raising an eyebrow, Feda looked at her quizzically.

"He was going to meet me tomorrow. Tell him what's happened - that I'm sorry to mess him about, but it wasn't my doing."

"Who's doing was it?"

"It was an accident."

"Are you sure?"

"No," Jude admitted. "We all have enemies. Planting a timepiece in someone's pocket isn't all that different to trying to kill them. It's just a question of degree."

For several seconds Feda looked at Jude's face. "I can't make you out," she admitted. "I'm glad they didn't squash you into that floor, but I reckon you're playing with fire somehow. Who are you really looking for? Not some old flame that's for sure."

In surprise Jude turned away, wondering how to answer. Once you started to lie it got more and more complicated. She would much rather be a simple, straightforward Family Support Officer. "I wanted to join Tuecer's lot," she whispered.

Feda sewed a whole seam before answering. "How do you know about Tuecer?" she asked.

"I've heard people talk - and seen his name. It was on the hospital wall." Jude's wrist was aching and she rubbed at the bone.

"You've been to the hospital?"

"It's a right mess, isn't it?"

Feda sighed. "All that wonderful equipment and it was only open two months. The firm went bust, and Sector Council just left it. Everyone signed petitions but nowt happened." She glanced nervously at Jude. “Now some charity’s come forward and wants to open it again. It’ll make them very popular.”

“And Tuecer’s money’s behind it?” Jude hazarded. Though Feda did not answer, it was clear the guess was a lucky one. “He would do something like that.”

“You know him - personally?”

“I know people who’ve met him, when he’s been down south. They reckon he’s trying to sort things out - bang heads together... Just what the country needs.”

“We’ve certainly had enough of the war lords,” Feda agreed carefully.

Though Jude was bluffing, her companion’s expression was easy to read, giving clues at every sentence. “I’ve heard the Reivers are even worse here,” Jude continued, “and they were always causing trouble round our way, raiding across the border. I reckon if this Tuecer fellow really can sort things out, I’d like to join up - or whatever else you do. I feel I ought to be doing something to make things better, and I’ve had enough of SecureCity already.”

“I wouldn’t talk about such things if I were you,” Feda warned. “Tuecer’s on the banned list.”

“Why? Surely if he’s trying to get a bit of stability... That’s good isn’t it?”

“If your power comes from being in chaos, stability’s the last thing you want.” Frowning, Feda began to gather up her mending. “Yakim might know how to put you in touch,” she whispered. “But if I were you, I wouldn’t get involved. I’d find safer things to do.”

Rising, she touched Jude’s shoulder in warning. “Stop worrying about things, and enjoy yourself a bit more,” she advised. “Go and see your cousin. He’s quite a dish. I wouldn’t mind getting to know him myself.”

Afterwards, Jude returned to her bed and did some careful thinking.

Starting with Molly calling the meeting in the refectory, she went over every minute of the previous evening. She got as far as finding herself alone on the eastern side of the atrium, and then stopped. Why had she been so afraid of the autowash above her?

For a couple of hours she had worked quite happily. No one liked having to walk under such heavy equipment, but in a Refuge you had to get used to such things. Then some instinct had come into action, warning her that she was not safe. Instinct alone would not have saved her, though. Having been forced to go forward, she would have died if she had not heard someone shout...

“Oh Lord!” she said to herself. “You stupid woman!”

Joel had been in the atrium because he had been guarding her. When he saw the hawsers cut, all he could do was shout to warn her.

Whatever angle Jude considered, a line of connections led her to the same answer. "Jude, you're a security officer -" The words echoed in her mind. They implied that Joel, too, was in a similar role - and for him to be guarding a member of the Triumvirate, he must be an important member. Why else was he in a soldier's uniform, rather than that of a Refuge medical officer? Presumably he was travelling incognito, but not for the Refuges. Feda had virtually admitted Tuecer's money was reopening Oldcastle hospital. And if Joel really was the Doctor Simeon the children spoke of, he visited that hospital regularly...

She had done him a terrible injustice. He must have known that in calling out to warn her, he would draw attention to himself.

Deep in Jude's mind a memory was struggling to the surface. Two men were flinging her backwards and forwards between them. Their hair was shaved in jagged patterns and they had letters tattooed on their fingers. "Fancy a game, Hunter?" the older one called.

Each time she tried to recall why the men were pushing her between them, her memory flinched away. Something awful had happened while she was walking with Carrie and the others back to the Refuge. It was to do with Hawkboys and a barn full of pigeons, but she could not remember what. Her only certainty was that Joel had saved her then, too.

Chapter Sixteen

The pain in Jude's back was excruciating that night. When the doctor told her she had suffered damage to her spine, she was not surprised. She would need further, and more difficult surgery. The thought frightened her more than any risk she had taken in her work. She felt sick deep in her stomach.

She had to make peace with Joel. Just in case...

Nurse Millom nodded. "You'd be wise to do so," she agreed. "Of course we hope the op. will go well, but you never know... You might need your cousin's help." She looked at Jude curiously. "Has there been bad blood between you two in the past?"

"Our parents didn't get on." Persuasively, Jude smiled. "It's odd what your subconscious can do, isn't it?"

"It is, my dear, particularly when you have a nasty blow to your head. Mind you, I can imagine people were jealous, with him being adopted and doing so well."

Jude tried to look as if she knew what the woman was talking about. "Do you know his background then?" she asked.

"Oh - I wouldn't pry of course, but you get talking when you're working together. I'm from round here you see, so I know the Andersons' estate."

"Is it very big?" Jude bluffed.

"The biggest in this sector - absolutely beautiful, with its own boathouse, and beach. If I were you, I'd apologise to your cousin very, very nicely. You never know what he might be able to do for you."

Briskly, Nurse Millom went away to make the appropriate calls.

Lying back, Jude stared at the ceiling. The name Anderson was vaguely familiar to her. Soon after she returned to her Refuge, Joel had written a long letter about being allowed to use the Andersons' library. He must somehow have won their help in other ways.

Ten minutes later, Nurse Millom was back. MRO Anderson would be willing to see Jude for a few moments. One of the ward orderlies would accompany her, to see she was all right.

When they reached the laboratories, the reception officer was waiting for them. "Officer Anderson asked me to bring you through," she said. "He thought you might like to look round."

"That's very kind of him," Jude replied. She was wondering how to get rid of her escort, when the clerk offered him a cup of coffee, leaving her free to follow the receptionist through the infection locks, and into the hydroponic centre.

"We have to operate a sterile environment," the woman explained chattily. "Mr. Anderson insists on it." She glanced at Jude, but was far too polite to ask questions.

Joel was working at the other side of the gallery. As she waited for him, Jude looked about her in delight. The air was filled with the scent of plants, and as tranquil as a summer's day. Even the humidity that often made the hanging gardens unpleasant was controlled, though water trickled down a thousand glass plates, and flowed along channels beneath. Jude had been in similar research areas before, but compared to this, they were places of routine and regimentation. Here, flowers were in bloom everywhere, bright purples and blues, yellows and reds. She had never seen so many colours together.

"You like my garden?" Joel asked, coming towards her.

"It's beautiful."

The receptionist watched curiously.

"I came to apologize," Jude continued carefully. "I don't know why I said what I did."

"I understood," Joel insisted, and smiled.

Still the receptionist lingered, pretending to sort some papers on one of the benches.

Jude tried to think of something appropriate for a distant cousin to say. "Why do you need so many plants?" she asked.

"My research draws on ancient remedies. I need my own supplies." They began to walk through the rows of screens. "Like these two here…" Joel indicated a couple of unassuming trays. "Woundwort and milfoil. We have to make medications more cheaply. At present, only the rich can afford what doctors prescribe. Even in the Refuge, we're having to cut back on prescriptions."

"They would only allow me a couple of days' painkillers," Jude remarked. Out of the corner of her eye, she could see the receptionist beginning to get bored.

"That's why I'm working with plant bases. They're the best renewable resource I know."

As he talked, Jude could hear the boy she had known years ago, telling her about some old wives' tale he had heard, and how well it had worked. "My supervisor said you invented that stuff against the plague," she remarked.

"Provene was one of those ideas that come in the night. And take three years to perfect."

At last the receptionist went.

Joel sighed in relief. "We can talk safely here," he said. "There's no surveillance. I convinced management it could lose them a fortune on the black market."

Extending his hands to her, he invited her closer, and further away from the door. "Would it hurt too much if I held you?" he asked gently.

"You can try. My back's the worst."

Cautiously she moved against him, and put her head against his shoulder. "I'm so sorry," she said. "You saved my life, and I was too stupid to see it."

"I helped you to save yourself. That's all. What made you think I could kill you? You're the last person on earth I would harm - deliberately."

"I thought you'd told me to look through the window, so that it would turn my mind. It nearly did - whatever you meant."

"I wanted you to see what we're up against. That's all."

Despite the pain, she let him comfort her. "I thought for a moment you were dead," Joel said. "I nearly howled - there in the atrium. It wouldn't have been wise."

To Jude's amazement she found that she was crying. For the first time in years she was weeping openly, tears of pain and fear and gratitude.

"Shh -" Joel said.

They could not stay long like that. The door might open any moment. Two chairs had been pushed against a workstation at the far side of the gallery. "We'd better sit down," Joel advised. "Tell me what you've been doing - apart from dressing up as a menial."

Holding her breath to steady it, Jude calmed herself. "They made me a ward of the Refuge after I returned," she explained, "And then sent me on a high-flyers' course. After that, there was Academy and Officer Training School. I work for Family Support now." Her wrist had begun to ache again and she rubbed at it crossly.

Taking her hand, Joel massaged the bone. The sensation was unexpectedly soothing. "Funny isn't it?" he asked reflectively. "I never imagined you'd grow up - or be so - beautiful. But it doesn't sound as though you've had much fun in life."

"Enough. The facilities at East Five are excellent. And I enjoy my job."

"Any special friends?"

"No. No one who matters to me. And you?"

"I was very close to a colleague, but Personnel realized, and packed her off to West One. We tried to keep in touch..." Glancing round the laboratory, Joel shrugged his shoulders. "This is my love now," he added.

"I still can't imagine how you ended up here," Jude admitted.

"Why?" Joel asked sharply. "Until General Rowles came to power, my mother was a doctor; my father a botanist. My career is logical, a combination of the two."

She had wounded him. "I'm sorry," Jude apologized. "I know your family weren't ordinary squatters. But there's a lot you need to tell me. Otherwise, I'll keep putting my foot in it."

Joel nodded. "Sorry. I'm a bit defensive," he acknowledged, "about my background at least. There's not a lot I can tell you at the moment. I did something that pleased a wealthy landowner round here, and he offered me a job. After a year or two, he was treating me like a son. I wouldn't agree to legal adoption, but I took his name." There was warmth and respect in Joel's voice. "Most of what I am, I owe to Tom Anderson," he added.

There was a difficult silence. Finally Joel smiled. "I've been extremely fortunate," he continued. "I've had two fathers, both of whom have done their utmost for me. But I couldn't go on living off others. So I joined the Corporation."

"And now you're risking everything," Jude pointed out, "Leaving the Refuge in secret."

"Leave's been difficult to get lately. With the fever spreading in town, I can't just sit here - not when I can help. The Corporation refuses to do so, and that makes me mad. They'd rather let children die, than share their knowledge."

It was an acceptable explanation, but not, Jude could tell, the whole one. Curiously she considered him. "You've grown at least ten centimetres since I last saw you," she remarked. "The girls downstairs say you're quite a dish."

To her amusement, Joel flushed. "Give over -" he said.

"You also have a reputation for honesty. They like that too."

Ruefully, Joel smiled. "That's not necessarily a good thing. My position as the man who discovered Provene's protected me in the past. Now it's the hope that I'm about to come up with something equally important. If I don't - or I find the answers too quickly - I might have something heavy falling on me too."

Jude shook her head in alarm.

Abruptly Joel got up. "Come to my dwelling tomorrow night," he invited, "and I'll give you the information you need. If I write out a pass-note, Security'll let you through."

"I didn't think fraternising with menials was allowed. Won't it damage your reputation?"

To Jude's surprise, Joel laughed. "It'll probably enhance it," he replied. "I'm viewed as a bit of a cold fish - a nice bloke, but works too hard."

Just as they were about to part, Jude managed to tell him. "I have to have an op on my spine tomorrow," she said, trying to sound casual.

Joel was not fooled. "You'll be all right," he said.

But as they began to walk back down the gallery he was very quiet. "Jude -" he said hesitantly. "There's something I should prepare you for - as a friend. You could be about to experience something very unpleasant."

"What do you mean?" she asked in alarm.

It was a long time before Joel replied. When he did, she knew he should not be doing so. "I don't mean the op. I'm sure that'll be OK. Just remember one thing: fear of being afraid is worse than fear itself."

*****

As soon as the woman in black appeared in the corridor, Jude knew the test had begun. No one had told her the rules, but it was vital she pass the examination.

"I'm glad you've decided to come," the woman said, as matter-of-factly as if Jude had accepted an invitation to tea. "We'll have to hurry. We don't have a lot of time."

"But I can't just walk out," Jude protested. "I'll be missed."

The old woman smiled. "It's quite all right, my dear," she assured her. "We have the whole afternoon together. Follow me."

There seemed to be no possibility of Jude refusing. "At least tell me where we're heading," she pleaded. "In case we get separated."

"You'll know when we get there."

Briskly, the woman in black set off. The corridor was empty. Jude risked calling out to her. "Who are you?" she demanded.

"Your tutor. Senior Magdala. You asked me to take you to your father. Don't you remember?"

They went down the moving stairway together, Senior Magdala always a few metres ahead. By the time Jude had reached ground level, the old woman was walking across the atrium, towards the main door. In amazement Jude followed her. No one challenged her. They seemed to accept that it was perfectly normal for a menial to cross the holy of holies, and during work hours at that.

The sun outside was dazzling, and Jude could not at first see where her guide had gone. Then she saw her, heading across the lawns. Running to catch up, Jude followed. Cautiously Senior Magdala looked around, and then darted out of sight, around the eastern side of the service buildings. Presumably transport was waiting under the platform.

At the river however, there was no sign of boat or guide. "Come along dear," Jude heard a voice call.

Mystified, she stepped under the platform. Sunlight flashed on the river's surface and glowed on culverted walls. On so hot a day, the smell was sickening. It rose from the water itself, and from the piles of rotting vegetation trapped at the foot of the columns. Something was rustling amongst the rubbish.

"Where are you?" Jude called in alarm.

"Come along dear. The path's quite clear."

Jude followed the voice. Within a few metres of the outer edge of the platform, the light began to fade. Like a metal forest, the perma-steel columns stretched off into the distance, each line becoming paler and duller as it receded. The sparkling river changed into a sullen chasm. For an instant Jude saw the old woman's hands and face against the surrounding gloom, but in her black suit and boots, Senior Magdala was virtually invisible. Still she walked on, right under the complex.

"I can't follow you anymore," Jude shouted. "I can't even see you."

"Nonsense, my dear. You can see as much as you wish. Or are you afraid?"

Sighing in exasperation, Jude stared into the darkness. A few scattered cracks of light showed where pipes and vents were set into the platform above. Every few seconds, water surged down one of the culverts.

Yes, she was afraid, Jude admitted to herself. She was desperately, sickeningly afraid. A path was becoming visible ahead of her. It ran along a thin, raised wall that marked the edge of the river channel. Spiked wire had been coiled over it, and then looped across the river to the other side. In the light from a grating above, the spikes looked like hooked thorns. A small space had been forced between them, just big enough for someone to crawl through. That was the path the old woman had taken - and the route she expected Jude to follow.

Jude hated enclosed spaces. Height was what she was used to, part of her daily life. Even as a child, she had nightmares about crawling through narrow tunnels. Now, standing with a colossal building resting above her head, she could feel her chest tightening in panic. If the struts snapped, she would be crushed so small not even archaeologists would find her bones. A warm shape brushed against her leg. Her skin stiffened in fright. "It's only a water vole," she told herself urgently. The animal had been far too large however - the size of a brown rat.

Turning quickly, Jude started to walk back towards the edge of the platform. "I'm not staying here," she shouted. "This isn't my idea of fun."

Then she paused, hearing her own voice echoing off the columns. It sounded thoroughly childish. "Fear of being afraid is worse than fear itself," Joel had said. That was precisely what she was avoiding now - the fear of what might happen, not any actual threat. If she gave up so soon, she would never respect herself again.

With a growing sickness in her stomach, Jude turned back, towards the darkness. "All right, damn you!" she agreed. "But you'll have to slow down. Somebody tried to kill me the other day. I'm not exactly on form."

"I'm so sorry my dear," the voice replied. "I'd forgotten how new to us you were. Use the light from the gratings. It's quite sufficient."

Jude stared hard into the darkness. A dull glow of perma-steel marked the position of each column near her. Using the pillars as a marker to the left of her, and the sucking sound of the water to the right, she set off along the path. "It can't be far," she told herself. The Refuge complex was large, but not infinite. They must ultimately come out on the northern side.

Suddenly the river vanished. In the faint light, Jude could see it rushing down some sort of grated entrance, and out of sight.

"Which way?" she called urgently.

There was no answer.

Squatting down on the mud, Jude put her head in her hands. A thin circle of light flashed from around a cluster of pipes. For a split second she saw the path again, on the opposite bank. The only way to reach it was by wading across the channel.

Within seconds she was up to her waist in water. The soles of her boots were slippery with mud. A strong current was pulling her to one side. It took all her strength to remain upright. Then she slipped. For several frantic seconds, she threshed about, struggling back on to her feet.

"Now what are you doing?" the guide's voice demanded. It reminded Jude of one of the children's officers after her parents died. "Can't you get anything right?"

Furiously Jude waded her way across the culvert. By the time she stumbled up the other bank, she was in a flaming temper. Her back was so painful it felt as if a door was opening and shutting in her spine.

Senior Magdala was waiting for her.

"You would have let me drown!" Jude shouted.

"Do be quiet dear," the old woman said, "Or the lost ones will hear you."

Startled, Jude looked where her guide was pointing. The path came out only a few hundred metres from the forbidden settlement. Ahead of them, in the sunlight beyond the platform, hundreds of people were rummaging amongst mounds of rotten food.

"If we can get under the platform, why can't they?" Jude asked in surprise.

"Their fear limits them, my dear. Only a few dare go under the lobe."

"But that's stupid! They'd stand some chance in the city. Here they'll starve."

The old woman smiled. "The city is a foreign place," she said.

A boat was waiting, moored against a single tree. As soon as Jude and her guide had boarded, it set off, towards the town. In the sunshine, Jude dried her clothes. She had lost her boots, and the deck was hot under her feet. "You're not making this easy, are you?" she commented.

"You like things to be easy, do you?"

"No," Jude answered hurriedly. "I want a proper test. I don't want anyone saying I cheated."

The old woman nodded. "Then you must face your worst memory," she replied. "Have you the courage?"

"I hope so. If there's something I don't know about myself, I'm only half a person." In irritation, Jude shook her head. She could not express what she meant.

A small queue was waiting at the Dispensary window. "Is Doctor Simeon here?" the woman in black asked.

"In the main waiting room, Missus," a girl in a long coat replied. She was carrying a toddler in her arms. "Tell him I must see him soon. Our Tilda's took real bad."

"I'm too old to get through any windows," Senior Magdala whispered to Jude. "You'll have to go on alone."

When Jude turned to protest, the woman had gone.

The pigeons were even more trouble by day than at night. They flapped against Jude's head when she climbed through the window, strutted round her feet as she walked down the corridor. One flew straight into her face. "Get away!" she shouted, and hit at the air. Feathers floated downwards, making her cough.

"Through here," Joel's voice called. "We're in the room at the back."

For an instant Jude froze. She could not go through the waiting room.

"Are you afraid of birds?" she asked herself, aloud.

"Yes," an inner voice replied.

The waiting room became a barn, and the pigeons were flapping among its rafters.

"You stealing our supplies?" a voice demanded.

In panic Jude turned round. The man's face was red and full, like a boy's, but his body was grotesque, a shapeless mound of flesh. He was wearing a blue shirt open at the chest. Across his skin was tattooed the word, 'Hawkboy'. As soon as she saw him, Jude knew she would be lucky to get away alive.

"Don't get mad, Mister," she pleaded. "Please don't get mad. I was hungry."

"Look what I've found here, Lahm," the man called. "A brat stealing our bread."

A second, older man appeared in the doorway. He had the same heavy mouth and lazy eyes. They could have been brothers.

"Oh yeah?" he asked. "What a shame!"

In terror Jude looked for a way out. A service hatch swung open in the wind. If she could reach it, the men would be too big to follow her through.

"You can have your bread back," she pleaded. Urgently, she emptied her pockets onto the bench. "It wasn't for me. I've got children to look after. They're hungry." She was talking too quickly, saying anything that came into her head.

The older man roared with laughter. "Bit young to be a mother aren't you?" he asked.

"I'm looking after them," Jude repeated. "We're trying to get home."

Moving towards Jude suddenly, the man pushed her against a bale of hay. His hand gripped her arm until it hurt. A blue letter had been tattooed on each of his fingers.

"Fancy a game, Hunter?" he called.

As if he was about to join in a bout of kick-about, Hunter crouched with his arms open. His brother half threw Jude across the barn towards him.

Five times the men pushed Jude back and forth between them, tormenting her. They had evidently played the game before. Though she tried to escape, they were too strong. In fury Jude kicked out at their shins, or bit into their hands.

"We've found ourselves a little fighter," Lahm laughed. Instead of pushing Jude forward the next time, he held onto her, putting his hand over her mouth. "I'll teach you to kick at grown men!" he vowed. "Clear off, Hunter: I rather fancy this one."

"She's only a kid!" his brother jeered...

Standing marooned in a derelict waiting room, Jude tried to drive the memory from her. Her face and hands were clammy with fear. Sweat prickled on her upper lip. Littl'Un reappeared beside her. "Doctor Simeon isn't here," she said.

"But I heard him," Jude insisted.

Big walked out of the inner room. "He'll be at t'other place," he predicted. "We'll go and find him. It won't take long."

The other children wanted to come too. "I can't carry our Tilda all that way," the girl in the long coat protested.

"The missus will carry her - won't you?"

Jude was exhausted already, but she could not refuse. Taking the toddler, she tried to make her comfortable on her back.

Just as the sun was dropping, they arrived at a village. An old church stood against the sky, its spire like an accusing finger. Two black mouths opened in the hillside beside it. "That's the caves," Big said. "We'll go first. You'll block the light."

Once again, Jude found herself fumbling through darkness, with only voices to guide her. Tilda's weight was beginning to make her feel sick. "I have to rest," she insisted and squatted on some steps. At once, the images started again.

Too shocked to cry, she struggled beneath the man's weight. Suddenly Joel was hitting out with a spade. It caught the man hard across the shoulders, knocking him to the floor.

"Run!" Joel shouted.

Then the younger man reappeared in the doorway. "What the Hell?" he began, and stopped.

His face white with fear, Joel turned to face him...

The force of the memory began to weaken. There was no sign of the children.

"You took your time," a voice mocked.

Startled, Jude looked up. The steps led down into in a huge cave. In the middle of it, a brazier was burning. Its light cast flickering shapes on the walls and ceilings. In the far distance, almost hidden in shadow, a man was seated at a desk.

Jude completely lost her temper. "What is it now?" she snapped.

"You must come and meet your father."

"My father wouldn't put me through such a silly rigmarole," Jude retorted. "I'm tired out, and my back hurts. I've got covered in mud, nearly drowned, and had rats crawling over my feet. That's what I call a swine of a day."

Even as she spoke, Jude saw the funny side of her complaint. "Just let me go home," she ended lamely. "If I have a home to go to anymore."

"You are indeed my child," the man said, rising to greet her. "And your home is with me."

Chapter Seventeen

"How are you feeling?" Feda asked.

Jude stared at her, not understanding. "Have I been away?" she asked.

"You had to have further surgery. Remember? You've been back a couple of hours. If you ask me, they should have kept you in another night."

Jude could only recall walking between rows and rows of pillars.

"I was wondering whether to wake you or not. You're supposed to be going for a meal with your cousin. Shall I ask Molly to say you're not fit enough?"

Jude sat up carefully against the pillow. As she did so, she expected to feel the usual ache, but her back moved easily. Swinging her legs onto the floor, she tried standing up. The pain had gone.

"They seem to have found out what the problem was," she said in surprise.

Feda smiled. "I'm glad," she said. "I'll say this for you, you've got guts. I could see from your face how much pain you were in, but you never said awt. Rest a bit longer, and then go to your cousin's if you feel up to it. I reckon you deserve a bit of loving."

Jude flushed. "My cousin and I are just friends," she insisted, and heard how ridiculous she sounded.

"Take your happiness while you've got it," Feda advised. "That's always been my motto. I may have regretted things afterwards, but I've enjoyed them at the time."

Feeling unkempt, Jude glanced at herself in the hand mirror she kept beside her bed. Her hair had fallen from its braids and she pushed it back from her face. As she did so, she paused in surprise. Echoed in her own features she saw another face, very like her own. The dark eyes had come from her mother, but the auburn hair and shape of her face and mouth reminded her of someone else.

Frowning, Jude tried to recall who it was, and could not. "Are you sure you're all right?" Feda asked. "You seem to be only half with us."

"I had some sort of illusion yesterday. I keep trying to remember it."

Feda was looking at her curiously. "What do you mean?" she asked.

"Ignore me," Jude said hurriedly. "I'm talking nonsense. It must be the anaesthetic."

Afterwards she laid down again, considering what she had said. It was not nonsense. Somehow, while she was in the recovery room perhaps, she had been frightened by a vivid illusion, just as in the Rehabilitation Suite at East Five. This time only shadowy images remained in her mind, but the name Tuecer had featured again. She had been walking somewhere that had a lot of steel columns.

Trying to be rational, Jude listed the facts she did know. First, Joel had warned her that she would experience something unpleasant. His advice as they parted suggested she was about to be tested in some way. Clearly she could not have left the Refuge. People lying in hospital wards tended to stay put. Yet visitors could have come to her. One person had definitely been involved - the woman in black - the woman Jude had seen in the corridor earlier.

Until then, Jude had assumed the figure was a figment of her imagination, but some very strange things were possible nowadays - so long as you had the right technology. In the Chief Secretary's office people had quarrelled in the middle of the room, only to disappear at the touch of a control. The Chief Secretary herself had been afraid of the electronic equipment around her. What was it she had said? "I'm never at ease while these things are switched on. An expert could feed off their power. " There would be plenty of electronic equipment in a Recovery Room, measuring heart beat, breathing, all the vital functions. If it had been used to communicate with her that afternoon, there must be similar experts in Border Seven, who dared not contact her openly. Given that Tuecer had featured again, they might well be connected with him, or even have come to the Refuge with him. It would be worth finding out if there had been any visitors recently.

Trying to empty all other thoughts, Jude concentrated on the images that hovered at the back of her mind. It was like playing one of those games in which you tried to recall as many items as possible, after a glimpse of a jumbled collection.

Gradually she visualised herself walking between the columns. A face and hands showed in the darkness ahead of her. They belonged to an old woman who called herself Magdala. Ahead, there was a river Jude must cross, and a church with a spire like an accusing finger. She was carrying a little girl, who was holding onto her neck tightly. Some steps and a cave featured too, but where that cave was, Jude could not recall. It had something to do with a barn where pigeons flew round the rafters.

An analyst would appreciate that lot, Jude thought wryly. Some of the symbolism was pretty obvious. Though she had not given Kurt much thought lately, the child gripping her neck was probably a reference to their coming bonding. In her dream, Jude had only carried the girl out of a sense of duty, and the task had worn her out. It did not need a psychiatrist to suggest the inference - that she did not want Kurt's child, anymore than she wanted Kurt.

Jude sighed. She had already come to that conclusion on her own, without any silly illusions to prompt her. Still, her wishes were irrelevant. If she stayed with SecureCity Incorporated, she would have to accept the decisions of the Futures Department. Besides, she had given Kurt her promise, and could not humiliate him by changing her mind.

So where did the barn and the cave fit in?

Staring at a fly spot on the wall, Jude tried to answer her question. There had been other images: enclosed spaces, rats, unpleasant smells; a mishmash of all the things she disliked. If her tormentors were trying to break her by playing on her inner fears, they had not managed it. That presumably had been the point: to test her endurance. As Joel had advised, fear of fear was worse than fear itself. At first, each of the horrors had frightened her, but viewed in the cold light of logic, they had lost their terror.

One image had proved more enduring however. Something had taken place inside a barn, under a cloud of pigeons. It was odd how often pigeons featured in her dreams. When she was in the empty hospital, she had been quite irrational in her fear of them. Closing her eyes, Jude tried to focus on the barn. A girl was being held down on a bale of hay. A man was leaning forward over the figure, so that all Jude could see clearly was his shoulders and back. His hair was shaved into jagged patterns, and his blue shirt was stained with sweat.

As if she were in one of the game booths, Jude tried to bring the girl into close up, so that she could see the face. At first the man was still between them. Then he swore and recoiled. For an instant Jude saw the figure beneath him. She was wearing a blue dress, torn at the front. Her hair was an unusual rich auburn colour, though dirty and dishevelled. Biting and scratching, she was trying desperately to push the man to the floor.

Appalled, Jude stared at the memory. Blood surged into her face. The girl in the barn was herself.

For fourteen years, she had pushed the past so deep down, she had forgotten it. Now it was back with her, in every hateful detail. If she had been at home, she could have got up and worked, or walked, anywhere, up and down the corridors, anything to deaden her mind. Now, trapped in a dormitory, all she could do was remember. A timepiece clicked on a cupboard near her. The controlled air supply hummed. Each sound was magnified in the silence. Through them all,

Jude could hear a man's voice laughing. "Fancy a game, Hunter?" he asked.

It was the realisation that she was still being tested that gave Jude strength. This was her final trial. She must learn to accept everything that she had experienced, whether good or ill. Like all the other horrors of her imaginary journey, when stared at directly, even the barn began to lose some of its terror.

What had taken place there had not been so extraordinary. When she was a girl, such things did happen. Life in a Refuge had left her ill equipped for the harshness outside. None of the adults on that last day had predicted the attack on their camp, just as she had been unable to imagine what might happen if she stole bread from an apparently empty barn. Not even Joel had anticipated Hawkboys using a derelict farm as their base. They were miles to the north of Leodis.

She owed Joel so much, and she had never properly acknowledged it. When he saw the Hawkboys he could have slipped away. Even his parents would have understood. There was little he could do against two grown men. Instead, armed only with a spade, he had attacked a tribesman twice his strength, to protect her, and then fought off the man's brother. By the time he had squeezed through the hatch himself, he was so badly beaten he stumbled as he ran. Blood streamed from a cut over his eye.

As she buried her face in her pillow, Jude could still feel the bewilderment and helplessness of that afternoon. Comforting each other, she and Joel had lain beside the fire that Gary had lit for them. Ultimately they had fallen asleep, to wake time and time again, shivering and hurt. They both knew that the relationship between them had changed. All their lives, they would be closer to each other than anyone else. That was partly why she had driven the memory down. When her tutors told her to stop writing to him, she should have refused, but it was hard to defy a whole system. Besides, by then, she had begun to agree that a squatter's son was not worthy of her attention.

*****

Joel's pass-note provoked little comment - worryingly little, since it suggested how common such things had become. Only the last security guard raised an eyebrow slightly. Knowing Officer Anderson, he found the request out of character.

Joel himself was the perfect host, very polite, with just the right hint of embarrassment. “How are you feeling?” he asked. “I gather you had surgery again yesterday.”

“I’m a little shaky,” Jude admitted, “But the pain’s gone.”

“Do join me.” Joel indicated a table set for two. Beside it, several covered dishes waited on a trolley.” You could do with a holiday,” he continued. “Where do you fancy? Paris? Sydney?”

“How can you take me to Paris in an evening?” Jude asked, as a menial might.

“We have many wonders here. All you have to do is tell me which option to choose, and our technology will do the rest. You won’t actually go there, but you’ll feel as if you have.”

“Take me to Italy,” Jude asked. “They say the coast is beautiful.”

“Thank you for choosing our personal holiday programme,” the electronic voice intoned. “You are just about to leave your hotel room, and savour the delights of the Italian Riviera.” A pair of French doors suddenly appeared in the middle of the room. With a burst of appropriately romantic music, they opened onto a sunlit beach. “Have a nice fantasy,” the voice concluded.

Jude smiled. With wrap-round reality covering the walls, and holo-images filling much of the space between, surveillance would be impossible. They could talk as freely as they wished.

“Have something to eat,” Joel invited. “I don’t imagine the menials’ food is much good.”

“Better than they’d get at home,” Jude acknowledged.

“I owe you another apology,” she added.

“Why?”

“You must have thought me very ungrateful, never mentioning what you did for me years ago. I’d driven the memory down, so deep it’s only just come back to me - though it’s featured in my dreams many times. I should at least have kept in touch.”

It was some time before Joel replied. “I hoped it was something like that,” he admitted. “For years I was furious. I used to imagine myself graduating from medical school, with you in the audience. I’d look down and you’d go red. ‘I never realised you could do it’ you’d say. Fortunately I grew up”

“Why have you never had the scar removed?” Jude asked.

“It reminds me where I come from - and makes me a bit different. Not the usual perfect male.”

“Vanity, vanity...” Jude teased. Then she was serious. “You’re involved in something deep, aren’t you? - that could get you into an awful lot of trouble. You wouldn’t keep leaving the Refuge if you weren't, especially now with the new infection regulations. If there's anything I can do to help you, I will - so long as it's not - well, something I can't agree with." Pulling at some dry skin on her thumb, she paused. "I sound pompous, don't I? But you know what I mean."

For a moment Joel sat in silence again. Finally he got up and fetched a small personal entertainer from a games box in the corner of the room. "Watch this, and tell me how you feel afterwards," he asked. "It's the only piece of evidence I've dared record." Pointing at the space between the table and the wall he switched on one of the programmes. There was just room for the holo-image to appear, blurring strangely at the edges into the main image of the holiday programme.

At first Jude could not identify the subject, which seemed to consist mainly of a padded cover, viewed from about chest height. Then the padding became the side of a lift. Doors opened, and there were a few moments of bewildering progress across an enclosed area. Finally, the movement stopped at a reception desk. Jude guessed the images had been taken with a pen camera, clipped to Joel's lapel. She could hear his voice greeting the guards, and their response. They took a long time checking his ID, as if his visit were unusual.

Then the image changed to a windowless corridor, with rooms opening off it. Once, an open door showed a view across mudflats and water. A prefabricated duckboard lead away from the door. Everything suggested temporary accommodation - quarters that had been established hurriedly and at the lowest possible cost.

The rooms that opened off the corridor were clean but spartan, containing nothing but a bed, and a table and chair. It appeared that some sort of inspection was taking place, for Joel's voice was heard wishing the occupants good morning. Each was old and frail. Several had bad coughs, or found difficulty standing as their door opened. Joel asked them how they felt. "Very well, thank you, officer," they replied, one after the other. Their hollow eyes belied their words.

Jude's throat began to tighten. "How did you manage to get down there?" she asked.

"I got myself appointed as an official visitor. Management wouldn't give me a budget, so my visits aroused hopes I couldn't fulfil, and I only went a couple of times. I shall always wonder if I could have done more, but it was made clear to me that if I so much as mentioned the new settlement, I would find myself a resident."

To save time, Joel fast-forwarded the image. Now the scene became an office, with an official sitting at a desk. His words were not always audible, but the gist of them was clear: the accommodation Joel had looked round was only temporary, of course. It was regrettable that such measures had to be taken, but until the planned retirement Refuge was built, there was no alternative. Residents of the overflow settlement were well fed and perfectly happy. At their time of life, they had few needs. Having served the organisation faithfully all their lives, they understood the necessity for sacrifices, and had agreed to give up their accommodation in the lobe to younger members. As soon as possible, they would be rewarded.

"And when will the new Refuge be completed?" Joel's voice asked.

The man at the desk was not used to being questioned, but he smiled politely. "In a matter of months," he replied. "Budgets are fully committed until the next financial year, but building will resume as soon as possible."

"Some of your residents have chest infections. Are they receiving treatment?"

"In cases of economic benefit, of course. Resources are scarce, though, and younger members have higher priority."

Even in so blurred a recording, Jude could hear concern in Joel's reply. "And what about those no longer - of 'economic benefit'?" he asked.

"Officer, the average age of residents here is ninety eight. In the world outside, life expectancy is sixty-five. Difficult decisions have to be made, as I'm sure you are aware. Our success in preventing the normal diseases leaves us with increasing numbers of ageing members to support."

"I'm aware of the problem," Joel replied. "But I don't think these dormitories are the solution." His courage in expressing disagreement impressed Jude. If it had been known he was also filming the conversation, he would have been restrained at once.

"What solution would you offer?" the man at the desk retorted.

"Some of my colleagues feel we should let nature take its course earlier. With dignity and in comfort. It's not for me to comment. I do however find conditions here harsh. Can you assure me that no one will have to stay for more than a few months?"

"Completion dates are difficult to predict - and demand for places in the lobe is high. The situation is continually under review."

There was a pause as coffee was brought in. The image juddered slightly as if Joel had bent forward to take a cup. In the background, a window came into view. Through it, almost hidden by another block of accommodation, a cluster of lean-to buildings could be seen, and what looked like an open fire.

"Are there any other residents I haven't met?" Joel persisted. "I've heard rumours patients with mental problems are being transferred here. I would like to be able to reassure my colleagues."

"I am not aware of any being recorded on our lists..."

The image died abruptly.

"There's a little more to come," Joel said. "My recorder developed a fault."

The programme came to life again. Now they were further round the complex, the pattern of light and shade suggesting Joel had hidden somewhere under the platform. Already there was the beginning of sad little shantytown. Then the image panned to the area under the platform itself. The shanty dwellers had evidently lit fires in several places, leaving black marks on the mud and on the sides of the columns. Joel froze the image on one particular column. Within the black stain, Jude could see a faint, hairline fracture running up the perma-steel. Then Joel jerked the image forward again. The crack ran on, into the shadows.

"You probably know more about such structures than I do," he admitted. "There are several other cracks like these, and they're deepest where fires have been lit. Do they matter?"

Jude recalled the designs she had seen her parents poring over night after night. "They could do," she replied. "If there are enough of them, and the movement of the platform becomes affected. The fires won't be the cause, but they could be making existing faults worse."

"Everywhere you look, this place is going rotten!" Joel said bitterly.

"What was that about difficult decisions?" Jude asked.

"We have too many old and sick. First they were pushed out of the Refuge. Now there's a proposal that anyone who can't earn - or pay for - their share of Refuge supplies, be denied them. It's to be debated in a week or so. Many of us will vote against it, but I doubt if we'll have any effect. Nor do I think that will be the end of it. There's talk of "a quicker solution" being needed. If you want to help me - and all those out on the mudflats - take this recording to the Triumvirate." He passed the personal entertainer to her. "Make them understand what's being done in their name. I can't leave for more than a few hours, and even that may become impossible soon."

He had confirmed her own fears, but Jude could not see why the Triumvirate should be involved. "Surely all it needs is to alert National HQ?" she replied

"They must know about it already, perhaps have sanctioned it. It looks like similar proposals are being made at other English Refuges.

Most of them are a making a loss. If costs aren't cut soon, the Corporation will pull out, like it did in Japan."

"But we have more contracts than ever!" Jude protested. "Every sector council - and most businesses too. Where's the profit going?"

Joel shook his head. "Lord knows!" he replied. "It's being creamed off at every level - bonuses for management, ordinary members selling to the cities, organised crime. There's always been the odd syndicate feeding the black market, but bigger boys are moving in now. Management's response is to keep raising the targets, and bullying those who can't keep up. Individuals are trying to change things, but there are too many vested interests. They need help, or the English Refuges will start falling apart, literally. No repairs are being done, no maintenance, and shoddy materials were used in the first place. You saw those cracks." Impatiently Joel walked across the room, and then back again.

The prospect became more frightening as Jude considered it. "If the Refuges are closed," she reflected, "A million members will be without a job - or a home. So will the maintenance crews, and the menials. The Groundnet will collapse and nobody in the councils or public services will get paid. The cities will run out of food, water supplies will fail..." Involuntarily she shuddered.

"What services we have, will collapse," Joel predicted. "And General Rowles, or someone like him, will be back in power, saving us from ourselves. The Refuges have to keep going, but they must open up. While they keep everything to themselves, the Corporation rules the country, not the government. The trouble is, the syndicates aren't going to give up their power. Even honest managers won't co-operate. They want to struggle on, making 'difficult decisions'..." Joel's tone was caustic.

Returning to the table, he began to cover the leftover food. "We nearly got everyone who mattered together, to discuss the situation," he continued, "but the opposition made sure it didn't happen."

Jude recalled the fat man standing on the platform, and the conference that was cancelled because of the riots. "I'll help," she promised. "But how can I possibly travel to the Triumvirate? Wouldn't a report be enough? I think I could get one to them - I was going to send one myself before somebody dropped an autowash on me. "

"You can try a report, but it will probably be ignored until too late. The arrival of an attractive young officer, unannounced - now that might catch their eye." Reassuring her, Joel smiled. "Even if I could go myself, I wouldn't have half your effect. There's no need to worry about money and passes. I can provide those." He took out a packet of Melodine and passed it to her.

"I don't take that rubbish!" Jude protested. "It rots your brain." Then she understood, and tried pressing the base. It gave way to reveal a thin, flat packet under the capsules. Inside were high-energy tablets, a money card, and a miniaturised first aid kit. Folded between them were two travel warrants. Each had been made out in the name of domestic supervisor Sara Atkins.

"Transport across the lake is arranged," Joel continued, "but I haven't managed to get you exit ID yet. You may have to follow me down the waste pipe. It's not very dignified, but it's the only other way out of the lobe."

"I can sort my own transport out."

"And an exit permit?"

"I have a friend who can walk me through."

"Then you have very influential friends. For the past three months, exit ID's been like gold. Resources have managed to produce a disc that's virtually impossible to copy."

"But what about the partygoers?"

"It's like a school outing. The organisers count them out and then back in - for a fee of course. Believe me, if your friend can come and go at will, their ID came from a marketeer at least - someone with the money to get anything they want. You're mixing in dangerous company."

Jude considered his warning. In the pause between them, Joel picked up the entertainment control, and pressed one of the commands. At once, the wrap-round reality took them further up the illusory beach.

"What other evidence have you?" she asked. " I need names, amounts..."

"I can supply them. I need someone else to know them in any case - before it's too late."

"What do you mean?"

They both heard the faint clicking sound at the same time. "Please accept our apologies," the mechanical voice intoned. "In-house entertainment will be resumed as soon as possible."

Quickly Jude pushed Joel's personal entertainer inside her coverall. As the Italian beach faded from the walls, the surveillance would merely have registered two lovers holding hands across the table.

Chapter Eighteen

Though Jude slept only a few hours before the siren woke her team, she felt refreshed. Almost at once, she got up and followed her supervisor into the showers.

"You're early," Molly remarked cheerfully.

"I wanted some hot water," Jude replied. Since her accident, she was wary of talking to Molly about anything but the merest trivialities.

"You never feel clean in cold, do you?" Molly agreed. "How are you feeling now?"

"Fine." They splashed and soaped alongside each other.

"What sort of day have we got lined up?" Jude asked. "Anyone special to see to?"

"A delegation of V I Ps. Therese was doing for them, but she's sick. They're leaving today, so it'll just be a case of getting everything ready for the next lot."

Jude's pulse jerked forward and then steadied. Visitors from outside had indeed come to the Refuge. "Would you like me to do it?" she asked. "I wouldn't mind a break from old people."

"If you like. There's three men and two women. I don't suppose any of them will be around while you're working, but if they are, grovel suitably. One of them's the sector commissioner, and another's a chief justice. Apparently they've been here for a top-level meeting." Though there was no one else in the showers yet, Molly lowered her voice. "Maeve said they didn't seem very pleased when they arrived. She reckoned they'd come to lay down the law."

"What about?"

"Goodness knows. This place is a law unto its self."

The guest suite was empty when Jude entered. Travel cases lay ready packed on the stands. Nothing was named. Evidently the group were travelling incognito. While the security listing would show hour-by-hour details of everyone present in the Refuge, Jude would have no legitimate reason to consult it. Disappointed, she began to strip the beds.

One other possibility remained. On her way to her midday break, she called at the medical centre.

"I just wanted to thank you," she explained to the receptionist. "My back's so much better, it feels like a miracle. Is it possible for me to speak to the doctor?"

The woman smiled with pleasure. "We don't often get people saying thank you," she admitted. "Doctor Howard's busy, but I'll tell him you called."

"I was a bit woozy yesterday," Jude continued brightly. "I remember somebody visiting me, but I can't for the life of me recall who. I'd hate to offend someone. Do you know who came?"

The receptionist shook her head. "I'm afraid I wasn't given a name. I assumed it was a relative of yours. His hair was the same colour as yours - only going a bit grey."

As she took the rapido back down to ground level, Jude stared in bewilderment at her reflection in the panelling. The rich auburn colour of her hair was her most distinctive feature. When she was a girl it was fair, like her parents', and only darkened later. It surprised everyone, including herself, but as her mother and father said, the geneticists didn't understand everything yet.

They were not in the least concerned about her appearance, just pleased that she had 'turned out so well'. Even twenty-seven years ago, there was little likelihood of a Refuge woman taking an unapproved mate. True, bonding was much less formal in those days, more like an old-fashioned arranged marriage, and relationships before bonding were not forbidden. All the same, breaking her promise to her official partner would have got Jude's mother into a lot of trouble. Yet repeatedly during the past few weeks Jude had been asked to meet another man who was her real father. Now the receptionist's remark suggested he might actually exist.

Her mother was not the sort, Jude told herself angrily. She had been an upright and faithful member, choosing to stay with her partner beyond the ten years of their bonding, and dying alongside him. And yet - Whenever Jude thought of her mother, there was always that 'and yet'. She talked of love as if it was important, stared at sunsets with a wistful expression, got recorded by personnel as having a tendency to romanticise. There was an inner space in her that no one could ever reach. As she grew older Jude used to resent it. "You shut me out!" she had shouted once, and her father had smiled sadly.

"She shuts us all out," he had replied. "She doesn't even allow me near her."

It was one of the few occasions Jude had heard her parents argue. Now, for the first time, she tried to think of her mother as a woman, with her own hopes and emotions. Supposing she had loved another man before her bonding. She must have approached the ceremony with a sense of dread every bit as great as Jude felt at the prospect of her own. Steeped in the traditions of the Refuge, brought up to do her duty in all things, she would have felt torn in two. But to have borne another man's child - and to have kept it secret all those years... that was surely impossible.

Feda was waiting for her in the refectory. "Molly's got a letter from your bloke," she whispered. "She asked me to tell you."

In alarm, Jude looked up. If Joel had trusted Molly, he was a fool. Casually, she crossed to her supervisor. "I gather you have a message for me," she said.

"Your cousin asked me to give you this." Molly winked broadly.

Jude began to suspect some trick on Joel's part. He knew Molly had been in the atrium when the autowash fell. If he had given her a letter to pass on, he had probably intended her to read it.

It was an hour before Jude could find a private place to examine Joel's letter. As she had anticipated, the seal had been broken and then carefully replaced. Molly had taken the envelope straight to her superiors.

Written by hand, the message inside was unexpectedly long. At first Jude could not make sense of it.

> 'Dear Cousin," Joel began.
>
> "I wanted to thank you for the very pleasant evening we spent together. I hadn't realised how lonely I was until you arrived here. Your company has meant a great deal to me over the last few days.
>
> I regret that our branches of the family have had so little contact over the last fourteen years. You and I might have become friends earlier otherwise, when such things were possible. As things are however, I can see nothing but difficulties ahead of us. We are both the sort to wish for a lasting relationship, and that would never be permitted between us. All I would be allowed is a little entertainment, and I wouldn't insult you by suggesting such a thing. In the circumstances therefore, I think it would be best for us to stop seeing each other. It would please me greatly however if you would visit me one last time, to say goodbye. There may be more I can do to help your family, and you could take greetings to mine.
>
> I enclose another pass to enable you to come to my dwelling again. I shall be free all evening. If you decide to stay away, I shall understand.
>
> With very best wishes,

Joel Anderson."

Carefully, Jude read the letter again. It was cleverly done. By apparently being so open, Joel had provided himself with a perfect cover. The censors would merely smile at a Refuge officer being foolish enough to fall for a menial. They would allow him his one last meeting, and probably not even bother to interrupt.

Putting the letter away, Jude continued on her round.

*****

The in-dwelling entertainment was already playing, projecting an image of woodland around them. "I need to give you the names and figures you asked for," Joel began, and passed her a box of expensive looking comfits. "They're on a microdisc, under the coffee fudge. Don't eat it."

"We do end up doing some ridiculous things," Jude commented.

Smiling, Joel nodded. "I also wanted to say goodbye to you," he added. "Properly." Pausing, he adjusted the colour of the scene around them and they sat together, watching the wind blow among illusory trees.

"Almost like old times, isn't it?" Jude remarked.

"I've often thought of those weeks," Joel admitted. "And of you. I fell in love with you then, but never had the courage to tell you. Besides, you were too young. Now you come back into my life without warning, and I'm in danger of loving you again."

Jude did not know how to reply. "I don't know what you mean by love," she said at length. "Relationships outside bonding are forbidden - you know that."

"You don't believe rules can prevent emotion, do you?" Joel asked. Tentatively he touched her hand. "You seem very innocent, Jude. Like the heroine in a game I used to play - tough and feisty, but knowing little of the world. 'Find the Maiden' it was called. Do you remember it?"

"Yes," Jude replied uncomfortably. For a few seconds she watched his expression. "I don't know whether to take you seriously or not," she admitted. "I never did."

"Would this convince you?" Bending forward, Joel kissed her.

At first Jude was angry. "Last time you did that it was to distract me," she reminded him.

Joel sighed. "I mean it this time," he said softly.

They were moving onto dangerous ground and Jude did not know how to respond. In confusion, she looked away. "I'd like to learn what you mean by love," she admitted. "I feel as if I've been shut away from something all my life - something my mother knew about. Something you seem to know about, too." Putting her arms around him awkwardly, she kissed him in return.

"Relax a bit," Joel whispered. "Imagine they're real trees around us, and that's real sun shining..."

With a sense of bewilderment and pleasure, Jude let herself be drawn closer to him, while the illusory woodland flickered around them.

Suddenly Joel's communicator bleeped, startling them both. Sighing, he sat up to answer it. Afterwards, they settled back together, but within minutes it was bleeping again.

By the time had dealt with half a dozen queries, the mood was gone.

"Can't you turn that thing off?" Jude asked.

"No. I was put on call unexpectedly."

For a while longer they sat close, trying to regain the mood, but both of them were aware that they had begun to return to their normal, Refuge selves. "Damn it!" Joel said at last. "It's no use, is it? That wretched thing's started me thinking. We may be grown-up now, but I'd still be betraying your trust. I couldn't do that when you were thirteen, and I can't do it now. I'm sorry, Jude. I shouldn't have started it. Forgive me."

Jude put her fingers to his mouth, silencing him. "I was being an idiot too," she replied. "Wanting to know what it was like... But you were as good as any brother to me - and I'd rather go on thinking of you that way. Anything else gets too - complicated."

The communicator crackled again. "All domestics back to their quarters in half an hour." Putting his fingers under her chin, Joel lifted it so that he could kiss her again, but this time it was a brotherly, parting kiss.

"When you're back home, I'll visit you at East Five," he promised. "If I can."

There was no way Jude could say it gently. "I'm due to be bonded," she said. "My Chief Secretary got it deferred. As soon as I'm back, they'll fix a date."

Joel sat silent and still. "Do you love your partner?" he asked at last.

"There you go again," Jude replied, trying to sound casual and bright. "Talking about love. Kurt's OK, but if you mean do I have the sort of feeling for him Mum described - no. It'll be interesting, though, and I'm honoured to have been chosen. I should have told you earlier."

"Yes. You should."

For a little longer, they sat on the couch, neither of them knowing how to part. "I've never asked you if you've been chosen," Jude remembered. "You're about the right age - for a bloke."

"I carry an imperfect gene. The Futures Department were terribly polite, and wished me a nice day. I was quite relieved. I have no wish to be mated with a woman I don't love. With you - or Jennie - it would be a different matter."

Jude thought of Mark and Carrie, and understood how they must feel. "Maybe some time in the future we'll meet up again," she said, trying to smile. "I only have to stay with Kurt for ten years. After that, I can leave him if I wish. I'm quite willing to spend my middle age not asking questions."

Joel shook his head. "In ten years there may be no such thing as SecureCity Incorporated," he warned, "Wherever I am, though, I'll find you - if you want me."

"You should leave the Refuges," Jude advised. "You don't belong here, and you're putting yourself at risk. Go to the Eastern World. The Corporation has no power there."

"I can't. I'm about two weeks from finishing my project."

"What can be so important, as to make you risk ending up on level 40?"

"I'm developing a cheap wound-healer people can use before medical help arrives. It could save a lot of lives. If I leave here too soon, I'll have to start again, and that could take years. Besides, I have to get an important official out of here - a woman called Maria Levant. You know her as your Chief Secretary."

"She's here?" In amazement, Jude turned to him.

"She came to trace the Assessor she'd sent - a personal friend. It was Maria who left you the supplies earlier. She's ended up on '40, and I've been asked to guide her to safety."

"But that's an awful risk!" In concern, Jude shook her head. "How have you ended up doing such things?" she asked. "When I knew you, you didn't seem the sort."

"I'm not the sort now. I'm no hero, Jude. I lie awake most nights, too scared to sleep. But if people like me don't stand up against what's happening, the country will be thrown into chaos again. Then the same leaders who forced my family into the wilderness will be back in power, doing anything they wish."

Pausing, Joel got up and crossed to the workstation. "When I started, I didn't think things through," he admitted. "I thought it would be just a case of guarding a few important officials while a treaty was brokered - that everyone would want the country on its feet again. I never reckoned on such stupidity, or greed. But I'm in too far now to stop."

Tearing a piece of paper from his memo pad, he returned to her. "This is my natural parents' address," he said. "If I vanish off the staff list, would you visit them? They could cope with my death, but not with having me just disappear - particularly if there was some sort of charge laid against me. Try to soften it for them."

Jude took the paper from him. "And your adoptive father?" she asked, probing a little.

Joel smiled. "It would be difficult for you to reach him," he replied carefully.

"Then I wish you well - and safety," Jude said. She got up to leave.

For a second longer, Joel hesitated. "Jude -" he said awkwardly. "When it comes to your bonding, don't let them give you anything. No alcohol, or Tranquil - nothing to celebrate, or to help you through."

In alarm, Jude looked at him. "Why?" she asked.

"There are unpleasant entertainments on the black market. It would drive both of us mad if you were in one of them."

In horror Jude recalled Sabbattica Collins, holding a pair of scissors above her child's eyes.

*****

Feda was adamant. She did not believe Jude would return. "I know I wouldn't - not if someone had tried to kill me," she insisted.

"No one's proved it wasn't an accident," Jude replied. "And they've looked after me well since. All that surgery must have cost thousands."

"I still don't think you'll come back," Feda said, shrugging her shoulders. "Even if it was just because of your bloke - knowing the man you wanted was so near and you couldn't have him. That'd drive me crackers. I don't care what you do, Love. It's up to you. But if you go at night, they'll know you had exit ID. With me being your mate, guess who'll they'll look at? Sorry. I'd help you if I could, but not this time."

Jude could do nothing but accept. "All right," she agreed. "I shall have to go out before curfew and wait until Jonah arrives."

"Where will you hide?"

"Under the platform."

"They'll look there as soon as you're missed."

"Not right underneath."

"Rather you than me." Feda grimaced. "There are rats," she said. "And creepy crawlies. Tell you what. If you book one of the game booths, I'll take over from you and keep the programme running. It could be roll call before they realise you've gone."

Jude smiled. "Thanks," she said, and touched Feda's hand.

At nineteen hours, Jude walked casually to the Domestics' games area. She signed in, and asked for five programmes - sufficient to last a couple of hours. Then she walked down the corridor towards the booths. At the very end, a fire exit was signed in bold letters. Since it opened only into the domestic area, it was not alarmed. Softly Jude opened the door a couple of centimetres. Someone with a strong arm would be able to force it a little further from the outside, and squeeze through. Finally, she went down to her booth and shut herself in.

Twenty minutes later, Feda entered. "Ye Gods! That door was stiff," she whispered. "What you playing?"

"'Find the Maiden'." Jude smiled. She removed the sensor pads and passed them to Feda.

Slipping past her, Feda took over the control. "Well then, clear off," she said briskly.

"Thank you." Jude's throat felt tight. "You've been a good friend," she added.

"You're not coming back, are you?"

Jude shook her head.

"Did you find what you wanted?"

Not knowing how to reply, Jude looked away.

"Aw, come off it!" Feda persisted. "You had to be doing summat special. You were too healthy to be one of us, too sleek and well fed. Besides, you've got that sort of watchfulness about you - like you've been trained to know what to look for. Take care of yourself, wherever you're heading."

"Look after yourself too," Jude replied. "I'm glad you're getting a happy ending. Just keep out of the authorities' way, that's all - and watch out for a clamp-down in the Refuges."

Quickly, she kissed Feda on the cheek, then she let herself out of the booth.

Chapter Nineteen

"Just how long are you prepared to wait?" the secretary asked.

"All week if necessary," Jude replied.

The secretary sighed. "Well, I'll say this for you, you're persistent." Her English was perfect, with only the faintest hint that it might not be the language of her childhood. "I could call Security you know, and have them take you away for being a nuisance."

"What harm am I doing?" Jude asked, very politely. "I'm simply waiting for the Triumvirate to see me. Every Refuge member has a right to see line management if they have a grievance against their supervisors. My grievance concerns the topmost levels. Since the Triumvirate is our ultimate management, it's logical I should speak to them. Neither you, nor Security, have the right to refuse me. Only the Triumvirate can do that."

The secretary sighed again. She found Jude's argument difficult to answer. "I'll try someone else," she agreed.

Jude could just about follow the woman's end of the conversation. "She's still here. Yes, Sir. Two days. Goes away at night and comes back first thing in the morning... I know, Sir. She won't. I've told Security, but they say if she's just sitting here playing games, they don't see there's a problem." There was a pause. "It would look bad, Sir," the woman continued. "She's invoked the grievance procedure."

This time the pause lasted several minutes, as if the person the other end had gone to see someone else. To fill the gap, the secretary began punching figures into a statistica. Finally the communicator clicked on-line again. "I really am most grateful," she said in surprise. "Will you send somebody down?"

Flicking the communicator off, the woman looked at Jude. "You're in luck," she said.

In delight, Jude got up and put her personal entertainer away in her pocket. "I will see all three of them, won't I?" she asked.

"You never get all of them together, except for special meetings. Decider Anesto is the only one in today." The secretary lowered her voice. "It's not worth making an issue over it," she advised. "He makes all the decisions, even when the other two are around. They just want a quiet life. Goodness knows where either of them is at the moment. Playing golf I imagine."

For an instant Jude hardly had the strength to get up from her chair. Then she called herself a fool. Of course three such important people would rarely be together. Taking out two copies of her report, she passed them to the secretary. "See the other two get these please," she begged. "It's vital they read them."

Dubiously, the woman took the two packets.

A brisk young man guided Jude through corridors and up escalators, to the inner sanctum. At each level, their ID was checked at least twice. Finally they came to a small waiting area. Three doors opened off it. "Stay here," he ordered, indicating a chair beside a coffee table. "If you're considering anything else, you won't manage it. You're under constant surveillance."

Jude waited. It was half an hour before one of the doors opened and a middle-aged man came out to greet her. Immaculately dressed in the uniform of senior management, he was exceptionally handsome, and knew it. Tall and greying at the temples, he could have been the ageing hero in a reality game. Offering his hand to Jude, he invited her to sit down again. He himself remained standing.

"Well, officer," he said, quite kindly. "You seem to have created a stir. We don't often get attractive young women camping in our reception area."

The man's manner was friendly, but to Jude the politeness seemed well acted rather than real. "It's good of you to see me," she began.

"I'm always interested in initiative," he replied. "You took a risk making such a nuisance of yourself. You could have been disciplined, or mistaken for an intruder."

"I assumed you'd protect me," Jude explained, and smiled her most winning smile. She was alarmed, however. It sounded as if her earlier report had not been received. Perhaps she had misjudged Jonah, and he had failed to mail her package. Perhaps she had expected too much of Linda Vass. "My rank is Family Support Officer; serving number 11690," she reiterated. "I'm based at East Five, England. I sent you a micro-disc by real time delivery. It contained information about malpractice at Border Seven - close to the Scots English border."

"So it was you who sent us that?" Decider Anesto's tone suggested surprise, but Jude was certain he had known already. "We were most intrigued." His expression became more stern. "You made serious accusations, my dear. You mustn't go round saying such things."

"I can supply you with names and ranks," Jude insisted, "and a full description of how goods and services at Border Seven are being misused for personal gain. There are also disturbing questions about the treatment of sick and elderly members."

"You were sent there by your Chief Secretary I believe - Maria Levant. Are you aware she herself faces charges of corruption?"

Jude could only nod in acknowledgment.

"Senior Levant was also suffering from creeping paranoia - a most advanced form of height sickness. Had she stayed for treatment, we might have been able to help her. Poor woman!"

Jude was determined not to go away without completing her mission, yet aware that the man in front of her was the most powerful in the whole Corporation. "Will you consider my reports as a separate entity?" she asked. "The facts are verifiable, regardless of Senior Levant's condition."

"Allegations are always investigated." By remaining standing, the Decider dominated even as he smiled. "You must have been very observant to acquire names and details yourself," he remarked. "Or did you have assistance?"

"I have sharp eyes, sir," Jude replied guardedly. "If you send investigators to Border Seven, I'm confident they'll confirm my conclusions. I also have some additional evidence with me." Pausing, she reconsidered. The record of level 40 could only have been made by a small number of people. Joel was one of them. "A few extra names and so on," she said instead.

"If there are any queries, we can contact you. I've been looking at your file, my dear. I see you were due to be bonded, but that the date was deferred. We also have a note that you were disciplined for over-familiarity with your clients. Am I right in assuming that was Maria Levant's doing, so that you could act on her behalf?"

Warily Jude nodded. "I would be most grateful if you could remove that from my record," she replied.

"I think you deserve more than that. A junior officer has no right to question a superior's orders, and you couldn't know Senior Levant's mental state. I shall ask for the disciplinary mark to be removed, and a commendation circulated instead." Smiling, Decider Anesto looked down at her. "Your record is excellent. Had you been staying on, you would have received promotion. It seems unfair to overlook you, simply because you have agreed to serve the Corporation another way. An additional point on the scale will improve your pension, and increase your chances of resuming your present role when your child is old enough."

"I'm most grateful," Jude said, and felt herself going scarlet with pleasure.

"Now I'm afraid you must excuse me. Resources will arrange for you to be escorted back to your base."

Jude was already rising from her chair. "That won't be necessary, Sir," she assured him. "I travelled here on my own."

"Nonsense. These are dangerous times. So attractive a woman should have an escort whenever she travels. In a few weeks you'll have your partner to care for you, but until then we must make other arrangements to ensure your safety."

"I appreciate your concern," Jude replied uncertainly.

"Not at all. The Corporation is always concerned for its members, especially those who are, shall we say? - a little innocent of the ways of the world. You will stay here a night or two in the guest suite. I'm sure you must need a rest before you travel home."

Pressing the communicator button, Decider Anesto called Security. In alarm Jude watched him. Beneath the charm, there was rottenness, and a faint odour of decay.

A young man answered promptly.

"Escort Officer Shah to Resources," the Decider instructed.

"My things are still in Reception," Jude pointed out. "I shall need to get them first."

"You will be provided with anything you need for your stay."

"But my bag contains equipment issued in my name."

"It will be delivered to you."

Turning abruptly, the Decider went back into his office.

Jude had no choice but to follow the young man down the corridors. He stayed with her all the way to Resources, and waited until not just one, but two clerks had appeared.

The clerks clearly had instructions to treat Jude as an honoured guest. She was allocated a beautiful room, with a window overlooking a hanging garden. One of the creepers just beside the air vent was in bloom. Its heavy scent floated through the ventilator, making the air sweet. Everything Jude could need for a few days had been laid out for her: a change of uniform, cosmetics and a hairbrush, sleep suit and toiletries. There was no communicator however, and no terminal - not even a link to the in-Refuge friendship net. When Jude activated the entertainment system it offered only soothing images. The news channel had been deleted. Standing in the centre of the room, she held her breath to steady it. Everyone had been polite to her, she reminded herself. Her sense of being imprisoned must be purely imaginary.

For a while Jude occupied herself having a shower. It was certainly pleasant to get out of the uniform she had worn for several days, and to be able to put on new clothes. Then, after she had dressed and plaited her hair, she looked round for something else to do. Staying in that close little room was already getting on her nerves. She was not a prisoner, but a guest, awaiting transfer back to her base. If she wanted to explore a bit, there was nothing to stop her doing so.

As soon as Jude went down the corridor, a domestic assistant appeared. "Is there anything wrong Ma'am?" she asked.

"It's very warm in my room," Jude replied. "I thought I'd take a walk."

"Perhaps the air control isn't functioning properly. I'll see if it needs adjusting."

The woman was strongly built. Though she smiled, there was ice in her expression. Reluctantly, Jude agreed. "That would be very kind of you," she said.

They returned to Jude's room. In less than a minute, the domestic assistant had adjusted the air control. "I'll put the entertainment on for you," she said cheerfully.

The morning lottery show was reaching its most fevered point. The audience was howling to know the winner. Settling down on the couch, Jude pretended to watch.

The bag had not yet arrived. All Jude's equipment was in it: her pacifier and her protective jacket, direction finder and enhancers. Though she had kept her return warrant and money card on her person, without her bag, Jude was unarmed and very vulnerable.

She began to feel afraid, not only for herself, but for Joel. By pleading the personal entertainer included her favourite games, she had managed to prevent it from being taken from her. How long she could keep others from wanting to use it was another matter.

*****

The escort reminded Jude of the child care officers who used to take her to the Academy. Introducing herself as Ingrid - "Just Ingrid my dear" - she had brought plenty of refreshment for the journey, together with a pack of games for Jude to play.

They sat at a table in the waiting room, drinking coffee together. "You must be quite excited," Ingrid enthused. "Going back to be bonded. I'll bet your feet hardly touch the ground."

"They manage it most of the time," Jude replied dryly. "Did my bag ever turn up?"

"Not yet. It really is most annoying. They promised me faithfully they'd send it on."

"I'm responsible for the equipment in it," Jude pointed out.

"Your supervisor will understand."

Jude looked away. She felt patronised. "I shall need the body vest as soon as I'm back," she persisted. "It was made specially to fit me. A borrowed one won't be safe."

"Oh - I don't think you'll need protective clothing now, my dear. If that's all that's worrying you, you can put your mind at rest."

In annoyance, Jude turned back to the woman. "Why?" she asked.

"They'll put you on light duties straight away. No more climbing up and down ladders for you. You might do yourself some damage."

"It's strange how protective everyone's suddenly become."

"You're very precious, you know. Almost perfect in every way - and with stamina and a strong character too. Of course the Corporation wants to look after you. In such as you, our future lies."

"You make me sound like breeding stock," Jude retorted.

"Don't be so sensitive, my dear! You should feel absolutely delighted, and very privileged. I know I would have done, if I'd been chosen. When you get back and you're arranging your party and planning your new dwelling, you'll feel a lot better. You won't have much time you know. Three weeks will absolutely fly."

Jude felt the breath swell in her chest. "Three weeks?" she repeated stupidly.

"They've brought your bonding forward. Your partner is growing impatient."

"But that's not possible." Jude flushed. "There are practical reasons why it has to be longer."

"Not nowadays dear. They'll give you booster injections. Anything's possible now."

Jude could not trust herself to reply.

"Don't look so surprised," Ingrid teased. "Of course your partner doesn't want to be kept waiting. Take a look at yourself in the mirror. You really are rather special; even better with that new hairstyle. When Personnel take it into their heads to give someone the treatment, they don't spare any expense. You could have come straight out of a reality game."

A nerve in Jude's cheek had begun to jump, and she pressed it with her fingers. "You flatter me," she said.

"I never flatter anyone. You should value yourself as a woman more. Work isn't everything."

For the third time, Ingrid got out her travel warrant to check it was safe. "Let me see yours," she instructed, as if she were speaking to a child.

Silently Jude passed the warrant over.

"You did well to get hold of one yourself," Ingrid commented. "For international travel too! They're like gold. How did you get it?"

"I had contacts."

"Nice! I wish I had contacts like that. Friends?"

Jude began to suspect Ingrid's interest was not mere curiosity. "No," she replied.

"They must have plenty of money."

"I couldn't say. I hardly know them."

It was nearly time to board their transport. "You'd better take one of these," Ingrid remarked, and passed Jude a small pink capsule.

"What's that for?"

"Travel sickness."

"I travel very well thank you," Jude replied coldly.

"So they all say - and I've ended up with some pretty uncomfortable ladies. I always insist on my charges taking a capsule. Go on. While you've still got something to drink."

The reply was apparently pleasant, but Jude heard menace in the woman's tone. Urgently she tried to think what to do. She would be unwise to alienate her escort further. If the medication was only for travel sickness, it would do her no harm. If it wasn't, she could tell by the taste and get rid of it. Taking the capsule, she pretended to swallow it with her drink. For a minute or so it should remain intact under her tongue.

"Now swallow," Ingrid ordered.

Jude adopted a hurt expression. "Why do you doubt me?" she asked with her eyes.

"I said 'swallow'," Ingrid repeated. "Not that it matters really. The outer casing dissolves in thirty seconds, and you're not going anywhere in that time."

Unable to speak, Jude sat in terrified silence, staring at the flight screen. With the woman watching her every movement, she could not take the capsule from her mouth, or go anywhere else to do so. Rapidly the casing dissolved.

"Right," Ingrid said cheerfully. "Off we go."

*****

The journey passed quickly enough. Within minutes of boarding, a pleasant tiredness began to seep over Jude's brain. Travel sickness remedies always made her feel dopey, which was why she avoided them. Trying to convince herself she was interested in the other passengers, she fought the temptation to doze. It was too powerful. Her eyelids became too heavy to hold open. Still fighting to stay awake, she slid into sleep.

Special transport had been arranged from the terminal, to connect with the next service into East Five. Even the warrants were handled by her escort. Jude woke up enough to walk between the two, then fell asleep again. Only when the deceleration hit her at the end of the tunnel, did her head begin to clear. Crossly, she rubbed her eyes. It was silly of her to sleep so deeply on a journey. It always left her feeling groggy.

Kurt was waiting to greet her. "Good to have you back!" he said and kissed her.

"Good to be back," Jude lied. She was having difficulty focusing on his face.

In surprise, Kurt considered her. "You look different," he remarked.

"Personnel gave me the once-over."

"It looks great. I didn't realise I'd got myself such a stunner. Did you miss me?"

"I'm afraid I was too busy."

"Well, I missed you. I liked having you call me sometimes." Kurt laughed. He seemed genuinely pleased at her return. "They've brought our date forward. Did you know?"

Jude nodded. "I gather you were bored with waiting," she replied tartly.

An expression of surprise came to Kurt's face. "Me?" he asked. "To be honest, I was enjoying being free a bit longer - no offence meant."

"Then why have they brought our date forward?"

Kurt shrugged his shoulders. "Presumably Futures haven't met their quotas," he said softly. "Do you mind?"

"It wouldn't make any difference if I did. I shall just have to make my arrangements a bit faster, that's all."

"That's my girl! Never one to moan." Putting his arm around her, Kurt kissed her again.

For a few more moments they were allowed to talk, then a brisk young officer took Jude to level 151. She would not be returning to her usual dwelling he apologised. That was exceptionally large, and seeing as she would only be needing separate accommodation for another few weeks, it made sense for it to be allocated to a newly bonded couple. Her possessions had already been transferred. He hoped she understood.

There was no point in arguing. Her head aching, Jude looked round her temporary home. She still felt heavy with sleep. Going into the bathroom, she splashed cold water on her face.

The mirror over the sanitary unit reflected her image back to her. Ingrid had advised her to take a look at herself. Smiling at her own vanity, Jude did so. Whether she was beautiful she could not say. She had never really associated beauty with herself. The last few weeks had given her more confidence however, and she stood straighter, with the dignity of a senior officer. The hairstyle felt strange, but it was softer and more feminine. Kurt had liked it. He had been quite attracted to her, in fact - for the first time genuinely wanting her.

Jude frowned. It would have been better if management had not lied to her. She could have accepted that the Futures' department needed to meet their quotas. Giving her the impression Kurt wanted her more than he did, was not a service to either of them. Picking up her brush to do her hair, Jude leant a little closer to the mirror. Then she paused in bewilderment. Her pupils were dilated. The bathroom was well lit. Her eyes should not look as they did.

It took Jude a few seconds to work out what was wrong. Slamming the brush down, she nearly howled in anger. Her eyes were dilated because she had been given a sedative, to get her back to her Refuge quietly. Her sense of being imprisoned at Headquarters had not just been paranoia.

Urgently Jude looked round for somewhere to hide Joel's recording. Then she remembered that she could be being watched. Trying to act casually, she went into the other room and unpacked her things. Finally she dropped the personal entertainer amongst the other bits and pieces of games equipment in her storage box.

Chapter Twenty

It was well after eight thirty before Jude woke the following morning. Even then she had to force herself to get ready for duty. Whatever her escort had given her, the effect was long lasting.

"We didn't expect you in today," Overseer Pera said, looking up in surprise. "We were told you'd be resting."

"I'm fine thank you," Jude replied, and felt anything but. Her head seemed to have been stuffed with cotton wool. "I'm afraid I have to report the loss of some equipment, including my safety jacket."

"Don't look so worried." Overseer Pera laughed. "You won't be needing safety jackets now. It's light duties for you. Number work I'm afraid, and a bit of training. You could pass on some of your skills before you leave us."

Jude listened and nodded and felt as if she were a hundred miles away. When she was a child she always used to cut herself off when she was in trouble. Now the sensation was even stronger. None of this could be happening to her. It was not just that she was playing a part. Over the past few weeks that feeling had become familiar. Now it was the knowledge that she was being written right out of the play. For ten years she would be on nobody's budget - except through Kurt.

"I'd enjoy doing some training," Jude replied and tried to smile.

Her overseer looked at her curiously. "Promotion, and a commendation too," she remarked. 'For special duties'. I never did believe you'd been disciplined. You were far too good an officer."

Jude smiled in pleasure. "Thank you," she said.

"You've done very well. Whatever your mission was, from your point of view, it obviously turned out right."

For the first time, Jude considered the suggestion. Viewed selfishly, her assignment had been a success. It was not her problem if no action would be taken as a result. As a good Refuge member, she ought to be able to accept that management would do whatever was necessary, while she settled down as Kurt Hammel's partner and the mother of another perfect child. The trouble was, it was not in her nature to keep silent when people were profiting at the expense of others. Nor could she allow an ideal to be dragged down - an ideal she had grown up with and that her parents had died for - without putting up some sort of fight.

"I guessed you'd have been sent up north," Officer Pera continued. "With all that trouble over water supplies, and you speaking the dialect..."

Jude smiled guardedly. "You've heard about the problems, then?" she asked.

"It was on the Newsline - didn't say much. They never do. Just that the war lords were threatening to cut off supplies to the cities, and someone who calls himself Tuecer was acting as arbiter. I wondered if you'd been asked to contact him -"

The remark startled Jude. Until then, she had never heard any Refuge official use the name. She considered trying to find out more, but decided against it. "I can't answer your questions," she replied. "Security and all that."

"Of course."

The conversation had intrigued Jude, and she was still thinking about it as she took her things out of her locker. "What's this number work you've got for me?" she asked.

"Budgets and statistics."

For the rest of the day, Jude worked on a grindingly boring set of figures. It was hard to maintain concentration. There was too much in her mind: the man called Tuecer, water supplies, Border Seven... Most of all, though, she thought about Joel. Somehow she must warn him that the Triumvirate was unlikely to take action. Then perhaps he would leave, while he still had time.

That evening, Jude made out the list for her bonding party. For a crazy minute, she considered inviting Joel, but the excuse that they had known each other in the past would sound thin, and draw attention to his background.

She could think of no other reason to contact him directly. Once again, Carrie seemed the only possible source of help. Working out in advance what she would say, Jude called Mid Two's personal net.

Carrie was as pretty as ever, and delighted to hear from her. "I've thought about you a lot," she said, smiling broadly from the screen. "I kept wondering if you'd got back safely. Then I saw your name on the Newsboard. You haven't half done well! A commendation! And promoted! You must be ever so pleased."

"A bit stunned actually." Jude smiled. It was good to see Carrie again. "I wanted to invite you to my bonding party," she continued. "Put your recorder on. I know how you forget details."

Carrie's eyes showed an instant of bewilderment, then she was laughing in reply. "OK. When is the great event?" she teased.

"Thursday week, at fourteen hours - until dawn, if anyone can still stand. Could you come over in person? I'd love to have you here. Shouting at each other over the air isn't quite the same."

Carrie laughed again. "I've got some leave owing me," she replied. "I'll ask my line manager. It's earlier than you expected, isn't it?"

"Yes. They're making special arrangements."

"How do you feel?"

"Nervous." Conscious that they were probably being monitored, Jude laughed. "But I'll get used to the idea," she added.

"What sort of present do you want?"

"Not baby clothes. I shall get plenty of them from others. Something for myself."

There was an awkward pause while Jude tried to remember what to say. "I'm contacting as many old friends as I can," she continued. "You remember Jay? You know, the lad who always used to lead in the cross-country? I bumped into him recently - doing well in medical research. The trouble is, I can't for the life of me remember his patronym. His mother bonded again, and they moved somewhere near Border Seven. Jay took his stepfather's name. I think it began with an 'A' but I'm not sure. Do you know?"

"I might be able to find out."

"He doesn't get a lot of freedom, what with extra work and teaching the local kids canoeing," Jude continued brightly, "But I'd like to send him an invitation. We used to talk for hours, putting the world to rights, but you know how it is - we didn't manage it." She pretended to break off with a laugh. "If you do trace Jay, tell him I shall understand if he can't come, but I really think he ought to get away if he can. He was looking very tired, and goodness knows when he'll get another chance."

"Sure, I'll pass the message on," Carrie replied. It would take her a while to work out all Jude meant, but she was beginning to get the general idea.

For another five minutes they talked about Jude's plans, the dwelling she and Kurt had been allocated, and the date her child would be born. Then they wished each other good night. As the screen went blank, Jude discovered her hand was shaking. So long as Carrie could contact Mark - and he could find a way of speaking to Joel - all might still be well.

*****

The following morning, Jude took her party list to Personnel. They would see to sending out the invitations and make arrangements for refreshments.

The chief clerk glanced through the names. "It's quite a short list," she commented. "I suppose with you having no family, it's bound to be. Who have you invited as your support?"

"An old friend of my mother's. There -" Jude indicated the name. "Veronica Gale. She and Mum worked together before they were bonded. She's been as good as any relative to me."

"Wouldn't you like to invite a few more? What about your friends at Border Seven?"

Jude managed to keep calm. "I didn't realise my posting was current knowledge," she replied. "I was ordered to tell no one."

"Everything about you is known to us. It has to be. If you'd like some of your contacts during your assignment to be invited, it can be arranged - unobtrusively of course."

Jude made a show of thinking about it, and then shook her head. She suspected other motives behind an apparently innocent question. "I was working as a menial," she replied. "I didn't have a lot in common with my colleagues. One woman was very kind, but she wouldn't want to come to a party like this. She'd feel out of place."

"And what about your cousin?"

The question nearly threw Jude. Again, she pretended to think, giving herself time to control her voice. "I could invite Joel I suppose," she said, "But it'd be a bit awkward."

"Why?"

"I told him I'd been thrown out of the Refuge and was earning my living as a menial. I had to say something, to preserve my cover. If I contacted him now, I'd have to explain why I lied. Besides, we got a bit too close, and I don't think Kurt would like having him around."

The personnel officer was surprised by Jude's openness. Clearly she did not know how much to believe. "Of course," she replied shuffling some papers. "It's entirely up to you. Now, my dear, if you'll come with me, you have an appointment at the medical centre."

Jude's stomach lurched within her. "I'm on duty in half an hour," she replied.

"The Futures Department has brought your final tests forward. Your duty is with them today. Your manager has been advised. It'll only take an hour or so."

"Ah - Officer Shah," the receptionist said, and ticked Jude's name on a list. "Wait here please."

For the next five hours Jude did a great deal of waiting. She sat around in cubicles or studied notices in hot little rooms. Each time she was moved on, she was greeted by a cheerful orderly who told her how privileged she must feel. Then she sat down again with a dozen or so more women, all of them silent with nervousness, or talking too much. After another wait, another orderly came into the room and called their names, one after the other, until it was Jude's turn, and she was escorted outside, to another hot little room. There, a man or woman in white asked her a lot of questions, and told her to undress again. Each time, the verdict was the same. She was almost perfect. Just what the department needed.

Time began to lose all meaning. One minute it dragged, the next it ran too fast. Twice Jude had a flash of hope that she might, after all, be refused. After the facial analysis, her features were declared imperfect, but it was decided other attributes compensated. Then, later, there was a question about her low blood pressure. Fear, however, had raised it that day, and the reading was declared to be within tolerable limits. By twelve o'clock a nerve had begun to twitch in her cheek. She was shivering, though her hands and face were sticky with sweat. There was no companion to crack silly jokes and take her mind off the waiting. When she tried to play a couple of games in one of the waiting rooms, her hands were too unsteady to operate the controls.

The indignity was harder for her to bear than for most, Jude admitted, though not in self-pity. From being a respected officer, she had been recategorised as a mere female, a body to be examined. No one told her what the measurements were for, or explained what they were doing. If they asked her how she was feeling, they did not want to know the answer.

If she could have run, Jude would have done so, but there was nowhere to run to. Besides, she could not go far in a paper gown. All she could do was to switch off her mind, as she used to do as a child. The part of her that was Jude Shah and no one else, was safely sealed away. No matter how many doctors and geneticists saw her, they could never touch that.

"Don't look so worried," one of the orderlies said towards the middle of the afternoon.

"I'm getting very tired," Jude replied. Her voice sounded small and frightened.

The woman smiled. "You'll feel much better when you've had a cup of tea," she said. "There's just one more person to see, and he's only going to ask a few questions."

"More questions? What about?"

"Attitudinal issues. There's some concern about how well you'll fit into your new life. It's harder for a senior officer - you're used to independence - and in your case, you've lived an exciting life until now. It wouldn't be surprising if you resented having to settle down. You could be a disruptive influence."

"I shall do my duty in all things," Jude replied doggedly.

"You'll try my dear, I'm sure. But it may be that you could benefit from special preparation."

"I don't understand you." The nerve in Jude's cheek was jumping again.

"Classes to teach you how to slow down - to be more content with ordinary things. It's up to your Lifestyle Adviser of course. I imagine you'll also be prescribed pleasure therapy for a few months."

"No!" Involuntarily Jude got up from the seat.

"Where do you think you're going, you silly girl?" the orderly asked. "I don't know! You face all sorts of dangers in your work, and panic at the thought of something most people enjoy."

Staring straight ahead of her, Jude sat down again.

The orderly smiled. "Tell you what, let's see if we can find out what sex you've been allocated. That'd be nice to know, wouldn't it?" Keying in a request, she waited. "Well, isn't that nice!" she said in delight. "A little girl! It would have been such a shame not to pass that lovely hair on to another woman."

*****

As soon as she got back to her dwelling, Jude threw a pair of shoes at the wall in fury. It was a useless gesture, but it made her feel better. Then, not even stopping for a drink, she switched on the Newsline. As Officer Pera had remarked, it didn't tell you much, ever, but at least it was something to think about.

For once, however, the update report implied a great deal: "Tensions in the Border areas are easing, following advice to the sector council from government allies. The small minority of antidemocratic elements responsible for last week's disturbances have been arrested, including several so-called Hawkboy groups. Water supplies to the south have been re-established. There is no cause for concern."

When a Newsline report said there was no cause for concern, you started to panic. "Government allies?" Jude wondered. Did that mean Tuecer, as Officer Pera had suggested? And why specifically mention Hawkboy groups? The ultimate anarchists, Hawkboys lived off the land, not even registering for social benefit schemes. The only time they had become involved in civil disturbances was when General

Rowles was taking over the sector parliaments. Then, they had done his dirty work, eliminating anyone who dared to oppose him. If the Hawkboys were active again, somebody was probably using them to cause trouble.

Jude had begun to shiver again. She must try to think of pleasanter things, or fear and anger would begin to take her strength. Sitting at her workstation, she called up the leisure programme.

The first game was called "Endurance." The title seemed particularly appropriate, and Jude began banging away at it furiously. Her scores were down, though, the sedative still having a deadening effect. Almost crying with frustration, she put her head onto her hands.

For a few moments she seriously considered the idea of death. It would be easy enough. Knowing the fire escapes as she did, she could walk out onto an open balcony, and throw herself down. That would be better than spending the rest of her life feeling like a prisoner, and knowing that she had failed not just Joel, but herself, and Big and Littl'un - and Feda - and everyone like them - her parents too; everyone who had believed in the Refuge ideal...

Then Jude began to think more clearly. Her death would hardly be noticed, except as removing an obstacle in the path of whoever was trying to silence her. She had to fight back.

Sitting up straight, Jude started the game sequence again. For half an hour, she played, over and over, refusing to accept that her mind could not be brought back to its usual clarity. Gradually her score rose. By the fifteenth attempt, it had almost returned to her usual high figures.

At the end of the half hour, she was exhausted, but calmer. Her anger and fear began to seem out of proportion to any actual cause. Since her return, everyone had been very kind to her, even complimentary. The only ill treatment Jude could cite was being forced to take medication on the way back from Headquarters - and that could be the doing of a lazy escort, who liked her charges to sleep, rather than talk. Even the threat of pleasure therapy had not been carried through, just suggested, and then by a junior official.

True, the bonding date had been brought forward, but by deciding to stay with the Corporation, she had accepted that her personal feelings on any matter were irrelevant. Even painting your balcony bright mauve, might offend your neighbours on the levels opposite. Everything was a question of balance. The words of one of the tutors at Junior Academy echoed in her memory: "A termite can't suddenly decide it won't follow the column, or that it would prefer to be Queen. On its own, it would be a mere speck lost in the desert. But by working together, termites can survive in the harshest conditions.

When you consider the difference in scale, their towers of sand are almost as big as our Refuges. We, too, must work as one..."

Even at eight, Jude's whole spirit had rebelled. "But I'm not a termite!" she had called out. It had got her into dreadful trouble. That was partly it, Jude admitted. She was afraid now, because she could feel herself being reduced to that termite. However much she valued the ideals of the Refuge, she still wanted to keep the core of individuality that made her, herself.

Keying the programme to a more routine setting so that she could play while thinking, Jude began trying to create a scenario for herself, as she might do for a game programme she was writing. Supposing one of the 'bigger boys' - as Joel had called them - had moved into the Corporation, buying even the Triumvirate, or at least one member: Anesto. They would block all investigations that might lead to the ending of their monopolies. But why leave her alive? She could easily have met a misfortune on the way back. Why let her go on living?

Because she had information? About Joel perhaps? No - That could be got from her by force, however hard she tried to protect him. She must have some importance in herself. Because she was 'almost perfect', perhaps? No again. The Futures department could find another woman to breed from, however much difficulty they might have in meeting quotas. In any case, they could use her, and then destroy her, once her child was born.

The suggestion made Jude go cold. She must not let herself think like that. Her scenario had to include some reason why she was worth keeping alive beyond then, something that made her unique. What about the illusions in the Rehabilitation suite and at Border Seven? Could she build them into her story?

In both illusions, a man called Teucer had featured, and called himself her father. Supposing he actually was her father? Officer Pera had said Tuecer arbitrated in the dispute over water supplies. For his name to have been removed from the banned list, he must now be trusted by the government, and presumably by the warlords too. He would want to curb the power of the Refuges, and therefore be a threat to the people Joel was trying to expose. Was she being kept alive in the hope that she might lead them to him? Or that he might come to her?

Jude's scenario suddenly became possibility. If her mother had already loved someone before she was bonded, she must have watched her preparation weeks tick by with a similar desperation to Jude's now. Since she aroused no suspicion, she must have gone to Jude's real father on the actual day of her bonding, or more likely, the night before. From what Jude could recall of her mother's character, it was probably an act of defiance rather than weakness, a refusal to accept a system that would not allow her to choose her partner. But later, she would have dreaded the shame her act could bring her, and probably regret hurting Joachim. She had come to respect perhaps even love him, too. It was not surprising she kept her unfaithfulness secret from everyone, including Jude.

Jude had always been good at drawing portraits. Picking up a stylus, she tried to recall the man she had seen in her illusions.

The first sketch was not difficult. The rehabilitation programme seemed to be burnt into her mind. She could see a man protecting her, while crowds surged on the other side of the rail. Then there was the receptionist's description of Jude's visitor when she was recovering from surgery. Once again his hair was a rich auburn like Jude's, but going a little grey. Thoughtfully Jude shaded her sketch. Finally, a third image came to her mind, of a cave, and a flight of steps leading down to it. Beside a fire, a man was standing, holding out his hands to welcome her.

In surprise, Jude looked up. For the first time she could recall the man's face. Quickly she sketched it in - not particularly handsome, but pleasant and kind, someone you could take your troubles to, and who loved life himself.

Afterwards, Jude stared at her drawing. It was familiar to her. She had seen such a man when she was a child, though there had been no grey in his hair then. When was it?

He had been introduced to her by her mother, that was it. They were at the survey camp, and had just set up the temporary units. Who was he? Some sort of local official. A lawyer? He was angry... not at all pleased to have a Refuge party nearby. Her mother had met him before it seemed, on a previous survey of the area, when she was younger. Try as hard as she would, Jude could not remember the visitor's name. When they were introduced, she had hardly listened. She had been much more interested in the peculiar atmosphere between her mother and him, the sense that each wanted to say much more and could only mouth politeness. The man had looked hard at Jude, and then turned away.

It still did not make sense. If she was his child, he ought to have seen some likeness to himself, and at least lingered, trying to get to know her. Then Jude recalled how cold it had been that day. Her face and hair would have been hidden under a hood.

It was time she had a talk to Aunt Gale. Taking a printout of her drawing, Jude folded it carefully and put it in her pocket.

Chapter Twenty One

Mrs Gale was working when Jude arrived, but happy to take a break. "How lovely to see you!" she said, and kissed Jude on both cheeks. "Thank you for naming me as your support. I was quite touched. I wish Claudia could see you. She'd be so proud."

"I've been thinking of her a lot lately," Jude admitted. "You're one of the few people who remember Mum, and I'd like to know more about her."

"Of course. Sit down and I'll make us a cup of coffee."

"I think I'd rather have a walk together," Jude said, and smiled. "Like we used to before I got so busy."

"What a nice idea! You can tell me all about your promotion."

They went down to the pleasure area together, talking of old times. Jude let the conversation drift, waiting until it was safe to ask more important questions. Veronica Gale had been her mother's closest friend. If anyone knew her secrets, she did. Finally they were in the middle of the gardens, out of the reach of the surveillance.

"Did my mother love anyone other than Dad?" Jude asked abruptly.

The question took Mrs Gale by surprise. "I couldn't say," she replied.

"But you'd know," Jude insisted. "Please. My own bonding is to take place in less than two weeks. I have a right to know about my parents." Taking out the drawing, she passed it to Mrs Gale. "Who's this? Is it someone Mum knew?"

The paper remained in the open for barely a second. With a gesture of surprise, Mrs Gale folded it up quickly, and passed it back to Jude. She was about to say something, but could not find words.

"Is that man my father?"

Taking Jude's hand, Mrs Gale pulled her to one of the seats, as far as possible from other walkers. "I don't know," she said softly. "Claudia would never tell me."

"But you think he may be? Tell me. I have a right to know. I'm not going to discredit my mother's reputation. It would damage mine."

There was a long pause. Then Veronica Gale nodded. "Where do I start?" she asked, shaking her head. "It's all so long ago."

"Tell me how they met."

Watching the light flickering on the roses, Mrs Gale looked into her past.

"We were on a survey together," she began. "Just north of where Border Seven is now. One of the Reivers let us camp on his farm. He had two sons, both of them studying in London and home for the summer. They used to bring the milk, arrange for fuel to be delivered to us, that sort of thing. We saw a lot of them. It was quite innocent at first - four young people enjoying themselves. Claudia and I had had so little freedom, just to sit looking at the stars was wonderful, and Dan and Tom were excellent company, well educated and full of fun."

Pausing, Mrs Gale smiled at her memory. "The Corporation tells you love is just foolishness," she remarked. "I suppose they have to. With members in such close contact with each other, emotion has caused no end of problems in the past. Reason is much safer, but that summer, Reason didn't matter to any of us. I was mad over Dan, and Claudia used to say being with Tom was like being with herself - that he knew what she wanted, before she did.

"After three months, the survey came to an end. Dan and I had always known we would have to part, but Tom and Claudia wanted to stay together. When his father died, Tom would inherit the estate, and he had good prospects as a trainee lawyer. He asked Claudia to be his partner. The Corporation didn't give her chance to be tempted. She was ordered back, ahead of the rest of us."

"When was this?" Jude asked.

"Let's see - we were both 19 at the time, so that would make it 2130. I forgot Dan - or tried to - but I was heartbroken when I heard he'd been executed by General Rowles during the purges. Claudia kept in touch with Tom. She spent most of her leaves with him, though she kept it very quiet. I used to wonder why she didn't run off with him, but your mother had a very strong sense of duty, and she'd signed her lifetime contract. I think she hoped she could go on forever, serving the Corporation and seeing Tom in her holidays. The Futures Department was quite new then, and neither of us dreamt we would be amongst the first women to be chosen. When we were, we were devastated. Ultimately I gave in, but Claudia pleaded a prior commitment. You had to admire her courage. Management came down on her from a very great height."

There was another long pause.

"I suppose in the end, she had to agree," Jude prompted gently.

Mrs Gale nodded. "Joachim was kind and understanding, and would make a good partner. Claudia accepted him. But the last week of her preparation, Tom turned up at the Refuge, on some sort of delegation. He pleaded with management to let her leave. Futures wouldn't hear of it. They'd invested too much in her. So the bonding took place, and Tom went away."

Jude's hair had started to come undone, and Mrs Gale plaited it again, as she used to do when Jude was a child. "You had dark blond curls when you were little," she said. "It wasn't until you were about ten that your hair started to change. I can remember distinctly the day I realised you looked more like Tom than Joachim. You were sitting at the table doing your homework, and the light was shining on your hair. I looked up at Claudia and I knew I was right, but we never spoke about it. Your mother was a very private woman."

Jude felt her throat going tight. "Poor Dad," she said. "I shall always think of the man who brought me up as my Dad, even if he wasn't. But this Tom - he must have felt pretty bad too."

Mrs Gale looked at her curiously. "How did you do that drawing?" she asked. "Have you met him?"

For a second Jude considered the question. "Yes," she replied. "At least once." A discrepancy in Mrs Gale's story caught her attention. "You knew a young man," she pointed out. "I drew someone I saw recently. People change."

"Tom's not aged a lot."

"You've seen him recently?"

"Just before you went off - wherever you went. I presumed that was when you met him."

Jude shook her head. "No. He kept out of my sight." Her brain was too sodden to take in all Mrs Gale was saying. There was something she was missing. "What sort of business did he have here?" she asked.

"He represents the sector councils. Tom's a powerful man, Jude - led the opposition to another Refuge being built along the Borders, and won. The Corporation treats him with respect. He always gets the VIP suite."

"Did he recognise you?"

"Oh yes. He was very polite - and very cold. He blames me for persuading Claudia to stay with Joachim, but it was her own choice - truly." Sighing, Mrs Gale shook her head. "Odd isn't it?" she commented. "With some people, love can go on for years and years." She tucked the finished plait back inside Jude's hair-band, and then kissed her on the cheek. "Take the advice of an old friend," she advised. "Go on thinking of Joachim as your father. Your life is here, and if you start looking outside, you'll end up pulled in two."

"Have you been happy with Uncle Chris?"

"Very. I know it doesn't feel like it now, but Futures do know what they're doing. They match you with a man you can live with as a friend for years, rather than merely love for a few months. Even your mother came to recognise that. You'll come to respect your partner, just as she did."

Jude nodded, but somewhere inside her, a small voice was crying.

*****

That evening Jude was allowed to see Kurt for a couple of hours. They arranged to spend the time in the main lounge on level 209, where the terrace gave a lovely view of the gardens below. Being such a popular meeting place, it was also possible to talk without too much fear of surveillance. Kurt found them a couch, and they sat together awkwardly.

"The evenings have been a bit empty without your calls," he admitted. "I knew you must be doing something special. You never answered my questions. I began to wonder if your messages were being sent automatically, to make me think you were OK."

In surprise, Jude glanced at him. She had underestimated him badly. "I can't answer you," she replied. "I'm sorry."

"Was your mission successful?"

"I don't know. I doubt it," Jude replied. "Don't ask me questions. It isn't safe."

"But they've commended you."

"To keep me happy."

Uneasily Kurt looked around them. "You sound depressed," he remarked.

"Then cheer me up. Tell me what's been going on while I've been away."

"Oh - the usual sort of things. Millie's been promoted, and Beah's applied for a transfer. There was an outbreak of fever on '143. Our lot were running in circles to get hold of enough antivirals. Fortunately it died down. Everyone was ordered to keep quiet, but you know how it is, word soon got round. Members have been jumpy ever since."

Jude nodded. After the strain of the last few weeks, it was pleasant to sit looking at the view, and talk about ordinary, everyday things. Kurt, in turn, seemed genuinely delighted by her return. In any other circumstance, Jude would have valued his friendship. She recalled Mrs Gale's advice. All she could do was make the best of things - just as her mother had done before.

"Yes - but what about Sabbattica Collins?" another part of her mind whispered. "Remember her? Shut inside with a man she hated?"

Jude shivered slightly.

"Someone walking over your grave?" Kurt asked.

"Just thinking."

"I've been doing a lot of thinking myself," Kurt said softly. "We've been asked to clear the top level. All the dwellings are being emptied."

"Why? Because of the storms?"

"I dunno. Some members don't mind the sway, and it's not all that bad now - not since they installed the new stabilisers." An expression of unease passed over Kurt's face. "Management won't tell us what they're planning. There are some worrying rumours though."

At once Jude was fully awake. For a few seconds she could not trust herself to speak. "Are they moving the old people up there?" she asked.

Kurt stared at her in surprise. "They say sick members are being sent too. How did you know?"

"It's happening elsewhere. The Corporation can't afford unproductive workers anymore, and the city authorities won't take them off their hands."

Kurt studied Jude's expression, unsure if he understood her properly. "If what you're saying is true, none of us is safe," he answered. "My own grandfather's sick. He's a nice old guy. I wouldn't want to think of him stuck up in the clouds, with nobody to visit him. It's good to have you to talk to again. I can admit things to you, when I can't to others."

"I'm glad," Jude replied, absently. She could not stop thinking of people being moved from their dwellings, far into the skies. They would be terrified. And all she could do about it was sit on a sofa and whisper to Kurt...

"We don't get on too badly, do we?" Kurt asked and smiled.

"No," Jude acknowledged. "We could have done worse."

"Did you miss me?"

"I'm afraid not."

Kurt raised an eyebrow. "I hoped you would," he admitted.

"I was too busy." Remembering the list of guests Personnel had prepared for her, Jude decided to tell him a little more. "I met an old friend," she added. "Nothing much happened between us, but I did get quite close to him. Are you hurt?"

"A bit - but I've no right to be. I know you'd rather not be bonded to me. I'm getting to like the idea though."

"I'll try to make you happy," Jude promised. "So long as you don't make a fool of me. I'm not holding the baby while you chat up some junior clerk."

Kurt laughed. "That's more like it!" he remarked. "I was wondering when I'd see a bit of the old fire again. You've been worrying me. It's not just your hair that's changed. You seem vague - distant somehow."

Once again, Jude was impressed by his sharpness. "I'm being made to slow down," she whispered.

"Whatever for?"

"They're afraid I'll be a disruptive influence on other mothers."

An expression of anger passed across Kurt's face. For several seconds he watched the tiny figures in the gardens below. "I haven't asked them to change you," he said. "I want you as you are."

"Disruption and all?"

"I know what I'm letting myself in for. My counsellor's warned me you're too independent. I told him I was proud to be given a partner people respect, and who's achieved so much. I meant it."

Jude could not reply. She was near to tears.

"Come here -" Putting his arm around her, Kurt comforted her. "They're mad to try and break your spirit," he whispered. "If they'd left you to your own sense of duty, you'd have done everything expected of you - and more. Instead, they're likely to make their own prediction come true. Then I really will have trouble."

*****

The next few days settled into an acceptable pattern. At eight hours, Jude went to work, having been transferred permanently to the day shift. Though the statistics Overseer Pera asked her to provide were mindlessly dull, it was good to be back amongst friends. At eleven hours there was her daily realignment class. At first, Jude's stomach lurched when she entered the parenting centre, but as each day passed, the sessions became almost enjoyable. In the evenings, she spent an hour or so with Kurt, getting to know him better. They went swimming or played badminton, or simply sat and talked. There was usually plenty to fill the time.

At night, however, she could do as she wished. As soon as possible, Jude sat at her workstation and played games, did quizzes, read learning programmes, anything that would sharpen her mind. For the first couple of rounds, her score was always way down, worse than the day before, and she had to breath deeply to stop herself despairing. Then, as she persisted with the programme, her score improved. By the time she moved on to the next game, her total was almost as high as the night before.

By midnight, Jude was too tired to continue, and would fall asleep easily, but at five or six in the morning she would wake up, and lie staring at the ceiling. No matter how hard she tried, she could not stop herself thinking of Joel, and wondering if he had got her message in time.

She thought a lot about her father too - the man called Tom. Until the last few months, he had kept out of her life. Then suddenly he had made contact with her. Mrs Gale's stories had helped her put together a sketchy image of him, but there was some other fact she was missing, Jude was sure of it. Like a blind woman feeling her way around a room, her mind kept reaching towards it. Whatever it was, it linked all the separate fragments together. If she fumbled long enough, she ought to find it, however much cotton wool was stuffed into her brain.

By the fifth day, replies to Jude's invitations were beginning to arrive, together with gifts from those who could not attend. There were good will messages also from families Jude had known through her work. When she opened a box of toiletries and found a note from Sabbattica Collins, she was deeply touched.

For several minutes Jude stood at her window with the gift in her hand, and looked at the levels circling in front of her. She wondered if she would have the nerve now to climb down a fire escape and jump onto a balcony. She doubted it. Her reactions would be too slow.

"Something for you to spoil yourself with," the card said. "Thank you for giving me the chance to be happy."

Jude smiled in pleasure. When she had the time, she would call on the Sabbattica, and find out how she was coping.

A message flashed on the receiver. At once, Jude went to see what had come through. It was another acceptance, from a former colleague, but not the one she wanted. Carrie's silence was becoming ominous. Anxiously, Jude considered checking the staff lists, to see if Joel's name was still recorded, but she decided it would be too risky. Her request might be noted. It would be safer to call Carrie again.

"I'm so glad you contacted me," Carrie said cheerfully. "You seem to have a fault on your receiver. Helpline said your number wasn't accepting external calls."

"I'll bet it wasn't!" Jude thought, but she managed to look suitably puzzled.

"Really?" she asked. "I'll have to get the receiver checked. I thought it was funny you hadn't replied to my invitation."

"I'll be there, don't you worry. I wondered if I could bring another old friend of yours. Mark? Remember him? I bumped into him last week, and told him about you getting bonded, and he said he'd love to see you off. Would you mind?"

"Of course not."

Jude looked at Carrie's eyes, trying to read what she meant. "Shall I send him an official invitation?" she asked.

"If you would. He'll need it to show his line manager, so that he can apply for a travel permit."

It sounded as if Carrie was trying to arrange for her and Mark to obtain leave on the same weekend. Jude was intrigued.

"Did you manage to trace Jay?" she asked.

Carrie's expression could not help but convey the concern she felt. "I'm afraid not," she said. "He isn't working with the same outfit anymore, and no one seems to know his new employer. One of his friends thought it might be a small place, on a long-term contract. There was some sort of disciplinary proceeding. I gather Jay didn't talk to people afterwards. He was never very forthcoming about things that mattered."

Jude's hands had gone very cold. "Perhaps his family know where he is?" she suggested.

"I couldn't trace any family, just a guardian. All he'd had was an official memo saying Jay had been disciplined, and struck off the register. I checked the judgement lists, but couldn't find anything about the case there."

"Had his guardian been told the charge?"

"Gross misconduct with a patient. Doesn't sound like Jay at all."

"No," Jude agreed. Her voice was beginning to take on a strangled note that might arouse suspicion. "Thanks for trying, any rate," she said. "I'll cross him off my list."

As the picture died, Jude stared at the empty screen. "A small place, on long term contract..." The meaning was clear. Joel had joined the ranks of the Lost Ones. His friends believed he had been imprisoned, but did not know where. It would be virtually impossible to find out. No formal charge had been listed, and therefore no sentence. Carrie had also hinted that Joel had been questioned, and was refusing to talk. Clenching her hands tight, Jude went into the bathroom and leant against the vanitory unit. At least she could grieve there for a few moments, in peace.

For an hour afterwards, Jude lay on her bed, pretending to rest. She did not dare cry anymore, in case her watchers made a link between her grief and her call to Carrie. Anger throbbed in her mind, and along every vein. Whoever Joel's enemies were, they could not even invent a credible charge. If they had accused him of theft of Refuge property -

whether of medicines or his own ideas - there would have been some foundation for it. But gross misconduct - the idea was absurd.

But why had he not been simply expelled, or handed over to the civilian authorities? Whatever Joel knew, it must be of great importance...

Turning towards the pillow, Jude tried to control her emotion, and almost failed. Her grief for Joel was beyond any experience she had known, or the Refuges taught. It was not rational. No single individual could have so much value.

"Oh come on!" Jude said to herself in anger. If she stayed inside that close little dwelling much longer, she would suffocate.

Going out, she went to the relaxation area at the end of her sector. For a while she sat at the bar with a drink, but she could not settle there either, and walked on through the lounge, to the main route to the terraces. As she looked down the curving line of the corridor, a sense of such appalling desolation afflicted her that she had to stop and catch her breath. She had never felt so utterly, terrifyingly alone.

Turning round, Jude walked back along the corridors to her dwelling.

An official was sitting on the couch near her door, waiting.

"My! You're late back!" the woman greeted Jude cheerfully. "I thought you'd decided to stay out all night. My name's Nurse Barrett. Futures asked me to have a word with you."

"I'm sorry. I wasn't expecting anyone," Jude replied. "Can't it wait until the morning?"

"It'll only take a few minutes, my dear."

Beginning to feel alarmed, Jude let the woman in. Brisk and cheerful, Nurse Barrett sat at the kitchen table, and indicated Jude should join her. "I need to check a few details," she explained. Taking out a viewer she called up Jude's file.

Wondering what the real point of the visit was, Jude confirmed her personal record.

"Well, that all seems to be in order," Nurse Barrett said and smiled. "We're getting a bit concerned about you, officer. You're pushing yourself too hard. Your overseer says you're hardly slowing down, and you were playing games most of last night and the night before. What are you trying to prove? That your score is still as good as ever?"

Too surprised to answer, Jude felt a deep flush rising up her face.

"You don't need to prove anything to anyone, my dear" the Nurse chided, and touched Jude's hand. "Not even yourself. Of course your reactions will be slower. It's nothing to be ashamed of. You should be relaxing and enjoying yourself. I'm sure your partner wouldn't want you to be tired on your big night."

"I am not tired," Jude replied. She could cheerfully have hit the woman.

"Well you sound it, my dear. Roll your sleeve up and I'll give you something to calm you down."

"I'm quite all right," Jude insisted.

"That's for me to judge, not you."

The tip of a restrainer stuck out from the woman's breast pocket. Panic swelled in Jude's mouth. "I'll go to bed early tomorrow night," she promised.

"Roll up your sleeve. Or do I have to persuade you to co-operate?" With the slightest of gestures, Nurse Barrett touched the restrainer in her pocket.

Silently, Jude rolled up her sleeve.

Chapter Twenty Two

After that, the world became a little blurred. Jude could work, but only slowly, plodding through the figures her overseers gave her, without understanding more than the general drift of what she read. When she went home, all she wanted to do was eat and watch the in-house entertainment, until it was time for Nurse Barrett to make her regular call. After that, Kurt claimed her. She listened to him and smiled, and replied as well as she could. Everything was remote from her, a long way away.

Kurt was a nice man really. He took her swimming and played badminton with her, and they walked a lot in the gardens. The roses smelt so sweet Jude felt intoxicated by them. Even if sounds did echo oddly in her head, the warmth of the evening sun was comforting, and she liked to sit with her face towards the light. A long time ago, she used to rush around doing clever things. It wore her out. Or was that someone else? She could not quite remember.

There was something else she had to do, Jude recalled. It was terribly important, and she ought to be making serious plans and thinking serious things, but it was so pleasant to drift contentedly. Besides, with her party to arrange and her new apartment to furnish, there was such a lot to do. She couldn't do it all. Perhaps when her bonding was over, she would remember what the important thing was, and find the time.

Kurt could remember more than she could. He did not like her as she was now, and said so. The evening before her party, they almost quarrelled over it.

"I wish you'd wake up," he said. "Half the time you don't seem to be with me."

Jude frowned. What did he mean? They were sitting right next to each other. "I'm sorry," she apologised. "I don't mean to displease you."

"Well, you do! Snap out of it! And change that bloody hairstyle. It's not you."

"If you wish," Jude replied.

"'Yes, Kurt. No, Kurt'," he mocked. "I've always imagined the perfect woman. Now you're beginning to sound like one, it gives me the creeps. I liked the old Jude better."

His bad temper cut through the wool in Jude's head. "Who am I now?" she asked.

"I dunno. Someone without a brain, I know that."

Appalled, Kurt stared at her, frightened by what he had said. "Oh hell -" he whispered. He drew her closer to him and soothed her hair, as if she were a child. "Are they giving you any medication?" he asked softly.

"Of course. To prepare me for you."

She was puzzled by the distress in his eyes. "What else?" Kurt persisted.

To Jude's surprise, he pinched her hand, hard. As the pain passed into her brain, she caught her breath. It was as if a cool breeze had blown through it. At once, she understood his question.

"A nurse comes every night and gives me an injection," she managed to say.

The fog was descending on her again and she watched in bewilderment as Kurt took a packet from his pocket. Quickly he pressed one of the capsules out of its foil. "Take this," he whispered. "It's only Activate. I keep them with me, for when I'm on double shifts. Have the rest later."

There were walkers all round them, and he closed her hand over the packet. People were always giving her things and saying she should be a good girl and take them. Mechanically, Jude slipped the capsule into her mouth. It was hard to swallow and stuck in her throat.

For several more minutes Jude sat, watching the world go by. She could not understand why Kurt seemed to be waiting for something. Then, gradually, the stimulant began to work.

"Don't move," Kurt whispered. "Stay close to me, as if nothing's changed."

The noise in the pleasure area was almost more than Jude could bear. People were shouting all round her; fountains were roaring like torrents. "Oh Lord!" she said. "Where have I been?"

"I don't know - but you're not going back there, not if I can help it. Jude, why are they picking on you? Several of my mates are getting bonded, but their partners aren't being destroyed like you are. It breaks my heart to watch."

Her mouth felt stiff, but Jude forced herself to speak. "I know things I shouldn't," she replied. It occurred to her that Kurt could be being used even now, to make her talk. In despair, she put her hands to her face.

"There must be some way you can fight back," Kurt said. "When you get home, take two more of those capsules to clear your head, and then decide what to do. I don't want to lose you, but I don't want a beautiful, smiling shell. It'd bore me to tears. In ten years, I'd be half mad myself."

They walked back across the pleasure area. The shock of the stimulant affected Jude's vision and she missed one of the steps. Kurt had to support her. "I'll go right up to your dwelling with you," he whispered. "Don't forget you're being watched."

For two precious hours, Jude could think clearly. Tomorrow was her party. All afternoon, people would be round her. There would be no chance of disappearing then. After that, only two more days remained until the bonding itself. She would virtually be in solitary confinement, pampered and cosseted like royalty. All she had left to herself was tomorrow morning. It would be long enough to walk out onto one of the fire escapes and step into space. Nobody could make her talk then, but if there was such a thing as an afterlife, she would be flaming mad for most of it.

*****

At twenty-two hours there was a call on the communicator. "Who is it?" Jude asked.

"Only me," Kurt's voice replied. "I thought we might go swimming together."

"Now?"

"The small pool's open. I often swim when my shift's finished. We'll have it almost to ourselves. Get your things."

His voice shook slightly, as if with emotion or fear, but Jude could not say which. She had lost the ability to judge such things.

The pool was lit by a blue light, the fountain at the shallow end glinting like a huge aquamarine. Only three other people were swimming, plodding up and down, keeping fit. In the past Jude would have dived straight into the water, but now she lowered herself in gently, fearing the cold on her skin. It was an effort to force herself to swim to the deep end. Lying on her back, watching the reflection of the water above her, would have been far more pleasant.

With a crisp jump from the boards, Kurt joined her. "Swim with me to the bar," he instructed. "Halfway up, where we're both in our depth."

Obediently, Jude did as she was told.

"Can you understand what I'm saying?" he asked softly. "Are you still with me?"

"Just about." Splashing water onto her face, Jude tried to clear her mind.

"You've got to get out of the Refuge - before the fifteenth."

"Why the fifteenth?"

Looking round him quickly, Kurt checked the position of the other swimmers. He was shivering.

"I've been doing some checking. A year ago, I worked out how to tap into staff records. You can find entries for six weeks ahead. It can be useful to know who's on the way up, and who's going down." His voice caught in his throat. "I wanted to know what the charge was against you."

"What did you find?"

"Next week Jude Shah exists, commendation and all. The week after, you're merely my partner. On the fifteenth of next month, your death is recorded."

Jude's mind was clear now, as cold as the water in which she stood. "How do they intend to kill me?" she asked.

"Lubitzin poisoning. Liver failure, after two days."

"And do I do this to myself, or does someone help me?"

"It's recorded as suicide."

Fearing that she might faint into the water, Kurt put his arm around her. "There was a bit afterwards that horrified me," he whispered in her ear. "'Child saved and awarded to surrogate'."

"What do you mean?"

"They're keeping you alive Jude, for the sake of your inheritance. I can't be part of such a thing. It makes me feel physically sick. How can I get you out of here?"

It was as if knowing that she was about to die, Jude came to life again. She watched Kurt's face, and knew that he would help her. "There's one possibility," she said. "The grey-water outlets. So long as there's a gradient, I ought to be able to make my way down one of the pipes, and out to the discharge point at the river. "

"You'll drown."

"It can be done. Can you get me past Surveillance, down to the service area?"

"Only if Security don't check your ID."

"Then we need a distraction." Intensely awake, Jude considered the possibilities. "Could you tap into the bulletin board?"

"Perhaps. Nothing's secure against an insider."

"I'll start a rumour fever's broken out," Jude suggested. "You put a notice calling everyone for booster injections. Don't give any appointment times. That should cause chaos nicely. We'll join the throng, but go past, down to the service area."

Kurt smiled. "I'm not surprised they want rid of you," he remarked.

As soon as he spoke, Jude saw the danger. "They'll trace the call back," she warned.

"I could bounce it off one of our suppliers. Make it look as though it came from outside."

"That'd only delay things." The risk was appalling. Jude could not ask him to take it for her. "Forget it," she said. "I'll think of something else."

Kurt shook his head. "Anything you think of, will put someone at risk. It might as well be me. It's time I left -"

"You've always said your future was here."

"I thought it was. When I was a kid, being the member of a Refuge was the greatest honour anyone could have. My grandfather used to drill it into me. Now where is he? For the past two days my parents and I have been looking for him. He's on the top level Personnel says, but we're not allowed to see him. OK, he was old - and pretty sick. There's no point in being sentimental, but I liked talking to him, and he played a mean game of chess." Kurt paused. "Things are happening here that I can't accept. If I stay, I shall have to pretend I can. Someday I'll lose my temper and get sent for treatment myself. In any case, once this sort of thing starts, it doesn't stop with one or two. We'll all be at risk."

The water splashed and glinted in the fountain. A party of young people were entering the pool, their voices echoing around the tiles.

"You'll have to leave quickly," Jude warned.

Kurt watched the young people. "I've got some annual vacation owing me," he said. "If you disappear, they should let me take it, on compassionate grounds." He frowned, seeing another difficulty. "How am I going to explain what's happened to you? Your party will have no hostess."

"I'll make it look like I threw myself in one of the boilers. We've had a couple of women do it lately. There's no trace afterwards, unless you test for carbon."

Kurt shuddered. "You'll have to leave a note," he warned. His voice caught in his throat.

"I'll say I loved another man."

*****

Even Jude had not anticipated such utter confusion. People were pushing and shoving on the escalators, cramming into the turbo lifts, determined to be at the medical centres before the supply of antivirals ran out. It was impossible not to be carried along by the crowd. Kurt held her hand so that they would not become parted, and they headed down the levels, as fast as the throng would allow. Above them, the central communication system was already exhorting everyone to return to their dwellings. It stood about as much chance of being heeded as a whisper in a hurricane.

Jude and Kurt managed to turn out of the main thoroughfare, to rest for a few seconds. "Shit!" Kurt whispered. "If one announcement can cause this, what will happen in a real epidemic?"

Smiling ruefully, Jude paused. "I'm not going to know," she replied. "Either way."

They rejoined the crowds, and continued on down, towards the nearest medical centre. The appeals echoing round became demands. "All members are ordered to return to their dwellings," the mechanical voice repeated.

A burst of crackling silenced it, and a medical officer intervened. "There is no epidemic," he shouted. "Go back to your levels!"

A Security squad had arrived at the end of the corridor, and was trying to close the lifts. The result was even more panic, as two hundred people tried to work out which way to go. A woman had fallen and neighbours were trying to pull her to her feet.

"This way," Kurt said urgently, and turned down another corridor.

Below the medical centre, everyone was trying to go upwards. It was hard to push against the tide, and for a terrifying minute Jude became separated from Kurt. "Family Support!" she shouted, flashing her ID. "Let me through!"

A gap widened enough for her to squeeze past, and onto the 'Down' escalator.

Outside the service area, the corridor was unnaturally empty. "Now we see whether my pass works," Kurt whispered.

To Jude's intense relief, the door opened.

They stepped inside, under a canopy of pipes and tanks. The noise was deafening. Water swooshed and rushed, purifiers throbbed.

"Those are the outlets," Jude said, and felt her stomach tighten as she pointed.

"You really think you can get down one of those?"

Considering the gradient of each outlet, Jude tried to sound businesslike. "That looks the best," she said. "It's a bit steeper than the others. I don't fancy getting stuck halfway down."

"I wouldn't fancy it at all."

Jude smiled. "You're sure you won't come with me?" she asked.

"Perfectly. I'd rather walk out on my own two feet. Besides, I'd be in the way. You need to finish whatever you were doing."

Putting her arms round Kurt's neck, Jude kissed him. "I think I could have learned to love you," she admitted. "You're a very nice man, even if you are terribly handsome."

Kurt held her tight, then he kissed her once more and let her go. "Do you need me any longer?" he asked. "I ought to report for duty. There was an appeal as we came down the stairs."

"You go. I'll never find the nerve while you're here."

With a wistful smile Kurt nodded, and walked through the door.

Jude pulled herself up onto the funnel-shaped collector, and waited for the next gush of water. She had expected to be terrified, and found instead that she felt rather foolish. "You do end up doing some daft things," she told herself.

Above her, the outflow opened. Taking a gulp of breath, Jude lowered herself downwards. She had an absurd impression that she was a child again, launching herself into one of the water slides at the Aquarama. Then the wall of water hit her.

Just as she began to feel her lungs would burst, Jude was dumped unceremoniously on to a patch of mud. For a whole minute, she could not stop laughing. Joel had been right about the indignity of such an exit. She felt like a drowned cat. Above her, the outflow pipe protected her from sight. In front of her, only a few metres separated her from the river. There was no one about.

No one would expect a Refuge escapee to strike straight across country. Walking to Border Seven would take weeks of course, but without documents, Jude would be foolish to use public transport. Besides, other than keeping her promise to visit Joel's parents, what plans did she have for her life? While she was skirting Leodis, she could call on Linda Vass and thank her for sending the reports to Headquarters. It was not her fault the Triumvirate would not listen.

Before the next deluge of water could descend on her, Jude pulled off her sodden uniform. Under it she was wearing the lightest of her lounger suits. That too was soaked. Since a bundle of clothes would lead to immediate suspicion, she rolled her uniform into a tight parcel. Then, keeping low down, she slithered down the bank and into the water. If she were missed, the Refuge dogs would not scent her there.

Chapter Twenty Three

Dressing as a wisewoman was never a deliberate decision. The trader who sold Jude the second-hand dress joked that it made her look exotic. All Jude needed was a scarf round her hair, and she could earn her living telling fortunes. By the time the young soldier approached her, Jude had forgotten what the trader had said.

"Do you tell the future?" the soldier whispered.

"Why?" Jude asked in confusion.

"Is my partner going to die? Tell me - please..."

Jude could not answer such a question. Neither could she turn the young man away. He was too distressed. She suspected he had been unfaithful, and guilt pained him as much as love. Smiling, she offered what advice she could. "Stop thinking about your second woman," she said. "And spend your savings on a doctor. Otherwise, you'll feel bad for the rest of your life."

The man was so surprised, he stared at Jude in alarm. "How did you know?" he whispered. Then he thrust every coin he had into Jude's hand.

Until then, Jude had feared she would never reach Linda Vass. The journey had become a nightmare of endurance and worry, about her own future, and Kurt and whether he would leave the Refuge safely, about Joel... At times, she was almost delirious with tiredness and hunger, and found herself imagining she was a girl again, leading a group of children across miles of wasteland. But after she unbraided her hair and bought herself a bright red scarf, travel became much easier. People were nervous of leaving a wisewoman beside the road, in case she cursed them for their neglect. Rarely did Jude have to walk more than a few kilometres at a time. Twice she was offered accommodation - in outhouses admittedly, but it was better than sleeping rough.

With everyone she was scrupulously honest. "I don't know the future," she would insist. And then she would make a few general opening remarks, while watching their responses. After that, they interpreted what she said according to their own hopes and fears. It took her only a week to reach the Sheffield zone, and one lucky question to find Linda Vass' address.

At first Linda did not recognise her. She was carrying a pile of bedding to a battered old carrier. The whole courtyard was full of activity, people coming and going with household goods in their arms, while neighbours watched. The Vass family was moving out. Jude had only just caught them in time. Pushing her way through the onlookers, she walked towards Linda. "I have a sign for you," she said.

For a second there was fear in Linda's eyes. "What do you want?" she demanded. Then she recognised Jude.

"Yes. Tell my future," she replied. Urgently she guided Jude to the back of the carrier.

"What on earth are you doing here?" she whispered. "Dressed like *that*?"

"I've fled my Refuge."

"I thought you'd never leave."

"So did I," Jude agreed. "But we all have our sticking point, and I'd reached mine. I came to thank you for helping me."

"Did your report do any good?"

"Not that I've seen. Hopefully the right people will receive it in the end, but I didn't dare wait. That wasn't your fault though, and I'm very grateful to you. I wanted to be sure you were safe. Where are you moving to?"

"The Vale of York. Dad owns some land there. It was rented out, but the lease comes to an end this week. We've decided to claim it ourselves." Though the young woman tried to keep her manner businesslike, her tone suggested excitement. "Rick and Dad have been talking about it for months, but I don't think they'd have done it if I hadn't come back. Dad's college is still officially open, but most of the time, it's shut. The lecturers are paid by the class so he's not making much, and I haven't found work myself yet. We've decided to make a fresh start."

"What doing?"

"Growing vegetables. We've found someone to rent this place, and managed to get a travel pass. Our luck's begun to turn."

"If I'd known how hard things were," Jude said, "I wouldn't have troubled you."

"I'm glad you did," Linda replied cheerfully. "It made me feel better about leaving the Refuge. Until then, I'd been wondering if I'd done the right thing. Our family's part of a new wave of migration, you mark my words - not having to move like the squatters, but choosing to do so. If we stay in the city we'll starve. I know it'll be harder than living in a glass tower, but a lot, lot freer." She laughed with happiness. "There's not a lot to stay here for, is there?" she asked, looking round.

Jude saw respectability, and growing poverty. "No," she agreed.

"Come and meet my parents. Or are you in a hurry?"

"I'm trying to get to the north, but a few hours won't hurt."

"Then help us to eat up the scraps, and ride with us in the morning."

That night Jude ate until she begged for mercy. She felt confident enough of Linda's family to admit where she had come from, but not why. Besides, she did not want to put them at risk.

"A friend of Linda's is a friend of ours," Dr. Vass announced. Spoken in his deliberate, mellow voice, the cliché sounded true. "We're glad of your advice. It doesn't matter how many books you read. There's nothing like meeting someone who's lived outside the city themselves."

His daughter-in-law had finished feeding her baby. She looked curiously at Jude. "Do you think we're mad?" she asked.

"Yes," Jude warned. "But I think you'll make a go of it. It sounds like you've got fertile land, and having someone working it beforehand will help. You won't have to spend your first year grubbing up nettles." In contentment, she pushed her plate to one side.

Mrs. Vass could not stop worrying. "What do we do if the Smiths won't leave?" she asked.

"You'll have to be ruthless," Jude advised. "The government has decreed anyone reclaiming family land must be given support. If you have trouble, go to the police and demand an escort."

"But what will happen to the poor Smiths?"

"That's their problem, not ours," Rick insisted. "It's every family for themselves now, Mum. The land belongs to us. It's been in Dad's family for a century. Now we need it back."

Mrs. Vass sighed. "Yes, dear," she admitted. "If your father could have got that post with the Academy, things might have been different, but it wasn't to be."

Linda caught Jude's eye and winked. She had heard it all before.

"I'll tell you your fortune, Mrs. Vass," Jude said gently. "In ten years' time, you'll be successful market gardeners, with fields full of strawberries. You'll have a little stall outside, and a pony cart that takes vegetables to the market. It won't have been easy. You'll have had pests and frosts, and at first you'll have had to dig with old-fashioned spades, and carry water in buckets. But you'll have had a laugh while you did it. And in three years, Linda will have found a handsome young farmer, who's bursting to give you his tractor, in return for her hand."

Everyone laughed, though Linda looked a little mortified. "How did you know what I was thinking?" she asked. "About the man I mean, not the tractor."

"It was written in your face."

The following morning, they set off, very early. A steady downpour pattered against the carrier. Despite Jude's protests, Dr. Vass insisted on a detour, so that he could deliver Jude safely.

They passed several other groups reclaiming family land. Such newcomers were easy to tell from their clothes and makeshift tools. One man was wearing bathing trunks to hoe a vegetable patch. Another was pulling a handcart full of firewood. To Jude's delight, a little boy was sitting on top of the wood, holding a cord around his grandfather's waist like a rein. Both were laughing, though their thin, city suits were soaked. For a long time Jude savoured that image of hope.

Finally they neared the address Joel had given her. She was surprised to find it was marked on the map as an established farm. When she knew Joel's family, they had been squatters on an area of derelict greenhouses. Though they were restoring the greenhouses and growing enough to sell at the market, they could never have saved enough to buy a farm, unless it was very poor land.

"It's just beyond this ridge, "Jude called to Dr. Vass. "Drop me anywhere now."

"Are you sure you'll be all right?" Linda's brother asked.

"Of course. I expected to have to walk for another couple of weeks."

"It was the least we could do," Dr. Vass insisted. "If your friends aren't there, come to us."

Jude wiped herself a clear space and looked out. With so many of them in one carrier, there was a lot of moisture settling.

"Good luck," she said to Linda. "If you can't get work, it's pointless hanging round the city. Maybe you'll be able to return to your career later. Things are bound to get better soon." Impulsively, she gave the girl a hug. "There are nice people in the world," she admitted, "Even if I haven't met many of them lately. When I've got myself settled, I'll pay you a visit."

"Take care," Linda warned. "The Corporation can claim you back. Pretending to be a fortune teller won't work for ever." Unpredictably, she laughed. "I shall never forget seeing you standing there. It quite unnerved me."

Dr. Vass stopped the carrier near a security fence. "Can't we take you all the way?" he asked.

"You've come far enough," Jude insisted. "You need to be off the road before dark."

Getting out, Jude waited while Rick passed her bag down to her. With a strong smell of recycled fuel, the carrier turned round. Jude had a last glimpse of a young woman waving to her, then the Vass family were gone.

*****

Rounding a bend in the track, Jude saw Houghstones Farm beneath her. Even in the rain, it was clearly good land and well kept. She turned away, thinking she had mistaken the address. Then she saw a girl come out of the front door, and start calling the fowl.

Fourteen years ago, Lisa Denovitch had been little more than a baby. Now she was tall and straight, dark haired like Joel. In relief, Jude walked towards her.

Warily, the girl watched her approach. "Can I help you?" she called.

"I've come to see your parents," Jude replied. "Are they at home?"

Putting down the bowl of chicken meal, Lisa went indoors. "Mum - there's a wisewoman to see you," she shouted upstairs.

Dr. Denovitch came to the door. Her hair had gone grey, but her face was a pattern of good health and respectability. "Do I know you?" she asked Jude in concern.

"My name's Jude Shah. You were very kind to me when I was a girl," Jude replied. "I had five small children with me."

In amazement Dr. Denovitch stared. "But you belonged to the Corporation!" she said.

"I used to. Not now. I come with a message from Joel."

An expression of pain came to Dr. Denovitch's face. Anxiously she looked behind her. "He's not here," she replied. "We don't know where he is."

Joel's father appeared. "We don't talk about our son," he said curtly. After more than thirty years in England, he still spoke like a foreigner.

"I come from Joel, not to see him," Jude insisted. "Did you really believe the charge against him? Things are going on in the Refuges that would horrify you. Joel knew he had enemies who would discredit him. That's why he asked me to come, to assure you of his innocence."

"What did I say?" Joel's mother demanded, turning on her husband.

It was not a quarrel Jude wished to join, and nodding in farewell, she walked away.

She was a hundred metres up the track when she heard Lisa Denovitch running after her. "You must come back!" the girl shouted. "You can't just disappear!" Catching up with Jude, she stood breathlessly beside her. "Mum's been crying her eyes out," she said, "I think Dad has too, only he pretends he hasn't. How can you be sure my brother's innocent?"

"I worked with him in Border Seven. We were good friends before that. Ask your parents to tell you the story."

"They have, lots of times. It's because of you we own this farm."

In bewilderment Jude stared. "Why do you say that?" she asked.

"When the new Refuge was built, the Corporation paid us top price for our land - because we'd helped you. We couldn't have afforded this place otherwise."

Jude smiled uncertainly. In those days, SecureCity would not even have paid them market value for their land. There was no need. The Junta welcomed any new Refuge as a source of employment, and cared nothing for those it dispossessed.

"When did you last hear from Joel?" she asked the girl.

"Five weeks ago. He sends vouchers for my schooling, but the last lot didn't arrive." Lisa's voice caught. "Then we got this awful letter. It said Joel had been disciplined and struck off the medical register. After that, there's been nothing." Nearly crying, she searched in her pocket for a handkerchief. "I've never known my brother well," she admitted. "I was only four when Mr. Anderson took him on, but he's been very kind to us, and I like him a lot."

"So do I," Jude admitted. "Do your parents really want me to come back?"

"Please." Curiously Lisa looked at Jude's clothes. "Can you tell the future?" she asked. "Will I see Joel again?"

"I hope so," Jude replied gently.

That night, Jude sat beside the fireplace and ate lardy cake. Her hosts were equally hungry, but for information. Jude tried to find the right words. "I believe Joel's been imprisoned," she said. "He criticised management at Border Seven, especially when the old and sick were expelled. The policy was supposed to be temporary, but lots of people are being removed from the lobe. There's a whole shantytown of them, on the mud flats. Joel could be there, but I don't think so. He was too senior, and too likely to cause trouble. I imagine he's still in the Refuge itself."

There was a great deal more that could have been said, but Jude left it at that.

"We knew something was not right there," Professor Denovitch agreed. "Too many Refuge people are crossing to the city, and the water-folk have seen fires under the platform."

There was an awkward silence. They sat together, watching the flames.

"Joel's always spoken his mind," Dr. Denovitch said, shaking her head. "And he would have the courage to speak out. Not knowing what's happened to him is the worst. Not even Justice Anderson can find out."

"It's like the years of the Junta," her husband agreed.

Jude tried to piece together the story, without obviously probing. "Joel said one of the local landowners gave him a job," she began. "Was that Justice Anderson?"

Dr. Denovitch nodded. "In those awful times, there were lots of private armies, and word got around about what Joel had done. Even before he reached home, he'd had offers it was dangerous to refuse. He asked the Andersons for protection. They gave him food and shelter, then escorted him home, but with a letter inviting him to become one of their retainers -"

"We were dead against it," her husband cut in. "We wanted more for our son than serving in some warlord's private army. We'd had our careers taken from us, but Joel was born here, and we'd been giving him lessons regularly. He stood a chance of a scholarship. But then old Mr. Anderson himself came. He said his family needed to protect themselves, and Joel's local knowledge would be useful to them. In return, they would see he was properly trained, and if he wanted, let him continue with his studies. Joel himself begged us to agree. He wanted to earn his keep until the Junta fell and he could go back to school -"

His wife took up the story. "The trouble was, the Junta lasted longer than any of us had dreamt, and we feared Joel had become just another mercenary. But the Andersons kept their word, letting him do the lessons we sent him..." Her voice snagged, and she had to pause to control her grief. "Then Mr Anderson was appointed as a Justice, and asked to investigate the attack on the Refuge surveyors. He interviewed local people, and some of the older children in your party."

Jude recalled her child-care officer telling her to write an account of what had happened. "I think I was on a course then," she said.

"It took nearly a year, but Justice Anderson determined which tribespeople should be punished, and who should be rewarded - including us. It seemed to draw him and Joel closer, because he started to treat him more like a son than a retainer - got him a tutor, encouraged him to go to medical school. I suppose he was lonely. His brother and both his parents had died, and he was left with a great estate, and no family of his own. We didn't like Joel taking his name, but it gave him chances we couldn't, and it was clear Tom was genuinely fond of him. He was as broken hearted as we were when Joel joined the Corporation, but he needed the resources the Refuges could provide, and we all understood that."

"Tom?" Jude repeated. The name echoed in her mind.

"Mr Justice Thomas," Lisa replied and smiled. "But we know him as Tom."

Tom Anderson. Crumbling the last bits of her lardy cake, Jude stared ahead of her. Joel himself had told her the name, but she had forgotten it until now. Mrs. Gale had said a man called Tom could be Jude's natural father. If her brain had not been so sodden, Jude would have seen the link at once. "If you don't mind, I'll go to bed now," she said. "I'm very tired." Her voice sounded odd in her ears.

"Of course, my dear. If there's anything you need, just ask."

Afterwards, in a room smelling of lavender and clean linen, Jude sat on the bed with her head in her hands. So many facts that had seemed unrelated began to cohere. At first, Joel must have established himself with the Andersons on his own merit. Later, if Tom Anderson had somehow learnt that he was Jude's father, he would have felt grateful to Joel for leading her and the other children back home. The Corporation would not have paid for the Denovitchs' land, but Jude's real father might have done, as a reward for helping her. Then a year or so afterwards, when she and Gary described how Joel saved her from the Hawkboys, Justice Anderson's gratitude would have become respect. He could not claim his daughter, but he could treat Joel as a son.

She must have been meant to work it out. In everything else Joel had said to her, he had been scrupulously careful. When he mentioned Tom Anderson's name, he could only have been acting under instructions.

"Most of what I am, I owe to Tom Anderson..." How much did that include? Defending one of the Triumvirate at the station? The whole double life Joel was leading?

Jude recalled her illusion in the rehabilitation suite before she set off on her mission. "It's that unifier man!" a woman had shouted. "Reiver! Reiver!" the crowd had chanted. Everything else in that illusion had proved to have relevance. The Hawkboys had not only come from her memory, but were a threat she needed to consider before she crossed Leodis. Why should she dismiss the final words as mere fantasy? Or ignore the other peculiar messages she had received?

The rain had eased. A watery moon reflected in a small mirror beside Jude's bed. Picking the mirror up, she looked at her own features, trying to see the father she had never known. There was one more piece of information the illusion had given her. "I've seen you before!" the rodent woman had shouted, pointing at Jude's father. "You're Tuecer!" Then she had turned back to the crowd. "It's that unifier man!" she had shouted to them. "He'll give us water!" they had chanted in reply.

Tom Anderson and the Reiver leader known as Tuecer were one and the same. That was what Joel knew, and why he had been imprisoned rather than eliminated - in the hope that he would tell someone Tuecer's identity. Why? Because Tuecer was unifying the tribes and the sector councils, against the Corporation? No, not the whole Corporation, Jude reflected, but a corrupt group within it that was prepared to see England plunged into chaos rather than lose their income. The remnants of General Rowles' Junta were actively fermenting that chaos so that they could return to power. Both had distorted what Tuecer was trying to achieve, and painted him as a ruthless warlord who must be captured. A desperate struggle was going on, between what was left of the old tyranny, and a weak, newly elected government supported by men like her father, and Jude had become involved, without even knowing how, or why.

Trying to calm herself, Jude began to unbraid her hair. For a minute her instinct was to run, back down south perhaps, anywhere, so long as she could hide. She wanted nothing to do with warlords, or syndicates, or politics. If she could no longer serve her Refuge, she wanted no more than to make a living somehow outside, unnoticed. Then she began to feel ashamed. She could not pretend that what was happening was nothing to do with her. Already someone had tried to kill her. Someone else had tried to turn her into a smiling fool. Even if she hid, she would probably be found and it might be third time unlucky for her. Her fencing trainer used to repeat, "The best defence is to attack." Joel had said something similar: that he had to fight to defend himself. All right then, she would find a way of doing so.

At least she ought to learn what her father wanted.

Chapter Twenty Four

Nervously Jude waited at the outer gate until the security check was complete. "I would like to speak to Mr. Justice Anderson," she announced.

"Your name please?" a mechanical voice asked.

"Jude - Claudia Artuso's daughter."

There was a pause, and Jude looked around her. The house was old and beautiful, a gracious nineteenth century residence built on a headland above the ings. She was nervous to the point of fear. The mechanical voice crackled again. "Come through please," it invited.

As soon as Jude saw the terrace with its view over the water, she knew she would like the man who owned it. Little boats came and went across the horizon, while moorhens dabbled through the reeds beneath her. To the east, the huge tower of Border Seven dominated the sky, but if she looked west, everything was at peace.

A door opened behind her, and Jude turned towards the sound. Standing at the other end of the terrace was a dignified, middle-aged man. His hair was the colour of her own, but greying at the temples. Though his self-possession and clothes suggested high rank, there was nothing overbearing about him. He was as nervous at the prospect of meeting her, as she of him.

"I believe you wanted me to find you," Jude began. "I'm sorry I've been so long, but it took me a while to work things out."

For a long time Justice Anderson stood beside the conservatory door, considering her. Then, crossing the terrace, he came nearer her. "I assumed you wanted to stay with the Corporation," he said. "As your mother did."

Jude heard emotion in his voice, and closed her eyes briefly, in relief. "The Corporation didn't want me," she replied. "Today should have been the date of my death. All the while I walked here, I kept thinking how beautiful the world was. Even the insects crossing my path were the most fascinating things I'd seen." In embarrassment, she stopped, began to feel confused. The house was so big, and so beautiful, and she was dressed like a wandering fortune teller. "You did want me to come, didn't you?"

"I've wanted you to come for years, but it hasn't seemed right to ask you until now."

"I'm a bit untidy at the moment," Jude apologised.

Her father laughed. "You're all I could wish for," he assured her. Stepping forward, he held her to him.

In delight and relief, Jude let him do so, and for a long time they stood close, not needing to speak. Finally they sat on a swing seat together, looking over the ings. A cool wind promised rain, but under the shelter it was warm.

"When did you find out about me?" Jude asked.

"A long time ago. I knew from the start that Claudia had a child who might be mine, but she said nothing to me, so I respected her bonding." An expression of remembered loss came to Tom Anderson's face. "But ten years is a long time," he continued. "And Claudia grew to love her partner. When I contacted her, she said she wanted to stay with him."

As she walked from Houghstones Farm, Jude had tried to imagine the man she was about to meet. She had never visualised feeling compassion for him. "You didn't recognise me when you met her again, did you?" Jude asked gently. "I remember. It was very cold and I had my hood up."

"No, and she assured me you were Joachim's child. I think she was afraid I would take you from her - so I went away. A few days later I saw a news bulletin about your family surveying for a new Refuge, and from the pictures I knew she'd lied to me. That was just before the attack."

"You must have felt terrible," Jude replied softly.

"I knew Claudia had died, but there were stories about some of the children surviving, and being guided home by a local lad. I was desperate to know if you were one of them. When I talked to Joel himself, I found you were. Ever since, I've looked for notices about you - made discreet enquiries, watched your progress... You belonged to the Refuges and I accepted that. All I did was watch over you - until I discovered Maria Levant was using you."

In surprise, Jude was about to speak, but her father shook his head.

"Nothing is completely secret," he warned. "Travel arrangements have to made, passes obtained. The woman wanted the same things as we did, whatever her motives, so it made sense to support her - and help you. I would have wanted to protect you in any case, but personal feelings sometimes have to be ignored."

Jude recalled standing against the window while the Chief Secretary whispered orders. It seemed like years ago.

"I keep telling myself that about Joel," her father added quietly. "I had no way of knowing what we were up against, but I shall never forgive myself for involving him."

"I need to know what that involvement is," Jude replied. "And what we can do to help him."

Her father nodded. "First of all you need to eat something and refresh yourself. Then I'll take you to meet some of the people who are trying to trace him. Believe me - we're doing everything we can - but if you think of other ideas we'll welcome them."

In acceptance Jude watched a group of mallards dabbling around the jetty below her. She would far rather have been Joachim Shah's child - nice, sensible Joachim. It would have been a lot simpler, but her mother had loved this man first, and whether she wished it or not, she was his daughter. Besides, being a member of a pro-democratic group during the Junta was virtually a badge of honour. He must be worth knowing as a man, not just a father.

"You're listed as a warlord on the Refuge cyclopaedia," Jude remarked. "You're not, are you? I couldn't bear to think you were just after power and money, like the rest of them."

"I'd make a pretty poor warlord. All that strutting around and camping in the wet. I like to be comfortable, and use peaceful means to get what I think is right - not just for myself, but for those I care for..."

"Like funding hospitals?" Jude prompted.

"If that's what's needed. Someone has to help ordinary people round here, and I have money to spare - and influence. The sick aren't even safe in the Refuges now."

"You've heard about level 40?" Jude asked, nodding towards the tower on the skyline.

"It's more serious than that. There are rumours that the mud flats are to be cleared soon - 'so that Refuge members should not be distressed by the sight of the idle and uneconomic'... It's not clear where the people are going; all we've gathered is that it's 'a natural solution'. I imagine that's why Joel disappeared, because he wouldn't keep quiet about some proposal."

There was a long silence between them. It was going cold but neither wanted to move. Instead, they drew closer for warmth.

"Why did you choose the name Tuecer?" Jude asked at length.

"I read it in a book, and it sounded good."

Jude laughed. "And there's me trying to read all sorts of significance into it," she admitted. "But how did you get involved in all this political stuff?"

As if he were telling a story, her father began to fill in the history Jude had never known. Like other Reiver families, her ancestors had raided along the border for years, until in her grandfather's time they no longer had need. They had more than enough water. That was one resource the hills did offer, in increasing amounts. So her grandfather had exploited that resource, first from his own streams and then by buying derelict valleys nearby and turning them into reservoirs. It made him rich but got him into trouble too. About the time her father first met Jude's mother, the Andersons were caught up in an argument with the Junta. They wanted the southern cities to pay for the water they took, instead of just piping it away for free. When the Junta tried to silence them, they joined a group agitating for democracy, known as the Unifiers. Soon afterwards, General Rowles made it a capital offence to belong to any dissident group. Her father's older brother, Dan, ignored the ruling. Her father was more cautious, deciding he could achieve more by becoming a lawyer. He kept his head down, and obeyed the General's rules.

Jude could sense the pain such memories caused, and touched her father's hand in sympathy. In response, he sighed. "Ten years later, Dan disappeared," he explained. "It was the time of the purges, when people did just vanish. I hunted for a month and then Dan's body was dumped in one of our fields. I decided I had to fight back."

"Were you involved in the Uprising?" Jude asked. She was discovering she might have a hero for a father. People in the north still spoke with respect of the small band of men who had taken on the guards at a Leodis prison and triggered a revolution.

Her father merely nodded. It was clearly not something he talked about, and there was silence between them again. Finally he smiled. "They were heady times, Jude," he admitted. "We thought a brave new world would dawn once we'd got rid of the Junta. But it's been ten years now and the country is still in a mess, with everyone trying to grab what they can and no government lasting more than a couple of years. If things go on as they are, some army general is going to step forward and say they can sort things out - just like Rowles did thirty years ago. If the Refuges close, it will be inevitable. We need to negotiate a deal that keeps them open and shares their skills - and to get the tribespeople to work together instead of fighting. Basically all I'm trying to do is bang a few heads together."

It was definitely too cold to stay outside and the dark clouds across the horizon warned of an imminent storm. Unexpectedly, Justice Anderson got up, setting the swing seat swaying. "Come on! We both need a cup of coffee," he said.

The sudden change in his manner lightened the moment. "I could murder a piece of cake," Jude admitted.

*****

As they went inside the house, Jude looked round her curiously. There was little obvious sign of wealth. Antique books and pictures were the only luxuries, and they had been chosen for the pleasure they gave their owner, not to impress visitors. Standing on the tape stand was a holo-still of Joel on his graduation day, looking awkward and embarrassed, but happy. His presence was elsewhere in the room too, in a press release about Provene, and a small carving of a fox he had made years ago. Her throat going tight with grief, Jude picked up the ornament. It was unexpectedly good.

Her father asked the housekeeper to bring them coffee and cake.

"What you're trying do is common sense," Jude agreed as soon as they were alone again. "So why can't you act openly?"

"I do try to. But there's only so much I can do as Justice Anderson. The tribespeople assume any lawyer is acting for the government, and I wouldn't be able to enter the Refuges if it was known I was trying to make changes there. Besides, the last thing some elements want is stability. If I make too much noise - openly - I may well end up in the lake. By playing at being Tuecer I get ordinary people's confidence and some measure of safety."

His answers reassured Jude, though she still felt sick with nervousness at the implications of what he was saying. "Tell me one thing more," she asked. "Why did you put me through that unpleasant experience at Border Seven? It was you, wasn't it?"

"I had to know whether I could trust you. Friends in the Refuge set you - a few tests. I'm sorry if you found them distressing." Looking away, Justice Anderson sighed. "I never intended to risk your life," he said. "None of this affair has turned out as I planned. The Triumvirate should have taken some action by now. They have sufficient evidence."

"I wasn't able to deliver Joel's recording," Jude warned. "I had to hide it in my apartment after I returned to East Five. If you have anyone you can trust, get them to look in the games box in Dwelling 136b. But be careful. The syndicates have at least one of the Triumvirate in their pocket - Decider Anesto. It has to be him who ordered my imprisonment, and presumably my death too."

Sitting up quickly, her father looked at her in alarm. "We would never have asked you to go if we'd known," he said. "Oh Lord! Joel doesn't stand much chance if the syndicates have bought the Triumvirate too."

He rubbed his eyes in a tired gesture. "My father invited a boy to become a retainer," he said, "because he was impressed by his courage. I never dreamt he would become like a son to me - or that one day I would be afraid he would betray me." The storm had reached the ings, rain lashing against the bay windows. Crossing to them, he looked out. "And yet -" he added wistfully. "Part of me argues that we're worrying unnecessarily. Joel won't give any of us away. If I could help him without endangering others, or jeopardising an agreement that's about to be signed, I'd try, but there's no way of getting to him."

The lights of the Refuge had come on automatically, in response to the failing light.

"There may be," Jude replied thoughtfully. "Have you any idea where he's being kept?"

Opening the window, Tom Anderson stepped out onto the terrace, despite the rain. He looked towards Border Seven. "Somewhere inside the lobe," he replied. "On the night of the twenty seventh, Joel helped Maria Levant off level 40, and showed her the route under the platform. Levant tried to persuade him to come with her, but he refused, saying he had important work to finish. He's not been seen since, but the domestics tell us officials have been coming from Headquarters to question someone important. Joel's research has also continued. His assistant takes the credit, but it's doubtful she had chance to learn enough before he vanished. He may still be at work."

"There's a disciplinary area in every Refuge," Jude remarked. "Tell your sources to look for a corridor with permanent surveillance, and a high concentration of guards. If they find somewhere that fits that description, we know where to start."

A tray of coffee was brought in, with a plate of cake. It was all very civilised, contrasting starkly with their conversation.

"What resources do you have?" Jude asked.

"Enough for most things, but not an attack on a Refuge."

Smiling slightly, Jude shook her head. "I was just planning a little diversion," she said. "Something I've been thinking of for weeks. Part of my brief was to prove local management weren't doing their jobs properly - so that HQ would remove them. I kept trying to think of something dramatic that would force them to act, something like structural failure perhaps - because money for repairs was going into private pockets. We might manage that and get Joel out at the same time." Pausing, Jude relished the sweetness of the idea. "We might also get some of the people on the mud flats off too. The fit ones at least. And alert the city to what's going on before any elimination order's put into effect. That'd achieve an awful lot in one go."

"How?" An expression of amused anticipation came to Tom Anderson's face.

"By putting deteriorators under the platform. They would have to be in the right place. Too far one way, and hundreds of people would get hurt. The other, and we'd be twiddling our thumbs. If you've got a stylus handy I'll show you what I mean." Jude tried to remember the images on the personal entertainer Joel had given her. She recalled, too, the time she had sheltered under the lobe, waiting to cross the lake. "There are cracks in the steeltite supports under the platform," she said, sketching the lobe and the platform that supported it. "Here. And here - behind the shanties on level 40. If it rains much longer, the hydraulic mechanisms under the platform will come into action, lifting the lobe to keep pace with the water rising underneath. Like this -"

On her diagram, Jude added upward pressure lines. "Normally a few fractures wouldn't matter, but if one side of the platform rose, while the other jammed because the collars couldn't pass over broken steeltite, you'd get a lovely tilt. So long as you did it on the north side where there are no dwellings, you would hurt anyone, but you would cause quite a sensation. For an hour or so, you could walk in through the atrium, and knock on Joel's door."

Her father laughed. "No wonder they call you a trouble maker," he remarked.

Jude flushed. "I want to bring that lobe crashing down," she admitted, "but ordinary, innocent people would get hurt if I did. Those cracks wouldn't have appeared unless inferior materials had been used. The whole place has been built on corruption, and my parents died to make it possible." Anger had made her speak louder than she intended, and possibly give offence. "I'm sorry," she apologised. "I shall always think of Joachim as my father, even if you are too. Revenge is a bad motive I know, but I want to hit back, not just for what was done to me - but to my partner, Kurt, and Joel - and everyone on the mud flats outside... to an Adviser I knew - all the frightened people I heard on my rounds..." She could not go on, and closed her eyes to check her emotion. "I'd like to finish the job I was given, too," she added lamely.

For several moments, Justice Anderson considered the diagram. "It looks feasible," he agreed. "There would have to be an evacuation while the structure was checked and straightened. A lot could be done in the meantime." Taking the diagram, he smiled. "I'll discuss your idea with a few friends," he promised. "Now eat your cake."

*****

All that night it rained, waking Jude in the early hours. Absurdly, she found herself longing for the security of the menials' dormitory, and Feda sleeping beside her.

"You're never satisfied!" Jude said to herself crossly, and getting up, went to the window. A grey, streaming dawn was spreading across the lake, and towards the ings. The night-lights of the Refuge glowed in the sky, with a scattering of smaller specks around its base. From such a distance, the lobe looked like a mysterious, fairy-tale tower, a place of pilgrimage and desire. Jude had to remind herself that on the inside, it could feel very like a prison. For Joel, it was exactly that.

"May I come in?" a voice asked.

Starting, Jude pulled her robe closer round her, and answered the door.

To her surprise, her father was standing there, fully dressed. "I heard you were awake," he explained, "Can we talk? I have to leave early."

"You're going away?" Jude asked in surprise.

"For a few days - touring local sessions. I would have much preferred to get to know you."

"I'll leave too," Jude offered hurriedly.

"There's no need," her father replied, setting the tray on the table. "My home is yours. Stay here until I get back. You can trust my staff, but don't take risks. Your management is not convinced you're dead. They're looking for your partner too."

"Kurt? He got away?"

"Officer Hammel left your Refuge on official leave and hasn't gone back. He appears to be following your route. He's in Leodis now."

"How do you know?" Jude asked quickly.

"We have friends... The man could become a problem, Jude. Would you like him to be - discouraged?"

Jude could not reply at first. She was not sure what she did want. Then she thought of how Kurt had helped her, and what he had risked for her. "No," she said, "Not if you can avoid it. Just keep an eye on him, please. See he comes to no harm."

Her father nodded. "Haven't you slept at all?" she asked him.

"I'll sleep during the hearings. No one will notice." He smiled.

Looking out over the water, Jude watched the first ferry of the morning leaving the jetty. "I can't stay here on my own," she protested. "I didn't come expecting charity."

"And I wouldn't dream of offering it. I've left a stack of papers for you to summarise - if you would be so kind. My secretary is also behind with some statistical returns. Your first priority though, is deciding how to get into that place." Turning towards the lights on the horizon, Justice Anderson nodded. "My colleagues are happy for you to pursue your idea."

For an instant his voice caught. "Get Joel back," he asked. "But do it safely. A man known as Phil will meet you at eleven hours tomorrow. He's worked with Joel and has asked to help. Phil also knows the lake well and could make a crossing by canoe, if that's any use. Two other men will be made available to you."

Jude could not help smiling. "Three men should be enough for any woman," she replied. Then she was serious. "Could you get us Refuge ID?" she asked. "And maintenance uniforms for later? The surveillance will pick us up otherwise."

"Phil will organise such things."

Justice Anderson paused. "Are you intending to go in yourself?" he asked. "I've only just found you. I don't want to lose you again."

"I know my way around, including the domestic areas. Do you have anyone else who does?"

"No."

Sitting on the window seat, Jude drank her tea. The ferry had reached the first stop along the lake, and was picking up passengers for the Refuge. Feeling rather sick, she glanced at her timepiece. It was five thirty.

Drawing Jude to him, her father kissed her goodbye.

Chapter Twenty Five

At eleven hours exactly, Phil arrived at the meeting place, an old warehouse just outside the city. As soon as he entered, Jude was sure she had seen him before. Older than Joel - in his mid thirties perhaps - he reminded her of the leader of the canoe group she had watched crossing the lake. Though she had never seen that man's face, Phil's physique was similar, and as her father had predicted, he knew the lake intimately. If she went back to the clubhouse on the lakeside, she could probably work out his proper name, but that would be unwise.

He had brought a colleague with him, who could also be a member of the club, though his bulk would have difficulty fitting into a canoe. Introduced as Rexel, he was a powerful man, and looked as though he could guard half a dozen rescue parties. The third man would come later. Newman was an expert in metals and would advise on the technical side of things.

Jude was surprised by the softness of Rexel's voice. His heavy frame suggested a big booming tone, and the contrast was unnerving. Smiling, she nodded, and tried to hold on to reality. Both men were very polite to her. They could have been meeting to discuss a business venture, rather than an attack on a Refuge.

Since it had stopped raining, they went into the yard, so that they could look towards the lobe. "I've made a drawing of the lake and the area around it," Phil began. Clearly used to explaining things to others, he opened a hand-drawn map across the table. To keep the edges flat in the wind, he put a stone on each corner.

"As you can see, it's not to scale, but the islands and the platform are marked accurately. The ferry links are shown in green, and the supply ship and waste container routes in blue. These can vary a bit, according to the time of day and the tidal inflow from the estuary. In addition, there are several mud banks and currents to avoid. The safest and quickest crossing would be to this jetty, here. With the kind of diversion you have in mind, you could probably land a double-decker transporter and no one would ask questions, but leaving would be a problem. A couple of thousand people would be trying to pile on. The other obvious possibility is to land on Willow Island - here - and paddle a small boat across, but I doubt if Simeon would be in a fit state to paddle back."

"Simeon?" Jude asked, then remembered. "Of course -."

"We use pseudonyms at all times. Rexel and I both have an idea who our friend is, but we avoid using his proper name, in case it ever slipped out in front of others. Your pseudonym will be Nina."

Jude nodded. Her father had denied that he was any sort of warlord, but there was clearly an organized militia behind him, in which Joel had a respected position. "I gather Simeon's quite important to you," she remarked casually.

Phil replied with careful vagueness. "He's well respected, Ma'am. I've worked with him several times, and enjoyed doing so." Returning to the map, he stood looking at it, an expression of regret softening his face. "It may be partly my fault he's in trouble," he admitted. "There was an outbreak of fever in the city, and I knew he could help. I allowed myself to become emotionally involved in a project we were developing, and I traded on Simeon's' kindness."

Jude thought of the derelict hospital, and the clinic amongst the pigeons. "It's hard to turn sick children away," she remarked.

Startled, Phil glanced at her. "I don't know who you are, lady," he replied, "But you know an awful lot." Briskly, he opened another map. "We're wasting time," he said. "Let's get on."

His manner was so like a teacher's Jude smiled. A medical researcher and a teacher could find a lot in common, particularly with their shared love of water, and of the outdoors.

"This shows the Refuge platform itself," Phil continued. "It's easily approached, so long as you avoid the security fences. Half the water folk know the route by now. We could try taking a skimmer right under the lobe and entering via Level 40, but with such heavy rain there mightn't be sufficient headroom. In any case, we don't know whether our ID would admit us from that angle. Simeon's the only one who could have told us. I suggest we use the river to take us just under the platform, and leave Rexel to guard our means of escape, while Nina and I walk round to the front. No one will be asking questions."

"There's a path round the platform, to the front atrium," Jude volunteered. "Through the gardens. I should be able to find it."

"Then that's agreed," Phil replied. "We'll keep it to the three of us, or the skimmer will be too heavily laden on the way back. There'll have to be a second group to deal with the people on the mud flats. The lake's high for this time of year - it must have been raining a lot in the hills. I doubt if you could wade through the river under the lobe - particularly if you were sick or old. Group two will have to access the flats from the lake, landing on the north side of the lobe. The fences will be cut in readiness."

Glancing towards the lake, Jude saw what Phil meant. The water level had risen since she looked out of her bedroom window. There must have been a storm up river.

Then she understood. "They've opened the sluice gate!" she said in horror. "That's their 'natural solution'. At this rate, it'll only take a week before the mud flats go under, and the shanties with them. Those who don't drown will die of exposure. Of all the hateful - " She could not find words.

The two men looked at her, sharing her horror.

"Well, we'll have to intervene, won't we?" Rexel said finally. His control was admirable and brought all three of them back to business. "How are you going to get into the lobe - when everyone else is coming out?" he asked.

It was a good question.

"Use one of the contract workers' entrances," Jude advised. "They'll be the last to be allowed out - apart from the poor souls on Level 40." She felt the two men looking at her. "I was a menial myself for some weeks," she explained. "I know how little they're valued. Once our friend is safe, I'd like to pause long enough to open the dormitories. Then the last shall be first - for once."

"But how do we get Simeon round the platform?" Rexel persisted. "Even if he is alive, he's not going to be in a very good state."

The man could be very irritating, and very useful. "We'll take high energy medications and first aid," Phil replied, "But if necessary, you'll have to help him."

"Simeon won't accept help, Sir. He's a proud man."

"He'll damn well have to!" For the first time, Phil's friendship rather than professionalism took over. Then he regained command. "If it's humanly possible, our friend will walk round the platform on his own two feet," he insisted. "But if he can't, and he argues, stun him - anything - but get him onto that skimmer."

Rexel nodded. "And then where?" he said, thinking aloud.

"What about the water folk?" Jude asked. "There's a man called Yakhim who sounds pretty powerful. If you paid him, he might arrange for us to cross to one of the houseboats, and hide Simeon there overnight."

To her astonishment, both men began to laugh. "What's so funny?" she demanded.

"Yakhim is the biggest crook in this sector!" Phil answered, still grinning. "But evacuations come expensive. I'm sure he'd like to have a few boats ready."

"Can he be trusted?"

"Sure. You can trust Yakhim, so long as he's paid."
"I'll make contact with him," Rexel offered. "He knows me."
"Tell him Feda's friend needs help," Jude asked, smiling in embarrassment. "And ask him to thank Jonah for the ride."

*****

For three days it rained on and off. The lawns in front of the house became a lush, vivid green, and the ornamental ponds beneath the terrace filled with water. If the rain kept up and the sluice gates were left open, the hydraulic mechanism beneath the platform would come into operation soon, Newman predicted. Then they would see what happened. The deteriorators had worked well. The steeltite around the metal columns was brittle already.

Though Jude had plenty to occupy her, she kept drifting back to the bay windows, pretending to read, but watching the colossal mass still filling the sky.

"Shift! Damn you!" she prayed continually. "Or I shall feel such a fool." And lose Joel too, she reminded herself.

When the platform did finally move, all four members of Group One were standing on the upper floor of the warehouse, watching the lake.

"It's going!" Newman shouted.

A sullen, grinding sound came from the direction of the Refuge, as if metal were trying to pass over other metal and sticking. The tower of light still filled the sky, but it looked most peculiar. It was slipping to one side, like a monstrous over-laden Christmas tree.

Flinging the window open, Jude looked out. At once, the grinding sound became almost unbearable, like an animal crying in pain. For a second she stood in horror, appalled at what they had done. If they had got the calculations wrong, every dwelling along the western corner of the lobe would have collapsed downwards.

Then she ran down the stairs, and out into the courtyard.

The sky was black with cloud, a fierce wind driving sheets of rain along the jetty. The path downwards was slippery, and Jude grabbed the handrail to steady herself. Phil and Rexel were preparing for a rapid departure. Taking the hand offered her, Jude joined them.

The skimmer cut straight across the ings, with the grinding noise echoing around the lake ahead of it. From all directions, the lights of small craft were appearing, blinking fitfully across the rain-lashed water. Anyone who dared was setting off towards the Refuge, brought by concern, or mere curiosity.

Visibility was poor, and Phil veered towards the city so that they would approach the Refuge from the south. A collision with one of the other skimmers could be disastrous, and he had to cut power several times to weave through the sightseers. As they turned back, Jude could just make out figures moving around the Refuge's jetties, their shapes outlined by the searchlights that still swept the complex.

The undertow of the river was strong, and Phil stopped the motor so that they did not rush too fast towards the platform. The level of the lake was a good two metres higher than the last time Jude had approached, and the mud flats she had stood on with Feda were almost under water.

Suddenly the current strengthened. They were getting too close to the conduit. Urgently Phil put the skimmer into reverse. The vast array of lights hurtled towards them, drawing them to itself.

For an awful moment they thought the current would be too strong. Rexel grabbed hold of one of the pillars, and the craft slewed round. "Hang on!" Phil shouted. He struggled to keep the skimmer steady. It veered to the left, tipping alarmingly. With a fourth person on board it would surely have been swamped.

It took all three of them holding onto columns, or pushing against them, to get out of the current. By the time they were safely among the pillars to the side of it, they were badly shaken.

"If we'd gone over, that would have been the last of us," Phil said. "You did us proud, Rexel."

They moored the craft firmly, and left Rexel to guard it. The climb up the platform was still passable, but only by keeping to the highest parts of the mud flats. On the other side, on Level 40, people must be crowded against the platform, trying not to slip into the rising waters around them. With the aid of Phil's illuminator and the searchlights, they made their way round the outside of the complex, towards the gardens.

A few officials were running between the rose beds, away from the lobe. "The lobe's falling!" one of them shouted urgently. Others were trying to push a gangway across to one of the supply ships, and there was a great deal of shouting. Until the central controls were released, most people would still be trapped inside the lobe.

Anxiously, Jude looked upwards. For an instant she felt giddy, crushed by the weight of the tower above her. Though the angle of incline was less than five degrees, it would be enough to make the floors of the upper dwellings slope to the north. The swimming pools in the pleasure area would be slopping to one side. Shoes would be sliding across floors; coffee cups drifting along tables. At the very top of the lobe, the gradient would be sickening, accentuated by the swaying of the wind. It would feel as if the sky had suddenly shifted.

With Phil to clear a way in front of her, Jude turned into the domestic area, through one of the side doors. Judging by the shouting and banging further down the corridor, the menials' dormitories had indeed been locked. At so low a level, the tilt was scarcely noticeable, and those inside could have had very little idea what was going on. Quickly, Phil led the opposite way, towards the atrium.

As they entered, Jude paused in horror. The panic she and Kurt had induced at East Five had been bad enough, but this was of nightmare proportions. Every escalator and walkway was crammed with people from the upper levels. They were trying to push past residents from lower down, who had come out to see what was causing the commotion. Set at highest possible volume, the public address system was echoing around the marble. It could scarcely be heard. "There is no reason for concern," the automatic voice repeated. "Instructions will be given." Nothing could have been more irrelevant.

The scene looked, and sounded, like a scenario from a reality game Jude used to play, 'Inferno'. Several of the turbo lifts had jammed, their sensitive balance upset by the gradient. Their alarm bells rang continually. No one seemed to be making any attempt to control the crowds. Officials who should have been trying to restore order had deserted their posts, and were scrambling to use their exit IDs, on doors that were jamming with overuse and the unaccustomed gradient. In their nightclothes and carrying their most precious possessions in bags, the ordinary members of the Refuge were being left to fend for themselves. Some of the children were clutching toys. Jude would remember those teddy bears and dolls for the rest of her life.

"We'll never get though that lot," Phil shouted.

"Head back through the service buildings," Jude called. "And then up the far side."

They reached corridor 293b in less than ten minutes. The doors of some of the dwellings had been left open, revealing rooms in which sleeptime entertainment still played softly. A sprinkler had been activated in one, and was flooding the floor. Urgently they followed the curve of the corridor round, to the main lounge. A few people still remained there - a sensible minority who had decided the lobe was not going to slip any further, and that they were safer remaining where they were. "What's happening?" one of them shouted.

"It's stabilizing," Phil replied reassuringly. "No need to panic."

Corridor 293c was not recorded on the dwelling finder, but logic suggested it must be further on, past a waste collection area.

A whole section of lighting had failed. As far as Jude could see, Corridor 293c looked ordinary enough. Beyond it, however, was a sign warning, 'Security Personnel Only'. To her intense relief, the door under the sign had jammed slightly open, and Phil was able to force it further. It was time to pull the maintenance uniforms over their Refuge ones. The surveillance could still be working, and maintenance crews would be expected.

Phil directed the illuminator ahead of them. "Keep it away from our faces," Jude warned.

Then they stepped through.

The smell of confinement and despair hit them in the face. Behind them, the public address system still echoed in the distance, but in that dark, silent place, every sound was suffocated. The walls were coated in some sort of soft material that absorbed noise; the floor felt spongy underfoot. No window allowed light to seep in, or appeal to leak out.

"This place is full of pain," Phil whispered. "It makes my skin creep." He shone the illuminator up and down the corridor.

Cautiously they walked forward. One of the rooms was obviously a staff rest area, with refreshment centre and games tables. Another was an office. The third was furnished with a table and two chairs, one either side.

"The interrogation room," Jude remarked unnecessarily.

Next to it was a small, square room, completely empty. As soon as Jude entered, she wanted to leave. The floor had been scrubbed clean.

"What the Hell's been going on here?" Phil asked.

Jude dared not reply.

The whole place was deserted, but at least four cells had been occupied until an hour ago. Jugs of water stood on the table; body foil lay where it had been thrown in haste.

They walked on, down the corridor. It was totally deserted. Jude was aware of Phil's disappointment, as clearly as her own. Suddenly, as they rounded the curve, Phil put his hand on Jude's arm, drawing her back. A faint light shone ahead. He switched off the illuminator, and very carefully they approached.

At the far end of the corridor, was a small duty area. It was lit by a separate emergency strip. Tables and chairs had been left exactly as they were, scattered when most of the staff abandoned the area. Only two men remained. They were sitting at one of the tables playing Balzique.

It seemed such an odd thing to do. Bedlam raged outside, but the two men were staring intently at the tower of glass they were building, apparently unaware of the world beyond them. To compensate for the angle of the floor, they had put food containers under two legs of the table. One of the men wore a guard's uniform and had his back to Jude and Phil. The other man was in the drab blue of the recalcitrant. As if sensing that intruders were near, he looked up. It was Joel.

They had feared that he was dead; expected at least to have to carry him out of the lobe. Instead he was sitting with a drink beside him, playing Balzique.

He had lost a great deal of weight. Dark shadows shaded his eyes and hollowed his cheeks. Yet he still had the presence of mind to chat amicably to the guard.

It was several moments before either Jude or Phil could think what to do. Taking out his pacifier, Phil stepped forward. They edged their way nearer, though taking care to remain in shadow. Then Joel heard them. For an instant his concentration faltered, but he looked intently at the tower of glass floating above the table. His control was impressive.

"Your move," the guard said, unaware of the soft approach behind him.

Joel added another piece, holding the man's attention. His hand became unsteady, but otherwise he gave no sign of what was happening. Finally, Phil was near enough.

"My game I think," Joel said quietly.

"I might win yet," his opponent replied, and laughed.

"I don't think so, Harry. There's three of us, and only one of you."

The guard took a second or two to understand. Leaping up, he whirled round. In terror, he stared at Phil, snatched out his weapon, and pointed it at Joel.

"Don't be daft!" Joel warned. "The other two will hit you afterwards." Completely ignoring the weapon directed at his chest, he pushed his chair back, and got up. "I'll be off now, Harry," he said. "Thank you for your company."

The man was shaking, bewilderment increasing his fear. "Where do you think you're going?" he demanded.

"To my family. Which is where I suggest you go. Don't use the lift. You might get trapped."

The guard looked again at the group surrounding him, and tried to smile. "No sir, I won't," he said and put the weapon away. Clearly he was a sensible man and not given to pointless gestures.

"When they ask you afterwards, say I just walked out. Don't mention my friends. They might come and find you otherwise."

"No sir - I mean, yes..."

"Goodnight, Harry. Off you go."

Not stopping to reply, the guard left.

"You took a risk letting him go," Phil pointed out afterwards.

"He was a decent bloke, doing his duty." Taking a last drink from his glass, Joel stood up. "I thought I'd better hang around," he added. "I didn't think the sudden tilt could be natural."

"We have transport waiting for you," Phil replied. Like Jude, he watched Joel nervously, unable to interpret his manner. It was too quiet. "Will you be able to get to the river?"

"Of course. I need to call at my laboratory first. It won't take long."

Bending down, Joel picked up his jacket from the floor. As he straightened up, he suddenly swept his arm over the table, sending the pieces of Balzique flying across the room. Glass splintered everywhere. The noise shattered the silence, making Jude start violently.

"Let's get out!" Joel said coldly. "Before I break the whole place."

Then he turned and walked down the corridor.

*****

They left the way they had entered, through an unassuming door. People must have walked past that door a million times, Jude thought, without realizing what lay behind it. For a few seconds Joel stood frowning into the brighter light. He considered the plain, unlabelled entrance. "What's the old saying?" he asked. "'Abandon hope all ye who enter here'?"

"I dunno," Phil said uneasily. "How do you get to your laboratory?"

By now, the whole corridor was eerily quiet. No one challenged them as they took the rapido down to level 127, and followed Joel to the laboratories. Though emergency striplights had activated, the main ones had gone out. The infection lock was still working, however, and Joel keyed in his code to gain access to the hydroponics area beyond.

As the door closed behind them, the emergency strip went out, leaving them in darkness.

"Put a light on!" Joel shouted.

The sudden darkness had startled them all, but the note in Joel's voice was of sheer terror. It went to Jude's heart, suggesting how much he had endured. Urgently Phil put his illuminator on, and shone it towards the door.

"Sorry," Joel said. "The darkness surprised me."

In concern, Jude glanced at Phil, but she said nothing.

In the hydroponics area itself, the air was cool and sweet, but water splashed everywhere, out of place. Drip screens were at an angle, and some of the hanging trays had slid to one side. Plants trailed down from them. For a moment, Joel stood in silence.

"I have to collect something," he said at last, and went through to his office. Carefully he propped the door open, so that he could not be shut inside.

Laid out on his workbench were six trays of seedlings - ordinary looking plants such as any genetic engineer would have lying around. Quickly he took the first, third and fifth seedling from each tray and wrapped them in a sealable bag. Taking out a drawer from his workbench, he turned it over, and retrieved three microdots he had taped to the underside. Finally, he collected a white coat from the hanger over the door, and put it on over the recalcitrant's uniform, to hide it. Becoming nervous as they waited, Phil and Jude watched.

Even then, Joel paused, looking at the ruin of six years' work. "Maybe I could have held on," he said. "The regime seems to have changed at the top. I might have been released." Picking up a fallen pot, he set it upright again. "But you can't predict these things can you? And I don't think I could have worked - not knowing what goes on a few levels away."

Phil put his hand on his arm. "Come on," he advised. "We need to get out."

As they went through the infection lock, Phil kept the illuminator on at brightest power, but even so, Jude noticed that Joel closed his fists tight.

By the time they reached the domestics' quarters, the banging and shouting had become frantic. "Let us out of here!" a voice kept shouting from the dormitory nearest the door. It seemed to come from underneath it, as if someone was lying down, trying to see out.

Some semblance of order was appearing amongst the crowds in the gardens outside. Security officers and some senior officials had appeared, and lines were being formed near the jetties, to await the evacuation being urgently arranged by the city authorities. In the darkness, the scene looked unreal, a nightmare of people and searching lights. For a moment Jude watched, working out the best route.

"Did you do all this?" Joel asked.

"The weakness was already there," Jude replied. "Just a few broken pillars... a little bit saved on materials..."

She nodded towards Phil. "You set off with Simeon," she whispered, then she ran back inside, taking care to leave the exit open.

Pausing at the door of the first dormitory she shouted, "I'm going to give you my ID. Open the other dormitories with it." Then, swiping the lock open, she shoved the disc in the first outstretched hand.

Running back outside, Jude joined the men on the path around the lobe. Slithering on the grass, they scrambled down to the platform. Rexel was waiting to help them

"Good to see you, Sir," he said and shook Joel by the hand.

It was only when they reached the entrance to the river that Jude realised they were likely to have a problem. Even in the light of Phil's illuminator, darkness filled the gaps between the pillars, and made menacing shadows on the mud flats. The river was making a roaring, sucking noise as it passed beneath the lobe.

"I can't go under," Joel said quietly.

"You have to," Phil insisted. "The skimmer's moored between the pillars. It's OK. The mud flats here are still dry."

Joel shook his head. "Go while you can," he ordered.

"Don't talk daft!"

"Bring the skimmer to us," Jude said quickly. "I'll stay with him."

"But you could be seen -"

"I'll risk it." She put her arms around Joel and kissed him.

Chapter Twenty Six

With so many craft around, Phil had had to weave back and forth until Jude felt sick. Joel was exhausted. Yet as he pulled himself up onto the old cargo vessel waiting for them, he declined the hand Newman offered him.

Jude had assumed her father would be there, and looked for him in disappointment. Then she realised she was being foolish. Her father's presence would have revealed too much. Instead an elderly stranger was waiting in the bow to receive them.

Introducing himself as Jacob, he shook hands with each of them in turn. "Tuecer sends his good wishes, and congratulations," he said. Putting his hand on Joel's arm, he indicated the gangway down to the cabin. "Come down and rest," he invited. "You'll be safe until morning."

"Thank you," Joel replied, with dignity. Then, turning to those who had released him, he nodded. "Thank you, all of you," he said. He had to concentrate to walk across the deck, but only a close friend would have known.

For a while Jude and her two companions talked to Newman, briefing him on what they had done and seen. In reply, he explained that Tuecer had asked them to stay on board until further orders were received. The boat would moor beside one of the islands until the lake was quieter, and then set off making deliveries, as if it was going about its business normally. To stay in one place too long might arouse suspicion. Group Two had been in touch. They did not yet know the number of survivors on level 40, but the flooding had not reached the dormitories. Even the outcasts living in the shanties had mostly managed to reach higher ground. It would take hours to get them all through the lobe.

Afterwards, Jude sat on her own against the stern. She had taken off the two outer layers of uniform, but her clothes underneath were soaked. Everyone seemed to have forgotten her. Rexel and Phil were talking quietly; Newman was lashing tarpaulin over a pile of boxes. There was no sign of the craft's owners. With tiredness and relief, she leant forward and cried, though silently, so that no one would know.

After that, Jude must have fallen asleep, for she started as a hand touched her shoulder. "Are you all right?" someone whispered.

In alarm, she sat up, and found Jacob beside her. "Yes. Just tired - and wet," she replied. "How's Simeon?"

“We’ve given him a shot of Quatrone, and a high energy solution. As soon as he’s had chance to recover we’ll leave the area. He needs to get away from this place.”

“Where will you take him?”

“Up country first of all - for a rest. I’m not sure after that. He’s asked to go to Lendal.”

“Why Lendal?”

“An important meeting is taking place there, in a week’s time. He was to have been one of the Refuge representatives. He fancies turning up unexpectedly, and seeing the reaction.”

“Politics?” Jude asked.

“As usual,” Jacob replied, and smiled.

Jude liked him. Looking at his face, she realised he was older than he seemed. His eyes had the wary expression of a man who had seen a lot of trouble, and learnt how to survive. He had probably lived through the chaos that led to the General Rowles seizing power, as well as the Junta itself. And now he was her father’s representative.. He didn’t give up easily.

“Good luck, whatever it is,” Jude replied. Then she paused. “Don’t expect too much of Simeon,” she advised.

“He expects too much of himself.” Sighing, Jacob watched the lights crossing the horizon. “Did he tell you anything on the way?” he asked.

“No. He can’t stand confined spaces, or the dark, but we could only guess why.”

The line of Jacob’s face showed in the lamp near him. Anger tightened his mouth. “We’ve arranged for a doctor to come across first thing,” he replied. “Tuecer wants a report of what was done. Someday soon, we’ll bring the Corporation to account.”

In the distance heavy transporters were crossing towards the Refuge. Dozens of smaller craft were heading from the city harbours too, families coming to the assistance of their relatives. Those who were collecting the old or sick would have some unpleasant surprises, Jude thought sadly. They would find them distraught and half starved, but at least they had been saved. What was to be done with them afterwards was another problem.

“I’ll have to go now,” Jacob added. He dropped his voice so that not even Phil would hear. “Your father asks if you want to come back with me.”

Carefully, Jude considered her answer. “It’s risky having me in his home,” she pointed out. “People are bound to ask who I am. I’ll go to Lendal and keep an eye on Simeon.”

The old man smiled. "Tom thought you'd say that," he admitted. "He's sent you a travel pack and some clothes. I've put them in the captain's cabin for you. It's a bit cramped, but a tramper doesn't usually have ladies on board."

As he smiled again, Jude saw a likeness to her father. The old man could be her father's uncle, or an older cousin - and therefore a relative of hers, she realized in surprise. The idea pleased her.

Putting his arm round Jude's shoulder, Jacob drew her to him. "Take care, my dear," he said. "No one could have asked more of you. I'll rejoin you tomorrow evening."

"Shall I see my father at all?" Jude whispered.

"Later - when we leave the lake and travel inland. He sends you his love until then."

Rexel and Newman appeared on deck. With a sense of utter, abiding relief, Jude thanked Jacob, and went to find her cabin. As soon as she had taken off her wet clothes, she stretched out on the bunk and slept.

*****

She seemed to have been there only a few minutes when a faint tapping woke her. "I know it's a daft question," Phil's voice whispered. "But is Simeon with you?"

"I don't think either of us would have the energy," Jude replied tartly, and opened the door. "You can't have lost him already!" For a second she panicked, then steadied herself. "He'll be on deck," she said.

"In this weather?"

"Wouldn't you want the air on your face?"

Understanding, Phil nodded.

They went up the ladder. A signifier lamp was fixed to the bow of the tramper, warning passing craft. It reflected across the deck, and onto the stack of boxes. Joel was lying in the shelter of the tarpaulin, asleep. "Let him be," Jude whispered. "We'll put some foil over him."

"He's not safe. If he gets up, he might stumble overboard."

"I'll stay with him until morning, and keep an eye on him."

Quietly they laid the foil over Joel. Even so, they woke him. Starting violently, he sat up. Being woken in the night was something else he had learned to fear.

"It's OK," Jude said. "Just us. You're going to get cold."

A cutter passed by, its wash setting the tramper rocking. Joel nodded and stretched out on the deck. Within minutes, he was asleep again.

Wrapping herself in another sheet of foil, Jude settled against one of the boxes. In the faint red light, she watched the man beside her. The collar of his jacket had pulled back as he laid down. Just visible under it was a dark bruise.

Jude leant forward, to see the mark more clearly. There was no doubting that jagged, oval shape. A restrainer had been pressed against Joel's neck, several times. 'Reasonable use' was permitted, and accepted by Refuge members. Some form of punishment was needed when removal of benefits did not deter, or a member became violent. But to have left such a bruise, Joel's punishment could in no way have been reasonable. Jude closed her eyes in anger. She remembered how he had watched over her, years ago, after the Hawkboys had attacked her in the barn. Then, she had cried in pain and fear, and he had held her to him, to comfort her. Now they were adults and she did not know how to comfort him. All she could offer was her presence.

For a long time Jude sat beside Joel, against the boxes, watching the river for danger. Her back began to hurt, pressed against the wood, but she did not like to move in case she woke him. As she sat, for the first time since she left Houghstones Farm she had time to think.

Her mind seemed to be revving into over-drive, recalling the events of the past few weeks and trying to make sense of them. Image followed image, sometimes blurring one into another. Often it seemed to be trivial details that her mind focused on: trying to lift a heavy bed frame while her supervisor shouted at her... Joel passing her a packet of capsules with something concealed in its base... Kurt talking to her while they swam up the pool together...

The thought of Kurt cleared her mind abruptly. He had got as far as Leodis. Why? His family were in the Mid Sector. She had expected him to go to them. Not for one moment had she imagined he would try to follow her, but he was clever and perceptive, a good security officer. He could well have traced her as far Linda Vass' home, guessing that such a contact would be useful. From their neighbours perhaps, he might have learnt where the Vass family was moving to, and set off further north to find them - and her. "Oh Kurt!" she found herself whispering. "Don't get into more trouble because of me!" In concern, she closed her eyes.

The rain stopped at dawn. As Jude opened her eyes, a fine mist was rising off the river, curling around the craft moored along the island. She was mortified to find she had fallen asleep, sitting upright against the boxes. Urgently she turned towards Joel.

He was awake, and sitting near her. "Don't worry. I haven't gone anywhere," he said. "I've been watching the lake. It's beautiful."

There was nothing particularly interesting about that stretch of water: a muddy bank, and the occasional tree, but Jude understood. "I spent a whole hour last month looking at ants," she agreed. "They were the most wonderful thing I'd ever seen."

The morning was cold, an autumn chill in the air. Jude drew the body foil closer round her.

"Come out of the wind," Joel invited.

Skimmers were passing up and down the channel, in the direction of the vast tower on the horizon beginning to emerge from the mist. The evacuation must have continued all night.

"Couldn't you sleep in the cabin?" Jude asked.

"I felt like I was suffocating."

In silence they watched the lake, while the old tramper creaked and groaned.

*****

At ten hours the doctor came. A thin, elegant man who had learnt not to ask questions, he was dressed in a fisherman's cape and hat that barely disguised his city origins. After introducing himself as Dr. Henry Reiss, he woke Joel gently and took him down to the main cabin. Half an hour later, he spoke briefly to Jude and Phil before leaving.

"Your friend is in a lot of pain," he warned. "Restrainers affect the whole nervous system. It's fortunate you called me so quickly. Whoever was responsible knew what they were doing. There's very little evidence, and it's fading fast. I've taken images though, and I'll make a full report of my examination. I'll also see a lawyer comes over before evening to take statements. We'll meet you at the old city harbour." He passed a packet to Phil. "Your friend will recover over the next day or so. Here are enough analgesics to last until then. Guard them well. They're worth more than that young lady can earn in a week." Then he was gone, climbing down into the waiting skimmer as carefully as if he were wearing his best suit.

"Who did you say I was?" Jude asked Phil afterwards.

He grinned apologetically. "The cook," he replied.

"Cheek!" Jude replied, smiling. Then she realized they had not eaten for over twelve hours. "I can take a hint," she added. "But my repertoire is small - eggs, or sausages and chips."

"Eggs for breakfast then, and sausages and chips for lunch," Phil suggested. "I could make us something myself, but Rexel needs me to help with the boat."

So once again, Jude found herself in a tiny galley, trying to provide food. At least it was something to do.

The rest of the morning was almost unbearably quiet. Several of the boxes needed to be off loaded. Picking one up, Jude risked going on shore. "Why are so many boats heading out to sea?" she asked an old man mending a net.

"Going round to Lendal," he shouted back. "The President's coming. Haven't you heard?"

So that was it. President Robins was still a popular figure in the north. Revered as the man who led the revolution against the Junta, with his game-star good looks and eloquence he was the people's choice to sort out the country. How much longer his government would survive depended on whether ordinary lives started to improve, or got worse, Jude reflected. And that depended on what happened to the Refuges... The President's visit could not be a coincidence.

"No, I hadn't heard," she replied, putting the box down on the quayside. "Is there going to be a procession or something?"

"A big show they say - to mark ten years of freedom. I reckon that deserves celebrating."

It did indeed, Jude agreed.

Presumably while the President was in Lendal some meeting was to be held, which Joel had made up his mind to attend. She would have to find a way of going, too.

They stayed moored as long as they dare. Then, just before noon, with a rumble of power, the tramper pulled away from its berth into the main channel. Newman was not an expert sailor, but good enough to steer them around the lake, while Phil and Rexel acted as crew. Putting on a sailor's cape and hood Jude went on deck, to help unload the cargo. Several police patrols were heading upstream, towards Border Seven. Fortunately they made no attempt to search any of the cargo vessels, assuming they were part of the evacuation. Far more likely to be of interest were the darkened skimmers that darted past, black marketeers, curious to see what they might get out of a Refuge in crisis.

Jude went below deck, to see if the movement had woken Joel. He was sitting on the floor staring ahead of him, with a stylus and note-taker in his hand. He appeared to trying to remember something. Softly she turned away, but he heard her and looked up. "I was trying to remember something," he said, "but my mind's sodden. I need a break."

Jude looked uncertainly at him. "Would you like a coffee?" she asked.

"Please. Bring one for yourself. I'd like to talk to you."

"How do you feel?" Jude asked as she returned with drinks. Joel's face was still thin and drawn, but the haunted look was leaving him.

"On the mend. I wanted to thank you. Any debt you may have felt you owed me is more than repaid." He took her hand and kissed it briefly. "I thought I was hallucinating when I saw you with Phil and Rexel. You're one hell of a lady."

"I don't feel much like a lady at the moment," Jude admitted. "More like a scruff."

"You look good to me."

For a moment Joel paused, considering how to word something. "Did your bonding take place?" he asked.

Jude flushed and shook her head. "Kurt helped me to leave," she explained. "On the morning of my party. There must have been an awful lot of wasted food."

"I'm glad you weren't forced into something you didn't want."

Jude could feel him assessing her reaction and flushed even deeper. "What were you trying to remember?" she asked.

"Doctor Reiss asked me to write a statement, but the details are jumbled in my mind. Besides, there are still things I can't say - but I have to be absolutely honest..."

"Are you going to bring a case against the Corporation?" Jude replied.

"If I can. It could be a useful bargaining tool."

"You intend to go back?"

"Not permanently. But I have to try to secure my freedom. I can't spend my life as a fugitive."

Jude nodded. She had been thinking about the same problems herself. "You stand more chance than me of getting a job outside," she remarked.

"If I tell people about those, I should get work." Joel looked towards the seedlings arranged around a bowl on the table. "They don't look much, but those bits of green are worth a fortune."

Puzzled, Jude looked towards them too. "You finished your project?" she asked.

"The day after you left. Fortunately, I didn't tell anyone - as insurance. I put a couple of timed glitches into my programmes, and fiddled my results. It bought me several weeks."

There was a pause between them. "Phil told me you visited my parents," Joel said afterwards.

"Yes. They were very grateful - and very good to me."

"Thank you."

For a few seconds Joel wrote something down while he could remember it. Then he frowned in concern. "Oh, Lord! I didn't have chance to send Lisa her school vouchers," he said.

"Your brother's paid the bills," Jude assured him. "He's doing well I gather."

"Yeah - I'm proud of my kid brother."

Once again, Joel recorded dates and names. Then he looked up and took her hand awkwardly. "We need to sort things out between us, don't we?" he asked. "I'll try to make space for us."

Nodding slightly, Jude turned to go. Then she paused, examining the plants in their bowl. "I hate to say this," she began carefully, "But whatever these plants are, the Corporation will claim them. You developed them while a member."

"I'm aware of that," Joel replied coldly. Then he apologized. "I'm sorry, Jude - it's a valid point. I could sell to the highest bidder, but if I did, I'd be running for the rest of my life. I shall try to get the patent, in compensation for the way I was treated. The rules of discipline were broken, and what for? - because I wouldn't agree to their plans for level 40? It would have been against my oath - and any principles I have left."

If the Corporation had hoped to silence Joel, it had failed.

Chapter Twenty Seven

Newman warned them that a representative from Tuecer was about to come on board. He wanted to speak to Jude and Joel. The rest of them would keep out of sight, so that no identifications could be made on either side. Ten minutes later, a darkened skimmer came alongside - a typical blackmarketeer. A figure reached out, and climbed the ladder that had been lowered to him. Waiting on deck, Jude watched.

"Any trouble?" the man asked. He was dressed as a trader.

"None at all," Jude assured him.

"How's Simeon?"

"Getting better, physically at least. He's recording evidence for Dr. Reiss."

The man nodded. "I've brought you some bits and pieces," he said, "to help pass the time. Let's go below."

As soon as they were in Jude's cabin, she recognized her father. She nearly laughed out loud in delight.

"You look surprisingly well," he remarked. "Considering what you've been up to. You've done very well, too. With all my heart, thank you." Opening a box he had brought with him, he took out an art screen and stylus. There were also two bundles of clothes, one for Jude and another for Joel. As he passed them to her, Justice Anderson smiled. "I had a visitor today," he said. "A young woman called Carrie."

"Carrie?" Jude interrupted in surprise. "How is she? Was Mark with her?"

"One question at a time," her father replied. Sitting on the bunk beside her, he tapped her nose. "Your friend and her partner turned up for your party. They found you'd apparently committed suicide. It put quite a dampner on things. Officer Hammel was distraught, so the guests went home - except for Carrie and Mark. They used the opportunity to disappear. Some friends of Mark's have been hiding them since. Carrie remembered contacting me about Joel, and thought I might find them work. I had to admire her cheek."

Jude laughed. "And can you?" she asked. "Find work?"

"I imagine so." Glancing out of the porthole towards Border Seven, Justice Anderson shook his head. "The Corporation's loss is our gain," he added. "The brightest and best are leaving every day." Taking her hands in his, he looked at her intently for a few seconds. "I need to talk to Joel," he said. "I'll come back to you before I leave."

After he had left her, Jude looked through the things in the box. There were even shampoo and a file of body oil. Delighted, she fetched a bowl of water from the galley and washed her face and hair. Then she smoothed oil over her skin, and felt human again.

The old cargo vessel was passing a settlement on the estuary bank. Children were diving from a small jetty, their laughter as bright as the sun on the water around them. For several moments, Jude watched them in pleasure. Then she took up the stylus and art pad her father had brought her, and began trying to draw the view from the porthole. Through the flimsy bulwark of the cabins, Jude could hear Joel and her father, talking softly. At one point there was quiet laughter. That they could laugh in such a situation suggested how deep was the bond between them.

Half an hour later, her father returned, knocking quietly on her cabin door. Before she could put it away, he had seen the drawing, and looked at it curiously. "Your mother could draw," he remarked. "She could have been an artist..." With a wistful expression, he glanced out of the porthole.

"I've never drawn for pleasure before," Jude admitted. "Just faces, for identification; maps, that sort of thing."

"I hoped you'd inherited Claudia's talent," her father replied. Abruptly he turned back to her, businesslike again. "I have a proposal to make."

In surprise Jude looked up. "Propose away," she invited.

"I would like to acknowledge you as my daughter, legally. I've dreamt of it for years, but it's partly self-interest, too. I've been asked to join the government as Chief Justice for the northern sector. It would be - let's say - difficult - if the opposition got hold of a scandal against me. If I acknowledge you before I accept the post, I should forestall that. I'll do it carefully and not until I know we're neither of us at risk. Once I'm in the cabinet, Tuecer will disappear and I shall be boring old Justice Anderson."

In surprise Jude considered her reply. She had never imagined such a situation.

"What do you say?" her father asked anxiously. "I know it's a lot to ask. It will affect your mother's reputation at least, if not yours."

"I would feel bad about damaging my mother's memory," Jude agreed. Then she thought about what Mrs. Gale had told her, and about what she herself recalled of her mother. "But I can't help feeling she chose comfort instead of honesty," she added. "When she went to you instead of her official partner, she made a decision. She should have followed it through, however much trouble it caused. She could have left the Refuge. It was possible then. "

"Is that a 'yes'?" her father asked.

"I think so."

Justice Anderson smiled with pleasure, his whole face softening. Putting his arms around her, he kissed her cheek. "I like having a daughter," he said.

For a while they sat on the bunk, talking about the timing of his announcement, and what form it should take. Then Justice Anderson looked at his timepiece and got up. "I must go," he said. "There's something else I should tell you first, though. If I do join the government, it'll be impossible for me to manage the estate. I've asked Joel to take over. That will include opening the Oldcastle Hospital again, and other projects I've started. Joel's agreed, so long as he can get his freedom from the Corporation." Tom Anderson's eyes betrayed anxiety, but he continued lightly enough. "And so long as things go our way over the next week. If the Refuges refuse to open up, the government will ultimately fall and personal plans will be irrelevant, but let's live in hope."

In increasing disbelief Jude nodded. Awkwardly she offered him her hand in a gesture of agreement, and her father took it and held it in both of his.

"Now to more immediate things," he continued. "We have two days before it's time to go to Lendal. Joel's asked if he can take you a walk, to somewhere he and I both love. It's to the north of here, so you'll be travelling overnight. On the way back, you'll be picking up a guest - Maria Levant. She wants to see you. I'll understand if you refuse. She's shown very little concern for your welfare till now."

"She couldn't afford to," Jude acknowledged. "What does she want?"

"To see you're safe. If you're willing, we'll bring her to you. Take care what you say, though. Officer Levant is an important ally, but you never know who you can trust. She's been asking after Joel - though she knows him only as Simeon. It'd be wise to keep it that way."

"She worked the link out herself," Jude warned. "It was on a list of names she gave me."

In alarm, Justice Anderson paused. "What did you do with that list?" he asked.

"Destroyed it of course. It probably saved my life, though, and she took a risk getting it to me. I can't say I liked the woman, but I think we can trust her."

Her father nodded, and turned to leave. Then he paused again. "See if you can talk some caution into Joel," he asked.

"I doubt it," Jude replied. "I'll try -"

Her father sighed. "He's never been any different," he agreed. "He makes up his mind he has to do something, and goes ahead, whatever the odds. But there's always a last time..."

*****

At seventeen hours Dr. Reiss met them at the old city port. Looking uncomfortably around him, a young man clambered aboard after him. He was not at all happy after a rough ride on a skimmer, followed by a scramble up a ladder. The old tramper rolled slightly, and he sat down as quickly as he could. Even so, he was businesslike and thorough, introducing himself as one of Justice Anderson's assistants.

There needed to be witnesses he insisted, both to the recordings he would make and to verify any written statements. All the evidence would be given to the local judiciary. Justice Anderson had a reputation for pursuing investigations without fear or favour. Confidentiality would of course be observed, unless there was a public inquiry. Even then, witnesses' identities could be concealed if the court thought they might be in danger.

Phil and Rexel were busy casting off the moorings and Newman was on the bridge. Jacob had not returned. The doctor looked at Jude. "I'll act as first witness," he offered, "but we must have a second. Would you mind, my dear? You won't have to do much: just confirm written notes haven't been tampered with, and validate the recordings."

Jude hesitated. It would put her at risk, but Joel's evidence could be vital. "I'll sign with a pseudonym," she said, "but give you my identity in a separate statement. Please don't reveal it unless you have to - or the country's sane again. "

In surprise both the lawyer and doctor looked hard at her, then nodded.

Together they went below to the main cabin, where Joel was waiting for them. "Do you have to do this?" he asked Jude in concern.

"No one else is available," Jude replied quietly. She noticed the plants in the bowl had gone, presumably taken to safety by her father.

"You don't have to read the pages," the lawyer advised her. "Just sign that you saw them handed to me, and that they haven't been altered in any way."

Joel had recorded names and dates, and described what had happened to him on each date. As she took the pages Jude tried not to read them, but she saw enough to make her feel slightly sick. The cabin was damp and cold, and she began to shiver. Pulling her cape closer round her, she added her signature to the doctor's at the foot of each page. Both he and the lawyer were taking a terrible risk, too, she reminded herself. The atmosphere in the cabin was heavy with nervousness.

The lawyer made the initial announcements of date and time, and Joel confirmed his personal details. Then, standing looking out of the porthole, he recorded an account of the past six weeks. At first he spoke with studied calmness, as if he were giving a report to colleagues:

"On the afternoon of 9th August, I was called to a meeting of senior personnel at Border Seven to discuss the problem of uneconomic members. I've listed the officers present. Management asked us to ratify a policy of expelling the elderly and sick onto 'level 40'. 'Level 40' is the codename for the mud flats around the Refuge complex, and the policy has been in force for some months unofficially. Together with Officers Hemmingway, Tallin and Fox, I voted against the motion, arguing that it was against Refuge rules, let alone human rights. We were in the minority."

The lawyer interrupted. "Can you pause a minute?" he asked. "I need to adjust the recorder." Then, when he had done so he added, "Please continue."

Still with his back to them, Joel did so. "That evening, I had an argument with my superior, Medical Officer Allerton. The following day I was charged with insubordination, and confined to my quarters for two weeks. The sentence was excessive, and clearly meant to shut me up. When the two weeks were over, an officer from Public Relations asked me to sign a document endorsing the exclusion policy. He said I was well respected, and my support would reassure others. If I didn't agree, I would be charged with working against Refuge interests."

Clearly Joel had rehearsed his evidence, but he remained at the porthole so that they could not see his face. "I had been to the dormitories on level 40 as an official visitor. I couldn't support leaving people to die out there. So I refused to sign, and tried to warn some of my colleagues. Within hours the enforcers arrived..." For the first time his voice became unsteady and he had to pause to regain control. "They told me my career was at an end if I didn't do as I was ordered, and put me in solitary confinement for ten days - to think about my future."

There was silence, broken only by the lapping of water against the boat's hull.

"Please go on," Dr. Reiss said. "We haven't a lot of time. What did you do then?"

"Sat in the dark trying to evaluate costs and benefits. If I completed my project, I might save a lot of lives, but to support what was happening on level 40 would make it possible elsewhere - in other Refuges. I couldn't decide, so I played for time. I pointed out that I had a patent almost ready, which could earn the Corporation a lot of money. After that, I was allowed to return to the laboratories during the day, but ordered to train my assistant to take over from me." By now, Joel's voice was going hoarse with tiredness and strain. "I owe a great deal to Delia," he added. "She was perfectly capable of taking over from me, but she spun everything out. When things got really bad for me later, she did her best to help..."

Getting up, Dr. Reiss offered him a drink of water. "Come and sit down," he advised.

So Joel sat on the floor leaning against the cabin wall, though with his face still in shadow. "It got bad after Maria Levant was missed," he said. "One of the old people on level 40 had been babbling about ghosts disappearing under the lobe, and Security realised someone must have helped her to escape. Apparently she has supporters in every Refuge, and because I was opposing management, it was assumed I was one. Two officials from HQ arrived to question me - I believe the woman was called Blakney, but I only knew the man as Dave. That was eight days ago I think, but my sense of time after that is hazy."

There was so much conveyed in that final sentence that Jude closed her eyes. The sound of the sucking and lapping of water became irritating, and she wanted it to stop. Instead, it grew louder and faster as the wake of a passing craft hit the hull.

Finally, the lawyer prompted Joel again. "Tell us some of their questions," he asked.

"'Who is Maria Levant working for?' 'Who supports her? Inside the Refuges? Outside?' 'Was it you who led her under the lobe?' They went on and on with the last one. For some reason they got it into their heads that I was the one who had helped her."

The lawyer was about to say something, but stopped himself.

"Each session got nastier," Joel continued. "I've recorded details in my notes. I don't want to say them now. Then something must have changed at HQ. Two days ago, the interrogators gave me one last going over, and left. After that, no one seemed to know what to do with me. The local guards had clearly been uneasy about what was happening, but didn't dare challenge it. Left to themselves, they treated me quite well. When the lobe began to tilt there was no one to stop me walking out."

Once again, the lawyer checked his recorder. "Do you have anything more to add?" he asked.

"No. The details are in my notes."

There was silence again, while the old boat pitched and rolled in another passing wake.

"Funny in't it?" Joel asked. His voice had taken on a harder note. "I wanted to hate the whole lot of them, but I couldn't. The guards were just ordinary blokes keeping their heads down. It's the two from HQ I want to see swing."

*****

After Dr. Reiss and the lawyer had gone, the boat plodded on, towards the mouth of the estuary. Then under cover of darkness, it changed direction and pulled back to shore, to one of the muddy inlets that surrounded the lake. A water taxi was waiting there, moored in the shadow of a pier and without lights. There was no sign of the owner.

Joel had slept most of the time after Dr. Reiss and the lawyer left, but now he woke and knocked quietly on Jude's cabin door. "Will you come with me?" he asked. "I could do with your company. It'd take my mind off things."

"Of course. If you want... Where will we be going?" Jude asked.

"Up river. It'll take most of the night. In the morning, if the weather's good, we'll take the day off."

With Phil and Rexel, they transferred to the waiting craft. "I suggest we both get some sleep," Joel said. "Rexel will drive, and Phil will keep watch."

In relief, Jude settled down in the cabin.

The slowing of the craft woke her. It was dawn, and they were pulling into a small natural harbour. Dense woodland grew right down to the edge of the shingle. "Are you awake?" Joel asked. Gently he pushed the hair from her face.

Stirring, Jude found she had been lying with her head on his shoulder. "Just about," she replied.

"We'll have breakfast on shore. Phil and Rexel will come with us to see we're safe, but we can have a walk on our own for an hour or two - if you want. We're in the Disputed Lands, though, so we do have to be careful."

Helping each other down from the craft, they crunched over the shingle, towards a path that led into the woodland. Joel clearly knew the way.

"Where are we going?" Jude whispered to Phil.

By now he trusted her enough to answer. "A hiding place arranged by Tuecer. I've been here twice before, on training sessions. There's a house built round an ancient tower. It belongs to one of the Reiver families who farm the water. Rich city folk can rent it and play at living rough. Tuecer books it sometimes for more serious things."

They came to some high metal gates. Early morning sunlight glinted either side of them, suggesting a fence ran right through the woods. "Don't touch the fence. It's live," Joel warned. Then he put his palm flat against one of the crossbars, and after a brief pause the gates swung open. "Come on through," he invited. "You have thirty seconds."

All four of them walked quickly through the gates.

The path widened to a rough track. Autumn was beginning to touch the birch trees with yellow, but the morning was a beautiful clear gold, warm in the clearing either side of the track. Even though they had right of passage through the area, Phil and Rexel were wary. Both were clearly relieved when they were well out of sight of the coast.

Climbing steadily upwards, they walked deeper and deeper into the forest. Light barely filtered between the densely packed trunks, though it splashed gold down the cleft of the track. There was the sound of water on all sides, trickling, oozing, swashing down ditches or over stone, but rarely seen. Once a flash of pipes startled Jude, and she could just make out the shape of a tank set in the earth. The forest was a living reservoir, a catchment for the rain that soaked the area most of the year. It was that brackish gold that gave the wiser Reivers power... and had presumably built her father's beautiful house overlooking Border Seven, she reflected, and would reopen Oldcastle Hospital. No honest lawyer could make such wealth by the Law alone.

Suddenly they were above the forest, onto bare hills. Tucked against the side of a valley stood an ancient stone building, more like a fortified tower than a farmhouse, with views across kilometres of heather and sky. The rear of the tower burrowed into the hillside, while the front windows looked straight down the valley. Even the cattle yard was protected by a marshy area that came right up to the stone walls. A livid green, the bog was covered with tussocky reeds and grasses. Out of them oozed a stream that meandered under a gate, and down what had once been a track. It would be impossible to approach without being seen. They could spend the day there safely.

Since the track was so wet as to be virtually impassable, they walked the last kilometre straight across the moor, beside a line of windmills that whirred quietly above them. By the time they had picked their way across the marsh, the sun was flooding the top of the ridge with light, and they were hungry and tired.

Though sparsely furnished, the main house was comfortable. Food and water had been left in the safe, and there was wood set in an old fashioned grate ready for a fire. Ravenously hungry by now, they ate breakfast together outside, sitting in the shelter of the courtyard. On the moor beyond, grasses blew gently in the wind, rustling and breathing. A flock of rooks crossed the skyline, cawing, but otherwise nothing disturbed the peace. After the confinement and anxiety of the past weeks, the beauty of the hills moved Jude almost to tears. She visualised the crowds and danger awaiting them in Lendal, and wished they could stay there forever.

It had not always been so peaceful, Jude reminded herself sternly. Fifty years ago, the Reivers who lived there had been hunted criminals. The tower would have been their hiding place after they had raided the farms over the border. Life then was cold and raw and violent - as it was still for many of the borderers, unable to accept that collaboration was needed now, not resistance. It was one thing to come on a holiday, in daylight, but she would not like to live in such a place, without the comforts of her dwelling.

Once again, Jude found herself thinking of Kurt, recalling how pleasant it had been to play badminton with him, or just to sit in the gardens talking. She was aware that she was turning two ways mentally, away from the restrictions of the Refuge, and yet back towards its safety. Joel had made his decision and would leave if he could, but what would she do?

"I'm going for a walk," Joel announced, getting up.

"Will you be safe?" Rexel asked. "What if tribespeople see you?"

"We have no enemies here. They can't cross the fence." Turning to Jude, Joel offered her his hand. "Do you want to come?" he asked her. "The fresh air will do us both good."

Nodding, Jude let him pull her to her feet.

They set off through an ancient gateway, between even older stone walls. A stony path led upwards, towards a smudge of trees that marked the line of a beck. Jude was not used to walking so far in the open, and at first could not overcome her fear of attack. "It's all right," Joel reassured her. "This is one place we're safe." He paused, looking back across the moor. "But I'd forgotten how steep it is."

"I get the impression you've been here lots of times," Jude remarked.

"A lifetime ago I trained here. I was the youngest, but I dreamt I could earn enough to go to college, and that kept me going. Your grandfather bought this estate forty years ago. He developed it to make a living from the water, and to train a private army to defend what he believed in. He was no more suited to be a warlord than I was to be a mercenary, but we both made as a good a job of it as we could."

"What was he like?" Jude asked curiously.

"I only knew him for two years, till he died. I found him generous and kind, but determined. He fought the Junta passionately, as your father did."

They set off again, walking in a comfortable silence until they reached the trees along the beck. "Do you mind if we rest here?" Joel asked. "I'm still a bit shaky, and I need to talk to you on our own."

A grassy bank was catching the sun, though hidden from below by the trees. Taking off his jacket, Joel spread it out for them to sit on. For a few quiet moments they watched the sky and the hills. Jude recalled sitting on other grassy banks with him, watching the clouds while Gary and the younger children rested. They used to play a game Joel's parents had taught him. Each would look at a cloud and challenge the other to guess what they saw in it. 'Cloudspotting' they called it.

"It's like old times, isn't it?" Jude remarked. "Sitting together in the open, hearing the wind and the grasses moving." Yet it was not the same, she realised, even as she spoke. They were adult now, and their last meeting at Border Seven had left a sense of unfinished business between them.

"I want to ask you something," Joel replied. "Give the first answer that comes into your head. Do you like your partner? - the man you were to be bonded to?"

The question startled Jude. "I don't know," she admitted.

"Come on, you know the manual," Joel said gently. "'If an officer's duty is unclear, they should evaluate the situation and give the first answer that occurs, devoid of emotion.' So - do you like Kurt?"

Jude began to feel irritated by his insistence. "When we were introduced I didn't," she admitted, "but then I found we got on well. And he risked an awful lot for me..." She paused, forced to analyse what she did feel. "I suppose I must like him," she added. "I'm worried sick about him. He tried to follow me, and I don't know where he is now - or if he's safe." Realising the implications of her reply, Jude stopped. "I'm sorry," she ended lamely.

"Don't be. It makes my course clearer." Turning away from her, Joel looked across the moors. "I've had a lot of time to think during the past six weeks," he said quietly. "I love you, Jude. I love you as I love myself. You're my past, and the one who's driven my ambitions. Even when I was angry with you, I kept on thinking of you. When you came back into my life so suddenly, it threw me. You were so beautiful... I wanted to show you my love. But I lost the chance. I got to thinking - that I was taking advantage of you... that it wasn't right. We're too close... too like Family. I can't get rid of that feeling. Do you understand what I'm trying to say?"

Silently Jude nodded. "I wanted you in return," she replied, "but a lot's happened since then." In confusion, she stopped, unable to explain. "We mightn't think clearly if we're too - emotionally involved," she agreed.

For a long time they stayed quietly together on the bank, watching the clouds scud across the sky. "I'm not sure what love is," Jude said at length. "But if worrying about someone is part of it, then I love you as well as Kurt. If you go back to the Corporation, I may never see you again. Take care. Please take care."

"What choice do I have? I have to get that patent legally. Otherwise the Corporation will hound me wherever I go - and prevent anyone else from employing me. Besides, if I can fight back somehow, I have to. I should never have entered the Refuges, but I saw it as the best way I could achieve something. When I developed Provene, I was promised it would be made freely available, but people still die of plague outside the Refuges. It makes me wild. The Corporation drains every country that invites it in, attracting its brightest and most - idealistic I suppose - then keeps what they achieve to itself."

"But what can you do?" In concern, Jude turned to him and considered his expression. The determination in his eyes frightened her.

"This is the best chance we'll get for years," Joel replied. "We need to throw everything we have against the Corporation. I was to have been one of Border Seven's representatives, and my name will still be on the list of speakers. They won't have dared take it off. If I turn up, they can't stop me speaking. I was to have seconded the motion to open up the Refuges. Instead, I intend to expose what's been going on at Border Seven. It'll at least liven up the meeting."

Shaking her head, Jude sighed. No warning she could give would alter his intention. "Then may your god go with you," she said. Putting her arms around him, she kissed him.

It was cold, even in the sun. "Let's not spoil a lovely day thinking grim thoughts," Joel advised. "I reckon I can make it to the top of the ridge. There's a fantastic view from there - right across the border."

Jude smiled. "All right - but first you must answer my question," she replied.

"What's that?"

"If they do open the Refuges, what will you do? - apart from manage my father's estate. Will you find the colleague you told me about? I'd like to think you were happy with someone."

To her surprise, Joel flushed slightly. "If she'll have me," he replied. "But I'm not sure she'll leave her Refuge for me -"

Jude cut him off with a laugh. "Oh, give over!" she chided. "You'll have a whole hospital for her to run. Won't that be bait enough?"

"I hope so," Joel agreed, smiling. He watched the clouds for another few seconds. "I can see an elephant up there," he said. "Didn't we used to say that was lucky?"

"It's not an elephant, it's a rhinoceros," Jude teased. "But that's lucky too."

Chapter Twenty Eight

The faint wash of a skimmer interrupted Jude's sleep. At once, she was alert. Hardly breathing, she listened as someone was helped on board.

Dressed in a water woman's cape and breeches, the Chief Secretary was unrecognisable until she let down her hood. Then the high forehead and heavy jaw were clear, even in the dim light of the cabin. Jude did not know how to greet her. "Relax, my dear," the woman said. Her manner was almost hesitant. "I wanted to thank you. You've been on my conscience a great deal."

"I appreciate your concern, Ma'am," Jude answered awkwardly.

"You've certainly discredited management here as I asked, dramatically. Well maintained structures don't collapse - and well controlled budgets don't depend on expulsions. I gather you've already reported the clearances in person to the Triumvirate. You've fulfilled your duties in an exemplary manner, and I shall see you're rewarded."

"Thank you Ma'am," Jude replied again. Once again, in her superior's presence, she felt a sense of unreality. They were both fugitives hiding on a smelly cargo boat, yet the woman talked of duties and rewards.

"You intend to return, then?" Jude asked.

"I've done so already, my dear. For the past year, I've been Decider Designate. With Paolo Anesto dead, I had to take his place as soon as possible -"

"Decider Anesto is dead?" Jude asked in surprise.

"He died five days ago. Of heart failure. I'd have said he was very healthy myself, but you can't see inside a man's arteries."

Jude looked at her uncertainly. "I didn't realise you were the next in line," she apologised.

"You weren't supposed to. I have a lot to do. Send heads rolling, sort out the Corporation's finances... Anesto was doing his best to ruin us. Clearly he was in somebody's pocket, though I don't yet know whose. Now someone's got rid of him. Do you know who that might be?"

"No, Ma'am. Why should I know?"

"I thought you might." Looking sharply at Jude, Maria Levant paused, "Did you trace the contact I suggested?" she asked. "The man calling himself Simeon?"

"Your information was very useful," Jude replied carefully. "He helped me a good deal."

"Yes. He helped me too. I would still be on those ghastly mud flats, but for him." Looking towards the glow on the horizon, Maria Levant shuddered. "He woke me one night, and told me he could lead me to safety. I shall never forget that walk. It was like your worst nightmare. Simeon kept me going, and then insisted on returning to Border Seven himself - because it might draw attention to my absence if he didn't, and because he had work to finish. That's what I call courage. I've often wondered what happened to him, and how much I was to blame."

It was the first time Jude had heard regret in her superior's voice. "Simeon survived, Ma'am," she replied. "I'll ask - mutual friends - to convey your thanks to him."

To Jude's surprise, the woman's face took on a pinched, haunted appearance. "At least I'll be able to describe what it's like to be thrown out as garbage," she said quietly. "Nothing's solved of course. The Corporation still has to find a way of catering for the uneconomic, but at least everyone can see what caring solely about budgets does."

She indicated that Jude should sit on the bunk with her. "I gather someone tried to kill you at Border Seven," she continued. "And that you were treated very badly at East Five. I shall need reports of all this."

"I've written them already," Jude said, and getting up, fetched the notes she had made. "I don't know who was responsible in either case, just that someone wanted me out the way. Perhaps I was onto things they didn't want other people to know." Awkwardly she stood beside her superior, trying to think how to word her explanation better.

"I imagine you were. As I said, you've done well. I look forward to working with you again -"

"I'm not sure I shall return, Ma'am," Jude interrupted.

"But what else would you do? Life's impossible outside. I can understand you feeling bitter, but anyone found to have misused their position will be punished."

"It wasn't just a few individuals. All sorts of staff must have been involved. Orders would have had to be drafted, budgets balanced. My death was even announced on the forthcoming list. No one queried it. I can't belong to an organisation that requires such unquestioning obedience. I'd sooner grow cabbages."

Maria Levant frowned. "Officer, you've served faithfully until now," she replied. "Because of you - and your friends - the Groundnet will hold, and the cities will continue to function. I'm asking for an amnesty to be declared so that all those who had to leave their Refuges can return. Please rejoin us. We need your sort to turn things round." Pausing, she looked at Jude shrewdly. "Don't miss a golden opportunity, my dear," she advised. "If I can get back to Headquarters safely, I shall have a lot of power. I'll need someone who knows Border Seven, and what's been going on there. I'd like to put you in charge of Security as the place is rebuilt. You'd be able to help your friends, and give your career a tremendous boost."

The temptation was almost too great to resist. Hesitating, Jude studied the woman's expression, sensing that despite her confident manner, she was appalled at the task facing her. She was probably on her way to Lendal, to the same meeting Joel and her father would be attending and worried about what might be decided there. If she was offered a bargain, she might accept.

"Ma'am," Jude began tentatively, "the Ideal still means a great deal to me, but I couldn't shut myself up again. I've grown too used to freedom. If I come back, it will have to be as a liaison officer, or an outside consultant - something like that."

Since she was not interrupted, Jude held her breath to steady it, and then continued. "No amount of tinkering with budgets will turn the English Refuges round quickly enough," she hazarded, "and the Corporation can't afford to keep them running at a loss. Besides, the mood's changed. People are saying our skills should be shared - that it's not safe for any country to be dependent on one provider. Sooner or later you'll have to do a deal with the sector councils or national government itself. Someone like me could be useful. I have a lot of contacts. Let me serve outside my Refuge, as a liaison between the Corporation and other bodies."

Maria Levant laughed, though it was more like a sharp yap than merriment. "You don't miss a chance, do you?" she asked. "Yes, we will have to do a deal as you call it, and yes, you could be very useful, but a member is a member for life, with no bargains. You'll be in a great deal of trouble if you don't go back to your Refuge."

Jude held firm, but only just. "I've grown used to trouble," she replied. "Too much comfort would be like a prison - as I imagine you may find also."

To her relief the Chief Secretary nodded, and then picked up her cape, ready to leave. "I probably will," she acknowledged. "Think about what you're doing, dear. So long as I can survive long enough, I'll see your allegations are thoroughly investigated."

"Send someone to East Five, Dwelling 136b -" Jude began.

The Chief Secretary cut her off. "The recording has been retrieved," she said. "I don't know who by, but it's to be presented in evidence at an inquiry next week. I haven't had chance to see it myself yet, but I'm told it's damning. Management at Border Seven will have to be removed."

For a moment longer the woman paused. "I don't know who your friends are," she admitted. "And I don't want to know. But we have a lot in common." Then she left.

*****

The blackmarketeer vessel they had hired carried some very sophisticated listening devices, and Captain Lester knew how to use them. Plump and round-faced, she looked more like a farmer than a blackmarketeer, but she could find out what was happening in a secret meeting many kilometres away. The preliminary discussions were taking longer than expected, she explained, and advised Joel to delay his arrival in Lendal. So, slowly and carefully, as if it had a power-line fault, the tramper plodded down the coast.

It gave them a precious extra three days to amass the evidence Joel needed. For hours at a time, he sat in the communications cabin, receiving coded messages from half a dozen different sources, all unnamed. At night, Jacob came across from the shore, bringing lists of names or testimonies. It was impossible for one person to sort so much material in so little time, so Jude took over the transcriptions, and then tried to bring some order to the separate, often unrelated shreds of information. Most of the time, she felt faintly sick. The tramper rolled convincingly, but it was not just the motion that affected her. It was what she was reading.

She broke down only once. As she entered up a list of names, she found herself writing one she recognised: Advisor Julia Nyall. For several moments she tried to control her grief, but it was too much.

At once Joel crossed the cabin to her and put his arm round her shoulder. "Don't do anymore," he suggested. "It's unfair of me to ask your help."

"But I want to," Jude insisted. "If I had any doubts before, they're gone now."

On the fourth day, Captain Lester announced that it was time to head for Lendal. The national conference would begin that afternoon.

Jude spent one last hour in the main cabin with Joel. They made three copies of his evidence, one for him to take, one for Phil as back-up, and one to be sent to shore later. Then they sat together while Joel rehearsed what he might say. If he managed to get into the conference and was allowed to speak, he had enough material to cause a sensation. If he was arrested on sight, they were probably all finished.

"Don't look so worried," Joel said finally. "I've been a lucky devil all my life."

"Your luck may not last for ever," Jude warned.

"It's not going to run out now," Joel insisted. "Still, we do need contingency plans. Wait for a full week just outside Lendal, then if there's no public announcement or I'm not back, slip out to sea. Don't risk yourself again for my sake. If you're not going to accept the amnesty, go to my parents and wait there a bit longer, in case I ultimately turn up. Your own father is likely to be very much occupied, possibly at risk himself. And whatever happens, remember - I love you, more than I can say."

Muffled by the steady throb of the tramper's power unit, they could hear the sound of other vessels nearby. Kissing her on the cheek, Joel went to his cabin to change into the uniform Captain Lester had somehow obtained for him. Afterwards, Jude went up on deck, to watch as Phil prepared the skimmer to go onshore.

At least a thousand small craft were crowded along the river banks approaching the locks to the city. It would be impossible to find space for a cumbersome old tramper, so they turned back, downstream for a few kiloms, and moored there.

"I didn't expect so many people," Phil admitted. "It's going to be some celebration."

"Would it be better to wait until the place is quieter?" Captain Lester asked.

By then Joel had come on deck too, looking like a perfect Refuge senior officer. Captain Lester had even managed to get him the medical officers' insignia. Phil and Rexel exchanged glances but made no comment.

"The amnesty runs out at the end of the week," Joel replied. "Even if I'm not going to accept it, I need its protection. Besides, if word gets out what's being discussed and the talks fail, there'll be trouble. I'll go now, while I still have the nerve."

Biting the skin around one of her fingers, Jude nodded. Her mouth was dry with anxiety. Turning away, she watched the muddy bank beside her. A duck was paddling beneath an overhanging tree. Every detail of its green and blue neck, its brown undersides, was vivid to her. She heard the skimmer lowered into the water, and the ladder being dropped down, but she did not look as Rexel took Joel upstream, towards Lendal.

After that, there was nothing to do but wait. There was plenty to watch: more and more small craft heading for the city, police patrols buzzing up and down anxiously, walkers hurrying along the riverside path. Then, finally, Rexel returned. He had escorted Joel into the city, but left him to go on alone, as asked. "The streets are packed!" he told them. "People must have been here for days. They've taken over the doorways - flasks, bed rolls, everything, like they were queuing for travel permits. I've never seen anything like it. I suppose it's a long time since there was a big public celebration - of something people wanted to celebrate, anyway. The President's expected later this week, but the authorities aren't giving the exact time or place - security of course."

All day they waited, moored beside an old jetty. All the following day, too. For Jude, the lack of occupation was the worst part. Lester spent the time listening intently to what was going on in the city, but apart from telling them that negotiations were coming to a head, she said little. Phil was busy keeping watch or working about the vessel, and Rexel cooked their meals. Though Jude tried to be helpful she felt utterly spare.

By ten hours on the third day, she had had enough. Since it would be safest to blend into the crowd, she found the old dress she had worn to travel to the north, changed and went on deck.

Phil was staring anxiously up river. "I'm going up to the city," she told him. "I can't stand this any longer, and we need to know what's happening. I won't take any risks."

"If you wish, Ma'am. I'd better stay here in case Simeon comes back."

Taking the baggage carrier so that the others would have the skimmer in an emergency, Jude set off. Though small, the craft was unwieldy, pulling to starboard continually and Jude took several moments to master it. Then she drove up river, avoiding the swirl of comings and goings. At the first lock, she found a gap between the jumble of craft moored downstream, and scrambling out, pulled the carrier up the bank and under some bushes. It was well hidden, and there was a good chance she would find it still there when she returned. Afterwards, she set off on foot, along a muddy path that led to the city precincts.

Rexel had not exaggerated. By the time the path had become a paved walkway, it was crowded with other walkers. When Jude reached the first bridge, the streets leading to it were packed, every alley jammed with people. Like an uneasy tide, the crowds ebbed and flowed, individuals carried forward and then back again. She had no particular destination and allowed herself to be carried along too, listening to the conversation around her.

For over a month, negotiations had been taking place about something important. The deadline for agreement was rumoured to have been extended twice. The unifiers, or maybe it was the government, had got all sorts of people together for a big meeting. What the negotiations were about no one was sure, though there were as many guesses as speakers. It seemed to be to do with the Refuges. They were going to be closed. No, more were opening... One of the Border Refuges had been attacked and there would be massive reprisals... The Reivers were shutting off the water supplies and all the northern Refuges would have to shut... Of course not, the Corporation was taking over the government. It had done a deal with the army, who were about to reinstate the Junta...

One suggestion made Jude's heart leap in hope. A young soldier said something sensational had happened at the national conference. Someone who was thought to be dead had turned up, and made allegations about management at Border Seven. Senior officers had immediately been arrested and there was a tremendous scandal...

Whatever was at issue, it seemed today was the final day. Everyone of any importance in the north had sent representatives: sector officials, civil administrators, the judiciary, academics, Refuge liaison officers. Even the larger militias were represented, several of the justices having been briefed by faceless men, to speak on their behalf. Jude could not help smiling. Her father would be one of the Judiciary. As Tuecer, he was presumably also being represented by someone else. He would appreciate the irony.

Since no one agreed on the venue for the negotiations, Jude decided to follow her own suspicions, and headed towards the former Assembly building.

She was not alone. Despite being converted into offices, Convocation House had become a place of pilgrimage. A plaque listed the names of those who had lost their lives defending the Assembly thirty five years ago, and fresh flowers were still strewn beneath it. Even as Jude watched, two more posies were laid carefully, so as not to disturb the others.

There was no evidence of any meeting at Convocation House itself, however, but there was an unusual amount of security around a deserted biotech factory off one of the walkways opposite. Unobtrusively, Jude walked as far round the site as she could, and then crossing the river, settled down in a doorway where she could see the entrance on the opposite bank. Occasionally she risked using her enhancers to check windows and doors for signs of movement. Any other empty building would have been taken over by squatters, but people feared the danger that might linger in such a place. The forecourt was deserted, covered in a film of city dust. There were footmarks in the dust, though, recent ones, heading inside.

She had been there less than half an hour when Jude saw a security officer approaching. In concern, she watched him, while pretending to adjust her shoe.

"Fortune telling is illegal in a public place," he announced harshly.

"Pardon?" Jude asked. She did not need to feign alarm.

"You heard. Telling fortunes is illegal. You're under arrest."

"But I haven't been telling fortunes," Jude insisted. She was not sure whether it was a joke.

In answer, the security officer grabbed her roughly by the arm, forcing her to rise. People nearby stared, then looked away. No one was going to risk trouble for a fortune teller's sake, though they might be willing to use her services. Urgently, Jude tried to think what to do. Another security officer was approaching. She could have thrown the one, but in so crowded a street, she would have trouble avoiding the other's fire. Ordinary people might get hurt.

*****

As soon as they were around the far end of the biotech factory, the two men pulled Jude towards a door. It opened as they approached, and then closed swiftly behind them. Jude just had time to register an empty foyer, then she was bundled down a corridor. Laboratories opened off it, still complete with benches and equipment. The place seemed to have been closed as abruptly as the hospital near Border Seven. She wondered if there were any pigeons.

Finally, Jude was pushed into darkness. Putting her hands over her head to protect it, she waited, crouched on the floor.

Somewhere, the far side of the room, there was the sound of movement. Simultaneously, the lights came on. "How did you know I was here?" a familiar voice demanded.

For several seconds, Jude could only stare at Maria Levant. Then, cautiously, she stood up. "I didn't," she replied truthfully. "I was waiting for an announcement - like everyone else."

"And you just happened to sit on the bank opposite?"

Jude tried to judge the woman's mood. "Yes, Ma'am," she replied.

With an impatient gesture, Maria Levant indicated that Jude should follow her. "Well, now you're here, you might as well meet your friend," she said. "He made quite a sensation, turning up from the dead right on cue. It was interesting to see some people's expressions. As for the speech he gave... Now that really set people running in circles. "An opening in the wall appeared. "Hurry up! I should be in the debating chamber, not sorting out Personnel's affairs."

In bewilderment, Jude followed her, past other laboratories, until finally they came to an apparently empty office. When the door slid back however, it revealed another door behind it, and light glinting around its edge.

Inside the room three Refuge officials and several police officers were sitting around a table. At its far end was Joel. Relief and the after effects of fright made Jude feel faint, but she managed to stay upright. Joel looked up and smiled at her. Then he returned to a pile of printouts he was reading. He appeared to be checking them for errors.

Looking from him to Maria Levant, and then back again, Jude tried to assess their body language. To her surprise, it was the Chief Secretary who seemed smaller, defeated, while Joel sat calmly passing the printouts to the clerk beside him. The clerk's manner towards Joel was unexpected too, respectful, even nervous.

"Give me the disclaimer!" Maria Levant ordered.

Without speaking, the clerk handed her one of the papers. After reading it through quickly, she passed it to Jude. "Verify the signature," she instructed. "It'll look better if we have an outsider doing so."

Cautiously, Jude checked the document. It was a contract, drawn up between SecureCity Incorporated, and one Joel Anderson, medical officer. In it he waived all rights to Refuge privileges, pension and facilities. In return, the Corporation granted him honourable release from his membership and possession of a patent to which he laid claim. "This looks like Joel's writing," Jude agreed, though her voice was unsteady.

One of the police officers was gathering up the rest of the printouts Joel had been checking. Those too were passed to Maria Levant. Briskly, she glanced through them. In surprise, Jude watched her. Despite her apparent efficiency, the woman could hardly bring herself to read what was there. "Fine," she said and clipped them together.

Sitting down, Maria Levant rubbed at her forehead in a gesture of weariness. "We have elements in the Refuges left over from the Junta," she acknowledged. "That I can understand, even if it makes me wild. But what beats me is the sheer carelessness..." She turned towards a senior security officer sitting quietly on the other side of the room. The man visibly winced. "It's on Officer Anderson's record who sponsored him," she pointed out. "One of the few Justices round here who couldn't be bought. Didn't it occur to you he might be gathering evidence? Then you allow an assault on his own rights! Weren't any of you watching what was going on?"

"Too busy taking trips ashore," one of the police officers suggested.

Sighing, Maria Levant turned towards Joel. "Whatever fault may lie with you - and there is fault - you served the Corporation faithfully. I owe you a great deal myself. I want that putting on record - and that you were right to oppose what was going on, however inconvenient it was for Finance. I appreciate their problems, but such a breach of Refuge ideals cannot be allowed. From now onwards, no new members will be admitted until the retirement Refuges are built."

Cautiously, Jude moved closer to Joel. "I told you I was born lucky," he whispered to her.

"I owe a good deal to you, too," Maria Levant continued, turning towards Jude. "The evidence you delivered to the Triumvirate is proving invaluable. Change your mind, and stay with us. I need you at Border Seven - to turn things round."

"I'd like to help you," Jude replied carefully, "But only if you give me my freedom. I was treated wrongly too, and I've left an account of my experiences with several friends."

"Blackmail, as usual!" With a gesture of irritation Maria Levant slapped the printouts down in front of her. "This time, I hope it's not needed. The Refuges are going to have to open up. My colleagues will be mad not to agree. The Reivers will shut off our water supplies if we don't sign, and without water the northern Refuges will have to be abandoned. Even if that threat's removed, the sector councils will take their contracts away. With a scandal like this, we can't talk about ideals anymore, or say we're serving the community, and they've discovered they can run themselves - with a little help from our competitors. Just agree to help me through this mess and I'll give you whatever fancy title you want - within reason."

In amazement Jude stared at her. "Can I have that in writing?" she asked. She saw Joel suppressing a smile.

Snatching a stylus and note-taker from the clerk's desk, Maria Levant scribbled a message and then passed it to Jude. It said: "If you will help me sort out the problems at Border Seven and act as my emissary with outside groups, I will appoint you as a liaison officer or consultant, the exact term and conditions to be decided later. Your freedom to come and go from the Refuge will be guaranteed.'

"Will that do for now?" the woman asked brusquely. When Jude nodded, she printed off a copy and passed it to her.

"You need to get back into the main chamber," Joel warned her. "I'm afraid my affairs have been distracting you. It's not only the Reivers threatening trouble. Some of the more extreme groups intend to attack Corporation employees on trips outside - or anyone who trades with them. If an agreement's not signed soon, there could be violence."

Getting up quickly, Maria Levant picked up a folder from the table. "I wish I didn't believe you," she admitted, "But you strike me as a very dangerous young man, who knows what he wants and has important friends. Thank you for your warning." Turning to the others at the table, she ordered, "The decisions of this meeting are to be made public. It must be known that the Corporation accepts responsibility for its errors. In addition to what MRO Anderson has requested, compensation will be made to him. That will have to be negotiated through Finance. Now I must leave, and see what's going on in the main chamber."

Closing the visiscreen in front of him, Joel stood up. His control was impressive, though relief showed in his voice. "I'll keep my word." he promised. "The Corporation's assistance will be acknowledged in anything I publish, or develop." He offered Maria Levant his hand in farewell.

Jude hardly noticed the corridors afterwards, or the deserted laboratories. She only really registered where she was when she found herself outside, blinking in the sun. Putting his arm around her waist, Joel stood beside her. "I told you not to follow me," he said, "But I'm glad you did. It's been a... difficult few days."

"I can think of other descriptions," Jude replied. Anxiously she looked at the crowds. "We need to get back to the river," she warned.

"Let's go to Minster Square first," Joel suggested.

"Why? Can't you ever rest?"

"I'll rest in the square. Beside, things are happening, and I want to see them."

Wearily Jude agreed.

Pushing their way down the street, they headed through alleys crammed with people. Even when they arrived at the square, though, they could find nowhere to sit. The great doors of the old Minster were open, and Joel suggested they see if there was any room there.

The building was a reality-drama studio now, but the owners allowed people inside, out of respect for the symbolism it still held. That day, whole families were sitting on the stone floor, or on window ledges, all of them quietly waiting, and hoping. Finding a small space in the former chancel, Jude and Joel joined them. Leaning against her shoulder, Joel rested.

"Cutting off the water -" Jude whispered. "Was that your idea?"

"Your father's. I don't know why none of us saw it before. However much the Refuges recycle, they can't survive without fresh supplies, and the Reivers are happy to do anything Tuecer recommends. For the first time we have the opposition acting together. Sensible people like Maria Lavant are gaining the upper hand in the Corporation, too. They're arguing that the government must be given overall control."

"We'd get a proper government then," Jude whispered back, "not just a Refuge customer. Oh Lord! I hope you're right. There'll be one hell of a party if they do agree!"

They had been there about an hour when the rumour began. "The decision's been made," it claimed. But what that decision was, no one could say even now.

For another half hour, nothing happened, though more and more people began to drift in through the great doors. There was a sense of tension, even fear, a conviction that an announcement was due, and that it had to do with the Refuges. Some of the whisperers were optimistic, but most feared that the Junta was returning, that the ten precious, chaotic years of freedom were over. Hardly able to breathe, Jude waited beside Joel. "It begins to look like you're wrong," she said.

"Surely not," Joel replied anxiously. "The Corporation will be mad not to sign."

Suddenly, the ancient bell above them began to toll. It reverberated throughout the building, a deep booming sound that had not been heard for fifty years. Everywhere, people leapt up in surprise. "That must be a signal!" someone shouted. At once everyone began to gather up their things, and push towards the doors. Anyone who remained on the ground risked being trampled on. Carried by the flow, Jude and Joel joined them.

Outside, the rumours were becoming wilder and wilder, shouted by people running into the square. "The government's bought the Refuges!" one voice yelled. "They've kicked the Corporation out!" another claimed.

"They say we're all going to live in Refuges!" a woman beside Jude told her partner. "Won't it be lovely?"

"Nah! I wouldn't want to be shut up inside one of them towers," he retorted. "But it's about time we all got a few of their comforts."

Abruptly, the public address system crackled into sound above the whole city. Rarely used since the days of the Junta, it stopped every movement. Those old enough to remember the bad old days seemed frozen with fear. Even the younger people looked in alarm towards the police squadron entering the square.

Then the crackle settled into distinguishable words. "Citizens wishing to hear an important announcement from the President are invited to proceed in an orderly manner towards Convocation House. I repeat. Please proceed in an orderly manner."

Still every one hesitated, not knowing whether the announcement would mean good or ill. As though an adviser had pointed out the need for reassurance, a second voice added, "There is no cause for alarm. To mark the tenth anniversary of the great uprising, a momentous agreement has been signed between the government and SecureCity Incorporated, which you are invited to celebrate. At sixteen hours your President will present the terms of that agreement, and address the world's media. Following this, there will be public celebrations. Music and dancing will be permitted."

"Yes!!!" A thousand voices shouted the word together. A babble of delight followed.

As Jude had predicted, the city was about to have the biggest impromptu party in its history. Two women were already dancing, their arms looped together. Others joined them. In amazement, Jude watched. She had never fully realised how hated SecureCity had become, and how long people had dreamt of it losing power. An old man near her was laughing, grabbing hold of the last dancer's hand as she passed.

"Let's go and hear the President!" someone in front of her shouted. Joel moved forward towards the speaker. Jude started to follow.

At once hands held her firmly from behind, preventing her from moving. In panic she struggled to get free.

"Shush!" a voice said. "Don't attack me. I've come a long way to find you."

"Kurt!" Jude cried in amazement.

The grip on her shoulders relaxed, so that she could turn to him. At once Jude threw her arms around him in delight. "How did you know I was here?" she demanded.

"Your friend sent for me. Neither of us expected so many people, though. I nearly didn't find you." The crowd was pressing all around them, and Kurt held her close to him to keep them from being separated. "I've been longing to do this for months," he whispered, and kissed her.

For several moments they held each other, oblivious to the people around them. The noise of voices, of shouting and movement blurred in Jude's ears. She was conscious only of Kurt's nearness, and that he had found her.

"Oi, you two!" a voice near them called. "Come and join the party!"

Startled, they returned to the world around them. The dance was growing, becoming the ancient ring of pre-junta times. Two young girls snatched at Jude's hands, trying to persuade her to join in. "I don't know the steps -" she protested.

"We'll teach you -" Grabbing her, they pulled her into the dance.

Urgently Jude snatched at Kurt's hand so that he was with her too. Round and round the circle swirled, growing bigger with every moment. It moved suddenly forwards, across the square, and then splitting into a hundred smaller rings, surged down the ancient lanes towards Convocation Square. Jude could not keep in step, but she laughed for sheer joy as she danced.

She looked for Joel, but he had disappeared amongst the crowds.